"Vampire stories are always gay but rarely are they so trans. Schrieve's tale of teen rebellion, friendship, and bloodsucking is ripe with hope for a better world—a world in which networks of mutual aid relationships support outsider communities, and people give and receive trust, pleasure, and magic outside of heterosexuality and government control. Buffy fans, this book will knock your socks off!"

—MAIA KOBABE, ALA Alex Award-winning author and illustrator of *Gender Queer: A Memoir*

"Some writers give us a couple of characters, but Hal Schrieve gives us a whole community. Hir characters breathe; they seethe; they're driven by rage and longing; and they're indelible. *Fawn's Blood* is unafraid of complexity and mess, and unafraid of love too. This is the queer vampire novel we deserve."

—ISAAC FELLMAN, Lambda Literary Award-winning author of *Dead Collections* and *The Breath of the Sun*

PRAISE FOR *OUT OF SALEM*

"Tension burns hot until the explosive conclusion, which begs for a sequel. On fire with magic and revolution."

—*Kirkus Reviews*

"Schrieve . . . provides incisive social commentary via monster-tale tropes. Any reader who has felt it necessary to hide their true identity will find strong characters to connect with in this fun, powerful story."

—*Publishers Weekly*

PRAISE FOR *HOW TO GET OVER THE END OF THE WORLD*

"No one writes the contemporary teen voice better than Hal Schrieve."

—COLLEEN AF VENABLE, author of the National Book Award Longlisted *Kiss Number 8*

FAWN'S BLOOD

FAWN'S BLOOD

a novel

HAL SCHRIEVE

SEVEN STORIES PRESS
New York • Oakland • London

Seven Stories Press
140 Watts Street
New York, NY 10013
www.sevenstories.com

Library of Congress Cataloging-in-Publication Data is on file.

ISBN: 978-1-64421-470-1 (hardcover)
ISBN: 978-1-64421-471-8 (ebook)

College professors and high school and middle school teachers may order free examination copies of Seven Stories Press titles. Visit https://www.sevenstories.com/pg/resources-academics or email academic@sevenstories.com.

Printed in the United States of America

9 8 7 6 5 4 3 2 1

AUGUST

1

RACHEL

When Cain bit me and put his own bloody fingers in my mouth, I did remember Mom being like, if a vampire ever tries to feed you his blood, don't drink. But in the moment, I was looking into his deep, bloodred eyes, and his bat-like nose was brushing my cheek, and I just thought, you know, *I don't want to die.*

It was supposed to be the raid where we killed Cain.

My mom came barging into my bedroom that Monday morning at the exact moment that I had been about to open my blouse and take a thirst trap, holding one of my mom's self-defense knuckle kitty keychains up, because I mostly don't post any pictures to Insta that aren't part of the Security Sisters viral marketing plan. This picture was for Brid, though. I held up the kitty keychain and punched toward the mirror, so the sharp spikes of the ears showed. The morning sun through my pink lace curtains was just right for a cute high-femme selfie. I was wearing the leopard print bra Brid had gotten me, and it showed a little bit under my blouse. Mom doesn't love the idea of me being sexual in general, but she knows that me being cute and using her products helps sell them. Of course, when you're killing vampires, the best thing is an old-fashioned stake. But there's plenty of other creeps out there too, and that's what the Security Sisters merch is for.

Mom never knocks. Good old Mom.

"New post? Can I vet?" Mom asked. I showed her the selfie. I saw a slight flicker of concern at the cleavage, and then her business face took over and she nodded. She took my phone and opened our marketing copy notes app. "Good. We've got a minimum order of 1,000 for these. Need to move them. Here, let me type the part about the product so you can work it in."

"Can I see what you've got?" I asked, because it was clear she'd stomped in to show me something.

She held out her phone, pointing at the Gothic font at the top of the fried screenshot of a photo of a flyer that had initially excited her interest and prompted her to pay Randall, our informant: CAIN'S BIRTHDAY BASH.

"Remember how we thought he might be based in that black house on Bagley, and then thought we were wrong because we saw those human kids hanging out on the stoop?"

"Yeah," I said, internally groaning that I'd probably need to spend a night sometime soon waiting on my stomach in a bush in front of a punk house. But I guess we need to. Seattle has long had one of the highest rates of vampirism in the country, due to our rainy season and how functional the government is at handing out blood to the creeps.

Back in the 1980s, when there were tons of vampire cults and everyone was getting their blood drunk and freaking out and slaying them, people argued the reason vampires were evil predators was because of lack of resources, and if only they had a little regular blood they'd be okay. The Department of Vampire Affairs says it's a two-way street: they donate some of their venom to stop hemophilia and fight AIDS and, nowadays, to help make new Covid-19 vaccines, and they get blood. Thanks to lobbying since the Vampire Recognition Act, any vampire who wants to can register with the government, promise not to hurt anyone, and get a bag a day of real human blood that could go to actual useful stuff if only our society wasn't so sick. And at night, even though they do have their trackers, they can go outside, and cops can only kill them if they catch them hunting.

In the last two years, though, things changed. At first it looked good. When Covid-19 hit, the government blood banks for normal people ran dry, and doctors thought vampires could be given just half of what they'd been getting. The President had this emergency order that cut blood rations for vampires, and there was this panicky thing going around in the vampire scene because they were convinced that without two bags a day a vampire will starve to death. Even though the government was still giving a totally excessive amount of blood, a lot of registered vampires ripped off their trackers and went into the woods or the secret tunnels under the city. It was easier to hunt them in the woods: you could lift their tarps off them in daytime, turning them into ash. We had to get good at finding tunnels. For a little bit in 2020, it looked like homelessness and blood bank shortages would cut the vampire population in half. We emptied dozens of camps of vampires. But Cain, a skeezy vampire club owner and Mom's nemesis, redoubled his efforts to increase their population ever since lockdown ended. For every registered vampire who had died of starvation during the blood shortage, there were, it seemed like, two or three new, young vampires who didn't even want to get registered. Who hunted.

Cain's parties weren't for the registered vampires. Every week, more vampires ditched their trackers, moved underground, and switched to drinking black market or fresh blood.

"I did a scout last night," Mom said, "and whatever that was, it was a red herring. Something *is* there. They were setting up sound system equipment in the backyard. The Bagley house is involved in this for sure. They're going to be at the house, and they're going to be *outside* for this."

Vampires' lives sure seemed shitty: a ratty punk house was where the most important one had his birthday.

"Outdoor vampire party in August? They'll only get like six hours of true darkness." Winter was the best time to be a vampire. The weak sunlight of sunrise often didn't do as much of a number on them even if they did stay out too late—they had a couple hours of blistering sunburn and devastating migraine before they started to smoke. Summer was brighter.

"Must feel pretty safe. They have to have an escape route to their afters. I think the current location of La Fang is in the U district now. I think there's a *tunnel*."

Her eyes blazed with all the ice-blue, sea-blue, sunlight-blue glory of Seattle's best vampire slayer. I was meant to match it. I was not feeling like planning for a major bust of a new La Fang or its adjacent stinky tunnels. Yes, important, but we never fucking sleep when we're going on a big raid. I was going to barely scrape a 3 in my AP classes. I have to make six or seven videos a week to promote Security Sisters merch, and then eight or nine more to keep people interested enough in my account to keep following—mostly martial arts training videos with Mom or Brid. And every time there's a really big raid, we risk the cops getting involved, since slaying vampires is technically illegal after the Recognition Act, and when we burn stuff, usually that's illegal too and landlords get mad. The donors to MAVIS aren't happy when we attract too much attention to ourselves—they like us shadowy. My mom shrugs that off, because she has a couple friends on the force and friends of Dad's from the military who she thinks would pull for her. But if I get arrested, I can kiss my Harvard dreams goodbye.

"Is Daylight on board?"

"Daylight Inc. told us that Cain's blood supply is a concern for them as they prepare to launch later this year, and they've given us some grenades."

She looked excited.

"What's my first task?" I asked, doing the polite Slayer Jr. thing, sitting down on the bed.

She tried to make it playful, the way she did when I was twelve; she took out her big knife, still sheathed, and anointed me on each shoulder, like a knight.

"You are my best recon officer. You and Bridget should scope for entrances to tunnels this week. I'll text you the address on Signal, and just sweep that whole area. Saturday afternoon, Sunday too if you can't find anything."

"Can we do day scouting and then have the sleepover we were planning?"

Mom tried to stay fun but pursed her lips. "Me and Molly are going to double our sweeps at night in Capitol Hill because Stacey and Robin are at the swim meet. We'll need you and Brid to cover the U district, Ravenna, and the cemetery near the hospital."

I dropped my head to my chest and dangled my arms like a neanderthal, melodramatically.

"When do I get to have a hot girl summer?" I'd said it many times, sometimes joking. Mom sometimes sympathized with me. She'd been slaying vampires since she was my age. Even with Dad, there had never been a time when her life had been whimsical; her girly image was her trying to take back some control in what was otherwise a grim fight with the devil. She adjusted her glasses to peer down at me with her "I've Been There" look.

"You know none of us can be normal until this vampire cult is destroyed," she said.

I wanted to get *laid*. Brid and I were supposed to have a sleepover without Stacey for once, since she was at a swim meet this weekend. Stacey is kind of a snitch, and since Mom didn't yet suspect Brid and me were flirtatious, a sleepover alone together was code for getting to majorly fool around. The only times I'd gotten to do anything real with her since we started secretly dating is when I got to touch her in her dad's garden shed. The raid would fuck it all up.

When I told her at school, though, Brid didn't seem too fazed.

"Funsies. We basically have a parent-endorsed date," she said.

"We have to learn to set boundaries with them about the slaying schedule sometime," I said, playing with the Campus Safety Cutie taser I carried on my keychain. "I want to like, stay home sometimes. I'm going to be a lawyer, not a slayer. Like, sure, it's important, but it's her calling, not mine."

Brid shrugged. "I mean, it's all our cause. Even the regular state department has admitted there's like, a vampire population explosion happening in Seattle. A vampire pandemic, practically. Imagine if we didn't kill five or six of them a night. There'd be like, billions."

"Their population is limited to the humans who already exist, and they'd need to keep some to eat," I reminded her. "I don't know, it just feels like maybe a team of women doing this a handful at a time isn't the way to move the needle. There should be like, a police force in charge of this. Beyond the people who raided the camps in 2020. A hunting patrol that looks for tunnels and bars. The laws should change so it doesn't have to be just vigilantes."

"At least she lets other people work with her and listens to Daylight when they tell her not to blow too many things up at a time. But hey," Brid continued. "I promise it'll be fun. I just like spending time with you. I don't care how. And I still get you to myself."

So, on Saturday morning, we made our way through the sweltering, summer-abandoned University District to our favorite boba place, Boba Gem, and then sauntered in a leisurely way down by the water on the bike trail until we got to the cross street with Bagley. We stopped to kiss on a bench, and her mouth was warm and wet and tasted sour from the super sugary drink. Up through the lazy, hot morning, past all these houses with drippy rhododendrons and Little Free Libraries, to the dilapidated house with black siding and a pink awning that you'd absolutely look at and be like: yeah, a gay vampire lives here.

Brid checked her watch and grinned. "We could just set it on fire now, right? Save everyone the trouble."

"Cain's probably not there now, and there's always like five or six little wannabe vampires that Cain has around. Human shields. Also, we can get more vamps if we get it at the party and block the exits."

In any case, I knew Brid hadn't brought her fire starters. We looked around on the quiet street for evidence of a tunnel. We heard only bees and Weedwackers and the distant highway. Maybe through a manhole, I thought, and checked the ones nearest to the curb. They were hot to touch because of the sun and locked tight, but Brid had a wrench. There was a profound stink when we opened them. Inside, there were a set of rungs leading down to a metal walkway. For vampires or city workers? Only one way to find out.

Down in the sewer, it was cooler by like ten or fifteen degrees than up above in the summer air. Brid clung close to me.

"Ooh, spooky," she breathed, on my neck. She put her soft hand under my shirt, on my back; it was warm against my clammy, sweaty skin. "What if I was a vampire? I'd bite you—" and she leaned forward and nibbled on my neck. It made electric shocks dance down my spine. Then she bit down, hard, with her dull human teeth. She pulled back, laughing.

I gasped. I wanted to kiss her, though the air also smelled like rotten eggs, metal, and poop. I turned on my flashlight. We walked on the metal walkway over the barest trickle of sewer water, holding hands, taking turns counting our steps, in case we got lost. If there was an entrance to a club, it would be near here—not a long walk away. Fortunately, I knew where to look for the signs. After ten minutes of little steps through the dark tunnels—an ancient-looking dusty trapdoor with purple, thick glass set into its face. It didn't look like it belonged in a sewer tunnel. A bat wing in spray paint decorated it with Cain's unmistakable sign. It was, unfortunately, also majorly locked.

Brid and I climbed out of the manhole cover, then tracked our path aboveground to the place where the door had been. It was an unassuming two-story brick building with a dive bar on the first floor, under a fortune-telling place. This was where the vampires would flee if anything happened at their party, and this was where we'd be waiting to stake them.

I texted mom: *We found it!*

"Mission accomplished," I said.

"We should go make out in Ravenna Park," Brid said.

The sun and smoke lifted the sewer-stink from our

skin. Among ferns off the trail, for the first time, I let Brid unbutton my pants.

"You act so Type A, but I know you're just a bottom," she whispered.

A week later, we were in position with our stakes and silver bullets and fire starters out to the U district, and that was the moment everything went wrong.

Mom was tense. I figured she'd found something out that complicated the raid, but she wasn't talking about it.

"June seems weirdly aggro," said Stacey to me quietly, as we looked through our binoculars to the house."

"She's just nervous about seeing her *ex*," Brid said sardonically. Which struck me as kind of mean.

My mom had a moment, the year before I was born, when she went kind of crazy. Dad had been stationed in Iraq. She was pregnant. Cain used her vulnerability and got close to her, and she let her guard down, and Cain fed her fake information about a vampire cell in Santa Monica that led to an ambush. She learned not to trust vampires.

My dad got killed in Iraq. Now we're living on 55 percent of my dad's estimated retirement salary plus the revenue from Security Sisters.

We watched the sun go down, the doors open, the lights come on in the vampire house.

Then the music started. It sounded like cars crashing, with a deep bass sound underneath. Cain's kids love sludge metal, noise music. The lights in the basement windows turned red. The people in the backyard were dancing; there were lights in the trees. But their shadows were wrong: vampires don't have shadows, and so only the shadows of humans in the crowd showed.

We had to wait and wait while the party went on, only staking the vampires that were leaving the party alone. That's procedure for these kinds of nights. We don't really strike till near sunrise, so there isn't time for vamps to retaliate. I was with Brid, waiting down by the water for vampires that took the scenic route home.

We'd been waiting hours, had only had one kill, and it was almost time to move back to the house, when I saw one older guy, walking with a younger girl. I could see from their shadows that she was undead, and the guy was dinner.

I staked the girl in the back as she wrapped her arms around the old guy and made for his neck. She disappeared into ash, the way they do. It blew into my eyes and made me cough, which was why I wasn't prepared for what came next. The old guy—and he must have been in his seventies—hit me in the face. Hard. I fell back and hit my ass on the ground and dropped my stake, and he tumbled after me, stomping at me. I spun and struck at him with the only thing on hand—one of my mom's Security Sisters window-breakers. He was screaming, totally incoherent. He was a big guy, and he was on top of me, which sucked, because we're not supposed to kill or hurt civilians at all. I was on the bike path by the bushes, and Brid couldn't see me, though I figured she could probably hear this guy's screaming.

"Slayer!" he shouted, as if it was a cause for alarm, and not relief.

"I just saved your life," I said to the guy. "That was a vampire."

"You killed my wife," he screamed at me. "I'll kill you!"

In the dark, yellow-black light of the water reflecting the streetlamps, his eyes were wide and insane. I pushed at him, but he got his hands on my neck. Which is why it was lucky that Brid ran up at that moment and hit him on the head with a wrench. She pulled me out from beneath him.

We looked at his form, crumpled on the ground. He was bleeding. This was a major problem, not least because the vampires in the area would smell fresh blood.

"I'll call 911 in a second. Don't tell anyone about this," Brid said. She's always been the more decisive one. I felt a lurch, and I looked at her in horror, but I was distracted by someone else running toward us. It was a vampire, fangs out, forehead wrinkly.

"Sam!" the vampire yelled. "Sam, are you okay?"

It saw us and stopped, its yellow eyes glowing in the night. Then it saw Brid's wrench, and my stake.

"Shit," the vampire said. Brid surged forward, wrench in one hand and stake in the other and tried to stake him, but he danced backward, facing us. He took out his phone and started to type. "You guys are slayers, huh."

"Damn straight," Brid said. She tried to get at his phone, but he circled her. I was back up on my feet by now, between him and the body on the ground behind us.

"Well, you fucked up," the vampire said.

This time, Brid got the vampire in the chest as he tried to run around us to get to the old guy on the ground. He dissolved into ash. Once you know the technique, vampires are really easy to kill. I coughed again. The guy had dropped his necklace when we staked him. I picked it up. It was silver-colored, but not silver. It was in the shape of a bent bat wing, shaped like half a heart. I stuck it in my pocket.

I felt my phone buzz, and saw it was my mom: *Where the hell are you? Get into position. Sunrise is in half an hour and I'm going to smoke these fuckers out.*

"We have to get back toward the house," I told Brid.

"Wait, we have to call 911," I said, and I paused, dialing. Brid was running ahead, so I jogged to keep up. I described the location of the body to the dispatcher; I said he looked homeless.

I should have told my mom we'd been seen. Then she could have made a plan.

The dew was wet on our ankles as we jogged back up through the dark, mostly quiet neighborhoods to the loud rancor of the house on Bagley. We were supposed to slide into position, hidden in a bush where the vampires couldn't see us, and then prevent the ones leaving the tunnel from going inside the house and vice versa. Brid was panting, exhilarated—and in hindsight, I should have known she wasn't thinking straight either. We both lay on our bellies in the bark. I kept seeing the wrench hit the old guy's skull.

I felt the boom under us as my mom's homemade explosives went off in the tunnel.

"I think I can start to see the sky getting light," Brid said, as we crouched in a rhododendron near the manhole.

I turned to look, and that was when I saw Cain right behind us, standing on the railing of the porch. I had seen him before, in pictures, but never in person, this close. If you glance at him from afar, he looks young-ish, a semi-androgynous, short, awkwardly proportioned guy, his chest narrower than his belly and hips. He wears velvet blazers that look not so much like they are Victorian as they are the 1970s remembering something Victorian, with really wide lapels. He had white hair flowing back from his face and slicked to his skull, pouty red lips, and a thin, scraggly goatee slicked to a chin already covered in blood. As we watched, his face morphed into his ridged, fanged form.

I turned and threw a stake, but he moved—too fast—and landed on me, wrestling me to the wet dirt before I could get my stake.

"You won't kill us this time," he hissed.

As he hugged me to him, I could see his skin up close, crinkled, mottled white, like glaciers run through with red rust. His nose flared out from its center as he smelled my hair, becoming like a bat's—wide, nostrils open, curves of flesh folded down and up. He bared his fangs in my face. He had known to expect us. The vampire we killed must have texted him.

"Run," I said to Brid, and pushed her, leaning away from Cain, trying to pull him off balance. She did run, turning and sprinting away, leaving me straining. I thought maybe she'd get my mom.

Cain's sharp fingernails hooked into my skin, and at the same time he reached out to press a button hidden in the paneling of the house, making the earth beneath us collapse. We fell into a hole. Cain's nails tore through my skin, anchoring me to his breast in the dark, dirt falling on both of our heads as we landed on hard cement. His nails grew longer as I writhed against him, webbing spinning between his fingers, Cain's forearms lengthening, his snout growing wolfish, the teeth jutting from his top gums down in the near-darkness. I hadn't known vampires could do that. White fur grew around his muzzle. Red tears dripped from his eyes.

"You killed my boyfriend, little one," Cain said, in the dark. His voice was like a chainsmoking college girl's. "You have been taught to kill and kill. Enough of it. Look up. *This* is the only image you will see while your heart beats." I looked up, and in front of the moon, I saw my mom, standing, holding a crossbow pointed at us. She wouldn't shoot, for fear of hitting me. Her shadow was dark, and I couldn't see her face.

"Get *down*, Rachel," she said, but I couldn't break from his grasp.

As his fangs sank into my neck, I thought I was going to die, though my screams died in my throat. He pressed another button, I guess, and a trap door slid slowly shut, slamming us into earthy darkness. His breath was cool, where Brid's had been warm. His lips, though, were hot—I guess from drinking living blood. He held me there for what seemed like forever, gulping my blood, far more than ten minutes, fifteen. I was dizzy in the dark. My knees were weak. Each time I tried to move, his grip tightened, and his fingers were longer around me, sharp.

"Drink from me. Eat well. I want you to know pain like me. I hate you, but I *know* you. I think you want it too."

He bit his own wrist hard, so the blood flowed thick, and stuck it, bleeding, into my mouth. I didn't want to die. I swallowed, and swallowed again, because there was dirt in my mouth. It wasn't my fault. I drank and came back from the brink.

And that's how I became a vampire.

MARCH
(Seven months later)

2.

FAWN

I didn't exactly allow myself to believe what I was doing was real until I got on the bus. This was, I thought to myself, a kind of vengeful, crazy, grieving friend thing. Not a real thing, not exactly. But if he was out there—I texted him, and then messaged him on Facebook Messenger, Tumblr, Twitter and Instagram. All the same thing: *If you've run off to be a vampire without me, and haven't told me, I'm going to be so fucking pissed, Silver. You absolute asshole.*

I watched the little gray bubble underneath the message turn blue. Read.

Probably his parents had his phone.

I hadn't seen the body, but the coroner had. He would have had to lie still a long time. And I wasn't sure if they'd have cut him open.

Next, I messaged Cain. I hadn't talked to him in months—he had liked a couple of my posts, but we weren't like, talk-all-the-time mutuals anymore. It was also embarrassing to have been such a huge fan of someone who I understood now to be probably kind of a fake person, a character. Nobody really was the way he acted. It was role-play. Crazy vampires who talked about vampires ruling the world weren't people who really existed, turning people, they were just something right-wingers made up to prevent vampire clinics showing up in their town. Probably Cain was some sad nobody somewhere, like me. Maybe not even really a vampire. I didn't know what I would say to him. I wrote, on Tumblr Messages: *Hey, this is weird and awful and feels really weird to write you about on here. Silver killed himself last night. His girlfriend said he had been talking about running away and living with you. I was just wondering, is that true? Have you been in touch with him? I'm not on good terms with his family, so nothing you say to me will make it to them. I just want to understand.*

One day after the funeral which I was not invited to, I walked—sleepwalked—to the cemetery, where I knew he was, or must be. It took an hour to get there, to the family grave where his grandfather was buried. The gravestone next to that one was new, and shiny. The name engraved there was not Silver. The last name was his. It was weird, I thought, to think of him there, cold, below the ground beneath the wrong name. I knelt to press my face to the earth, thinking about Mary Shelley and how she carried Percy's heart around with her until she died.

The earth beneath was muddy and, oddly, turned up.

I knew that new graves didn't get turfed over right away, and that the soil was often kind of loose initially, when they buried someone. But this was more than that. It looked like a huge mole had just burrowed out of it. Rocks and sticks and grass twisted at the edge. And something shiny, in the dirt, caught my eye. I bent down to take it.

A bat's wing, sharp on the edges, chain still dangling, snapped at the clasp. I held it up to my own necklace, and it made a perfect heart.

The coffin would have been closed; it couldn't have fallen out.

The mud around the grave was trodden on, and there were many sets of footprints. I stood there, holding the necklace.

The driver on the Greyhound bus didn't ask to see my ID, or my vax card, or anything. I just got on, and twenty minutes later, we left town, driving to DC, where the bus would veer west. The sun glimmered briefly through gray clouds and disappeared. I was one of just a handful of people on board. I had chosen my outfit carefully—I wanted to look like a girl, and look Goth, but also didn't want to draw *too* much attention to myself. I had my school backpack with me, two changes of pants, one skirt, and four shirts stuffed into the interior alongside my copy of *The Vampire Armand,* a pack of gum, a toothbrush, three KN95 masks, deodorant, a new set of razors—the girl kind with lots of blades—and a pack of Camels I thought I could maybe offer to someone in exchange for information on where to sleep. My hair was down. I had some eyeliner on. Most of my face was hidden under my black mask. The rest of my outfit was black and unornamented. I wore both halves of the bat necklace over my shirt.

I had not told Flo I was going.

I had my phone, which I had gone back and forth about. Ultimately, even though it could potentially be used to track me down, I did need a phone. On my blog, I had posted, *Do I know any mutuals in Seattle who could put me up?*

I had four thousand, two hundred and thirty-seven followers on Tumblr. That didn't mean that much, because a lot of those accounts weren't active anymore, and a lot of the other ones just followed me to re-blog my pictures of graveyards.

Cain hadn't written back.

And also—there was something else happening with Silver's Tumblr.

There had been *five* new posts on the blog since he died. All of the pictures in the mermaid series he'd been drawing—women with dark gills and frightening teeth.

All of them had been posted in the last twenty-four hours before I hopped on the bus.

That wasn't in itself proof that he was alive. His timed queue was still going, and probably would for a while. It was weird that he would have queued art to post like that, all in a row, but it wasn't impossible. If he had plugged them into his queue before committing suicide, there might be a weird message in there. Something he meant to share, after he died.

But the *likes* tab?

I was pretty sure that the last thing he had liked before

the funeral was a giveaway post that had this picture of this fancy dragon ring with a red stone. Now the first thing visible when you clicked on his likes tab was a picture of the full moon with pink text reading: *trans men who don't bind are valid.*

That wasn't something his parents would have liked when going through his Tumblr. I didn't even think that they knew how to access his Tumblr. Unless someone else had access to his account. But why would they?

I was straddling the border of reality and something else.

On his fifteenth birthday, back in 2020, we got suspended for wearing Dracula capes to school because it was too offensive. At his house that night I asked Silver what he thought it was like to drink blood.

"Like this," he said, immediately, and went to his knife collection.

He cut a little notch in his hand and I drank blood out of it, which was the closest my body had been to his body at that point. He tasted like salt and metal, like when I had licked the playground pole in kindergarten. Then I cut my hand and he drank. It was kind of funny—he and I could drink each other's blood and be totally normal humans, still, but if a vampire did it, it was illegal. The only difference was that vampires would have saliva that could keep the blood flowing longer and maybe cure your ailments, and their face would go monster-wrinkly, and their eyes would go yellow or red, and they'd need it more.

It would be cool, I thought, to have someone need the very blood in my body. To be useful just by existing. To be necessary for another person's life—even if it did nothing, physically for me. Even if it hurt me. I wondered if it felt different, if a vampire did it. With Silver, it felt good.

During sleepovers Silver and I stayed up all night on YouTube combing through interviews with people who were vampires, who were registered and got the blood bags in the big liberal cities that did that. The videos were from before the July 2020 blood shortage: the ones from local news channels in the 2000s were about how it was nice not to need to hurt themselves or others to live, and to have somewhere safe from the sun, and how nice it was for the cities to give vampires what they needed to live. Most of the vampires had already lived in big cities, before the Recognition Act. The municipal government videos said that once vampires had been given the option of bagged blood and banned from drinking blood from living people, most of them switched, so the cities were safer now for everyone. There were new vlogs by registered vampires who said that they were okay with living on one bag, now that the ration had been cut. There were some videos where people sounded more like Cain and talked about how the blood banks starved vampires slowly, and made vampires distant from each other, and housing was hard to find, and how there should be more humans who gave their blood willingly, because it was good for humans too. Usually, those videos got removed.

There was one channel from a guy who claimed to be doing interviews with really old vampires, who would describe historical events they'd experienced, but his channel got shut down by Google for promoting illegal activity because the vampires would talk about drinking blood and hunting. That was the thing with the more interesting channels—they usually got deleted. A lot of history and medical articles about vampires were behind paywalls, too. You could get the old *New York Times* articles from before the Recognition Act through the library. "VAMPIRE DEN BUSTED WITH A BANG," that kind of thing. The tone they used was somewhere between fear and humor, like in old vampire movies. Some of the old articles had photos of vampire ash. If you searched *vampire getting staked* online, there were shaky found-footage videos that were out there, on the same websites where the Saddam Hussein execution was. Silver watched those, had theories about where the slayers lived. I didn't like it when he talked about it.

There was one vlog that ended right after the guy making it, who was obsessed with vampires and posted a bunch of vampire movies with his commentary, got turned into a vampire. His last video was about the physical changes he was going through. He said he couldn't reveal anything about his sire.

"My life never made sense before," the guy said. "Now it does. I know what I am."

We paused the video, and Silver leaned forward, studying the hint of sharp bone beneath the vampire guy's forehead, where his vampire ridges would be when he was hungry. He'd gotten ridges tattooed on, before he turned. The real ridges were in a slightly different place. Silver and I looked at each other, after looking.

"Cringe, but hot," Silver said. I laughed. I'd been thinking the same thing.

That night was the first night we made out, even though we'd slept in the same room a lot.

A couple months later, when we were on lockdown and talking to Cain more, and Silver was writing letters back and forth with him, Cain had sent us the set of bat wing necklaces. It came with a letter about how his community was dying, the old ones being killed by the state because of the pandemic. I thought Cain was probably roleplaying, like Silver was, but I knew from news that the shortage was real enough. In Seattle and NYC and LA and Chicago, they had been feeding all these old vampires blood, and now they'd cut the ration because of the Covid-19 blood shortage. There might be hundreds that had starved. Now, Cain said, we would be a new generation of vampires, saving each other and the world. When you slid the two bat wing necklaces together, they formed a heart.

Silver was hooking up with Flo by then, but they hadn't started dating until later, and when they did start, he didn't stop wearing the necklace.

Forever, the text on the back of the bat wings said. I felt weird about Cain sometimes, because he was one of those internet people you really know nothing about, but he understood something about me. I had worn my necklace every day, and Silver had worn his, for the year and a half after that.

This was part of the reason I knew Silver wasn't really dead.

The first half-day on the bus was boring; the rain beat down on the windshield and then cleared as we drove into the dusty highways west of Virginia and then, at last, Ohio. My hope had been to stay on a bus the whole time, straight through to the west coast. At each stop I would run off, pee as quickly as I could in the women's restroom, fill my bottle, and climb back on to reclaim my seat. I was pretty scared the bus would leave without me.

At three PM when I'd been on the bus long enough to feel like I'd been born there, Flo texted me:

Fawn, where are you? Your parents called me looking for you.

This isn't funny.

I know you're hurting too, but whatever you're doing is probably stupid.

She was right, I knew. I only had two hundred dollars with me. Four hundred more in a bank account that my parents would probably freeze—but I had to keep it there for now, in case I got robbed on the bus.

I didn't trust Flo not to rat me out.

Fawn, she texted, at eight that night. *Your parents called the police to look for you. You need to come back. I can't lose you too.*

As if we had been best friends. Whatever. I could tell her and not tell her where.

Flo, I wrote. *I think Silver is alive. I'm going to find him.*

It was ten minutes later that my phone began to ring.

"Flo," I said, trying to keep my voice down. I didn't trust her, but I picked up the call on the strength of how she had held me when I'd broken down sobbing the day that we got the news. She had held me as if she cared about me, and when her mom started talking about how strong I was to live in this town as a trans girl, she had glared at her mom to shut up.

"Fawn, I don't know what you just sent me. Where are you going? Where are you?"

"I—Flo, I can't tell you more right now. I'm not sure if I'm right. But there's nothing for me at home. I can't be there anymore."

"Fawn, I don't think this is a great idea. And—when you say, like, he's alive—"

"*Might* be alive," I corrected. "Or un-alive rather."

"Fawn, I saw him. I saw his *body*. He is absolutely dead. He is not alive. We cried together. I think this moment can make us all go kind of insane, but I need you to not say stuff like that. I *saw his body*."

I had not, because I was not his girlfriend, and they thought I was selling him drugs.

"I know," I said. I tried to make my voice have a kind tone. It sounded flat.

"I saw him go into the *ground*. And you didn't, because you stayed home, so now you're saying—."

"I wasn't *invited*," I said. My tone got a little snippy. "Because I'm the evil transsexual."

"I can't believe you're making this my fault!"

"Flo, it's not your fault, but—"

"My boyfriend died!"

"We were hooking up," I said, which shut her up for one of the most glorious periods of thirty-second silence I had experienced up till that point.

"What?" Flo asked.

"Silver and I were *fucking*, Flo. Whenever he slept over. Since we were fifteen. He didn't tell you, because there were things he didn't tell both of us."

"What?" Her voice broke. "I don't—Why would you say that?"

"Here's the truth," I growled. "When I visited his grave, the ground looked dug up. Like someone had crawled out. And his necklace was there, on the dirt. The other half of *my* necklace."

A long pause.

"Fawn, this is insane."

"Go look at the grave. It's dug up."

"He's *dead*, Fawn! This is really messed up. You're delusional about a population of people who are *very sick*. They spend their lives with trackers on their feet going back and forth from the clinic or they're criminals in the woods, they're not *glamorous* or whatever. Please, come home. I need you. I can't go through this alone. It's too much. You have to come home. Your parents are worried. Are you on a bus? I'm going to have to tell them."

I hung up.

Then, after she called me twice more, I blocked her number.

It wasn't that Flo was a bad person. But she was from a different world, a safer world. Now that I was leaving, I didn't have to pretend to be in her world anymore.

I knew there was a possibility that the other reality that was opening before me was not actually real—that Silver was dead, and that the vampire world I wanted didn't exist anymore.

It was terrifying.

At the next rest stop, I sat down on the toilet in the combination Marathon and 7/11 and cried for a minute. It was true that I had no idea what I was doing. Who knew where Silver was? I had no idea where I would sleep when I got to Seattle, or how I would make money. Without my parents, I had no health insurance, or way to get to college. I was leaving everything behind in the spur of the moment, with no idea where I was going next.

But it was also true that I couldn't stay with my parents anymore. They didn't love me. They weren't even good people—my dad worked for a company that sold weapons to the government. They only tolerated me because they were sure at some point I would change completely into a man they imagined was there, inside me, that I would never be. The only reason I had been able to stand it for the last two years was because someone was nearby who saw me, touched me, felt as weird as I was. Silver's long info-dumps about blood, his hands grabbing my hips like my body was shaped the way I wanted it to be, rather than how it was. It wouldn't be enough, even if Flo tried. I tried to push away the ungenerous thoughts, like—*she sees you as a freak.* She used my name. But even then, what I was left with wasn't much to base a friendship on. She wanted me to share her grief.

I didn't want to do that. I would be homeless on the street before I did that.

I compulsively opened my phone, planning to block her on the other platforms before the bus left again.

She had messaged me on Tumblr:

Fawn, this is really dangerous. People aren't always nice. Some people out there can really hurt you.

I wasn't used to feeling so angry but having no idea where to direct my anger. I didn't know what to do with it.

I left the 7/11 to see the bus's headlights turning on again. Suddenly, I had a thought. If she knew I was on a bus, then she might know that I was on a Greyhound headed for Seattle. I thought it was probably pretty easy for cops to call other cities to search a Greyhound looking for a missing teen. My parents also might think to tell the police I might have boarded a bus.

I'd made it this far—I was somewhere in Ohio outside of Cincinatti. I hesitated. I had my bag with me, with all my stuff. I'd paid for the ticket, so getting off here I'd lose the money.

But if I got taken back to my parents' house—that couldn't happen.

I would hitchhike.

People still hitchhiked, right?

I just wouldn't let anyone assault me.

I massaged my temples, thinking about Silver's smile.

I hung back when the bus engine revved up. The afternoon shadows were getting longer, stretching over the distant parking lot's prairie-like expanse. I stepped out of the terminal and began walking along the long parking lot, towards the road. There was a Subway on the corner—the only food option off the highway. Birds wheeled overhead in the late afternoon sky. The scrubby grass that grew between the cracks in the pavement looked like it had survived eight or nine mass extinctions and would hang on for ten or so more.

I got a sandwich at the Subway because I hadn't eaten, and got ma'amed by the woman who worked there, which felt good. Then I sat outside, looking at the sky turning into sunset. I couldn't make myself walk down to the highway and stand on the side. That might get me arrested faster than being on the Greyhound bus. My best shot was to talk to people in the Subway.

I went up to a woman with a kid walking to her car.

"Hey, are you driving west?" I asked.

She turned to look at me over her shoulder, looked me up and down. Her eyes grew hard. "Get away from me, pervert."

I retreated to the bench by the Subway. I noticed the Blue Lives Matter sticker on the woman's car as she drove away.

When a big semi-truck pulled into the parking lot, I decided to take my chances.

"Hey," I said to the guy getting out. He was tall and thin, fiftyish, white, with a hooked nose and a tan on one side of his face and a sweatshirt rolled up around graying hair on freckled forearms. "Are you going cross country?"

"California," he said, and somehow made it three syllables.

"Can you take me?"

He gave me a quick once-over, rubbed his nose on the back of his hand with one quick swipe. He had a scar on his thumb. "Kid," he said in a warning tone. "I don't take passengers. Not trying to get in the middle of anything."

"Just for like, a few hours."

"Tryna get me put where folks don't come out. Shit. Dressed like *vampire bait.*" He turned away.

“I’m just Goth,” I said, trying to smile politely. How had he known? It was weird to feel like I passed, that way, even if he meant it as an insult. It made me feel good, and also fucked up.

He laughed a little, turning back to give me a second once-over. “Sorry. If you’re not vampire bait . . .Tiny thing like you, you got no business wearing that.” He pointed toward my necklace with a casual nicotine-yellowed finger. “Where’d you get that?”

“My friend got it for me.”

“People are gonna fuck with you one way or another out here. Call your mom. Go home. Bus station down there,” he said, and pointed the way I had come.

“Oh, is it? Thank you,” I said, trying to keep the edge out of my voice. I sat back down, humiliated—but also glad I’d at least gotten into an exchange with him. He could have just grunted and moved away.

The guy went into Subway, ordered, and sat in a booth. I thought I’d wait until he left until I talked to anyone else. I turned surreptitiously to watch him, trying to keep my phone in my pocket, taking out *The Vampire Armand* to read, like I wanted to be sitting at this Subway past sundown. I wondered if I could ask one of the workers there if I could sleep in the bathroom. The woman who had called me ma’am might be chill.

When he came back out, scratching his ass, he looked me over again, and I felt a prickle of fear. I had laid my cards out knowing nothing about this guy. His half-tanned face with dark eyes ringed underneath with lack of sleep squinted down at me. I looked at his shoes, not willing to glance up to his face.

"Kid," he said.

I grunted, setting my book down in the most non-desperate way possible. "Sup?"

"Don't sit out here all night, some asshole will fuck with you. You can come with me through Iowa. Making a stop there. But after that I'm going south. If you wanna go North, you gotta find another truck."

How to say "thanks, mister" without saying "thanks, mister"? "I'll pay for gas," I suggested.

He snorted. "My company pays for the gas. Just don't cause me any problems." He paused. "And put away that necklace. It's tacky."

I looked down at the bat necklace, and up again at him, still wondering about what he'd said earlier, but tucked it inside my shirt. "Okay."

He extended a hand. "I'm Paul."

"I'm Fawn," I said, which was not the best idea—I should have given a false name. But I didn't have another one to give, except the old one that sounded like death.

"Don't go telling everyone you meet you like vampires," Paul said.

"Why not?" I said, as if it was a casual thing, and not something taboo I had accidentally built my life around. "I think vampires are cool and hot."

Paul smirked. "That's a crazy thing to say. You know that, right? At least while you're a runaway teen, I would tell you the smart thing to do is keep that on the down low," he said. "Cops will be all over you. And most vampires mostly get really offended when you talk like that, anyway."

I was immediately more curious; any part of me that wanted to cut and run disappeared.

We climbed into the great turtle-head of a white cab which pulled the big white box on wheels—it was higher off the ground than I had ever been in a car. I tried to figure out what Paul might want with me. Maybe just company—it had to be lonely to drive all day and night. If I was perky and chipper enough, maybe he'd deliver me to a city where I could get a train or a bus that my mother and father wouldn't know to track. But I didn't want to be annoying.

It wasn't out of the question that he'd want something else from a weird girl-boy teenager he picked up outside a Subway. I didn't have any weapons. I calculated in my head exactly what it was worth to me to get West.

His big truck hummed and rumbled underneath us, shaking the flesh of my sides. It felt like riding a huge beast, a dragon. The seat beneath me had tears in the plastic cover, like we were at a small restaurant. I saw these trucks all the time and noted how high their drivers' seats were, but when you were in them it really did feel like you were looking down on everyone else. You wouldn't be able to see a small animal or a child just in front of the car.

"What do you deliver?" I asked, by way of making conversation, buckling my seat.

He grunted. "This shit's all packaged snacks and crap," he said. "We're with Trader Joes and Aldi. But it varies. Don't always drive for them."

"Is trucking a good job?"

Paul rubbed his jaw thoughtfully. He seemed to appreciate the question. "Before this I worked in Arizona, out in the copper mines. My dad did that too. This is better. If you like being alone, and you can stay awake a long time, not bad. Drivers get fucked over, though. You gotta have a good dispatcher who understands you can't drive in a snowstorm."

"That's real," I said, because I wanted to sound like I knew what I was talking about. "Snowstorms are intense."

This must have been the wrong answer, because Paul didn't talk to me for another half-hour after that. He turned on the radio instead. It was, kind of to my surprise, NPR. They were talking about how each year there had been fewer oysters along the coast of Washington State. I thought about Silver, his face dead white, lying like Laura Palmer among the dwindling oysters.

I had faded into the night-fog that draped our evening slog to Indianapolis when Paul said, in the half-light of the dim night highway,

"You're a transgender, huh."

I was dumb, I realized, as he shifted gears, merged lanes, loudly, the Walmarts and Targets of whatever sprawling town we were in whizzing by. I really had not had any clue what I was getting into; I would have been safer on a bus. I would end up dead, my body parts distributed somewhere—like any one of the hundreds of trans girls in ditches somewhere between New York and San Francisco.

"I'm trans, yeah." I said, wondering what kind of shit he'd pull next.

Paul nodded. "Right. That. My sister's kid is one too," he said. He took a slow breath, let it out. "Think about that kid a lot. 'S maybe part of why I picked you up. Younger than you. He was seven or eight when he decided he was a girl. Now he's maybe thirteen. Long hair. Wears dresses. Sister's homeschooling, because the kids were such little shits to him."

Something in my sternum shifted, and I felt maybe a little safer. Though maybe not. Maybe Paul would tell me next how they beat the kid to a pulp and he approved. My responses were on autopilot.

"She," I said. "If she says she's a girl, she is."

Paul nodded thoughtfully again, the long lines around his mouth stretching. "Guess so," he said. "Sorry. Doesn't really matter to me. Even the hormones, people get upset about that. But there's hormones in everything these days anyway. What gets me is people who get really mad about it. My thought is, if he's gay, let him be gay. Right?"

"Right," I said, though Paul had clearly missed the gist of my statement. "I, uh, think being gay and being trans are a little different. But I basically agree."

"I saw that show a few years ago, what's the show about the miners in England. Billy Elliot? That one."

"Oh, yeah," I said.

"It's like, you want to be a dancer, dance," Paul said.

That made me smile. He was sweet, I thought. Even kind of cute, in a ragged, rough old man kind of way. I stayed nervous, my heart sitting a little forward in my chest, rumbling like the engine.

"I'm trying," I said.

"You running away?"

I nodded. "I'm gonna go live with my friend," I said. "Parents—they're not like your sister."

Paul breathed out heavily through his teeth. "It's tough out there," he said. His brow furrowed. "They beat you?"

I considered how much to lie. It sounded better to have been beaten. My dad had not spanked me since I turned ten. He did sometimes raise his fist like he was going to hit me, and then would talk about how he was a better man than that.

"Sometimes," I said.

"My parents beat me and my brothers," Paul said. "Used to be normal. But it's no good."

"It's mostly that there's just nothing to do in my town. No way to make a living if you're someone like me."

Paul looked like he might have some respect for me. "Well, Seattle can't be all bad. Expensive, though. Worse than out in flyover country. Worse than DC area, even."

That was something I hadn't had to think about yet. "Kurt Cobain made it work," I said, trying to be funny.

"No, he didn't. Motherfucker's dead." He paused. "You shouldn't go looking for vampires."

"Are there—you seem to know something about vampires. Are there a lot of vampires out there, in Seattle?"

He scoffed. "I'd say so."

"You know—you know about vampires."

He grunted. "Sure."

"How did you meet them?"

"Wait to run after a vampire till you have some brains in your head. That's what I'm gonna say."

I felt offended but waited for him to say more. But his lecture, it seemed, only had one bullet point.

NPR had switched to the problems of Gaza, and how

they were impossible to solve, nobody's fault, and had been around for centuries. We drove on in silence.

I looked at Silver's blog on my phone and hit refresh. Out here, my signal was bad, and the gray circles turned and turned like a wheel rolling slowly down a hill.

Then the page reloaded.

This picture wasn't a painting. Nor had it been reblogged from someone else. It was clearly taken out of the rainy window of a car. An indigo, darkening sky loomed overhead, rife with curves and splinters of cloud, and, between it and a low, long beige building, a tall, blood-red sign that said IOWA-80.

The tags said #middle of nowhere #road trip #bloodbrother

This was something Flo *had* to see. Maybe she was staring at it at the same time. But I couldn't text her. It did vindicate me. Maybe she would see I had been right.

I thought of holding it out to Paul, to ask if he knew where it was, but I figured it wasn't a good idea. I couldn't place exactly why, except that it would give him more information about me that I didn't want him to have.

As the dark road wound on, I thought about how Silver had moved along this road, or a parallel one, not long before. I knew now that he was out there—though exactly what he was doing was beyond me. I was furious at him. The cloudy purple sky was like a bruise. I texted Silver again:

I'm so fucking pissed at you.

My eyes began to blur, and my head drooped. It had

been a long day, and my muscles ached. I let myself rest my face against the cool pane of glass that faced the road, even though it vibrated with the asphalt's texture.

3.

RACHEL

Here's the thing about being a vampire who's also a vampire hunter: you don't have a whole hell of a lot of people who are on your side.

And my girlfriend wasn't texting back.

I sat at the kitchen table in my mom's apartment, the downpour outside clicking on the glass, the metal vampire-tracker latched on my ankle clanking against the chair when I pulled it in underneath me or shifted my weight reading. On the table, next to a pile of glitter-encrusted tasers and bulletproof backpack inserts my mom was making a video with for a giveaway sat an unsealed half-bag of blood in a measuring cup, the sharpie drawn on the side to the place I was supposed to fill the cup up to. I'd had half the bag this morning. Stamps on the bag: Seattle Children's. You have to ration it carefully, so the hunger doesn't catch up with you.

You'd think Moms Against Vampires In Seattle would have come up with some ideas for what to do if one of their own got turned, but the consensus-based process they developed in the nineties was still working, after six months, on the problem of *me*. As a result, I was extremely bored, reading an old National Geographic and waiting like a useless kid for my mom to get home from the MAVIS meeting and take me to therapy. It made me itch. I didn't get to make videos for Security Sisters anymore, because Mom was worried the other slayer cells would clock my fangs, and their follower count had taken a little hit, because, let's face it, I was the face of the brand. Security Sisters got four or five messages a week asking what had happened to me, since my mom was the face of all the videos now, accompanied occasionally by Brid and Stacey. My mom messaged everyone back to tell them I was taking a break.

I hadn't gotten any updates about current kills from the Moms, though based on a slight numerical decline in classmates at the government vampire night school where I spent the hours of 8 p.m. to 2 a.m., Mondays through Fridays, MAVIS was getting on fine without me. Which kind of hurt my pride. I'd always gotten in at least three kills a week.

My phone beeped: Mom was outside.

I tried to look cheerful and "good" as I bounced down the outdoor stairs of our apartment complex to her car.

"Good news. Our corporate reps from Daylight were here tonight. They're in testing phase five, whatever that means. Got a treat for you, kiddo," she said, handing me another polyethylene bag. The liquid inside was brighter red than what I'd just drank.

Daylight Inc, who helps fund MAVIS, is working in their labs on a solution that can fix things—everything, if their annoying reps are to be believed. Basically, a synthetic blood that would free vampires from having to hurt anyone, would be free from demand pressures on medical blood, and would let them—us—go out in the day. They're a disruptor company. Because the blood shortage during the Covid-19 lockdown made so many vampires die and go rogue, Daylight argues that it's clearly a broken system. Their product, of course, will fix it. They say it will be available for sale to people, to cities, to the state, all over the world, within the year. They said that last year too. Right now, they're testing it on vampires who sign up for the trial and—because not a lot of vampires volunteer—other vampires we grab for them off the street. And now, me.

Bright, viscous red liquid in bags. It's interesting, because regular food tastes terrible now. Even meat. Steak tastes like farts. Sugar tastes like acid. The Daylight blood, though, tastes ok—just kind of sweet, like it's flavored with breakfast syrup. When nothing's sweet anymore, it *is* like dessert. This was my sixth-ever bag. I slurped it down as if it was an Italian soda before I thought better of it. My mom watched me edgily without turning her face toward me as we veered out of the parking lot.

Before MAVIS voted to report me to the government instead of killing me, I had stayed in my room for three weeks with no blood. I'd gone all vampire-wrinkly, with the ridges and red eyes and stuff, though I couldn't see myself in the mirror. Blood-hunger at its worst blurs your vision, it makes you ache all over, and it also makes you totally ready to tear into whoever is closest. For weeks until I got blood bags, it was all I felt. My spine stood up in my back. My hairline had receded in that fucked-up creepy way, and my teeth were long and horrible. I looked like death, and I felt like I wanted to attack my mom when she looked in on my room. Every time she came in, I got closer and closer to letting go, to killing her. After they registered me and got me blood, my nose felt normal again, and my mom told me my eyes faded from red to yellow to brown. I wouldn't know. The Daylight fake blood was comforting to have on top of the ration. I felt, after I drank it, like maybe I looked a little extra normal.

"So how was the meeting?" I asked. I was feeling the stuff kick in. I was almost warm.

"We talked about stuff, made proposals."

"Wow, riveting," I sniped. Before, she would have told me what the proposals were.

I ran my tongue over my teeth as my mom inched up onto the traffic-clogged highway toward Bellevue. Even after drinking the blood and now the bright viscous synth-blood, which I could still taste, sticky and sweet on my lips, I was thirsty.

What I hated was I was *still* so hungry, aching, all the time.

I could tell Mom could tell what I was thinking.

"When Daylight starts sending us more, it'll feel better. It's just logistical stuff, this last trial, then we get it every week, big box. They were talking about how the initial tests show it *is* increasing patients' resistance to sun."

I sucked the syrupy dregs—half a mouthful. "People are going to love it when vampires are out all over the place."

"If you don't have to drink human blood anymore and can slurp whatever fortified corn syrup goo that's in that thing instead, you can be out whatever time of day you want," my mom said.

I didn't want to drink blood *or* synth blood. I wanted to be eating cocoa quinoa puffs with Brid and Stacey. But I wasn't one of the crew anymore.

"How's Brid?" I asked.

My mom smiled tersely. "She misses you. She won the swim meet this Saturday."

"She hasn't texted."

"She *does* miss you," Mom said, and it was almost like I was a girl instead of a monster now, for a second. She was trying to be reassuring. "It's just hard for her. You have to get that."

"It's hard, yeah," I said. Mom didn't know we'd done hand stuff.

When Brid dipped her fingers under the waistband of my underwear, it made me feel like the whole world would never be the same, and it was like, not only are we badass vampire slayers together, we're now *girlfriend* vampire slayers. But like, now . . . I wasn't at meetings or on patrol or in school and her mom was for sure not going to let me come over now I was a bloodsucking leech, so I didn't see her. I'd tried, one time—snuck out, took the bus to her house—but she'd been out on patrol, and when I left a note for her to meet me the next night, she texted: *No, Rachel. That would be stupid.*

She was right. I should wait until I earned everyone's trust before trying to get with her again. But I wouldn't ever earn their trust, probably. She would still send a heart and a *:) good how about you* back, sometimes, which felt toxic because that was not an emoticon she would have ever used, but sometimes not even that, and she'd never reply to three texts in a row. She maybe regretted having fucked me right before I became a bloodthirsty creepy demon. Maybe we weren't really girlfriends anymore, though we hadn't *talked* about that.

"How was school this week?" Mom asked. "Any suspicious activity?"

"I don't know," I shrugged. "People are pretty dead-eyed."

"Har har," Mom said. "Seriously. There's not a good reason for you to be there if you're not going to gather information. You can't just be getting into trouble. Any of the teachers giving vampire?"

"Mom, they vet people like crazy. None of those teachers are vampires."

"Just keep an eye. Any students seem oddly well-fed?"

I had casual friends at my old school, not that they'd known about my life as a slayer. I wasn't at that school anymore. Those people probably thought I had moved and ghosted. Now I spent most of the day sitting in class assiduously avoiding eye contact—there's something even worse about looking into bloodred eyes and hollow cheeks knowing yours look just the same.

"I don't know about well-fed. But they're leaving or getting staked. Probably one person a week has disappeared from class since February," I said, shrugging and looking at her reflection in the dark car window instead of her face. "And only two new ones."

My mom scowled at a red light. "You didn't tell me that. I wonder whether they're getting staked or going underground."

"For sure," I said, thinking about whether there would be enough time between when my mom dropped me at the door to the therapist's office and when my appointment started for me to smoke one of my last four joints out front.

"You know she still wants to flamethrow you. You want to be in those meetings, you have to earn your way back. You gotta help me fight for you."

"What am I supposed to do, go up and ask where they go at night? *Vere* do you go to suck the *vlood*?"

My mom pulled into the dark, empty parking lot, where one yellow light indicated the door to Tammy's office. "Be strategic and stop setting stuff on fire at school so I don't have to drop you off in the middle of goddamn nowhere for some crunchy granola lady to talk to you about your feelings."

"Someone's being a hypocrite about setting stuff on fire."

I threw my legs out of the car and stood up, waving to my mom once as she left, opening the door like I was going in. Then I stopped, sat down on the curb outside Tammy's office, and lit up. I liked imagining the greenish cloud inside my strange, dead lungs. Weed at least still smelled and tasted the same. I wondered where I was going to get weed when these joints were gone, now that Brid wasn't talking to me. I inhaled, and under the weed smoke, I could smell the Sound, and distant humans' blood, and animals scurrying in the bushes by the Whole Foods parking lot.

Being majorly nocturnal and hemoglobin-dependent and incapable of going to school in the day with the girl I love and instead having to be around some undead dick-heads *is* why I had taken to smoking weed in the girls' bathroom at night school on Tuesday nights in January, which is why I accidentally caught the trash can on fire, which is why on this particular Thursday night in March I was headed to the most beige room ever, waiting for my appointment with the one therapist in the city that does exclusively night-time therapy for vampire teenagers. My school referred me. When you're in vampire school, you can't really ignore referrals. They have a tracker on you.

Tammy stuck her head out and saw me smoking weed.

"Rachel," she said, smiling a cool-with-it smile. "Come on in when you're ready."

I ashed my roach and dredged myself up to follow her in.

I cannot actually tell Doctor Tammy anything real or important about my life, because it would get my mom, June Sorkin, Seattle's Greatest Vampire Slayer, in major trouble with the law. People never think about this with therapy, the mandated reporter thing, and how it stops me talking about what's actually wrong.

Tammy was wearing fucking plaid again, like a cartoon of a badly dressed lesbian. She was kind of cute, in an old-fogey kind of way. She has a double chin and thick glasses and this kind of academic-y, don't-give-a-shit slouch.

Tammy had a turtle in her office. It sat quietly in its tank, looking dead, but I had seen it move twice so I knew it was alive.

"Last time," Tammy said, after I had sat silently for as long as I felt I could get away with and then some extra time that surprised me, "you talked to me about how you felt your relationship to the world had been forced to change, and being sad you couldn't hang out with your friends."

She waited, after that, to see if I had anything to say.

"Yeah," I said. "I guess I did."

I'm never hugely into therapy.

"Would you like to continue talking about that, or should we cover some other ground today?"

I know it would be a total bitch move to let her sit in silence the whole time, and would be wasting my mom's $120, so I tried to think of something I could talk about that would be useful to me. I was not bringing up Bridget. I was worried Tammy would tell my mom.

"Uh," I said. "Well, I guess I'm worried that everyone around me is going to think I'm evil now."

Tammy sometimes writes things down when I talk to her, but usually it's just a little chicken-scratch shorthand thing, so I can't like, crane my neck and see exactly what she thinks of me. She made a little scribble now. She looked back up at me. "Have your friends or family said things about vampires being evil?"

I shrugged. "Sure," I said.

"Really," Tammy said, judgmentally.

I bristled. "I mean, who doesn't? It's not like, an incorrect statement. When I don't have blood, I want to bite someone."

"Right, but you haven't bitten anyone."

"No," I said.

"Would you say you think vampires are generally evil?" Tammy asked. She put such a slight stress on it that it was *plausibly* a non-judgemental tone.

"Well, I think killing people is evil, and I think turning other people on purpose into vampires who live horrible, mutated lives and can't drink Jamba Juice is evil." I said, crossing my arms.

Tammy sat for a minute and looked very thoughtful and serious, and I realized that she thought what I was saying was wrong in some way. She talked to vampire teens all the time. She'd decided to work with vampires. Maybe other vampire teens were in here talking about how much they wanted to suck living blood, and she was nodding thoughtfully and encouraging them to find safe ways to explore that.

Mom would hate that.

"I don't think it's true that *most* vampires do those things," she said finally, as if she had made some kind of decision about her own ethics as a counselor. "In fact, I would say it is true, at least from my personal experience of the world, that vampires are more likely to be careful about other people's boundaries and consent and needs than non-vampires."

"Well," I snapped, without meaning to, "the asshole who turned me sure did it on purpose and I didn't want it."

I didn't say Cain, obviously, I told the state and therefore Tammy that he was a rando at a bus stop that attacked me when I was out for a jog. Tammy affirmed that I was right by holding her head down with her eyes lightly closed, her mouth pursed in this absolutely perfect "you are so right, and you hold such pain" expression. It was entrancing.

"Anger is good. It's a really productive way to respond to what you're feeling," Tammy said. "I don't know what that man was going through, but we know what he did to you is not okay. I want to suggest something. And I'm not trying to hammer it home, right. But there are many vampires who feel what you feel, whether they were turned yesterday or a hundred years ago. They don't want to do what was done to you, because it's also happened to them. And those people are in the world too. They want to end that kind of blood-drinking."

"Why don't all the good vampires kill the bad ones, then?" I asked.

Tammy looked at me with another serious expression. "How would you know who was a bad one?" she asked.

I shrugged.

She blinked studiously. "Your classmates in night school. Do you think they're evil?"

I briefly pictured the fifteen other vampire teens who sat nightly under the fluorescent lights in the basement of Roosevelt High School in my homeroom. Well, nine now. We all got locks for our lockers, which sat alongside the lockers of human students, and I had thought about whether they wondered, or knew, who used those lockers that were never open in the day. I hadn't thought about whether any of my classmates were evil.

"They're just like, freshly turned," I said. "Like me. I don't know. I figure most of them were accidental, like me."

"Hm. Have you talked to any of them?"

Tammy and Mom on the same page.

"But those are the ones in school. There are vampires out there that aren't registered."

"There are," Tammy said. "They can't access the blood banks, and they mostly live in the tent cities, and sometimes in sewer pipes or tunnels. Sometimes they live in SROs. I've worked with some of them. To try to get them some access to blood."

"Don't you feel bad about enabling them?"

Tammy looked at me. "They deserve to live, and so do you."

Which is not what my mom thought. But my mom was the one who was right.

4.

FAWN

When I opened my eyes, the truck was still. My mouth felt like I had swallowed battery acid, or week-old coffee. It was the middle of the night—my phone, which was now on 24 percent, said that it was 3:46 a.m. Paul was not in the seat beside me when I looked over. I squinted through the droplet-flecked window of the cab. Out in the dark, I could see other cars and trucks, parked along a long strip of lot alongside the highway. I could see a gas station sign, and the taillights of cars passing the place where we were parked. There was no sign of Paul.

I felt suddenly gripped by fear.

I worried about leaving the truck alone, but a number of awful possibilities were arranging themselves in my head: Paul was planning on turning me over to human traffickers. Paul had called the cops. Paul had been murdered in the rest stop.

And then I looked out the window again, more carefully.

IOWA-80, the sign above the long building we were adjacent to read, scarlet in the dark.

I opened the cab door and jumped the long distance down to the asphalt.

The truck door locked behind me—if I didn't find Paul, I thought, I could just wait next to it—and I tripped toward this place which Silver had also seen, not long ago. As I walked toward the entrance, I realized it was larger than it seemed from the truck. It extended on around the corner—and then on, like a mall, twice as big as the downtown area of Jarlsburg. Inside the first set of doors I came to, there was a food court, strangely bright and alive for so early in the morning. Not all the vendors were open, but it smelled like pretzels and hot dogs. Mostly truckers—mostly white men in jeans or sweats or uniform jumpsuits—browsed the aisles near the checkout stands for packaged snacks or stood in lines for coffee or sat at linoleum-topped tables. I caught a man's eye—he raised a quizzical eyebrow at me—and ducked toward a hallway that said RESTROOMS. The hallway was bright and yellow and much longer than I expected. I found the women's single-stall room and locked the door behind me with a sigh of slight relief.

There was a knock on the door. I sat to pee quickly and then glanced regretfully in the mirror while washing my hands. I looked worse than a mess.

I opened the door to see the most beautiful woman in the world looking at me.

"Sorry," I said.

"Thanks," she said, and brushed past me, before I could fully register what I had seen: dark, grey-streaked hair in a close-cropped buzz, a dozen silver hoops encasing the outer rim of both ears. Big arms and shoulders under a Carhartt jacket, and a jowly, square, sharp olive-toned face on a body of magnificent breadth. She must have been at least five foot ten. She was fat—solid and huge, like a tree, with big shoulders, like an ox. She had thick eyebrows. I had never seen a woman in person that looked like her. I had not, in a real way, realized that a person *could*. I knew about butch dykes, from the internet, but that was the internet. Silver and I had been the only really out queer people we knew.

My breath stopped for a minute, as I stood facing the bathroom, until I realized I'd look like a creep if I stayed there.

I returned to the food court and sat in a chair, looking around for Paul. I didn't see him. Instead, a few minutes later, I watched as the beautiful, huge woman walked out of the hallway and out of the double glass doors.

I followed her.

Outside, in the misty parking lot, I felt like a mouse following the shadow of a giant. I wasn't sure what exactly I would do if she saw me. I had a vague idea that I would ask where she was going, and if I could come with her. I walked a few paces behind her—and to my surprise, found myself walking back to Paul's truck.

I hung back, expecting her to pass Paul's truck and move on toward her own vehicle, but she stopped, circled the cab and walked around the back—where she unlatched the back with two twists of metal and hopped, with a dull metal-drum sound, inside.

Did you need a key to open the back of one of these trucks?

I stood by the truck, uncertainly. Paul—where was he?

I was also fairly certain that whatever she was doing in the back of the truck was going to be something that compromised Paul's job. He'd show up with a load of packaged snacks that was short.

I stood, staring. She probably wasn't stealing packaged snacks. That was absurd.

I heard a rattle from the back of the truck, and a moan. It was Paul's voice.

It was a noise of pain.

Paul had been paranoid about taking me with him. He had some kind of secret. I felt suddenly protective. He was a little bit transphobic, but I also liked him. Even if this woman was beautiful, she was fucking with my ride.

I flung open the back doors of the truck and switched on my phone camera to squint into the dark metal interior. Unexpectedly, the back of the truck was cold—refrigerated.

"PAUL," I shouted. "ARE YOU OKAY?"

"The fuck," a woman's voice said. It was wet around the edges, like her mouth was full of liquid. I moved my flashlight around to try to find the woman and Paul, and lit upon two pairs of shoes. His—sneakers, spotted with red. Hers—black boots. I moved the flashlight up their forms.

Paul was staring at me in frustration, his eyes squinting against the light from my phone. He had four precise holes in his arm, leaking blood. Not spurting. Just a dull leak, like you get if you stick yourself deep with a safety pin or a sewing needle.

"Kid," he said. "Thought you were asleep."

"I thought—are you hurt?"

I was having trouble taking in the scene. The woman's mouth was ringed in red—it was smeared along her chin. He was not struggling, or pushing her away. His hand was on her shoulder.

Paul's voice was dry. "Close the doors, kid. You like vampires, huh? Don't get Wanda in trouble."

There were two ways to close the doors—I could stay outside or jump inside with them. I did not want to be outside in the cold again, wondering about what I'd seen. I scrambled up over the metal lip, hoisting myself inside to the cold metal bed of the truck, in between long rows of huge cardboard boxes. Paul let out an exasperated sigh.

"Jeez, what, you want to watch, or what?"

"You got a daughter, Paul?" the woman named Wanda asked. She was pulling back from him, though her movements were reluctant. Her hand still gripped his wrist; her eyes were glued to the spot where blood welled at the pale fold of skin near his elbow. I could only see a diagonally illuminated white section of each of their bodies; my flashlight was pointed at the floor. They had been in total darkness before I arrived.

"She's a hitchhiker," Paul said, sounding both exhausted and a little nervous. "Trying to get to Seattle. *Don't* stop."

Wanda turned to me while placing two fingers over the welling blood on Paul's arm. "If you know what's good for you, you won't call the cops."

"I don't want to call the cops," I said, feeling indignation rise in my chest. "I love vampires."

Wanda looked amused. "She loves vampires. Well, I guess we get right back to it, then, huh."

Her unoccupied hand, half-lit, clasped at his hips, stroked his chest. Her eyes closed, and his too. I felt like I should turn the flashlight off. When I did, they both vanished into darkness, and the sound of the sucking became mixed up in the noises of the highway and the noise of my own breath.

After a minute, someone exhaled, and they drew apart—I knew, because of the clang of their boots on the floor of the truck. I felt Wanda pass me in the dark. She flung open the doors of the truck again, and hopped down, turning to face me as she did so.

"Well. It's extra hands to load cargo, isn't it."

Paul was rubbing his own shoulder, breathing hard. I moved toward him, wondering if he was bleeding, needed something—but he held up a hand to push me away. He was leaning on one of the cardboard boxes, slightly bending its edge.

"Go—hey. Make yourself useful, if you want to be a snoop. Go help Wanda with her boxes."

"Her boxes?" I repeated dumbly.

"You stupid or something," Paul growled, his mouth twitching into a haggard smile. "We're smuggling blood, you jackass."

I was taken aback—so much so that I did retreat, edge back down the length of the truck, and leap out onto the asphalt. I faced Wanda, who stretched her arms behind her back and looked down at me appraisingly.

"Cut my meal short," she said. "I like to take it slow with Paul. He's an old guy. You better help me move some boxes, or I might bite you too." She gestured to one of the boxes in Paul's truck. "Start with the back."

I didn't want to question her. I lifted the box, which turned out to be heavier than I expected. I staggered under the weight. Wanda grabbed two; one under each arm. She turned and walked ahead of me.

"What's going on?" I asked. I was following Wanda to a UHaul parked two spots down from Paul's truck. "Does Paul really do trucking for Trader Joe's?"

"Course not. You gotta know what questions to ask," Wanda said. "You're gonna get yourself in trouble fast, otherwise." She pushed her boxes into the mostly empty back of the truck—though I saw that there was a sleeping bag back there, and a wide plastic bin, and a tarp hung up to divide the back of the truck from the cab.

I put the box where she indicated and thought of a couple new questions.

"How does the blood stay cool?"

"Thermal packs in the boxes."

"Are you going to Seattle?"

"Vancouver BC."

That was close, I knew. Much luckier than I had expected.

"Can I ride with you as far as Seattle?"

Wanda looked sidelong at me. "Only way I'm gonna take someone with me is if they can drive. I can't drive in the day. Can make double time if you can drive, and I'm in a hurry. You can drive?"

"Yes," I said.

"And you *want* to ride with a vampire."

"*Yes*," I said, more emphatically.

She sighed a long, aggrieved sigh, and turned to stalk back to the semitruck, where Paul was gingerly lowering himself out of the back onto the asphalt.

"I'm not turning you, if that's what you're hoping for," Wanda said, slinging two cardboard boxes into the truck more gracefully than I could have thought possible. "I don't make baby bites. Seattle doesn't need any more of them, and I can't take care of them."

"Oh," I said. "No, I wasn't hoping that you'd turn me." I wanted to be as far from an imposition as possible.

"And I don't kill anyone either, unless they're trying to kill me. Not an interest of mine. So if you're depressed and looking to end it all, I can drop you by the highway and you can do it yourself."

"No," I said. "I'm planning to stick around. I'm running away. Can't make it work at home." The boxes were heavy, and I wondered how the blood was stored. I pictured it in big plastic bags, like the boxed wine my parents drank at the holidays. However it was stored, it was liquid. Most of the weight of a human body was water, blood.

Wanda turned to me and nodded. She had been moving fast. The number of boxes in Paul's truck was dwindling. My arms ached. "Sensible enough." She slammed another box into her truck, slid it along the metal floor. "Okay. I used to have a driving partner. Sure helps us move faster, and time is money with blood. But I knew that guy. Now, you understand that it's pretty crazy of me to take a stranger with me. You could kill me."

"I wouldn't do that," I said. I was panting, struggling with my fourth box.

"Sure. But I'm going to take precautions," Wanda said. "I got a padlock for the back where I sleep that locks from the inside. I'm gonna drive at night, and you're gonna drive during the day. You are not gonna fuck with me. Should only be one day, two nights of driving, maybe two days if we're slow. If you go off course, I wake up in Utah or some shit, I *will* kill you, and if I don't, my bosses will."

It struck me that she was being very, very nice to me. It was surprising. Was I lucky or unlucky? Was I stupid or naive? Should I be worried?

"I'll prove I'm good," I said, though my voice wavered. "I won't let you down."

"I trust Paul. He likes you. And I'm in a hurry," she said, with a grim little quirk of her mouth. "If you drive, the blood I have on me is less expired when I deliver it."

Maybe she, like Paul, felt protective of me because I was trans. It felt better coming from her than from Paul. I wondered when she had turned, and if she had always been butch, and what her parents had been like.

"Are—I can pay you," I said. "In—in money, or blood, or whatever works."

"Don't get too excited."

I grabbed another box and glanced at Paul, who had been leaning casually against the truck and trying to light a cigarette with hands that shook a little too much.

He gave me a thumbs-up as he took the first puff. "She's taking you, then," he said. "Good job." I had elevated myself in his estimation somehow, which made me oddly proud. Maybe he felt like he and I were the same.

"What you told me before—is trucking for groceries

really part of what you do? Do you make most of your money doing smuggling?"

Paul inclined his head to the side, eyeing me. "Careful. Don't look at it too close if you want to stay safe," he said. "We do regular cargo too, to seem above board. But the money's in the blood. Especially since the shortage."

"How'd you get into it?"

He shrugged. "Women like Wanda. Can't say no to 'em."

Wanda's UHaul van had a backpack on the passenger seat that she pulled off and lugged to the back before we got back on the road. It was about four-twenty in the morning.

There were a couple hours before sunrise; Wanda told me we would probably make it to Des Moines before we switched off. Her face looked green in the light of the dash.

"Winter sunrise is slower, and overcast, like now, it'd be seven or so before I started feeling nasty. But I don't think we can get much further than that. I'd say Iowa City, but that'd make it dodgy."

I didn't really have any idea where the places she was naming were.

Paul came over to the side of the truck, on the driver's window. He and Wanda said a few quiet things to each other through the window before he gave her a nod and tapped his forehead as if he was inclining a hat. We pulled away from the red sign back into the last part of the night.

"So," she said, as soon as we pulled out, "Paul picked you up. He didn't do anything funny with you, did he? Don't think I want to drink from him anymore if he did."

"Funny how?" I asked, faux-innocently.

She gave me a grim glance.

"I just want to make sure I have the right read on him. Been working with him a while. He treat you normal, is what I'm asking. You're pretty damn young."

"Yeah," I said. "He talked about how he has a trans niece and said that's why he picked me up."

"Hm. And you remind him of his niece."

"I don't think it was in a gross way. He just wanted to make sure other people didn't mess with me. And I guess I said I liked vampires, and he told me not to tell vampires that, because it freaks them out."

Wanda let out a burst of laughter. "He's okay," she said. "And he's not wrong, mostly. But we also need y'all. We need each other. Now, do I know for sure he didn't mean anything creepy by the trans thing? I do not. I *do* not." She drew out the second part of her *do* to make it three syllables.

"How long have you known Paul?" I asked.

"About eight years," Wanda said. "Long time for a human. He's a nice tall drink. But I'm not telling you anything more about myself till you spill the beans about what your deal is. You're a teenager, running away to Seattle to find some vampires?"

"Yeah," I said. I looked at the night-colored fields flying past us next to the highway and felt suddenly how tired and jumpy and *alone* I was.

"You just like danger?"

"No." I felt defensive, and I was eager for Wanda to understand me and sympathize. "My friend—I think he faked his own death. I think he's a vampire. On purpose. But he stopped talking to me. I think he's going to live with our friend in Seattle. I took a bus, but then I thought the police might be looking for me because I ran away, so I switched to hitchhiking."

Wanda's hands went a little rigid on the wheel. She grimaced a little. But she didn't seem to acknowledge the second part of what I'd said. "I *hate* people who turn kids that young," she said. "Whoever turned your friend's a shitbag in my book, just know that. You should stay away from him."

I thought about this. "I think it's a guy named Cain," I said. "If you know of him. Not that all vampires know each other."

Wanda looked away from the road at me for a second, and I grabbed the door handle as the van swerved slightly. "Oh, fuck," she said.

"You *do* know him." I couldn't believe my luck.

Wanda shook her head, maybe a little too vehemently. "Not personally. He buys from me sometimes through another guy. He's got a whole stupid—he runs this underground vampire club. The Pearl. He *loves* the baby bites. There's been way too many college students turned in the last few years 'cause of him. Combined with the gov supply drying up since '20, it's a mess in the clinics. Too many old people died, too many young people without any guidance. I think it's irresponsible to just turn kids. They don't know how to act, and shit's getting worse for us. Police are getting all excited to catch us drinking, they don't care if it's consensual or not, then there's the slayers. Makes everyone unsafe." Wanda scowled. "How do you know Cain?"

"This website called Tumblr," I said. I had learned to be slightly embarrassed when saying it to adults but wasn't prepared for her reaction. Wanda hissed through her teeth, and I saw the edge of her fang. "I didn't know he ran a club."

"All that Internet shit. *Web*sites. I can't wait till that fad's done with. Too many baby bites coming into the scene with no experience, thinking they know shit because of the World Wide Web. I hate even having a phone."

I wanted to ask when she was born, but something told me not to.

"What are baby bites?"

Wanda sighed. "I guess you're running out there like you got an expiration date. Might as well warn you." She squinted at the exit signs flashing past us. "There's different kinds of vampires in the world. Baby bite means baby. New." She shrugged. "You know. Cain is one of the vampires who thinks we have an *obligation* to make more of us. He loves when young people turn. He also . . ." she paused. "He hunts."

I tried to process the implications of her statement. I thought back to the exchanges I'd had with him. He was comfortable with Silver's passion for bloodlust, unlike other vampires who told Silver he was being vamp-phobic by romanticizing it. It did sort of make sense. "He attacks people?"

"He likes to *persuade* people who haven't done it before. Dumb as shit. It's always a search for someone who wants it. That's why blood banks, distribution networks—we need them. I had to hunt, back in the day, and it makes you feel gross. There's nothing pleasant about drinking from a person who doesn't want it, or who changes their mind. People scream, go to the cops."

"Right," I said. She'd said it with humor.

I thought about how it would be nice if she pulled over and threw herself onto me, the weight of her body impossible to fight against. How it might feel to have her teeth in my neck.

"Of course, there's the people who think what I'm doing is evil too. Drinking from people who want it like Paul." She turned to me. "He begged me, the first time. But that's how it's gotta be. I gotta be sure someone wants it."

"Yeah," I said, and felt the blush in my own cheeks rise with the memory. I kept seeing her teeth when she talked, and thinking about when Silver and I drank from each other's cuts.

Wanda seemed absorbed in her own thoughts. A scowl furrowed her brow.

"I make money selling blood to people who don't want to have to deal with the government clinic shortages and the ankle bracelets and don't want to deal with live donors, or can't afford them," she added, after a second. "It's plenty of people. Big cities, it's underground clinics that do the legwork. They get some from hundreds of people like me, some from suppliers in the hospitals. More people, all the time, are turning. I'm not worried about my people going out of business, but I am worried about people like Cain making the government crack down on us. Once in a while, cops remember that we're fun to kill. They go through a vamp camp, tear it apart in the daytime. We catch fire. They find a smuggling ring, make a big show on TV of having us all executed."

"My friend from my hometown thinks it's impossible that my friend Silver—she thinks he can't be a vampire. She said he's just dead. It's like she doesn't believe it's *possible* to be a vampire."

"Easier to believe, for sure," Wanda said. She seemed to consider. "Why do you think he's alive?"

"I went to his grave. It was dug up. And he left this necklace on it," I said, pulling out the bat wing necklace—both its halves glittering.

Wanda flinched at the necklace, as Paul had.

"Not many people dig out of graves anymore. Why don't you let your friend make his own mistakes, follow your own path? Why you gotta find him?"

"I just have to," I said. And then, because that wasn't a very good answer, "I'm in love with him."

Wanda nodded thoughtfully.

"You're a passionate kid," she said. It didn't seem like a compliment.

She pulled over in a rest area when the first blue of the dawn began to creep above the edge of the horizon. I wondered if it hurt—even that first, limited light. I wondered how it felt to feel daylight as a burning pain that could kill you. That was one thing I knew I didn't want. I liked the sun.

Wanda set up her bed in the back—a sleeping bag in a big trunk. She checked the tarp covering the divider with the front of the truck, taking out a roll of black duct tape and sealing a couple invisible cracks. Then she handed me the keys to the truck.

"You done long haul shit before? Remember what I said about Utah."

"I can drive long haul," I said, because I was eager to be useful. I had technically achieved a driver's license, though it didn't have a name or picture on it that I could stand to look at.

Wanda let out a short, barking laugh. "I'm trusting you, got it? You're a champ if you get me where I'm going. Don't get pulled over. Here's a map." She handed me a folded piece of paper, the thickness of which frightened me. "We're mainly going one road the whole way, and it's gonna be long, straight, and scenic starting soon. There ain't shit out here."

"Uh—can I use Google Maps instead?" I looked at the paper map. I hadn't read one of those before.

"Have the cops on us in a second, use one of those phones," she said. "Matter of fact, you should turn off your data while we travel. Use the map. You can do it. Live without the Google."

Then she saluted and got into the back.

I hadn't slept, and I realized I'd need to, after a full day of driving. I felt it in my back and aching shoulders. I needed to sleep *now*. But the idea of helping Wanda made me feel my sleepless night as a shock of electricity instead of a weighted yoke.

I thought of Silver *hunting* with Cain. Silver had always talked about that, idealized it—a pre-industrial reverence for the dark. He wanted to be the dark. I had always treated it like a game. Because in practice, Silver had treated my body carefully, like he knew what it felt even though it wasn't his. I couldn't really picture him grabbing someone and pulling them into an alley. For one thing, he was really short.

I turned the key in the ignition.

I hadn't driven much after passing my test—our family had two cars, but I had to ask permission to drive them and pay for gas. I didn't like the surveillance that accompanied my access to a vehicle, and I wasn't good enough at lying to use them for anything fun. I had never driven something as large as the UHaul truck. But it was highway driving—that was easy. I looked at the red pen which Wanda had used to mark her route. The part where I got to I-90 would be the hardest part—then it was just that one highway, for twenty or so hours. I put my phone on airplane mode.

I pulled onto the first highway, I-29, going north, feeling tired and incredibly mature. The pink dawn crept up over the edge of the flat plain in front of me. Around, there was farmland, with occasional rocky, gravelly-looking hills, and barns, and warehouses. I could see houses, far off the road, but each stretch of town was marked by signs for Dairy Queen, McDonald's, and Subway, with an occasional casino breaking the rhythm. I got onto I-90 late in the morning.

That was when I noticed the white van following me.

Following me?

Was it?

5.

RACHEL

My mom picked me up from therapy in her minivan. It was just past two in the morning.

She turned her key in the ignition. I had hoped that maybe there was another Daylight pack she'd give me, but no go, even though she had coffee next to her. My school says vampires don't have the same metabolism as humans—we aren't warm-blooded—so calorie needs don't exactly translate. I need, they say, about a pint a day to stay alive. I'd had that. I should be fine, even if my stomach was telling me otherwise.

"How was therapy?"

I felt pressure in my nose and almost started crying, but vampire tears are red, and it's way easier to hold it in than freak her out that way. When I cry in front of her now, she goes blank and cold. "I don't want to go to Tammy anymore," I said.

"Okay," Mom said smoothly. "'Long as you don't set anything else on fire. You've done five sessions, I'm sure that's enough for the bastards."

I laughed, relieved. "She doesn't really get what I'm going through. Dealing with the whole *member of a race of evil monsters* thing."

Mom looked sidelong over at me. "Speaking of, we have a mission."

I tried to be nonchalant. "Did I . . . get approved?"

"There's a tip about a basement in the U district," she continued, shaking her blond hair over one shoulder. "Cain or someone is doing—they're calling it a *clinic* on the Discord. Not legally authorized, more of a suck-fest. Apparently been around since at least last June. And MAVIS has decided that you're trustworthy enough to be useful to us." I heard the tension in her voice, the resentment that her friends, who mostly fell in lockstep with whatever she said, had been giving her pushback on the subject of little old *moi*. I knew she'd been advocating for me with the other moms. I could see why they would doubt her.

"I'm thrilled to be back on the team, but we can't do more arson, Mom. Even if the cops hate vampires, they don't love fires tearing up the U district."

"No arson yet. Not until we see what we're dealing with. Could be snake demons in there, ancient tombs, anything. And after the August fiasco, we want to be thorough. None of us could enter to scope it out, but you can get us ID on some of the people running it and tell us exactly where the exits are. We're going to send *you* in there."

That was not exactly what I'd been expecting.

"Sorry. You're sending me into a vampire bar?" I pointed at my ankle bracelet. "What about that thing?"

My mom produced something from her pocket and handed it to me. It was a set of three small round silver magnets, like the kind we had on our fridge—tiny, circular, and super strong, so if you put them on either side of your finger, they held fast there, through your flesh. Each was decorated with a sequin. "I did my research," she said. "Obviously we could cut it off, but then you'd be in trouble with the state when you have to go back for blood. But! The crap vampire monitors Washington hands out don't work if there are magnets close by. The interference usually gets read as a device malfunction. Joe from Daylight told me that's what they do when we give them new subjects, while they transport them, before they cut the tracker off. As we'll be doing tonight, if everything goes well."

"Mom, I could get in a lot of trouble! Especially if there's actually blood sales happ—"

"You won't." Lip gloss mom smile. Valley Girl removed from valley, steel in her heart. I was in, so I'd better stay in. "You're still my smart girl. You're only in there for a little while. Looking around, talking to a couple people, and then leaving. What do you have when you don't have anything left?"

"Myself?" This was one of her truisms. Not a particularly fuzzy one. It had helped a few times, when I'd felt really down or been really scared.

"Right. Now, listen up. You're going to go without contact with us for a couple hours. Only message in an emergency. Take note of the floor plan. Try to ask for names, figure out how it all works. Then you're going to walk through the Ravenna woods before you meet me at the other end of the trail, over by the playground near the mall, at five in the morning. We'll go over what you've found back at the house. Reese and Christina will Zoom in to talk."

"You didn't tell me about this before." If she had, I might have talked about it in therapy. I felt pissed, and trapped, and alone. She hadn't even mentioned backup. The setup was also such that it left us with only an hour to get me home before sunrise. I couldn't go home on my own. Not from here.

"We went over and over it a lot before we mentioned it to you. Everyone had to get on board."

I thought about this. On the one hand, I was being trusted. On the other, it seemed obvious to me that my mom had forgotten a couple major details. "Mom, I've been a slayer since I was fourteen. What if a vampire recognizes me?"

"If anyone asks, you've changed sides. They may be particularly interested in having a Slayer's daughter on their team."

I wasn't so sure that vampires would be totally cool with someone who'd been staking them for a few years.

"What if they expect me to drink blood from someone? I mean, there's probably uh, blood drinking there. Won't they think it's weird if I don't?"

"Take a pack if you can, if they've got packs instead of people. We can use it to see where it's from."

I grimaced. "Mom, I don't want to do this."

"Honey," she said. "I am going to go make a video

about my TikTok taser raffle winner giveaways at Diane's house, and we're going to film our May special reveal for the tasers, and then I'm going to loop through the graveyard. When I come back to Ravenna, you're going to be there."

She's fought her way out of Hell a couple of times. You don't cross her.

We pulled onto the highway, heading north. The lights of the city and its towering cranes whizzed by as we sped on the wide, gray road toward the university district. Up the hill, past the wine store and the homeless guys huddled on the sidewalk corner, past the lit-up strip of the Ave where the bars were bright, up past 45th, where the streets got wider and darker. Into a Fred Meyer parking lot. A lone old woman crept across the lot, pushing a cart towering with belongings.

The magnets thwacked on to my monitor, and I pulled my pant leg back down over it. How would I possibly be able to tell whether or not they were doing anything to it? I couldn't.

My mom handed me an address with a password written on it, and I looked down at it with trepidation.

"Rachel?" she said, as I checked my tote bag for my phone and wallet. My emergency stake was tucked into my bag, just where it always was.

"What?"

"Leave the stake. Don't want to attract suspicion."

"Can I take a Guarded Girly taser?" I asked, gesturing to the glittery taser that always hangs from her cupholder. We don't pack all the orders for Mom's business—most of them are drop-shipped from China—but Mom always has some around for videos, and as backup.

"No."

Defenseless, I slid the minivan door shut and walked out into the night. My mom winked the lights of her car at me as she pulled out of the lot. I turned up the hill.

The air was cool on my face, and I pulled the hood of my sweatshirt up, so my hair wouldn't show. I didn't want to be a mark. I might be immortal, but I'd felt weaker since dying.

I had seen vampire parties from a distance—heard the music and seen the red lights. I had even snuck inside the door of one a couple times, to disarm a bouncer before we bounced in. But I'd never been inside one. Now I'd have to pretend to know what I was doing.

When I reached the address, I didn't see anything, at first. It was a dilapidated, grotesquely peeling two-story shingled building with a boarded-up deli on the first floor. But when I stood and listened for a second, I heard vague, tinny music from beneath me—and when I sniffed, there it was. Blood. I saw light shining from around the corners of the loading dock entrance—one of those metal doors in the sidewalk.

I glanced back and forth, wondering if that was the way to get in. It seemed like it. I bent to try to open it, wrapping my fingers around the metal hinges—it creaked open on a long set of stairs. So much for the ADA.

I ducked into the opening in the sidewalk, and tripped down the set of steps to a desk in front of another metal door. It was lit by a purple LED light, where a pale bald woman sat in the chill basement humidity, vamp face on, looking like the Devil, her wrinkles ridged and in high relief.

"Clinic entry is ten dollars."

"Nobody said anything about a cover," I said.

She shrugged and opened her hands as if to say *not my problem.* I fished in my pocket. She stamped my hand in exchange for the cash.

The floor was sticky. With each step, I had to swallow back a marble of nausea as I felt the slight resistance on my heel.

I smelled so many people's blood.

There was blood drinking happening here right now. I just had to find out *where.* Then I remembered my mom—I couldn't stop it tonight. Whoever was being hurt right now wasn't our goal. My head pounded a little. That much blood. It was gross—and it also made something funny go off in my stomach, a tingle of excitement, of attraction, of hunger. I was glad I had just eaten.

The space was dark, but its ceiling hung with purple and ultraviolet lights, streams of them shining like the veins of a deep-sea creature between rafters and cables taped just a couple feet above our heads. There were flyers plastering the walls. I drew close to read three—

ANDIE'S 200TH BIRTHDAY BASH

Memorial for Sam Guisewhite

Missing: Ariel Ramos

The music sounded idiosyncratically like The Flaming Lips.

I listened.

It was The Flaming Lips.

It was being piped in at medium volume through the speakers. The vibe really wasn't very club-like, not like Cain's parties. More . . . waiting room? Cafe? Retail store?

The room had maybe thirty people in it. Every person I looked at was vamped out. Their ridges and inflamed browbones cast shadows on their noses and under their eyes. Fangs gleamed. I didn't know why you would want to look like that in public. But maybe if you were used to blood-hunger, it felt more relaxing to show it, knowing you were surrounded by other demons. I prodded at my own nose, reassured by its smoothness between my eyes. I felt my teeth with my tongue—canines were still sharper than they had been, but my true fangs were retracted, deep in my gums. I wasn't like these monsters.

Most of the people in the clinic were older than me—though it was hard to tell, with those vamp faces. I saw a lot of guys dressed like dads, with flannel and metalhead graphic t-shirts. I saw a foosball table through the double-wide door to the next room, a rack of magazines. There were beanbag chairs in the corner. The vampires stood or sat around with blood bags, sipping through purple curly straws. At least my outfit didn't feel out of place. I had on my jeans and pink tank top and cardigan. My puffy purple Sketchers sneakers. As I walked toward the low mirrored bar at the back of the room, where there were no bottles or espresso machines but just one big ominous fridge, I felt a turning-toward happen in my direction. I felt an absurd, rising panic:

There were a lot of vampires here.

I was used to grabbing a stake when I saw a vamp—now

my hand twitched involuntarily toward my pocket.

Three vampires by the unstaffed bar talked to each other loudly over the music. Two of them were short, athletic Asian guys in their thirties or forties with big muscles. One was balding and had shaved his head, and one had a bleached pompadour. Stacey would have thought they were hot—except for the huge fangs, warped browbone, and angled ridges above their noses. Their friend, a tall austere Black woman with box braids in a tight tank top and floaty scarf, with a tattoo in white ink on her shoulder, caught me staring. She glanced at me with red eyes and smirked salaciously at me. Her fangs were bright white, lit blue in the dark by the strange illumination above us. Her bow-shaped mouth was smeared with white lipstick, like it was the seventies.

On her, vamp ridges looked *almost* good.

"Now who do we have here?" she said, and there was no question she was speaking to me. Her two friends glanced in my direction. They raised monstrous eyebrows.

I felt my guts twist—and watched as she did an exaggerated turn to glance at the mirror over the bar. I followed her gaze: in the mirror, I didn't exist, and neither did she. The room was empty, in the other world of the mirror. She turned back around, and I accidentally met the woman's gaze again. To my horror, she leaned forward.

"Thought you were bait, honey. Had to check! I was like girl, you can't sell *here*! Why aren't you wearing your fangs out?"

Bait—a vocab word to report to Mom.

"I—um, I'm not used to it," I said. "And I just ate, so

they're not, uh, out." I tried to laugh.

"You haven't gotten the hang of shifting? How new are you?"

"Don't give her a hard time," said her friend.

"Uh. I turned . . . uh. In August. But I haven't . . ."

The woman, unexpectedly, put her arm around me. I jumped a little, and then tried to relax, since she might realize I was a slayer. She looked emphatically at her friends. "August," she said, in mock shock and horror, gesturing to me with her hand. I couldn't tell if she was making fun of me.

"*August*," the less-friendly bald-er Asian vamp repeated back archly. "Well, welcome, baby bite. I'm Ned."

"I'm Erica," the woman vamp said to me. "Honey. And you're my baby bite now, if your sire hasn't taught you shifting yet."

"Not if she doesn't want to be," said the friendlier guy.

"You're *new* new," Erica said to me, ignoring him. "God, the shit you have missed out on. Imagine coming in on this mess, after the fire. Welcome to the afterlife, baby. What's your name?"

"Rachel," I said, and then gulped, because I could have given a pseudonym. "I, uh, I snuck out. I haven't met any other vampires before besides who's at my school."

Erica's brows furrowed. "You're *registered*, then. You got one of those tracker thingys?"

"Yeah, but I put magnets on it," I said. "I read that that works."

Erica's mouth pursed. "Magnets?"

Mean Ned waved a hand. "No, Erica, it works. I've heard about it too, from the kids at the shelter. It fucks with the signal, or the wires, or some shit. The Gen Z kids are nothing if not ingenious. Bet it's a few months before the feds figure out a workaround for that."

"Long as it works. I guess ask Frankie, at the bar. He knows everything about helping you kids with your Big Brother shit. He can cut the damn thing off you tonight, if you're down."

Frankie was someone with power here, then. I looked around, but there was no focused center of the crowd, and nobody who looked in charge.

She fished out a significant-looking silver knife from her purse. It was in a holster, but the first half inch of blade gleamed in her brown hand. "The Kevlar part where it fastens is the weakest."

"I can't cut it off," I say quickly. "I've gotta finish school."

"They're only going to follow you around until you do something wrong. And I'm not ready to lose another baby to cops or slayers. Had enough of that. First the old ones, then the kids. Too much death. Too many people hauled off to die because they tasted fresh blood."

"I'll be okay," I said weakly.

"Ha," said Ned, deadpan. "You gotta stop being a good girl or they'll kill you. You can stay at my shelter, if you want. There's rooms down the street, through a tunnel. Safe during the day."

"Oh, I don't . . . need that," I said. Mom would love that information, though.

"Erica, put away the knife." Ned's smiley bleached-pompadour friend added. He turned to me. "I'm Mark. I'm glad you found your people. How did you hear about the clinic?"

I realized that this might be a test. Was I about to have a trapdoor open under me? "Um, a kid at school told me. On a piece of paper in my locker. I thought it might be a trap, but I came and looked and the guy outside . . . pointed."

Erica smiled at me, and I shivered.

"I remember when I turned," she said. "I was so scared, for so long. And alone, once my sire died. I'd like to think that these days you all have a better time of it, but I'm not sure you do. I never gave in to registration, and good thing too, because I'd have all their records on me whenever I went anywhere or tried to eat anything. As is I have a fake ID, which is enough for night jobs, though you can't do work on the Internet any more without a legal ID. You're screwed no matter what you do. I'm worried about the way things are going, with the attacks, the slayer raids. If I'm overbearing when I see a new face, that's why."

"Don't scare her," said Mark. He looked back at me, and his red-brown eyes had a penetrating intensity. "To the point, honey, have you figured out how to get blood that *isn't* from a bag?"

My salivary glands burned.

"No," I said. "I don't want to—" I paused. "I don't want to hurt people." I regretted it as soon as it was out of my mouth. I wouldn't *say* that, if I was a *real* vampire. I was a shit double agent. I looked at their faces and knew I had said something that cut. Mark's eyes were closed and his mouth tightened in a grimace.

"Oh boy," said Ned, and moved off down the bar toward the room with the books. "I'm sorry, I have to go. No offense, honey, but I can't do that conversation. You guys have fun with her."

Shit.

"I mean, uh, I'm sorry," I added quickly. "I didn't mean that *you* hurt people. I'm sure you, uh, ask nicely."

"Very nicely," Erica said, looking after him. "It's okay. I've heard worse. Ned's sensitive. Go on."

"Uh, I just get the bags, basically."

Erica was now standing stiffly staring over my head. "What happened to your sire? Why didn't they tell you anything? Get you someone who could give you blood?"

"My *sire*?"

There was a long, unpleasant silence, during which the guy from Weezer sang, *I'm dumb, she's a lesbian* over the sound system. *What* was this music?

"You didn't have a sire," Mark said, gently.

"I uh, I got attacked. Fed on. Very, uh, Dracula horror movie. Then he changed me at the end." As I said it, I felt a tide of weird, nasty feelings in my stomach. I felt seasick. I had been made wrong. I was *like* the people who hurt me, and I had felt the bloodlust they felt. Now, standing in front of Erica and Mark, I was thinking about them as Erica and Mark, not the monsters me and my mom would kill next week. I wanted them to look at me approvingly, even though I knew they were evil. "I um. I guess most of you guys don't do that."

"Not those of us here. I'd say mostly we come to places like this," Erica said. "Ten bucks, *two* bags a day. It's not adulterated with pig blood like some of the black market stuff from overseas you get in the encampments, or whatever stuff Daylight's going to sell when they launch that fake blood. Usually a few days past the sell-by, which is why we get it and why it's cheap, but it does the job. Direct action, mutual aid. Though three times a week I see one of my girls over on the Hill, and I pay a little extra to get it fresh."

I wanted to know what they thought of it. "What's Daylight?" I asked.

Erica snorted. "Tech bros. They think they're going to fix the Covid blood shortage problem by making fake blood and forcing us all to eat it. After letting the government kill all our elders. All the vampires who are registered keep getting ads about it on their phones. I got an ad on Instagram and knew it was time to delete socials and get a new email and phone number again—these Daylight people *knew*, somehow, even though the government doesn't have my name."

Mark rolled his eyes. "Erica, that's just targeted advertising because you were following vamp accounts. The government doesn't know you're a vampire, the companies just are using their algorithms. It's like how Instagram knows I'm gay and have a cat."

"Anyway, there's some trial programs I wouldn't touch with a ten-foot pole. I'd bet hundreds of dollars that they launch some crap that makes our teeth fall out and try to put registered vampires on it."

"I don't know about any of this," I lied.

"So, you haven't had *anyone* in your life who has talked to you. See, this is some dark shit," Erica said. "I'm like, who out here is turning kids and not even sticking around to take care of them? What the hell is *wrong* with them?"

I was starting to like Erica, even if she ate people. "You can say that again," I said.

Both of them sat down on ratty pleather bar stools as if I had knocked the wind out of them. Erica turned around toward the bar. "Frankie!" she called.

A very short, Danny Devito-y vampire with a bald pate stuck his head around the corner from a back room behind the fridge. He had a double chin and tufts of hair on either side of his big eggy head, and a gross little mustache, made more gross by his vamped-out forehead.

"Get me a bag for this one. She's been through it. Get me my second one too."

Who knew where this blood was coming from? But . . . even if it was a blood farm thing, at least they weren't asking me to suck anyone dry. It would help my credibility.

And besides, I wanted blood.

When the short guy came out of the back and handed me a bag over the bar, I was relieved to see it was printed with the Seattle Children's logo that my blood at home was. Nobody had been forced to give this up. They just didn't know it was getting served in a bar.

"Thanks," I said.

Frankie handed me a curly straw and winked. "Welcome," he said.

The blood was hot—which, it turned out, did make a difference. Did they heat it in a microwave? It still didn't taste as good as the blood I had drunk from my mom, but it was way closer. I was still hungry. My fangs dropped with a *shunk*, and I felt my forehead bend downward, and without thinking, I sucked at the bag like my life depended on it. Shifting—when your fangs and ridges come out, and you look suddenly ugly and monstrous—feels like when you're going to sneeze, and then feels like you're doing some kind of intense yoga stretch for your skull. There's a moment of sharp migraine, but then it feels like you've scratched an itch.

"There we go," Erica said, looking at me with approval.

I finished the bag. I felt—dangerous.

Daylight stuff made me feel more normal, but I had felt weak, kind of sick. Drinking this blood now, something changed in my body. I felt muscles in my back unclench, a shiver of pleasure shock through me. I felt kind of like I was actually alive. I could probably *run*, if I wanted to.

"And now you're living with your family still? Are they being okay to you?" Mark asked.

"Uh," I said, wondering what my double-agent answer was. But it turns out, I didn't have to think that hard. I knew exactly what the me-that-was-evil would say, because it was under there all the time. I let my anger bubble to the surface. "My mom hates vampires," I said. "It sucks. She hates me."

"And you've been on the starvation ration? Nothing else?"

"I'm fine," I said, sharply, feeling instantly in my gut that I'd just done something horrible, betraying my mom. "The blood's enough. And when synthetic blood launches, that'll be good, you know? I'll just use that."

"It *really* isn't enough," Erica chimed back in. "You can live like that for maybe five years before you conk out for good, but your bones'll get brittle and you'll get even scrawnier. And that synthetic blood shit is going to be crap."

"I've always been skinny," I said.

Erica nodded, looking frustrated. Then she took out a notebook from her purse, behind her on the bar.

"I'm going to stop being a freak to you in a minute, but I just need to say. If you need to talk, or need blood, or a place to stay, you can always, always text or call me," she said. She handed me her number.

I felt the thrill of her hand against mine for the second we both held the scrap of paper.

I walked through Ravenna woods, the night alive with color, reds and greens that humans would only be able to see in the day, past sleeping homeless people whose hearts I could hear sloshing somewhere in the brush. I thought about how good the blood in the clinic had tasted. Through the empty, dew-covered parking lot to where the car lights gleamed near the grocery store. I found my mother's van.

"They call it a clinic," I told her. "They've got expired blood bags in fridges."

My mom looked tired but nodded with some excitement—and relief, I thought. She leaned across the seat and hugged me, and I hugged her back. What would have happened if I hadn't come up with anything, I wondered.

"See," she said, "I fucking told Amber. You know, this is the kind of intel we couldn't get without you. You're our man on the inside. What's the floorplan like?"

I felt a migraine start to pulse behind my temple.

"There are some tunnels to safe houses, supposedly. One exit to the street. A security guard and a vamp inside to collect a cover. I talked to a vamp named Erica who thought I was a little baby vampire who needed help figuring stuff out," I said, feeling darkness rise in my stomach, unpleasant, like the blood was going to come back up, as warm as when it went in. I felt like I was betraying someone by naming Erica. She's a monster, I reminded myself.

"Excellent. So, we can send Stacey now to pick up a couple vamps to take to Daylight for testing." She tapped at her phone, then looked back at me. "Next week we could send you in there again, and after a couple times nobody would bat an eye."

"Yeah," I said. I hesitated. "I uh, I think we should wait before destroying the clinic. I think I could go back and get more information, broaden what we know. If people trust me I might be able to build connections to other spaces too. Erica offered to help me find people to drink from. It's a lead."

This pleased my mom even more. "Definitely," she said. "Still my little Sorkin strategist. Okay, awesome, baby girl. Next week we go to the movies."

6.

FAWN

I'm in *a hurry,* Wanda had said.

It was a big white unmarked van, sort of like mine, except not a U-Haul. I couldn't see through its windows.

I wondered whether to bother Wanda. I wondered whether I should try to lose them.

Wanda was my ticket to ride; I had to talk to her. She hadn't told me she was being followed, which meant she might not know.

"Wanda," I called into the back, through the grille. "You awake?"

She didn't answer. I wondered if it was true about vampires being like the dead when they were asleep. Did that mean I was just driving with a body in the back? What if they pulled me over? Were the people in the white van cops?

I regained control of my breath through careful dry heaves for a couple minutes, my hands rigid on the wheel. I got off at the next service station, got gas at a Shell and watched as the van parked at the store. Nobody got out. They didn't refuel.

I pulled back onto the freeway, and they followed me.

Surely, I thought, it was just that this was another early-morning trekker making a journey across the great American waste. You know, sort of a ships-passing-in-the-night thing. But it didn't pass me, even though I was driving ten under the speed limit. I played a game, counting the seconds when I couldn't see it in my rearview mirror. It never was more than twenty. I ignored it by blasting the radio, and looking straight ahead, at the bugs hitting the windshield. Every time I looked back, it was there.

I pulled over to pee around eleven. It pulled over too, in the same parking lot. It parked far away from me; I watched to see if anyone got out. A blond woman did; she went toward the bathroom. Just a regular cross-country driver, like me. After a second, I got out and went into the bathroom too. I'd needed to pee for two hours. The women's restroom stalls had low-topped doors that someone could see over if they tried. Those kinds of doors had been worrying me since I transitioned, but I sat, and peed, and got up to wash my hands. A normal young woman, I told myself. Nobody's following you. There's no reason to.

The mirror over the sink showed a tired, pink face. I stuck my tongue out at myself.

With a bang, the stall door behind me burst open, and the masked blond woman lunged toward my back, a pointed wooden stake in her hands that she swung toward me like a club.

Fuck.

I ducked down to the floor on my hands and knees, faster than I'd known myself to be capable of. The woman, who was bigger than me, tripped and fell over me, and the wooden stake clattered to the floor. I almost slipped on the wet, dirty tile, but I flung myself at the metal restroom door, crashing into it with my shoulder, and jogged back to the truck. Another woman in a KN95 mask and a long, dark coat was racing me to the U-Haul back door. When she saw me, she turned toward me instead, but I was closer to the car than she was. I jumped into the driver side as she lunged at the truck; I managed to get the key into the ignition. She backed away from the door, and by then my foot was on the gas pedal. I tore out of the parking space with a crazy screech. I could feel my face, red with exertion. I tried to focus tired eyes.

I thought—maybe the cops? After me? But that was ridiculous. More likely, it was someone on the trail of Wanda's blood-smuggling. I kept on the edge of my seat, waiting for them to put lights on the top of the car, to hear a *whoop-whoop* of warning. But nothing.

There was nothing out here, no cities to hide in.

I followed the route set out for me, and the white van was on my tail again ten minutes later. They'd accelerated, cutting my head start.

This time, they were riding my ass.

"WANDA," I yelled into the back. "PLEASE WAKE UP. FUCK!" I felt the tears under my eyes, threatening to run. It would be cool to die in service to a vampire smuggler. It would not be cool to be dead.

No response. I began to worry that she was gone. What if they'd somehow gotten to her in the second I was in the bathroom? I couldn't open the tarp, peel it back, and I couldn't unlock the back where she was staying.

If they were government people, maybe they were tracking the plates. We were deep into North Dakota by now. The road was long and rolling, each small hill masking the sameness of the horizon, with flocks of little birds diving dangerously close to the road. There were fewer stops, fewer gas stations, more bleak oil-well areas and prairie remnants and cows adjacent to the long highway. It was all cold and dead because of winter.

I pulled onto the next exit, which was just a loop-de-loop and then farm road; the white van followed me. How could I get them off my tail? Who were they?

I was exhausted, and I couldn't get too far off the interstate. I didn't want Wanda to think I was fucking with her when she woke up—she might kill me. I saw, up the long, sloping grey-brown hill, a dirt road looping up from the two-lane highway toward a low house. The entrance was masked by an out-of-place hedge. If I could turn around there, I might be able to outpace them back to the highway. I spun the wheel up the dirt road, towards a treeless incline with NO TRESPASSING signs spaced regularly across the brush.

I got far enough up the dirt path that the hedge and the angle of the hill covered me until the white van passed, and then turned and barrelled over the prickly long grass back to the main road. I jolted over rocks at the end of the drive, hoping Wanda would yell from the back and demand what was happening. I hoped I wasn't bruising her. I pulled onto the asphalt at the bottom of the long incline, the white van now up the road ahead of me, but

I guess I hit the gas too fast—the tires screeched, and a second later, they were doing a tight U-turn like we were in some horrible action movie, following me again. Racing me back to the freeway.

They pulled up alongside me on the narrow no-passing road with a ditch on either side, and one of their windows rolled down. Each of us was hugging one edge of the asphalt, wind rustling. I had my foot pressed down, trying to hit the gas to go fast enough to leave them in the dust. I heard the U-Haul's engine strain. I squinted through the corner of my eye at the blond, masked woman in sunglasses driving. There was another woman next to her, with shorter hair and pink lipstick, who might have been the one to chase me in the parking lot. Neither of them really looked like secret service agents, though the pink lipstick one had something Sandra Bullock-y going on.

I rolled down my window to shout at them. They maybe wanted to kill me, but I felt like I needed to yell.

"What the fuck do you want?" I shouted.

"We know your business," Sandra-y yelled.

She shot but missed; the whistle of the projectile hit my ear a second after I felt the thump of the wooden stake as it embedded itself in the inner plastic of the passenger side door. Window not broken—glad I'd rolled it down. I hit the accelerator. There was a keening, horrible sound as the truck tried to meet my demand. I took a curve better than I thought I could take it, the left-hand wheels of the truck barely leaving the ground at all. Distantly, I saw a big tank truck loaded with a fuel tank on the other side of the road, coming toward us. It was a little too wide for this road.

The double-wide semi was approaching, and I sped up to go around it. They tried to swerve too, but the semi wobbled, and they jerked like a toy car running off its track.

The white van rode off into the ditch.

Didn't hit a tree, there weren't any to hit. Didn't burst into flames. But there was a crunch. I could only see it in my rearview for a moment. The semi honked as it pulled over on the side of the narrow road behind me. Wanda didn't yell.

This was harder than driving lessons. I felt my palms soaked in sweat. My heart thudded in my chest.

I was shaking, but I got back on the freeway, following the green signs under the white sky, and I did not see the white van again. I won. I felt so worn out. The gradual grade of scrub into piney greenery, with its steep red butte cliffs, looked less and less like the bleak afterimage of *Little House on the Prairie* and more like a fantasy novel. The hours hummed together, my heart pounding in my ears. Astonishing how I felt more awake now than I ever had, even though I could still feel tired delirium riding on my back.

A big, blue sign along the highway read: WITNESS BLOOD SMUGGLING? NOTIFY THE AUTHORITIES. $10,000 REWARD! There was a number.

I drove on, thinking about Silver.

"You loved him," Flo had said, when we were crying on her floor, after we got the news that he had killed himself. "And you knew he couldn't live in this town."

This was such an idiotic thing to say that I choked on my own tongue. I was facing the half-ironic poster of Young Josef

Stalin that decorated her wall alongside a psychedelic picture of some mushrooms marching along a blue mountain ridge.

"Yeah, of course," I said.

"Not like friend love. Like love, love."

I was unsure what kind of conversation to have with Flo, then. I had appreciated the warmth of her breath and her arms until now, but the sensation of her so close to me began to feel awful, static-y and claustrophobic.

"Since I was eleven," I said, hating her. Her eyes brightened, and her tears welled again, and, though I absolutely did not ask for it, she pulled herself toward me and pushed her pretty, puffy face against my collarbone.

I hit Montana before dark, plowing on the highway through the Crow Reservation and through buttes that jutted up from hostile ground. I figured the women in the van would get back on the highway as soon as they could, if they weren't broken down. They'd speed up, try to catch up to me. Unless they had some kind of boss to report back to. To be safe, I pulled off at a rest stop an hour before I was intending to, to wait until the sun set. With any luck they'd pass me. I pulled into a town, turned into a McDonald's parking lot.

Wanda stirred as the winter daylight faded.

"Kid?" she called, through the grate. "Give me a read. Where'd we get?"

"Hardin," I said. It was like there had been a wire holding me tight, upright, and now I slumped into my seat. It was over.

"Not bad. Trusted you, you did right by me. Any trouble?"

"White van motherfuckers following me for a while," I said. "Yelled but you didn't wake up. Ran them off the road on a little road off the interstate, someone's farm, a ridge. They went into a ditch and I didn't see them again. They shot a stick through the window. Pretty good shot. Inside of the door has a mark."

There was a long silence.

"What?"

"Crossbow. Pink hair." I couldn't muster much, verbally. "Know them? I figure you could have warned me about them."

"The slayers." Her tone had completely changed.

"They didn't slay us. You, uh, maybe could have warned me."

The noise of the lock; a second later, Wanda came around, sat in the seat next to me. She examined the small hole the projectile had left in the soft plastic of the passenger side door. She looked a little more haggard than when she'd gone to bed, moving slower. Made sense; she'd been in the back of a truck all day. She was still astonishing to me, the width of her body, the proud angles of her square face, the way her shoulders moved. The way her mouth was always slightly open because of her teeth. She rubbed her eyes with her fists, then looked at me, her irises like garnets. "*You made the slayers crash their car*? Did they hurt you?"

"I don't know about crash. I made them swerve, go in a ditch. I yelled but you didn't wake up."

Her little kiss—a peck on the cheek—was over before I understood it had happened. "Fuck, kid. I'm sorry, I really thought I'd lost them in Pittsburgh. We gotta get you some dinner," she said. "I'm pretty dead during daylight. Saved my ass. I didn't know they had my route. That was why I was in a U-Haul, they caught me coming out of Philly with my regular truck. Gotta change my plates again. Shit. You sure they're gone?"

"Not at all," I said, feeling my face flush. "I just haven't seen them again." I noted the way she wasn't telling me much.

She nodded, jaw tight. "They probably weren't expecting me to move in the day, but somehow they got me anyway. Wonder if Paul's okay. I don't think that guy'd sell me out willingly." She stared darkly over the dashboard. "Place in this town I think has a club sandwich, a nice Reuben, all day breakfast. You've had a long day. Get out of the driver's seat."

I had felt like a desiccated lizard, but now I felt warm and glad inside again, the way I had when I first saw her, the way I had when Silver first cut his wrist open for me.

Wanda pulled the truck around the flat blocks of Hardin, the too-wide streets, past buildings that all looked like century-old brick or steel storage barns, and parked in front of a diner made out of brick with a little awning out front showing a lasso and a hat. Inside, there were white Formica tables and a big horseshoe on the wall. In the corner, an overgrown houseplant flowered against the window. It smelled like hot oil, salt, and meat.

"I think the Reuben on rye, unless you're feeling like breakfast," she said to me.

I realized I was enormously hungry. I'd been hungry and shaky for a while. The other diners were mostly middle-aged or older, mostly solid, red, Americana-looking white men in washed denim, with a few Latino guys mixed in. They shot occasional glances at us. Truckers, I guessed, like Paul. The soda and blistered fries that came alongside my sandwich made me feel whole again.

"Can you tell me more about what you're doing?" I asked.

"It'd only put you in more shit. Less you know the better. I'm driving next shift. You'll sleep. I'll do my damndest to keep you safe. Just eat."

Wanda stared at me or the window, silent, the whole time I ate. She'd ordered a sandwich too, but didn't touch it, and packed it into a box when it was time for us to leave. I felt sleepy and full, ready to collapse.

"Now it's time for me to have something," she said, climbing into the back of the truck. "Get me going."

I saw that she was rummaging in the cold-packed boxes.

"Don't you, uh," I said, and faltered. "You could drink from me."

She looked over her shoulder. "That'd be just what you like, wouldn't it? No, you'd pass out. You've been up too long. Eaten too little."

I thought of what she'd said, about Paul begging. "Please?" I said. I watched her, watching me. Do I have to ask three times?

She shrugged a wide, fuck-it shrug as she ripped the plastic off the top of a bag. A single drop was propelled out by the motion and landed on her cheek.

"If you really want me to, I can get my dinner from you later, after you eat that other sandwich. But you gotta synthesize some calories first."

She pulled a metal straw from her pocket and stuck it into the blood bag.

"What if you drank from me just a little bit?" I asked.

She rolled her eyes. "I know what I'm doing, hon. Sleep a while. That's final."

I thought about rolling around with the blood in the back of the truck. I wouldn't know what was happening if more white vans caught up with us.

"Could I sleep in the seat up here?"

"Sure." I saw her check the map, trace where we were. I felt very safe, even with the inch-wide circular wooden stake hole still in the door. No matter how little I knew, this was where I was meant to be. I'd thought it was all Silver's vision, and I was just there for Silver. But I wanted to go with her as soon as I met her. This was what Paul had meant by scaring people.

I still had no idea of where I was going when I got to Seattle, but I'd found the right person. Like fate had driven me to this spot. I knew I couldn't stay here, but this was what I was running toward.

I turned on my data and looked at Silver's blog. No new updates. Refresh, refresh. Empty blue screen, then the last post sliding up to the top again. Nothing.

I rested my head against the bumpy, cool glass of the window and fell asleep.

When I woke up, the dark outside had grown complicated with thousands of bright stars. We were somewhere in between two great rolling mountains, clinging to the rim of a valley that stretched on either side, of forests that were at least partly evergreen, the rough shapes of the branches etching a lace blue-black against the bigger black of space. It was four in the morning.

"Hey," I said.

She grabbed the second sandwich from between the seats and put it on my lap, tapped the water bottle in the cup holder, wordlessly. The radio was playing Charlie Parker, kind of scratchy. Who knew how far we were from any transmitter. I knew the song because my grandpa liked Birdland.

I wasn't hungry, but I took a few bites of the sandwich obediently, feeling the warm anticipation in my chest. Would she drink from me? I was a dog doing as it was told. When I finished, I crumpled the wrapper in the box and put it on the floor. I didn't ask again. I didn't want to make her upset with me or make her feel like I demanded anything. I stared out at the stars, the shapes of the rocks in the black night on the empty road. For a while a semi drove ahead of us, and then Wanda passed it and it faded out of sight.

A half-hour later, Wanda glanced over at me, and I noticed her eyes glowed wine-red in the dark of the cab. It was her eyes and the speed dial and the dim glow of the headlights on the road ahead of us. She didn't have her brights on, maybe because she could see in the dark. Her hand found my wrist.

There was a shock like I'd touched a spark plug as she brought my vein to her mouth. Her lips were cool, though her tongue, when it found the vein, was wet. I sat there, gripping my seat with my right hand, my left up, half-crucified.

"Sure you're all right with this?" she murmured. "I'm not going to pull over for now, gotta make good time."

"THAT'S FINE," I said, too loudly. I could feel her hand. I had never thought of myself as a lesbian before. I had been in love with Silver. But Silver had never made me feel like this. I was alive like a flame.

She bit, and the pain was like I had been stabbed just once with a large sewing needle. I gasped and gripped the side of my seat. I wanted to bend toward her, sideways, but I kept still, shuddering in my own body. After a moment, the pain was gone; I felt her tongue moving over the marks, and her lips kissed the place she'd bitten, and then her mouth was wrapped around the vein, growing warmer—I realized, with my own blood.

I watched the clock's green digital face count three minutes, then five, and the radio station played through "Ornithology" and part of "Well You Needn't." I became a heartbeat. The motion of her cool mouth on my wrist, the slight twinge when she sucked, the overwhelming, floating feeling of joy, the rush of a roller coaster thumping from my head down through my torso to my feet and back. She switched hands to navigate a curve, her left hand coming up to grip my hand, her fingers laced with mine. Then she pulled away.

"That's all I can take right now. Six minutes is about a pint. More than that's gonna fuck with you." She wet her red lips with her tongue, and then they were pale again. "You taste pretty good. Chalk it up to that Reuben, maybe." Her voice, which had been terse and straightforward, even when praising me, now had a sweeter edge. I felt like my body was dissolving into warm ice cream.

She set my hand down on her lap, still holding my fingers in hers. I gripped as hard as I dared.

"Thank you," I breathed, finally. "I . . . I wanted that . . . for a long time before I left home."

She laughed, her voice raspy in a way that sounded more than a little tortured and sad, and that, maybe as much as anything, made me burn with shame inside. "Good. Happy to help. Happy for the dinner, too," she said.

"Oh, god." I felt the words stumbling on my tongue. "I'd give all my blood if I could." I didn't quite mean that—I didn't want to die—but I meant the feeling.

"*Don't* say that. I already kinda feel like a monster for drinking from you. Okay, when we get to the next stop and switch off driving again, I'm gonna give you some cash. Eighty's the going rate for a pint of fresh, if that's okay."

"Don't *pay* me," I said, faster than my brain could work. Of course I could use the cash. "I mean, not for the blood. I wanted that. And you're doing me a favor, getting me where I want to go."

She dropped my hand. My heart fell with it, rolling around on the floor between our feet. I felt dizzy and out of my depth. I reached for the water bottle and took a long swig.

"Don't make me feel like I'm taking advantage here. You helped me out yesterday. You're in trouble in Seattle with an attitude like that, kid."

"I know how to take care of myself," I said.

"No, you don't." She shook a finger at the windshield, as if addressing a class. "First thing, *never* let a vampire drink from you for free. Anyone telling you otherwise is a psycho. Pardon me for saying so, you need the money. All of us know the rules, we know what fresh blood costs. Everyone's gonna think you're a narc or crazy if you don't charge. Take it, god damn it, and don't leave me worrying that you're going to sell me out to the cops. They won't register me if I'm smuggling blood. They'll take me in and stake me."

"I wouldn't do that," I said.

She looked sidelong at me, rubbed her eyes with her free hand. "Yeah, cuz you're a little baby lamb. Look, let me put it a different way. We *need* people like you. We know it. We're willing to pay, except for those Free Blood idiots. You run around saying *don't pay me*, you're asking for the very worst kind of people to take advantage of you, and you won't be around long. Someone will get you, cops or slayers or a seller who knows what their own blood's worth. Please be smart, if you love us so much. I personally would love to run into you again in fifty years."

Fifty years was a long time.

"I'd like to see you sooner than that," I said, and saw immediately from her jaw that there was something wrong about saying it. "I—I mean, like Paul."

"You're moving too fast for me, kid," Wanda said. "We oldsters take it slow. I'd like to give you time to grow up a little, figure out if this is what you want to be doing."

"Sure," I said. I thought: how old are you?

"I'll give you my number, though, how's that? You need help, need to go home again, I'm in Seattle pretty often. I owe you a lifesaving."

"That's—Thank you."

"No problem." Her voice was back to the rough, cool cadence. There had been warmth in it for a moment. I hadn't imagined it. "Hey, and if you find your friend, and he's a vampire, you know, maybe you can give him some blood."

I had a feeling she was trying to sketch for me what I should want, to redirect my attention away from her.

"Yeah," I said, and thought about how Silver had been so secretive, so evasive with me. How he had run, not given me any kind of thought, left the necklace behind.

The pink dawn was not yet here, but the barest hint of a lighter blue struggled at the ragged horizon.

"We can switch off again in an hour," Wanda said, scribbling an address on a receipt and handing it to me. "You're gonna drive in to Seattle, head to this warehouse in the U district. I'll leave you with my calling card and shit so they know to trust you." She removed a card from her pocket, stamped with a large, red letter 'W,' then went back to writing on the receipt. "The bite marks on your hand'll help too. I won't be up when you leave, so I'm going to leave you with an address for a hostel you can go to. Takes all kinds, they'll hopefully put you up for a couple nights for free if you give em my name. Then you can look for a place without sleeping on the street."

I wanted to tell her I loved her, then, but I just nodded. I wasn't going to be able to get close to her. I could just float on, in this truck on the way to a city full of people who might want me more.

7.

RACHEL

In spite of myself, my body was into how it felt with more blood in it.

I felt weird about the idea of us killing Erica.

I texted Brid about the clinic and told her everything that had happened—about Erica and the fat little Danny Devito vampire and how everyone was so goody-two-shoes about not hurting people. She took a day to text back, and when she did, she said,

They're really good at seeming good little girlypops, I guess. Maybe they knew you were a Sorkin. They want to confuse us.

I didn't think that was it, but Brid was top vampire killer, and I should trust her. I called her.

She didn't pick up.

I'm tired and gotta sleep, she texted.

I didn't know what to do with Erica. I had told my mom about her, because I was used to telling Mom everything. I wanted to meet Erica again, and that had sort of meant

I had to tell my mom about her. She'd find out otherwise, and then I'd be in trouble for keeping the secret, and then they'd all probably kill me.

"Five minutes," my mom said. She started the timer. The sun had just started to come up, and we were testing the efficacy of Daylight's synthetic blood. Since they didn't give us the info about it, we were using me as a source of original research. I hoped that soon I could go out in the day again. As soon as the Daylight synth blood was ready. I hoped that I would have evidence soon that it would actually protect me.

The Venetian blinds cracked open. Slats of light fell across my arm in two bracelets of sun. The rest of me was draped in a thick My Little Pony quilt; I could just see the faint hint of a glow around my feet, between the horses. The places where light hit burned hot with pain almost at once. I pulled in my toes and focused on not moving my left arm.

"Tell me when it starts to hurt," Mom said.

I wanted to show her that I was becoming less flammable, so I waited thirty seconds before telling her.

Erica just had seemed *nice*, and like, of course vampires could seem nice, that was how they got victims, but I believed the nice. It seemed *true*. How could it be true?

"Okay, four minutes left," Mom said. "You're getting a little dark. I was hoping this batch would be the time, but maybe not."

She slathered sticky, cold sunscreen on one of the bracelets of light, to see if that helped. The burning cooled for a second then heated again.

The five minutes was up; the blinds closed, and I heard the blackout curtains being drawn. I opened my eyes. The bracelets on my left arm were dark black-purple-red. I knew it would fade a bit when I drank blood. The ones on my right arm from Tuesday were light pink now.

"I think it's better than last week," Mom said. "I think it didn't get you as bad."

"I think you're right," I said, trying to smile so she would smile.

My mom handed me my morning half-cup. It was cold, and I tried to turn my head down from her as I licked the plastic measuring cup.

That Wednesday I went to a MAVIS meeting for the first time since I turned.

"The capacity of the clinic is about fifty people, not breaking fire code guidelines, but it was at less than half capacity," I announced to the members gathered around Diane's living room in the folding chairs she got out of her hall closet for the occasion. A cheese plate and a veggie-and-ranch Costco spread was set out on the ottoman. Her marble countertops gleamed, which was how she was always one-upping my mom. Our military-pension plus social media self-defense drop shipping income wouldn't have kept us in Seattle except that Mom inherited her apartment from my grandma when she died. Our apartment was not as nice as Diane's. Her husband worked for Microsoft and was never home; Diane assumed he had another girlfriend, but it kept him busy.

I held up the sketch I had made of the floorplan, and everyone leaned in to examine it.

"The clinic is a place for people to access cheap blood outside the hospital system. There is presumably a connection to Seattle Children's, as that's how the bagged blood I observed was labeled. No blood drinking happens from live humans on the premises. What I learned last night is that there are safe houses connected to the site by tunnels. Probably connected to the system we found in August, though those tunnels will be closed by now. If we pinpoint the houses, we could accomplish a targeted strike. What I think is more immediately important is using social connections to trace where *else* the vampires congregating here go for blood. The vampire I spoke to last night indicated that the blood she gets at the clinic composes only a part of her diet, and that she drinks from live sources where she can, at a bar on Capitol Hill. If you approve, I can continue my connection with her and potentially uncover more dangerous vampire hideouts."

I could still kill *bad* vampires, I thought as I said this. There were vampires out there like Cain.

They'll know, the next time you see them, a voice in my head said. *They'll know you aren't one of them. They'll kill you.*

Diane nodded thoughtfully, and my mom sat up straighter, holding her kombucha-in-a-wine-glass proudly. Stacey looked at me like she used to, like I was a team leader. It was almost like I wasn't totally filled with internal turmoil.

It was Amber who spoke up. "Didn't realize we let crypt-keepers plan missions now."

"Amber," Molly said, frowning. "She did exactly what we asked her to. She made a great presentation. Good job, baby." She gave me an approving smile, though I noticed her eyes float above my head.

I felt so mad, for a second, that I had to prove myself to MAVIS as if I was a vampire off the street. I was so mad at Amber. I was a victim. Now I had a terrible, incurable disease that made me have to fight against bad impulses and not be able to suntan.

"You can test me," I said. "If you want. Cognitive tests, or moral tests. Give me the fucking trolley problem. I don't know, put a kitten in front of me. I won't drink its blood."

I felt a horrifying sob well up. I looked to Brid, because she should be smirking at the kitten joke, but she was biting both her lips at once and looking down at her hands. She had olive green polish on, glossy and elegant against her bronze skin.

I watched Molly's supportive look freeze as she watched a red tear make its way down my cheek. I had my hand gripped tight, and realized my fingernails were pressing into my palm.

"Rachel, take a break. I'll meet you outside," Mom said. Her tone wasn't unkind, but it made something snap in me.

"I'm not a different person. I'm not a different soul. I still believe in what you believe in."

Amber threw up her arms. "We've been over this, Rachel," she said, but it was that *they* had been over it, without me. What had they said?

MAVIS takes forever with deliberations. I wasn't allowed to message Erica without their approval. I could have anyway. I didn't. I figured they'd say yes, and they did, though it took five days to vote on it.

During those five days, my five-minute stripes from the sun began to be plum color instead of scary brown-black. Mom had me package giveaway promos of pepper spray cans and pens with knives in them and sign them with little hearts and my name. People on her Insta account had been asking where I was since I turned; she'd told them I wanted to step back from the spotlight because of harassment from creepy guys but was still helping with the business.

My burn crackled against my long sleeves at school. My phone buzzed:

The vote's finally in: contact the vampire for an undercover scout sesh, Mom texted, when I was in Algebra II.

I had to stand in the hallway near the blacked-out windows of our basement school to get reception.

Hi, this is Rachel. From the clinic. I want to go again and I don't want my mom to know. Could you hang out there again?

Erica messaged back almost immediately.

I'm so glad you're still alive! Was thinking about you. I can do you one better. Let's connect with my friend Roxanne and get you some of the good stuff. Can you meet me at the Cap Hill station? What are your mom's sleeping hours?

Very menacing, very sneaky.

I can go on a weekend, I said. Otherwise I have to be at school from 8 p.m. to 2 a.m.

I texted my mom: *Can I follow a tip from the clinic vampire? Delay clinic raid? This is a blood bar, I think. Cap Hill. Won't take any action without you telling me. Just recon.*

I felt excited, like I was scheduling a date. It was so odd to hold in my mind simultaneously that I was going to report it all back to my mom so that she could kill Erica.

Got to check with MAVIS, make sure you take a camera, share your location. Probably, my mom texted. She had seen my recon of the clinic as a test I'd at least sort of passed; I hadn't run away, hadn't killed.

Let me know, wrote Erica.

I had a rush of happiness, seeing Erica's message.

In the hallway, a girl came up to me—I vaguely recognized her from my math class, though I hadn't really spoken to her, or anyone. She was Asian, maybe Vietnamese, with a kind of solid, rectangular chin. She had short hair and piercings running in a line down her ear. She looked kind of gay. If we'd been in regular high school, I would have been keeping half an eye on her.

"Hey Rachel," she said. Then, seeing my clear inability to place her: "I'm Whitney. I, uh, saw you at the clinic a couple weeks back. I'm going tonight, if you want to go."

I froze, my muscles tight. I hadn't thought about how other vampire kids might actually be at the clinic. And I didn't look at their faces enough at school. I was not a very good recon artist.

"Don't worry," Whitney said. "I won't tell anyone. I was glad to see someone I knew, even if I was too shy to say hi."

"I'm sorry for being so nervous," I said, and a thought struck me. "My—it's my mom. She's a huge hardass ever since I turned. I snuck out, and she didn't know . . ."

Whitney smiled. "Me too," she said. "I took a bus after my dad went to sleep." She lowered her voice. "I was starving before. And I felt so lonely all the time before I learned about places like that. I've been going for a few months, at least a couple times a week. I stick around and play chess with this guy Ray. Never seen anyone from our school before."

"I saw people playing foosball and stuff. It's like a community center. Kind of dorky."

She quirked an eyebrow at *dorky*. "They don't give us any time to get to know each other here, it's like we're prisoners. I felt like I was really dead."

"I know what you mean," I said, and really meant it. "I, uh, I've been having a rough one." I fell silent as a teacher walked behind us. I realized Whitney probably could smell her exactly as well as I could, could hear the salty blood pumping through her heart. What would happen if all the teen vampires turned on our teachers, hungrily devoured them in one great big adolescent massacre? Who would stop us, if we all acted as one? Of course, they'd send in special ops teams to kill us when it was all over.

When the teacher passed, I raised my eyebrows and mimed a relieved sigh.

"Anyway," I said to Whitney, "I'm a little worried about how much I want more, now I've had it." My nervous laugh was something I didn't have to fake.

"It's okay to want food. The gov used to give everyone two bags before the pandemic. Did you figure out how to cut off and reattach your tracker?" Whitney asked.

I looked down at her foot, as if expecting not to see the little metal gray box there, or to see a zip-tied DIY project. But her tracker, latched above her sock, looked as pristine as mine was. “No,” I said. “I used magnets. If you get super strong ones, it turns it off.”

“If you still have it on your foot, some places don’t let you in. I can show you how to leave it for real,” Whitney said. “You can put it back on after. Have you been to any of the house shows in Wallingford?”

The bell rang, and I realized the hallway was nearly empty. There were only sixty of us in the basement school. Most of us got to class on time.

“No,” I said. “The woman I met is taking me to a spot this weekend, though.”

“Is she *paying* for you?” Whitney’s eyes flashed with jealousy. “God, the privileges of looking like a Barbie, I guess. You know fresh stuff is crazy expensive.”

This was a new data point. I wasn’t sure how I felt about her Barbie comment. “I don’t know,” I said. “I guess I’ll . . .”

Another human teacher approached us.

“I gotta go to class,” Whitney said. “Anyway, I think I found you on Insta. Maybe I’ll see you again sometime. I know where your locker is. If you have a sugar mommy, let me in on it.”

I had, sort of accidentally, acquired a friend and another lead. It felt like white lightning, knotting in my throat.

Mom and Diane had been planning to track some vampires through the tunnels near the clinic tonight, assuming that I’d arrange for Erica to meet me there and then plant a tracker on Erica, but with my new mission, they’d turn their recon to the general Cap Hill area. They promised me they wouldn't tail me too close, so I would avoid detection—they'd be at least two blocks away unless I signaled. They wouldn't try raiding wherever Erica took me tonight, but they could rescue me if I needed, Mom said.

Erica met me at the light rail station, right as I was starting to feel awkward. I needed to pee. It was raining. After school I'd gone home, sucked down my allotted blood, and changed clothes: a black sweater dress a few inches above my knee with my puffy red crop-waist windbreaker on top, red sparkly Converse with heathered red and black tights. My small bag, again, contained no stakes. There would be nothing to protect me if I was uncovered as a Slayer agent—except my teeth. I always felt nervous on the Hill—for all the swank bars, there were just as many scary-looking dirty junkies hiding under awnings and in corners, dim alleys down steep slopes where I saw broken glass gleam.

"Hey, kid," Erica said from behind me. I turned to see her rising up the escalator, lit against the white wall like a luminous bird. Her dark hair was in one fat, textured braid coming down from the top of her head; her deerskin jacket and dark green dress complemented the gold bangle on her wrist. Her human face was on, classically model-gorgeous, Iman kind of gorgeous. You could *just* see the hint of where the bones of her ridges might be. She had a large umbrella under one arm. She extended the other out, a princess greeting a new subject.

"I—thank you for meeting me," I said, feeling my feet shift nervously, thrusting my hands in my pockets.

Her face moved from amused and a little condescending

to irritatingly empathetic and earnest. “I have to make sure the youth are okay,” she said. “Hopefully you find your people. But we’re late now, ’cause of me. Roxanne won’t like that.” She beckoned to me and began to walk at a brisk but passably normal pace down Cherry; I hurried to catch up, trying simultaneously not to catch the eye of the junkie-looking guy standing on the corner with a cardboard sign and a pit bull.

“I met another kid who goes to the clinic at my school today,” I said, eager to have something to say other than “my mother is a Slayer.” “I didn’t see her there, but she saw me. I guess she’s more plugged in to things than I am.”

Erica smiled with clear relief. “You should have asked her along,” she said.

I slipped slightly on the pavement. “Well, we’re not quite friends yet,” I hedged.

“Yet. But don’t get isolated. That’s what kills us. Ask her next time.”

“Next time” thrilled me. I was so good at this. Suddenly it occurred to me—was Erica doing this as a lesbian predator thing?

“So, we’re going to like, a bar?” I asked.

“Do you want to go to a bar?” Erica glanced down at me. “I don’t know how I feel about that. There *are* bars here. They’re less low-profile, though, and you’re all registered. I was just going to have us meet Roxanne and get her some dinner, then at her place we could have ours. It’s safer that way, and since you’re so new, you know . . .”

“Whatever is fine,” I said, quickly. “I’m easy.” Though part of me wished we would be in public. I wanted to see more vampires. I wanted to know what they did when there weren't slayers there. That was something I'd always wondered, even before I turned. My mom talked like all they did was sort of roar and come at you, but Erica clearly was also buying outfits.

"Of course you are," Erica said smoothly. She rolled her tongue around her mouth, as if feeling the points of her teeth. "I don't know. We have to get Roxanne her pizza, though."

"Roxanne's human," I realized aloud.

"Yeah," Erica said, lightly, snorting only a little. We were walking fast, and nobody was really looking at us. The sun was down, and the streets were lit in lamplight. There wasn't anything that unusual about either of us, except our age gap, and the fact she was Black and I was white, and the fact my tracker stuck out from under my sock. But maybe she was my mom's friend, or my TA, or an improbable work friend.

We passed another homeless person below the overhang of an abandoned storefront. This one's sign said:

I KNOW YOU HATE VAMPIRES

I HATE YOU TOO

BUT IF I HAVE MONEY I DON'T NEED TO DRINK YOUR BLOOD.

I felt a knot in my stomach.

Erica stopped in front of him, which forced me to look at him, though I turned my face slightly so I didn't meet his eyes. He was thin and junkie-eyed, though he wasn't vamped out—if he was a vampire, he'd gotten enough blood, one way or another, to avoid looking like a monster.

If I'd seen him before I turned, I would have wondered if his sign was a joke, the kind of confrontational shit psychos say on the train when they're upset nobody has ones to give them. As Erica talked to him, I realized he was for real.

"Nick, I missed you at the show."

He looked up at her grimly. "I screwed up with Drake. They won't have me back."

"I really hate to see you out here in this rain," Erica said. "Why not hit up the fund at the clinic with Frankie?"

"Frankie hates me."

"Frankie doesn't hate anyone. He's probably annoyed with you, that's all."

"He hates me. I stole stuff out of the fridge last time, he chewed me out."

"Well, you say sorry to him, ask him for some cash from the fund. You're going to get destroyed sooner or later with that tagline." She pulled a twenty from her purse and handed it over; he took it and gave her a cursory fist bump. He was looking at her like he knew her well.

"Better they know. Better they worry. Hey, you seen my bike? Forster stole my bike. It's orange."

"No, haven't seen Forster in a year. I'm sorry."

"You were right about him, he's a shithead. He hit little Angie, the other night, in some scuffle over a kid who was wilding. Hit her in the face. I said, man—"

"Nick, really, watch out for yourself. The slayers have been out in force recently. They got James in the train station last night."

"Shit. James?"

"Roy told me. Some bitch in Pucci heels dusted him when he was coming back from distribution. You haven't even got anyone else with you here. The cops are like four blocks away. They'll take you in for that sign and you'll be in central processing for days."

"I get in tunnels before it's light," the guy said. "I'll be okay. There's a tunnel right over there."

I let my glance follow his finger, to a manhole in the middle of the rainbow crosswalk that zig-zagged, faded, across the asphalt.

"Take care of yourself," Erica said.

"You don't believe in the revolution," the homeless guy accused, too loudly, and without thinking I pressed to Erica's side, tried to get her to move. She began to walk with me, and clasped a hand reassuringly over my own, but turned her head back toward the man in his filthy orange jacket.

"You gotta survive to see the revolution," Erica said, over her shoulder. "Look, just make sure you get someone to go with you when you turn in."

Nick flipped her off, but he shouted, "Love you," as we walked away.

We strode up the rainy hill. Twenty paces from the man she put three fingers to her temple, pushing in as if trying to press back a migraine.

"What's the revolution?" I asked.

She didn't answer for a second.

I briefly pictured her fangs coming out, her turning toward me red-eyed. "I know you're a traitor," she'd growl.

"It's this idea some people have, that there's gonna be

a day when vampires like, stop having to beg to be alive," Erica said, finally. "Some people are like, we'll raid the blood banks and keep doing it until the government gives us what we need, and employs vampires, and the supply shortage will end by mandate; some people are like, our allies will join hands with us and give us blood or synthesize a good blood substitute; some people are like, we'll attack people and drink what we want from them and they'll like it too much to stop us. I don't know."

"*You* don't want to attack people?"

"I used to, when I was starving for a while. You've felt hunger. You know."

"Yeah," I said.

"I didn't kill people, mostly, but that meant there were people alive who hated me. You can guess why it's dangerous to live like that. The allies thing, that's closer," she said. "I think there's lots of people who like us well enough. Who get something from us, like we do from them. If there was enough of them, we could fix shit, you know."

I couldn't understand her. I tried to keep up with her long strides, struggling to follow what she was saying.

"It sounds idealistic," I said.

She jerked her finger back over her shoulder. "I was there when that guy turned," she said. "Back in like '03. His name is Nick. He was an art student. He had a sire, this guy Pete Fioretto, weirdo Italian, had him living with him. Then Pete got staked sixteen months after Nick turned. Eight vampires working nights in the Italian bakery Pete owned, suddenly homeless. Nick was okay for a while, lived in his old house, but then the lease didn't get renewed because the landlord was selling the building. He got registered then skipped out during the shortage in 2020, can't get re-registered without serving time. He helped rebuild some tunnels, so he has a little credit to live on, he stays at the safe houses, writes weird blogs, and now he just walks around provoking people like that. It's like he wants to get killed."

"He seems like, kind of unpleasant," I said, and then realized that was a really bitchy thing to say. "I mean, uh."

"Didn't use to be."

I could imagine someone like Nick attacking people and drinking their blood. My mom would have staked him on sight. "I'm sorry," I said, though I wasn't sure what to add. I was beginning to understand that Erica thought I might end up like Nick if she didn't help me. She was a vampire who was looking after people. Maybe neurotically. It was hard to look after vampires, probably. I was a project. But she didn't suspect me, and for that, I was very grateful. "Is it safe to leave him out there? Should you take him to the clinic?"

"I'm not going to take him to the clinic."

"What about that synthetic blood app? We could sign him up for a trial, if he has a phone." I looked back.

"Even worse."

"But like," I hesitated. "Harm reduction, right? So he doesn't have to like . . . attack anyone?"

She looked down at me, and for a moment her mouth curled in contempt in a way that I found breathtakingly terrifying. Not that I had breath.

"I'm glad you know the phrase harm reduction, but

Nick's the one who's in danger of harm, Rachel. He can *get* to the clinic. Frankie won't turn him away, even if he has it in his head that he will. Though he's not going enough, by the look of him, because he hates actually talking to people or asking for shit from his friends. He's ready to die. I've seen it before. He's out here because he wants to make people look at him. And I get it. I want people to see me too, sometimes. But it's so dangerous."

"I'm sorry. I didn't mean. I mean, I know there's like, a vampire housing crisis?" I asked. I said it like a question, like we hadn't waded through ferns, ripping tents apart and laughing at the screams. Cain's old coven houses, logs of black firewood each going up in smoke. I'd seen so many mimosas drunk to vampire house destruction.

Erica laughed like a wolf barking. "Yes. Where do you think the kids who don't end up registered end up? Someone's couch, someone's basement, someone's closet that shuts so the sun doesn't get in. The woods. Lot of SROs with shady real estate shell companies."

"But not you, right?" I couldn't picture Erica—statuesque and designer—in an SRO.

"I'm lucky enough to have a basement, though we're sort of at capacity. I got there after years without a long-term place. I'm hooked up to one of the tunnels. Cain is crazy, but his tunnels have saved a lot of lives, including mine. Back in the fifties, I used to live in a crypt, just like the movies."

I tried to find it in myself to say something besides "When did you stop hunting?"

"I'm worried about what I'll do when I'm out of my

mom's place," I said. "We've put blackout curtains in. I don't know . . ." I trailed off. It had flashed through my mind before that my utility to the Slayers probably had an expiration date. Probably about the same time as all the other vampires caught on to my deal.

Erica looked sidelong at me. She was still holding my hand. She'd been holding my hand since we left Nick. "We'll make sure you're covered," she said. "Here, Roxanne's going to meet us on the next block."

Roxanne turned out to be a short, fat, white, middle-aged teacher-y woman with tan skin, a big port-wine birthmark on her cheek, huge gold earrings, and long, wet brown hair that hung over her black raincoat in the yellow streetlight. Her body was soft, sort of the shape of a gumdrop, and I could hear the wet pump of her heart against the gentle woosh of the rain and wind and the noise of the street. She looked like a crazy alternative person who had grown up a little. She reached for Erica's hand and clasped it in both of hers. She did not seem mind-controlled.

"Raina dropped by earlier," she said to Erica. "She's around if you want, and so's our new roommate, who's a seller too. You can both drink. Maybe you can even go for one me, one Raina."

Erica looked up and to the side, as if considering. "I can spring for it," she said. "Yeah. Okay. Thanks, Roxanne."

"No problem, hon." Roxanne leaned forward to kiss Erica on the cheek. "Always nice to see you." She did not acknowledge me at all, but jerked her head to the pizza place behind us, which had low purple lights inside and glowed with the flickering screens of arcade games jammed into the vestibule entrance. She held the door for us. The warmth of the place flared around me—I hadn't been in public really at all since I turned, and it was almost too much noise for me. There were families and some sweat-shirted college-looking kids gathered at tables. The smell of garlic and bread and beer and the sticky floor made me ache for normal food, and that made me feel hungry in a new way that I hadn't before. I hadn't been in a restaurant in months. I felt a headache coming on almost immediately, especially when the woman behind the counter looked at me. She didn't know what I was. She wouldn't like it if she did. I glanced to my side. Erica looked chill, so I tried to relax too. Roxanne ordered with Erica at the counter—beer and a vegan pizza slice. She kept looking slyly at Erica and slyly at me, not smiling but not frowning. Sizing me up. I felt scared.

We sat at a sticky, glittery Formica table, my leg squeezed against Erica in the booth. We were both cold, and it made Roxanne's warmth across the table bake into my skin even more. Roxanne sat back after the second crust disappeared into her rosy mouth, licked sauce off her black, oval acrylic nail, ran a slightly pizza-greased hand over her hair to fluff its wet curls like a pompadour, and began to drink her beer slowly, a pleased expression playing across her face, like a cat who's won the chase.

I suddenly noticed that a man across the restaurant was staring fixedly at my vampire tracker, which was just visible over my boot. I crossed my legs to hide it. I was allowed out after dark, legally, but only with a guardian.

"That's the best damn pizza. Thanks, Erica. It's nice to meet you, Rachel," she said to me. "Erica mentioned she was going to bring a new friend along."

"Haha," I said. "I just, uh, met her at the clinic, you know."

"I know," she said, her voice raspier than it had been a second before. "My understanding is you're being half-starved." She burped and gave me a half-smile. "Gotta fix that. Erica's looking out for you."

"I want her to know her options," Erica said.

"Well," Roxanne said. "What I'm going to say, is, right, the clinic is a good standby, especially when you're young and broke."

"Most of the old ones are broke too," Erica laughed.

"I have nothing against it. Not like that synth stuff. You seen the news stories?"

"Daylight Inc. I don't believe they're really able to make synth blood. I was telling you this before, Rachel." She turned to me. "Better you know it's bullshit right now. If they made blood that worked, that would be a huge thing for humans who need blood transfusions, and they keep saying they're doing it for that too, but nobody approves it for medical use, there's no stories about it being tested for that. And where did this company come from out of nowhere? Red flag. They're some venture capital bozos, gonna sell vampires crap."

"I can't make enough blood to satisfy all the boys and girls out here, and even if the number of sellers doubled, we still would need some stopgaps. If Daylight can keep y'all alive, even if it's like, Burger King, that's good. But it loses the *connection*. That's what it's about," Roxanne said, and turned a new, radiant smile on me. "It's why I got into this. Tell me, Rachel, what do you like to do with your time?"

What did I like to do? I had no idea. "See movies," I said, sounding stupid. Kill vampires. "I don't know. I go to school. I used to play tennis." What did I do? I made out with Brid. But not anymore. I smoked weed in the bathroom and set stuff on fire.

"That's so cute," Roxanne said. "You look like a cheerleader. You should start a night-tennis league."

I felt like I was falling down a well. She talked to me like I was five years old, and that made me upset. If I drained her she wouldn't see me as a child.

I wanted to.

When I spoke, my voice barely emerged from my throat. "I—uh, they tell us at school that it's not safe for people to donate more than a pint every couple months, and that's part of the reason for the shortage and the ration. is it safe for you to give . . . how much can you give, when someone . . . drinks?"

"They've been lying to you. That's only for IV donation. I get a pint or so of blood drunk out of me every other day," Roxanne said. "I used to give more, and it was definitely possible when I was in my twenties. It's all your saliva. It's got healing powers, helps the red blood cells multiply, regenerate fast. It prevents us from aging as fast. How old would you say I am?"

I thought. "Um. Thirty-ish?"

"I'm forty-nine. I take plenty of iron supplements, and it's fine."

"Is that—true?" I looked at Erica nervously.

"There's not really enough research," Erica said, propping her head on her hand and looking at Roxanne. "But you've been doing this how long, Roxie?"

"Twenty-three years. Never been anemic in the last ten, though of course I've had to find a doctor who doesn't see the bite marks and call the cops on me. Once I had to go to a court hearing about it and I lied and said I had been at the animal shelter working with aggressive dogs. Had my friend at the animal shelter write me a note to get the charges dropped. If you get caught selling, it's two to four years inside. My friend Maggie just got out."

"I have to be honest. All this kind of scares me," I said.

"Well, you don't *have* to drink from me," Roxanne said, smirking. "But it is a symbiotic exchange. If it's balanced and moderate."

"Punks are often kind of reckless with it," Erica said. "Free Blood kids."

She *didn't* like Cain. My dead heart swelled.

"I'm punk, and I'm good," Roxanne said, batting her eyelashes. She looked back to me. "One person *can't* meet one vampire's needs completely. If you try it, both of you will get unhealthy and sort of withery over time. But I can see Erica and Freddie each twice a week, and they see a couple other people and get bagged blood too, and it does us all good." Roxanne patted my chill hand with her warm one. "The thing with being a seller is you have to have a couple of good clients. You can find people you like. And this girl's *good*."

"It's the best version of this life I've had," Erica said, wryness around the edges.

They smiled at each other.

I basked for a second in the propaganda.

I knew what my mom would say about this woman—if she was really donating that much, she was hurting herself. She looked young, it was true, but she had to be sick. Yes, my mom would acknowledge, there were chemicals or polymers or RNA or something in vampire venom that could cure hemophilia and was useful in treating people with HIV and putting in Covid vaccines, but the doctors had to synthesize it out of the vamps when we went and bit a sponge in a clinic every month on our check-ups. They did stuff to it to make it useful. Science stuff. It wasn't like we were naturally useful.

Mom's answer would be, "Don't let Roxanne do that to herself. Tell her she can change."

It was hard to hold that in my head, because she was sitting there so confident and assured, warm and with such an insistent heartbeat, wrapped in this energy of being grounded, like she was made of the body of Mother Earth.

"I—how much do you charge?" I asked.

"I got you," Erica said.

"Eighty a pint," Roxanne said. "Sixty for Erica because I like her. Real different from the blood at the clinic, but I gotta make rent. Barista'ing doesn't do it all anymore, and being a poet doesn't pay shit."

"Eighty's well worth it," Erica said. She turned to me. "You get people charging more these days. Don't get mad at them, even if you can't afford it. There's a shortage, there's demand. They're doing something dangerous, legally speaking, and it's their body."

"I do *like* it," Roxanne said. "Not everyone gets the high, but a lot of us do. It feels *good.* I just still gotta make money to live. I wish I didn't."

Erica tilted her head slightly, a strange expression on her face.

I felt so hungry now that I was gripping the edge of the Formica table. My head hurt so much that I was going to drop onto the ground and hold my skull in my hands.

"I have to go to the bathroom," I said.

In the dirty stall, looking at my shoes against the checkered tile, I texted my mom on Signal.

The vampire took me to a pizza place to meet a seller. She's saying that vampire venom helps heal humans and that she's been doing this twenty years. Erica wants me to drink from her.

My mom texted back by the time I flushed.

This is pretty good stuff, she said. *That's closer to a network than we've gotten in a while. The clinic, too. You are going to be their best baby vampire friend. You don't know anything about the big scary city and need them to help you. Stay with them as long as you can. Get as many names as you can. We won't act tonight. Get them to promise to take you somewhere else. If you need to drink a little to keep cover, we just won't pass it along to MAVIS. Good job, baby.*

My mom's permission shot through me like a flash of lightning. *Good job, baby.* I was so grateful to her that I sent another text, without thinking:

There's a vampire tunnel under the manhole at E Denny and Harvard under the rainbow crosswalk.

A few seconds, and then a reply: Great. *We'll hit it tonight with Brid.*

I thought of Nick, his narrow, brutal face, Erica telling him to be careful when he went to the tunnel.

He wants to die, I thought. Erica said so. But if she could be trusted at all, I wasn't sure that Nick deserved it. If he was almost starving, hitting the clinic just enough not to die, he wasn't really a priority—not like Cain. He was basically just homeless.

Maybe he'd go another way. Maybe he'd fall asleep in the doorway, and the wind would blow his sign so its incendiary words pressed against the wet gray of the sidewalk, and my mom's high heels would stomp by him without pausing.

There was a tinge of dark, mildewy fear in the idea of my mom or Brid thrusting a stake through his heart. I felt the future flicker before me: a time when they would not need me.

I fluffed my hair up and back over my forehead, like Roxanne had, staring at the empty place my face should have been in the dirty glass mirror. I thought the hair flip might have made me look less little-girl, more minx. More predator? I was glad I could not see myself in the space behind my head, the ACABs and FUCK JENNY DURKANs written in Sharpie on tile.

Roxanne grabbed her purse when she saw me, planted her Blundstones on the sticky floor. "Let's skedaddle, if you're ready," she said. Her beer was empty.

I followed Roxanne and Erica out of the pizza place. The cold, rainy night felt good on my face, and I felt more at ease, like this was where I should have been the whole time, anyway. Cold creature of the cold night, of the black woods, et cetera. I wondered what it would be like to be an equatorial vampire—warm, sticky darkness.

8.

FAWN

I left the van locked the way Wanda asked me to, in the drive-in storage unit her buyer would visit her in when dark fell. Before I did, though, I tried opening the back door of the truck—after closing the orange rolling door of the storage unit. It rolled up this time; she hadn't padlocked it from inside like before. I stared at Wanda's sleeping face. She looked dead. White and cold, surrounded by boxes of bagged blood. I wanted to kiss her, but I didn't.

I walked through the sloping hill of the university district alone beneath a faint drizzle, checking my phone. My email had several messages from my parents—I had blocked their texts and calls before leaving. I didn't block their emails, since if they found out where I was they might tell me through email. But I couldn't open them up to read them. My phone was low on battery again, so I navigated to a cafe with a long, dark interior, bought the biggest cinnamon coffee I could, and plugged it in.

The stool of the counter was so tall that I could mainly

sit hunched over, the cord stretched just far enough so I could turn the phone toward my face and not show anyone sitting next to me. Silver's post about Iowa was gone; there was another one now. It was a photo of him in front of an empty mirror. His face was in unflattering, white light shining down from directly over the grey tile sink he stood in front of—fangs bright.

I refreshed the page again, and then started texting him again—a longer text. I had to open my notes app to write it. I rewrote it three or four times, never sure how to start it or finish it. I didn't know if I was asking him to find me, to love me, or telling him he had hurt me. I wanted to warn him that if I could see his posts, so could his family, so could the police. I wrote three paragraphs, and edited them down again until there were just two sentences.

I wish you understood that I loved you enough to follow you, I wrote. *I want to see you. I'm reading your blog.*

Cryptic, petulant. I sent it anyway and thought about where I was going to sleep tonight.

The address Wanda had given me was also in the U district, off the Ave, above a Chinese bakery—but it wasn't marked in any way as a hostel. It looked like the door to an apartment. When I rang the bell, there was a long silence, and I wondered what to do next. I could find a bench to sleep on. I could sleep in the park. I thought about whether I could find a museum and pull the trick from *From the Mixed-Up Files of Mrs. Basil E. Frankweiler.*

"Ned's House, hostel for the lost," a bored voice crackled.

"Um," I said, looking back over my shoulder. "I—Wanda sent me?"

"Wanda who," the voice said, still bored. "You covered with a tarp or something out there? You sizzling?"

"I, um, no. I hitched a ride in her truck, she was driving out here from Ohio. She said that if I mentioned her I could stay here."

"You're gonna have to talk to Ned," the voice said, but then the buzzer sounded, and I pushed the tinny metal door inward. The brown-carpeted stairs creaked and squished slightly under my boots as I walked with the moisture of past travelers. At the top of the stairway, there were two doors, one with a pile of mail in front of it and one cracked open. The latter opened as I got to the landing, and a brown-skinned androgynous goth in a hoodie that went down to their knees and jeans that seemed to be made of mostly ripped fabric leaned out into the stairway and pulled me by the hand inside. I get nervous when people touch me and jerked my hand back from theirs. They held their hands up as if to say "I'm unarmed."

Inside the apartment, purple blackout curtains covered every window, but the lights were on. The floor was covered with miscellaneous rugs that were all the same shade of creative tan-beige in different patterns, as if they'd been pulled from a handful of different showrooms in a department store. In one corner was a couch, and a counter with a coffeepot. There was only one apparent door besides the one I'd come in by.

A welcome mat inside the door had eight pairs of shoes sitting next to it, but I saw no sign of anyone else.

The goth studied me as I looked around, and I guessed that they were at least in their thirties, with fine lines over their eyes and under them. They might have been a dyke or a prettyboy South Asian Robert Smith lookalike.

"Wanda doesn't usually take hitchhikers," they said. "Ned's coming. We've had slayer action out here in the last few weeks, so we want to be careful. If you are a friend of Wanda, that's probably fine, you can stay a couple days."

"Wanda was getting followed and needed another driver. We got chased by some slayers in Montana," I offered. "They broke a window in the van with a crossbow thing."

But I spoke to their receding back. A second later, I heard a door open and close, and a clatter. It sounded like someone descending a fire escape, and a breath of cool rainy breeze blew through the hallway back to me.

My feet were sore and I hadn't really slept much. My face was a mess. But I felt my heart speed up a little, at this new place. I was definitely closer to Silver now, and also to—I thought about the way I'd felt with Wanda. When two figures climbed back up the metal steps that I could hear and not see, and turned the corner, I tried to crack a smile.

Ned was holding a blackout curtain above his head. When the door shut, he shed it on the ground. He was a balding Chinese guy; he wore a ribbed undershirt that showed a buoyantly muscled chest and a considerable number of tattoos, including a large red heart dripping blood in a spiral down his tricep. He was barefoot. He walked toward me, holding out a hand, squinting at me as if trying to suss something out.

"Wanda sent you to *me?*"

"I hitchhiked with her," I said. "I—I did the day shift driving so she could go faster." I shook his hand awkwardly.

"You use girl pronouns?" Ned asked, which wasn't what I'd expected him to say.

"Uh. Yeah."

"Name?"

His brusqueness rattled me. "Fawn," I said.

"No last name? Like Madonna?"

"I'd prefer not to. I ran away."

He raised his head toward the ceiling. "God, we're going to be overrun if we get the human runaways too. Nothing against you, honey," he added, looking down again at me, "but this is supposed to be a resource for vampires, you feel me? I don't know. I guess we can put you in Room F, there's a bed there."

"I'm sorry," I said. "I just didn't have anywhere else to go."

"Of course you don't." He put a hand to his forehead. "I don't suppose you'd want me to call the regular LGBT youth shelter to see—No, it's fine. We can do that tomorrow. I cannot say, 'Oh, you can stay here three weeks,' but I can say you can definitely stay here two nights. I'll call some people, see if someone can put you up while you look for something else."

"Thanks," I said. "I do really appreciate it."

"Wanda must like you." He turned his back to me but beckoned, and I followed him and the silent goth attendant back down the length of the room toward the door at the end. It opened out to a screened-in metal stairway; slats of rainy light came through, and Ned hoisted the blanket back over himself as we descended. At the foot of the steps was a yellow light and a trapdoor, which opened with a creak. I could see it was faintly lit inside; that was a relief.

"I'll go first," the goth said, and went down. I followed and found myself at the end of a cinderblock hallway lined with linoleum. It was surprisingly clean and colorful; the cinderblocks were decorated with spray paint images of rainbows, clouds, and suns wearing sunglasses, baring fangs. A line of waist-high cubbies lined the right side, with locking doors bearing a collection of band stickers that looked like they'd accumulated over time. The hallway parted ten or so meters down from where we stood into two hallways that angled down away from us, sloping deeper beneath the ground. It was cold.

Behind me, Ned said, "We'll put you in F. Close to the surface. There's just other teens in there."

I followed behind him, then turned to the goth and whispered, "What's your name?"

"Millie," they said, which made me think they might be a girl. "I don't know if F is the best idea, but Ned runs the show. If they give you crap—"

Ned looked back at Millie with a scowl that silenced her.

"They won't give her crap. They signed an agreement."

The door we turned into was a deep red; inside, there were a set of bunk beds, all occupied. Ned lowered his voice to a breath, raising a finger to his lips to let me know that I should be quiet. "Everyone's asleep right now," he said. "So don't make too much noise."

"I kind of need to sleep too," I whispered back. "I drove—"

I found a rough terrycloth white towel pressed into my hands. "That's your towel," Millie said. "Shower's back down the hall that way, but you can't shower more than four minutes or the drain backs up."

Ned covered his eyes with his hands again, and I realized the light was hurting his eyes. "I *really* need to go back to sleep. Fawn, I'll need a phone number from you so I can text you some stuff when I wake up. We're gonna make sure you're okay as far as your next spot. That's what I can do."

"That's huge," I said. I wrote down my number, and Ned took the clipboard back and turned away.

That seemed to be that. Millie retreated, her face a mask of passivity. Ned preemptively had the blanket over him again.

In the silent room, nobody breathed; the four people who were laying in sleeping bags and under the thin purple blankets around me were still as stone. It was cold in here. I climbed into the sleeping bag over my mattress and checked my phone again. Silver's selfie had disappeared. It was like he was teasing me. It was just one in the afternoon. I might have a chance to get a nap and then hunt for a job.

I faded out of consciousness, and came to with a mouth on my arm.

A cold mouth, a sharp one. Not Wanda's.

I screamed and pushed up, kicking up with a leg at the same time. The mouth, which hadn't bitten me yet, retracted. I threw a punch, a kick in the dark, against the figure. They landed, and the body fell back with a cry and a thud. My heart was thumping in my chest.

“What the fuck?” I managed, finally. “What the fuck?”

“What’s going on?” someone else’s voice said, from deeper in the room, and a light turned on. I clutched the blanket to my chest and saw one teen boy sprawled on the floor next to me, where I’d kicked him, and another, a lank-looking fat blond girl, staring at me from a bunk bed.

“This—he tried to bite me,” I said, my voice wobbly.

“Fuck,” the kid on the ground said, starting to sit up. “You got me in my fucking ribs.”

“Are you *human*?” The girl in the bed squinted at me, sniffing. Ridges on her forehead rose and then settled as she did. “They’re putting humans in with us now?”

The guy on the floor sat up, rubbing his head where it had hit the floor. “Thought you wanted it. Your necklace, you know.”

At this, the blond girl rolled out of the top bunk and fell onto the boy on the floor, her hands bared like claws. “Fuck you, Jay. I’m going to kill you,” she said. “I’m going to have Ned kick you the fuck out on the street! I’m going to stake you myself! You misogynist, rapey prick! Get *control of yourself*!”

Jay was under her, holding his hands over his face as she scratched and flailed heavily at him.

“Stop! I was just kidding! I wasn’t trying to freak her out!”

“The fuck you were!”

I leapt up from the bed and ran for the door, but the girl turned her attention to me and said “Don’t fucking move. Why the hell are you here? Who let you in?”

“I—just for a day. Ned let me in. I didn’t have anywhere

else. I had a friend who recommended this place because she knew it."

"Well, that's a shitty idea. Clearly Jay can't fucking control himself. He can't room with humans. He's been vamped for a *week*. It's not safe for you to be here. The fuck are they thinking? Get the fuck out."

"I—I didn't know that," I said. Her hand, I saw, was tight on Jay's throat. He was grasping at it, trying to remove it. "Stop—stop hurting him. I'll leave. I'm leaving right now." I bent forward to grab my bag from the bed, retreating backwards toward the door.

Jay made a noise like a dying fish.

"He doesn't need to breathe," she said, rolling her eyes, and focusing down again on Jay with the gaze of a raptor. "He needs to learn."

Jay looked at me, mouthing, but I couldn't tell what he was saying. His face was all lizardy, ridged and hard. His pale bare foot twitched, kicked out helplessly under the bed. I pressed myself against the door and took a deep breath, then opened it and ran outside, up the stairs. It was dark out now, and as wet as it had been earlier, the steps barely visible. I banged on the door. My legs shook.

"Help, help, help," I said. The door wasn't loud enough. My fist couldn't connect with it hard enough. "Help." My voice wouldn't come out as loud as I wanted it to. I tried to make it louder. "Help."

Millie opened the door and looked at me. "I'm almost done with my shift. What happened?" she asked, kind of cautiously.

"I—uh, quick. Please. Uh, this blond girl is trying to kill

the other guy, Jay," I said. "I don't want it to be my fault. You have to stop her. You have to."

Millie pushed past me and hurtled down the steps, sweatshirt flapping, leaving me at the top. I was too scared to follow. I stood, hovering, in the room, and finally sat down on the floor in the corner, hugging my knees. I was crying before I knew what was happening. Big tears.

I managed to stop by the time Millie came back; it looked like stress was curling her hair. She was hauling Jay and the blond girl behind her. They looked smaller in the light of the front room. Both of their heads were jammed down between raised shoulders, the ridges of their faces contrite.

"Angie, Jay, this is . . ."

"Fawn," I said.

"Fawn," Jay said. "Okay. Hey. I'm sorry I freaked you out. I wasn't really going to drink from you. I was just messing with you. You know, people mess around."

"Uh," I said.

"Not good enough," Millie said. "Not fucking good enough, Jay. You're on two strikes."

"That's not *fair*," Jay said, turning to her. "I should be on one. I came back late because of my *job*, the person wasn't opening their door, it's not my fault the condo-dwelling techies can't be bothered to accept a delivery—"

"Two strikes. Again. Fawn trusted us and woke up to something that probably felt really frightening."

Jay looked at me but couldn't hold my eyes. He looked down at the ground, pursing his lips. "I acted really wrong," he said. "I uh. I got a little out of control. It's bad. I didn't expect a human to be there."

"One more time," Millie said.

"Okay, okay, I'm an evil rapist and I should go die in a hole," Jay said, looking at Millie. "Got it. Got it, everyone, Millie the human queen of morals says Jay's fucked up, he wants to—"

"Jay, that's *not* what—"

"Just *stake me* if you want to so bad," he said, to Millie, who blanched.

Angie punched him so hard he fell back, and Millie wrenched Angie off him.

"Angie, strike one. I'm handling this."

"You aren't! He's being a *monster*!"

I stood up.

"I'm gonna—I'm gonna go," I said. "I don't want to cause trouble. I really don't."

"She's going to call the cops on this whole place!" Angie screamed. "And she should, because you just acted like a *menace to society*!"

"Fawn, please hold on a second," Millie said. "I'm going to talk to Ned."

"I hate the cops," I snapped. "I don't want to mess anything up. I don't want to make problems. I'm sorry I'm a problem. I'm just out of here. I'll find another place. This was a mistake. I'm sorry."

"Fawn, we said it was okay, and we should have—"

I hurtled, head down, toward the door, through it, and out onto the street, in the rain, my throat hot. I heard Millie's voice behind me, but she didn't follow me. The slam of the first metal door and the second rang behind me. My heart was tapping inside my ribs like a bike gear out of true running down the hill. I got a couple blocks into the rain with my bag and then ducked into an alleyway, clutching it. I stared up at the dark sky. I put my hand into my shirt and found my bat-heart pendant, held it till it cut my hand. I rifled for my phone—

—my phone.

I couldn't deal with turning around. But I couldn't do anything without my phone. I slumped down, looking at my shoes between my legs, feeling how I still hadn't had a shower, still hadn't eaten anything since the sandwich with Wanda. The rain was making my hair wet. Cars splashed past on the street, and university kids strode by under umbrellas, busy with their real lives.

The footsteps rounded into the alleyway. I looked up at Jay.

He had a half-shaved head, floppy black hair falling on the opposite side. He'd unvamped his face, and now his long, curved nose fell into relief against his smooth, sloping brown forehead, with the yellow light behind him. He was pretty. If he'd been at my school, I might have crushed on him. So might have Silver.

"Hey," he said, holding his hands up like he was showing me he was unarmed. "Nobody's gonna hurt you. It's all a misunderstanding."

"Yeah," I said. "I just don't like those." I glanced to see if there was a way out of the alley I was in. It did look like there was a parking lot on the other end. I started to back away from Jay.

"I'm serious. I wouldn't have drunk *much*."

I wasn't practiced enough at all this to know what to say

back. "Okay," I said. Then I remembered what Wanda had said. "I mean, if you did drink, you'd just owe me eighty bucks, that's all."

Jay reeled back. "You're a seller?" He said it with a tilt I couldn't parse. He shook his head. "You're like, my age. You have the necklace. You're a *seller*?"

"I'm not giving shit away," I snapped back, trying to make my voice hard, clutching the necklace. "Can't afford to. And not while I sleep. Where I come from, people are polite enough to pay for their fucking meal."

"Y-you think you have something on us," Jay said. "You think you can have us all come running for your blood any time you want, charge us whatever you want."

"I didn't ask for you to come at me fangs out. I just needed a place to sleep."

He leaned back, looked at the sky. "You're wearing Cain's necklace then trying to charge people?"

I looked down at the necklace. I put on the voice I had used when people fucked with me at school. "You think this necklace means *anyone* can drink from me for free?" I didn't want to look weak, or stupid.

"That's exactly what it means, you fuck," Jay said, snarling, his vamp face emerging like ruts in a wet trail, water running down the apex of each ridge. "It means you're an ally. Someone who'll keep us alive without expecting that we owe you, because you know it's good for you too. Not exploit us. Have you even *read* Cain's writing?"

I spluttered for a second, because I had. On his blog. I just had sort of thought the whole thing was a bit he was doing. But I knew the answer to Jay's challenge.

"The necklace is about a *bond*," I said. "I can have a bond with one person and not another. I don't owe you just because I let another guy drink for free. I have something valuable. I'm not a public resource."

I tucked my bat-wing heart inside my shirt again. Jay looked so wounded that I knew I got him. He deflated. I relaxed a little; things weren't so different after all, between vampires and high school. Everyone had weaknesses.

There were more footsteps.

Millie stood there, panting. Her day had spun out of control. "Three fucking strikes, Jay," she said. "Three strikes. Stop it. Get out of here. Not okay to chase this poor girl. This ain't what it's about. This is really bad. What the hell are you thinking?"

"Just trying to make it right," Jay said. "I'm the one trying here."

"Leave," Millie said. "Just walk away. Ned's gonna call you later. You have to make a plan. You're in violation of the housing agreement."

"I didn't agree to anything," Jay said. "I didn't agree to having *sellers* in the hostel. You're both sick. Ned's a shithead for letting humans run the damn place. I'm out."

He turned and started to storm off, down the street.

"Jay, you may be undead, but you live in a society," Millie shouted. "Talk to Ned, Jay. That's all you need to do. You need to make a plan to make this better."

She turned to me.

"He hurt you?"

"No," I said. "He got mad because I told him if he wanted to drink my blood, he had to pay."

Millie rolled her tongue inside her cheek. "You sell, huh. That's why he's pissed?"

"I wasn't trying to sell while I was at the hostel," I said, since that was against the rules, obviously. "I was just saying it was messed up of him to come at me while I was asleep."

"Of course it was," Millie said. "No, of course. Hey. Do you need a hug?" She stretched out her arms, her face a thousand times more open and sympathetic than it had been during the day. I realized, all at once, that she was definitely trans, like me, and she knew that I was trans too. I felt my heart almost burst with it.

"No," I said, taking another step back.

She lowered her extended arms, put her hands on her hips, and looked back over her shoulder. "The young ones can be like that. They're all jumpy and angry and righteous . . . I don't know. Gives me a huge headache." She put her hand to her eyes, as if to exemplify the huge headache. "You're a seller. That explains Wanda. Okay, but this gives me an idea. Come back, get your phone."

I hesitated.

"Come on, come on," Millie said. "I don't want to keep your phone. At least come get it. I'm gonna call this girl we know, ask if there's room for you at her place. But if you don't want to stay with her you don't have to."

I walked slowly back with her through the rain. There was no sign of Jay on the street. "Will he try to attack someone out here?" I asked.

"Better not. If a slayer doesn't get him, Ned will."

"That a big problem? Slaying and stuff? How many are there?"

Millie's mouth went tight. "Huge problem for how few of them there are. They dusted a bunch of people this winter, this area. Mostly kids. Cops don't give a shit, obviously. Cops don't do a lot of vampire slaying directly, except when they bulldoze a squat house, then they pretend it was just never there. Slayers kill directly. My friend Shawn got staked. My friend Sam. Lot of newbies like Jay who are wilding out. Their families never get told. God, if he does attack someone, he's done for."

"Jay's probably fine," I said, feeling my stomach turn. "He's not a bad guy, I think."

"I don't know. Most of these kids don't actually hurt anyone, they're just indiscreet. Jay got kicked out of his housing a few days ago because he bit this drunk girl at a party," Millie said, glowering at a red sign that blared NEW SAIGON over a window filled with plants. "At intake Angie told it like he was high, had missed getting his ration at the clinic, didn't know what he was doing. I don't know about that now, seems like it's maybe a pattern with him. It's harder to control when you're new, so I hope that's all. Hopefully he talks to Ned, Ned puts the fear of the devil in him, we see if he can get control."

"Angie seemed like she was gonna kill him over it," I said.

"They're best friends. She's trying to protect him from himself. She's just scared. Those two are some of the Cain kids. It's not right how he turns kids so often now. He wants more young people around him so he doesn't feel sad, I think. It's irresponsible."

Back up the wet gray stairs with my wet bag, into the wide room with the pictures of naked women, where I stood, dripping on the floor, until Millie came back with my phone.

"Should have had you wait to sleep until the vamps were awake," she said. "Though I guess you maybe want to be nocturnal too. I'm going to make my call."

It was all very strange.

When she left the room and went to sit on the rainy back stairs, the door closed behind her so all I could hear was the muffled noise of low conversation.

After a few minutes she returned.

"My friend Raina says you can stay with her and her roommate Roxanne," Millie said. I wasn't sure when she'd come back in from the rain. "Least for a couple weeks, maybe more if you can pay rent. She's got a tiny three-bedroom and uses the third for work, but the office has a couch. It's over in Cap Hill. I told her you're a seller too, she made room."

She put a bottle of pills in my hand. "Also. These are estrogen. A month worth. You should go to a doctor for more, but I switched to injection so you can have these."

I was only a seller in the sense that I had eighty more dollars because of Wanda, but that made the whole thing real enough. I took the number Millie offered me, and the estrogen, thanked her while looking at my own shoes, and went to find a bus.

9.

RACHEL

Roxanne took us to her apartment building, and we entered through the back alleyway, where there was a smashed bottle on the ground, signs of trash and bums and all the seedier, sadder things in Seattle—but then we went up quickly through a warm, yellow-and-gray hallway to a hot pink kitchen with ancient cracking linoleum on the floor.

"Come in," Roxanne said, and the beads over the doorway parted.

There was a poster of Jean Loves Jezebel on one wall and one for a Maggie Rogers show on the other. Roxanne kicked off her shoes. There was a noise, and a door opened. A goth, round-faced, shaggy black-haired head poked out. A boy-y girl, or girl-y boy; I couldn't tell for a second, until I realized that there was the shape of a padded bra visible under her shirt. She had long hair, but was otherwise basically dressed like a metalhead guy. Brid would always get embarrassed when we saw a gay person who looked so bull-dykey in public, but I liked looking at them. It was like them being there let me be there. Seeing people like that was how I knew gay people existed.

"Fawn," Roxanne said. "Brought you a customer. That's sixty toward rent."

"Thanks. Not to be rude, but I thought it was eighty," Fawn said to Roxanne in a scratchy voice, brow furrowing—my conviction wavered, was she really a boy?—and then turned and looked at me, and I watched her huge, dark eyes widen. Not crazy or anything, but I know that look, especially in girls. She was definitely a girl—the way she smiled shyly at me left no doubt. She extended a hand to me politely. "I'm Fawn."

"I can do eighty," Erica said quickly. She handed the bills to Fawn, who promptly handed them to Roxanne. "Nice to meet you, Fawn. How long you been here?"

"Uh, about a week."

This seemed like a sketch operation to me.

Roxanne plopped down on the small green plastic-covered couch and patted the cushion next to her. "Come sit here," she said to Erica, and they were instantly wrapped around each other, Erica's mouth climbing up Roxanne's arm. Erica appeared to totally forget about me for the moment. I averted my eyes quickly.

Fawn stood in front of me. "You wanna go to my room?" she asked, nervously.

Her room seemed to be a futon and a computer on a desk and a bookshelf. A backpack spewed its myriad contents over the floor. She closed the door on the weirdly horny scene outside, sat on the futon, and pulled out her phone. She set a timer for six minutes and then held out her arm to me. After I waited, for what was clearly too long, she took my hand and put it around her wrist. I could see the blue vein climbing through her light freckly skin, as if it was a river viewed through sunset clouds.

"You can drink now," Fawn said, and she sounded as nervous as I was. This didn't necessarily feel okay. She didn't seem to know what she was doing. But when I moved my fingers up her arm, tracing on either side of that blue vein, she sighed softly. It was definitely a girl sigh. It had been a minute since anyone wanted to touch me. I wanted to grab her hips where they edged up out of her jeans, pull her toward me, straddle her.

The thing so close to snapping snapped. I touched her arm lightly with both hands, running my fingers up and down. She smiled.

I brought my face close to her neck. I felt disgusting, and I also smelled the warm, rich iron of her blood, and the faint other notes of her—salt and the sort of red, pungent, cumin-y sweaty smell of her insides.

My mom's voice in my head, *It's okay to drink to keep your cover.* Her earlier voice, *Any vampire that bites a human will kill someone eventually.*

I bent, and felt my ridges come out, my fangs come down. I bit her neck, like a pit bull.

The puncture wounds were not deep, I thought, but my right upper canine was in her artery. It was weird how natural it felt, like I had been born with the instinct. I wrapped my lips around the wound as her blood flowed, sucked like I was giving a hickey to Brid at our first sleep-away camp when we were thirteen, feeling as innocent and free, for a moment, as I had then—before slaying, when we could push each other under the water beneath the docks and take turns pretending we were in trouble, grasping each other, gasping for air. I gasped into Fawn's throat, her moaning, my tongue moving by compulsion, my eyes closed but the purple swish of the blood filling the inside of my lids. In my mouth, she tasted like metal pouring from a forge. It was so hot. It was the sun, pouring into me, not burning. I felt a drumbeat of pleasure in my heart, gripped her harder, pulling with my mouth at her soft skin, more, more more more—

The alarm went off, ringing. I grasped her more tightly with a hand, and she laughed and made no move to pull away, but then there was the noise of a door opening and Erica said, loudly, in the door behind me,

"Okay, honey, cool off now, that's gonna be enough. The neck, too? You're going to get monsterface."

Kill someone

"Sorry!" I felt a needle of shame jolt through my gut. I leapt back, off Fawn, and tumbled backwards into the desk. My head collided with the carpeted floor.

"Just checking in on you kids," Erica said, laughing. She walked over to me and bent to take my hand in hers, gave it a brief squeeze. "It takes practice, stopping. That's why it's best to have someone around to help you set limits at first. And I think it's harder, stopping, when it's from the neck." She helped me stand, and then moved me to a chair near the window, which she cracked open. A ripple of cold breeze came in. "How do you feel?"

The gold of the forge receded, and I was there, on the banks of the river, wanting to be in it again.

"I gotta think about it," I said.

She laughed. "I'll leave you guys alone a second. Just don't go back for seconds. Not good your first time."

She closed the door almost all the way and I heard a clank of an ice machine in the kitchen and her talking to Roxanne again, then both of their voices laughing.

"How *do* you feel?" Fawn said, nervously, and I realized she couldn't be older than me. "What is it like?"

The answer was—physically better than I ever had, even alive. I felt like Superwoman. I spent a lot of hours in the gym with my mom, training, to get this. It was different than being just *not* hungry, *not* tired. I would have drunk until she died. I was sure of it.

I felt like my feet were lifting from the ground. I had to glance down to see they weren't.

Bad—the word was taking on new meanings.

"I mean, I don't think I realized I was so hungry," I said, trying to make it sound like nothing.

"The hunger was nice for me," Fawn said, raising her eyebrows and laughing awkwardly, and I looked over and realized that I maybe liked butch girls. Was she butch or just androgynous? Whitney was butch too. Could you actually tell who was butch and who was femme? I hadn't thought about it before, because nobody in MAVIS was butch, and the masc girls at my old school didn't realize I was gay, so they had never looked at me the way Fawn was looking at me. Her eyes were big and inky deep brown and pretty, and she looked more solid than me, looked almost like a boy—though she would have been a pretty, really gay-looking boy. There had been a girl at tennis camp like her, blustery and tough.

"How—did I hurt you?"

"No." She put her hands behind her head and looked up at the ceiling, so I could see the whole length of her esophagus. She was smiling. "I feel floaty."

I wanted to drink from her throat and then have her straddle me and kiss me, the blood pouring down her neck where I could rub my face in it. And all of that was bad, bad, bad. Where her bruise was purple, I could see the blood under the skin, even though the wound had closed up with my saliva—

—my saliva, all over her neck.

"Bad" in this moment meant: this will fuck me up with MAVIS. Will fuck me up with Brid. I wasn't even thinking about actually bad. Bad inconvenient. It was impossible not to know that about myself.

I wanted to fling myself back onto Fawn, and it had nothing to do with knowing her specifically, just with how her skin felt against my mouth and how good her blood had tasted and how soft she was and how hungry I was, had been, would continue to be. I knew what it was like now, and it was really at least eleven times better than drinking blood from the bag. I felt my face with my hand—all ridges, all hard, monstrous. I couldn't change back, and it was like having my face stuck in a smile, in a rictus, and it was sort of scary that it burned in a *nice* way, felt good. My fangs were still out, still red. I looked at Fawn, searching for signs I had destroyed her, or weakened her. She had her eyes half-lidded and was smiling this huge, simple, smile with her round face and soft chin tilted back like she was stoned.

"You're looking at me really dumb," she said.

"I'm not looking at you dumb. You're looking at me dumb," I said, before thinking.

She laughed and looked down at my feet, putting her hands up to hide her face. "That was a mean thing to say."

"I didn't mean actually dumb." I realized I wished I could be her friend. Her freckled pink was undiminished. I felt so bad for wanting to rip her apart. "Are you for real okay?"

"Yeah, I'm all good. Erica probably made you stop too soon. You stood there like a minute of the timer before starting drinking. I could probably go and go."

"Oh, good. Okay. Phew." Normal blood drinking, not weird or intense at all.

"You want to sit down next to me a minute?"

She opened her soft arms at me. Could I just curl up on her lap?

I wanted to hold her, but that wasn't why I was there, and I knew my mouth was trying to open at her, gaping and full of fangs. My teeth were aching, growing, something. It was sending strange flares through my temples. I stood up, my hand over my top teeth. I had to leave. I had to leave, or I would eat her. I turned and walked briskly out into the other room.

"You good?" Erica asked, from the chair where she sat with an arm around Roxanne. They were petting a weird little dog, with wiry hair, that turned and let out a yap when it saw me.

"I think I have to go," I said, my whole body tingling. "I feel weird and my mom will know I'm gone."

I had my hand on the doorknob before Erica said, "Slow down!"

At least it wasn't weird that I was being nervous. I was supposedly sneaking. I needed to rush home for normal reasons.

"Chill, chill, chill," Roxanne said, leaping up and coming over. I could smell blood on her, inside her, against the sweet smell of pizza that no longer agreed with me.

"No," I said, and went through the door. "I, next time. Thank you, Erica. Sorry. Bye!"

Down the carpeted hallway, boom boom boom, and my teeth had to be past the edge of my jaw. It felt like my bottom teeth were jutting up past my nose. They were huge, and they were splitting my skin back, making new shapes in my face, it was like my face had elongated—I felt my nose and felt how it flattened. I didn't get it. Why was this happening?

A car alarm went off across the street, and someone cursed.

A moped drove by.

The fire exit door banged behind me.

I clattered up the hill to the sidewalk, past someone with a grocery cart of plastic bottles wrapped neatly in plastic bags, and after a minute of holding my hands over my face the night was good and cold around me again and my heart had stopped hurting and my body had stopped feeling so warm and pounding. I looked at the muddy stars behind the mist and inhaled, exhaled, which I probably hadn't done since before I bit Fawn.

I imagined myself, chomping down on her the way I knew I wanted to, and her terrified scream. The blood just bursting forth in waves.

"Hey!"

I turned.

Fawn was panting, climbing the hill behind me.

"Hey! You forgot your bag!"

I turned. I realized—I had had a purse. Oh, god. Fawn's face was screwed up with exertion. She'd run after me. I felt like dropping through the cement. I couldn't read if there was any emotion at all on it. But if they'd read a message from my mom . . . I had nobody to back me up if they'd discovered me and were closing in from all sides. I had nobody to call to on a walkie talkie. I had walked into this and exposed myself the way I'd been taught never to do, all because I was overtaken with need to drain a girl of blood.

I was spinning.

"You had a text from your mom, also," she said, meaningfully, and pulled my phone out of my bag. "It buzzed as soon as you left."

She was less than three feet away, holding my own screen toward me. Oh god. I backed away from her. What had she seen?

I looked at the screen, squinting in the dark against its brightness. In message previews, my mom's text read: Hey, aaawesome news. Daylight's sending us some big cases of samples. They have the formula now, for sun resistance, for nutrition. It's what's going to market.

She looked at me with a furrowed brow. "That's good?"

"It's good. Yeah, it's good." Phew. "It's, uh, there's a study for synthetic blood." I was so not suspicious.

"Oh, cool," she said. She laughed. "So you don't need to come see me again."

"I, um, I."

"I'm sorry for in there when I asked if you wanted to sit down with me. I didn't mean anything. I just thought you looked jumpy."

"I uh," I said. I should tell her to get out of this business, that everyone she met wanted to eat her. She was nice, and cute. "I think I'm not cut out for this life, is all," I said.

"For vamping?" She laughed as I took the purse from her. "Are uh. Are you new?"

I let out a forced laugh that became a real one when she giggled. "Very, very new." I remembered that I had wanted to tear her throat open. "I, I'm like, kind of not in control and it feels scary."

"You seem in control," Fawn said. "I thought you controlled yourself very well. Maybe like, even a little more than you need to be."

Undercover. Act normal. "I mean, I'm like, you know. I'm not exactly well socialized. I've basically been in a basement for months. I just . . . I never thought I would need to do that to live."

She nodded thoughtfully. "It has to be weird. It changes a lot, even if you were prepared."

I hated her thinking of me as someone who had intentionally chosen to become something that could hurt her.

"I wasn't prepared, I didn't want this," I snapped, before I could stop myself. "I got attacked."

Fawn looked so surprised that I felt bad. "Oh damn. I'm . . . I didn't think. That's terrible. Wait, so that's why Erica's looking after you."

Erica really was trying to look after me. And I wanted to know that Fawn hated Cain as much as I did, and just tell her. But I didn't feel like fabricating an alternate version of the story where I wasn't a slayer. "I don't want to talk about it."

Fawn. I stared at her, feeling the pain in my jaw gradually subside. She had freckles and smooth dark hair and looked really exhausted. She looked very cuddly and teddy bearish. I could smell each beat of her heart.

"I have to go," I said. I worried I had missed another buzz on my phone. I also wasn't sure that somehow my phone hadn't given me away some other way. What if they'd really, really fast downloaded my entire photo history? Seen June Sorkin on my Instagram contacts, seen the videos for Security Sisters I had made? They could be vampire hackers.

"Roxanne said to tell you. You look kind of vamped right now. She said maybe come in for a second till it's gone?"

I realized that my face hadn't shifted back. I had been talking, this whole time—my teeth had been scraping against my nose and chin. I felt at my nose. A wide, furry bat's nose, with flares and folds.

Gagotron. Gross.

I felt the tears come and pushed them down, but I was crying anyway. A strange shriek escaped my strange mouth.

"Hey," Fawn said. "Shit. Shh. Uh." She put an arm around me and I felt myself shaking against her. "Do you want to like, sit next to me a minute? On the steps inside?"

I followed her in, and the door shut more softly this time. We sat on the dirty, dirty carpet, surrounded by stray pieces of ownerless mail. I stared at her soft upper arms, exposed by the sleeves of her t-shirt.

"Like, maybe just, um. I guess not take breaths. Or do you?"

I laughed because she was so awkward. "I do. I can."

I bent my face toward the floor and looked between my legs at the carpet. I let the breath move slower than it would have if I'd needed it like I did when I was alive. Just focus on the feeling, I thought. Just the motion of the air, moving into me. Moving around in my dead lung.

I felt the plates of my face quiet, stop burning. I felt the lodestar of shame in my chest dim a little. Fawn was still sitting next to me. I still felt like sobbing, but the ache in my mouth and the buzzing all through me stopped.

"Okay," she said finally. "I think you're normal?"

I looked up at her, and she smoothed a thumb over my face, studying me with dark eyes, and there was only a flicker of terrifying jumpy electrode in my upper teeth.

"Normal Rachel," I said, and laughed, and felt a bubble of snot too close to the edge of my nose. I felt in my purse for tissues.

"Go home, Normal Rachel," Fawn said.

10.

FAWN

After Roxanne brought Rachel the anxiety queen to me, I failed to get my blood drunk for a couple weeks. I took estrogen every day. I was trying to figure out Craigslist. People kept emailing me and then ghosting or saying creepy stuff. Erica came over one night and paid me for a pint after she had one from Roxanne. But I didn't get any other customers, and I spent my days walking around Cap Hill and going into thrift stores and not buying anything. Then, after Raina caught me eating her cereal, I went out and wrote my number on five bathroom walls. I wrote it in women's bathrooms because I didn't think I wanted any men drinking from me. I was hoping Rachel would text, but she was on the synthetic thing, I guessed.

The first text I got from writing my number on the pizza place's wall came from a Massachusetts area code. I realized I didn't really have any kind of security process in place, but the text came in when I was feeling depressed about having no money to add to the fridge's sad repository of grocery items. One hundred sixty dollars isn't actually that many dollars; with Wanda it was $210, but it wasn't that anymore because I'd bought food. I kept the last twenty from Wanda like a token under my pillow, just in case. I had not become best friends with Raina and Roxanne. They seemed to regard me like a benign dog that happened to owe them money. They were sort of my landlord, and they didn't ever ask me what my favorite movies were. I would have told them.

Rachel the pretty vampire probably didn't have any money either, so really it was fine if she didn't want to be my friend, I told myself.

The selfie that this vampire with the Massachusetts area code sent me was of someone visibly much older than Rachel.

This woman's name was Richeza. Her skin was wrinkled and pale but had a purple tinge—the light?—and a long, tight grey braid trailed to one side of her head. Her face was striking—wide and heavy. It was like the bones beneath her furrowed skin were less closely formed, as if there were plates underneath spreading apart like continents, and the effect was something other than human.

I rode the grey elevator up to the sixth floor, and she let me inside. The door cracked open and she was there, immediately, taking my arm. She was stocky and barrel-chested and just above my height. The smell of her room was of oppressive clove and licorice. The room was tiny; a minifridge in the corner was the only hint of a kitchen. There was a pink lamp with a lace shade. She was wearing a long white crocheted robe that draped over her big chest to her stockinged feet; when she opened the door and reached nonverbally to stroke my cheek, the knit patterns trailed against my face. There were no windows, which made sense, but it gave the place the feeling of being inside a dollhouse. One wall was taken up by a glass case of porcelain dishes and trinkets, like a grandmother might have: little dogs and birds. She didn't look quite like a grandmother, but there were webs of wrinkles around her eyes, rust-red against purple-tinged skin.

She handed me eighty right away, from somewhere in the fold of her robe; no tip.

"You smell good," she said. "Better than I expected. Usually there is veiled distaste."

She had a necklace of paper-mache beads covered in newsprint alternating with wooden ones—an art-teacher necklace.

There was not room to draw breath, to answer.

She launched herself at me hungrily, her mouth descending to my wrist, nose flaring into winged chiropteran fringes, and it was the moment of hunger that I had been looking for. It was uncontrolled, selfish, ravenous. I shivered against the door, feeling four teeth scrape my arm. She had me trapped, forehead and cheek to my belly, no words exchanged. She knelt at my feet, both hands wrapped around my wrist.

I felt a terror grip my spine when she bit. After two deep breaths, the fear subsided, but you saw, looking at her, the thing that everyone was frightened of. I realized I was, okay, yeah, working a dangerous job.

Only the noises of thirst, her bumpy, boned ridges emerging larger and larger from her white skin in waves with each swallow, looking almost like little Sagrada Familia spires. It felt more animal than Rachel's mouth had. I was able to drop into the starry sky, and feel the cool dryness of her long-fingered hand as it crept around and held my back under my shirt. I looked at the pink lamp. It was easy to be part of the flow of it once it started. There was always something electrifying. It wasn't always world-changing, but it was always there. It was like lightning touching you. She dropped my arm, and I wanted more, but I was surprised when she rose creakily to her feet and kissed my neck tenderly with dry, chill lips.

"Sometimes it can feel good here too," she said, tracing a line to the left of my esophagus with one acrylic nail. "I will give you twenty more dollars. You had that before?"

Her voice was heavy with an accent that I might have called Italian, but it was thicker on the consonants. It was from somewhere else.

"I haven't," I lied. "Twenty seems low."

"Chickenshit youngsters only drink from the wrist. It is not dangerous to drink from the neck, though. It is the same small bite. I want a little more. And okay. I can pay thirty. Do you want it?"

I balanced the feeling of wanting to give her what she wanted, feeling scared and kind of guilty for lying and extorting her, wanting to know how it felt, with wanting to make money, to hold out. What could I bargain with? What did I need? I scooted around her further inside, sat back on the small, navy-colored bed pressed between the ceramic doll case and the minifridge. I wouldn't be drunk from against the door again. I tried to look composed.

"I'll—um, give you a couple minutes there, if you give forty and tell me everything you know about the vampire Cain."

"Cain. You're ruining my appetite," she said. "Annoying man."

"Everyone hates him, I know. I just need information. I'm new in town."

She shook her head as if to say, exhausting. "Of course." Was her accent Russian? No. She walked over to her wallet, pulled out two twenties, and then, pressing it into my hand, leaned forward and grazed my neck with her teeth. I realized if she wanted to take without paying, she could. I could probably push her off, but I wouldn't. Desire or paralysis or curiosity would stop me. This was going to be a problem if I was going to be doing this for a living.

"Promise before you bite," I said. "I'm looking for information."

"Promise, whatever," she said, and bit.

It did feel nice, her lips like a warm rush of sunlight on my throat, two deep slices of cold pain, and I felt my back arch up a warmth suffusing me as her hands grew long, narrow claws that wrapped around my wrists. A webbing began to stretch between her fingers as she drank. I watched, heavy-lidded.

When she retreated, her face gave me a start: eyes wider, bigger, ridges and spindles like a white desert lizard, her nose flattened and expanded into a wrinkled, wide batlike one that flared with her smile. Soft fur sprouted around her face, across her cheeks and down her neck, downy like a baby goose. She held her hands up for me to see. The webbing was translucent, like the rubber of a balloon. Her ears had grown long, with deep points. No blood ran down her face: she licked around her mouth with a long, thin tongue to make sure. She looked monstrous. My eyes went up and down her body. Furry down, everywhere.

"Neck drinking is just better," she said, shaking her head. "You see how I am now? There's more power in it, like in the old days. The children are scared of what happens when you drink from the neck."

"Oh," I said. "Yeah." I thought about Rachel's face changing, batlike.

"Unbraid my hair."

The enthusiasm in her voice startled me. I reached out and touched the braid proffered to me as she undid the scrunchie on the end. I ran my hand cautiously through the silver hair, and it came undone. As the black and grey tresses fell around her face, they began to rise with static electricity, to stand on end, moving as if in a wind, blown out on either coast of her wide cheekbones. It was like she stood on top of a metal plate. She stood, looking at me with a strange smile. She reached up with her hands to feel where her hair stood out.

"Up like the mane of a lion." She giggled—a low, primordial noise. "Your blood is especially good."

"It is?"

"You're of the old kind. Take pride in that."

She looked down. Her shoes had left the carpet, and she was floating an inch in the air, the fuzzy shadows beneath her moving of their own accord. She laughed and reached out to me and touched my face with one long clawed hand.

I took her hand, finding it more lovely the longer I looked. Her fingers were now twice the length they had been, and ended in prolonged, purple-stained claws.

"This scares you?"

"No," I said. Now that she was like this, I was beginning to feel for her the way I'd felt for Wanda, for Rachel. I watched her skin as if something new might bubble forth from it.

She floated, and I sat, holding her hand. After a minute, her feet touched back down to the carpet.

The fingers shrank as I stared, her claws turning slowly back into ordinary acrylics. Her nose dwindled, returned to how it had been before.

"How come not everyone changes when they drink?"

"We all used to do things like this. I remember what it's like to not be so restrained when most don't," she said, laughing, collapsing down onto the bed. "I'm older than anyone else in this city has ever been, except maybe Ron down in the South Side. I won't tell you what century, you wouldn't believe me."

"I won't make you tell me." I tried to picture her in another era's fashion, or untended, living in a rotten shell of a house or a cave beneath the ground. That was where people like her had lived, right?

"Cain pretends he's one of the oldest, he impresses them with his transformations and pretends he is the leader of the future. He is not special."

"Cain isn't one of the oldest?"

She began to comb her long fingers through her hair, rebraid it. "He says he has ancient secrets. Did you know he was born in 1945? I've heard him say he was alive in Spain during the Thirty Years War. All of the newest ones. They think the way to live is to pretend they're part of a pretend history. And many real old ones are dead—were killed by slayers, by sun, by the Covid-19 blood shortage. I have seen many die. I had to move so that police didn't find me, when they were looking for me. I cut my tracker off. I have a fake ID now, or I'd have been starved."

"Cain—so he's only like, seventy something?"

She lay down next to me and placed her nose against my wrist on the bed. The nose widened again into a creature-shape and snuffled flexibly. She seemed like she wanted me to hold her but wouldn't say it. Her fingers clasped my knee and grew longer again. Could she control it, the change?

"Do you know about vampires, child? How we started?"

"No," I said.

"We were once something else," she said, pressing her face into my leg like a cat. "It was a different thing. Many different things. There is no one history. We were called lugats and kallikantzaros or kukuth or shtriga, where I was from. Estrie is another word. With horns and hair and hoofs and tusks and wings. I say us, but almost all of us thought we were almost alone. We were different from each other. The other places, some of us had long necks or tongues, or holes in the back of our heads, and jumped or flew. The places we are from shape us differently. We turned into beasts. We were those who were touched by darkness, desire. The sun hurt us, but we lived in deep places, like wells, or caves, and some people loved us. Some of us found lovers in darkness, were made strong by them, our bodies changed with the magic of their love, and others' fear. Some of us had no lovers. But there were many kinds of us, different everywhere. Some plagues were blamed on us, and some of us were silly and believed we could stop people hating us, or find protection by giving the gift of our darkness by spreading our magic, and tried to persuade rich people to love us that way. But those people did not help us, only used the magic to hurt others. Mostly they did themselves in. They don't know what love is. More people turned against us and told stories of how they see us until we have forgotten the best parts of being what we are. We become less. Now we are just sick people. I am too, even if I can change. That's the only way for me to exist now, here."

"Did you say wings?" I asked. I felt hypnotized, while she talked and looked up at me, her ridged downy brows like mountains. But she rolled over away from me. Looking at the wall, she continued talking.

"Cain, this boy, he imagined he is an aristocrat. He thinks we have an aristocratic legacy, which is never what it has been about. He started doing some bull-shit . . . down in Mexico, in the 1970s," she said. "Said it was family, a new world being born. No family. He stole blood and money from tourists, that's all. His children down in Mexico got hunted down and he didn't help them, just ran. If he were old as me, he would have protected them or died with them. But he came up here with his dirty cash after they all were dusted and got everyone on his side all the same, listening to him. He and that Sorkin danced about each other. People turn on him in waves. I saw him have that moment in the 1990s. Everyone hated him, but now all those people are dead, and the kids don't know any better than to trust him. I suppose he is only a child too. He says the Free Blood children will build a new life for us, but they will be weak, because they are scared of what we really are. Including him. He wants to be a god, a world-saver. He's scared of being only a strange creature."

"Okay. So, vampires—if they drank from the neck, their face does that. How do you have wings?"

She gave me a sly catlike glance. "Just drink more. Do you want to see?"

I did. I nodded.

She raised up onto an elbow, fanged mouth smirking. "You don't mean that. I've drunk too much from you today, more than recommended." There was a purr of derision in her smile.

"Oh, uh, I guess you're right. Uh, maybe another time." Did I want it? "Have you heard of a boy named Silver?"

"No. Friend of yours? Lost to the Dark Prince?" She rolled her eyes and sat up, her face ridgeless now. She was back to looking like a woman at the farmers' market whose facial bones were a little too big. "He'll come back eventually. Cain alienates his closest friends every few years. Just be patient."

"What bars does he own now? I know he doesn't let sellers in," I said.

"Just one right now, out of a grocery store basement, down on Pike. Damalbi's. Old basement. He calls it The Pearl. Smells like fish. The building is from the frontier days, so it has the old world feeling the young fakers like, and it's connected to a theater that closed down. Sellers can go in, even if they say they can't, but you must not be advertising, not make a show. I have been in there a couple times, but it's dangerous. They say free blood, but those children have complicated relationships, and they get angry when you take their favorites from them." She chuckled. "Also, the slayers in this town want to kill Cain, so if you're ever at one of his things you never know when the whole thing will get blown up. Just like the Castle did."

"What's the Castle?"

She paused, sat up, stared at me intently. "You're very young."

"Thought that was why you wanted my blood," I joked.

"I like blood. But most young people, eh," she said, waving a hand. "They resent us, fear what they want from us. You're curious. I tasted it. How do you like it?"

"I don't know," I said. "It feels good."

"Are you sure?"

"Yeah. Even if I'm a little scared when you bite me." I felt the wad of cash in my pocket and wondered if she would ask to drink again. I thought I wanted to give her more. I was ready to ask for more money, though maybe I'd compromise if she didn't have it.

She smiled, without opening her mouth, the indents of her teeth shaping her lips. I looked at her until I couldn't anymore, and then I looked over at the corner, where there was a basket of thin white yarn. I wondered if she had crocheted the long white fuzzy robe she was wearing.

"You want to be one of us?" She licked her lips. "Someday? I could teach you the old ways. I saw you looking at me. You think it is beautiful, the way my face changes. I see it."

"I do think it's beautiful," I said truthfully. "I don't really want to turn, though. Not now, anyway. I want to do . . ." I gestured at my arm, my neck.

She licked her lips just slightly. "That suits me. Well, Fawn. I can text you again the next time I have the eighty."

I took that as my cue to go. "See you then," I said. I stood up.

She held up a finger. "Wait." She crossed to the shelf where the shiny ceramic dogs flashed in the half-light, and for a second I thought she was going to tip me after all, but she pulled out a box with different cascading strands of string and chain inside. She drew out a bracelet made of leather cord, with one steel strap in the middle. She held it out to me shyly.

"This can mark you as one of mine, if you want. I say mine, but I only mean that I drank from you and I like you and I will avenge you if another kills you. You owe me nothing."

I considered it, thinking of the bat necklace and how it had gotten me in trouble. Richeza saw my hesitation.

"It will get you a free bagel and coffee at Gefen's down on Cherry," she added. "That's the main thing. Tell them Richeza gave it to you."

She was so sober-faced the whole time, so serious. It would have been ridiculous to ask questions. I felt like I had met an alien from an unrecognizable past. "Thank you," I said, and put it on. The steel said something in what I thought might be Greek. She smiled and showed her teeth. I realized that it wasn't just the canines that were sharp. It was all of them, like the mouth of an anglerfish. Her red eyes glowed.

11.

RACHEL

There was a new girl at Diane's house, and she was making a Security Sisters promotional video with Brid. I had never seen her before in my life, not even at my old school. She was using the glitter nunchucks that I'd helped select from our dropship vendors, had customized myself. Brid was pretending to be the attacker. Diane was filming, and Stacey was cheering from the sidelines. They'd done two or three takes in the side yard behind the tall new fence, and Brid looked flushed and exhilarated as she did a backflip away from this mystery girl, whose long hair whipped around in a dark braid as she kicked Brid in the solar plexus. I felt a deep well of anger rise in me, watching them. I had expected one newcomer at the MAVIS meeting: Joey from Daylight, Inc, who was coming to make an announcement. I had a feeling I knew what the announcement would be, given the box of synth-blood that had arrived at our house, which I had been drinking for the last few days. It tasted the same as the old shit.

Sweet. But the test stripes on my skin from morning sunshine through the slats were barely pink.

The new girl came over to me, looked at me, and did not greet me. She greeted my mom. My mom shook her hand, and I could tell they had the same firm grip.

"I'm June Sorkin. I hear you've been staying with Diane and Amber and want to join our Scooby crew," Mom said. "Tell me about your situation."

The girl snapped the gum Stacey had just given her. "I'm Flo. I'm here to find my ex-boyfriend. Or whatever is left of him. I found out a lot of things in the last two weeks. I found out his internet friend is some vampire cult leader. The Slayer Sisterhood in Chicago was who I was in touch with first. Based on their info about Cain, I came here."

She'd rolled in on a Greyhound bus just over a week ago, I learned from Brid when I followed her to the kitchen to help grab snacks. Why had Brid not told me? Shrug, shrewd fake apologetic look. I was handed a platter of cheese.

"She said she'd killed three vampires between Maryland and Seattle. Sounds good to me."

"Why was she doing the video with you?" I heard the raw hurt in my voice, even though I had resented how many social media promotions for cheap plastic junk Mom made me do.

"June just needed someone new on the team for Security Sisters, someone cute and good for the brand. She's middle-aged, and she wants to get young people too, so they have self-defense supplies."

So they spend money on mace that won't defend them against a vampire, I thought, but didn't say anything. My mom's business was kind of a scam, but it had been our thing. Together. I was still packing up promo giveaway orders, writing notes that said Thanks for shopping with a woman-owned business!

We set up the meeting room. All the moms got wine and kombucha and filled their plates with cheese. They didn't talk about business except for Amber showing off six vampire tracker cuffs that she'd bagged in the last week after stakeouts. Brid was looking at Flo and smiling a little around the corners of her mouth, and that made me hate Flo.

When the meeting started, Flo was still the center of attention.

"Everyone, we have a new recruit," my mom said. Flo stood and repeated what she had told my mom.

"What skills have you got, Flo?" Molly asked, leaning back and taking a fizzy sip of rose kombucha. "What are you bringing? And don't worry. It's okay if it's just enthusiasm."

My mom laughed. "It's not just enthusiasm. We've got a new fighter, based on what Amber's been telling me."

"She's got a pretty solid round kick," Brid volunteered through a mouthful of cheese.

"Flo can man the flamethrower. I showed her how in the backyard today." Amber has a burned-out gravel bed behind her house where she tests out the more pyromaniacal weapons.

Flo sat there, silent, but nodded, chewing gum. She looked over at me. I looked down. I felt a noxious horror—they had replaced me. Nobody was saying it, but they wanted me to know.

Joey, who had just arrived, wearing athleisure in a weird shade of puce, an earring in his eyebrow, and a tight, trim haircut, coughed. "All right girls," he said. "June Sorkin, my favorite collaborator. Let's hold off on logistics for a second. If we're ready to start, I can make the announcement."

We were gathered around in the Beaumonts' garage, which held no cars but did have all these totally grody tupperware bins of weapons and confiscated vampire trackers. My mom sat next to me, the laptop in her lap, taking notes on the encrypted platform she uses for meetings.

"Go for it," said my mom. She looked at me, smiling.

Joey smiled back, and he rummaged in the tidy leather shoulder bag he'd brought with him. "Okay, girls," he said, his voice lilting. "It's been a long time coming. I think you all know what I'm here to announce. You know," he said, pointing to me. Everyone turned to me. "And boy, has this year been a wild ride. But—she's here!"

He drew out a little bag, plastic like the ones he'd sent to our house, resembling a hospital blood bag—but pink, with a label that showed a bright sun against a rainbow cartoon Seattle. The liquid inside was still much brighter than blood—a lurid pink-red. It was stickier looking too. Slicker. The new samples I'd had tasted more or less like the first samples. I couldn't tell immediately if the new stuff tasted better or worse than the clinic blood, though there was a certain gelatinous blobbiness; three a day of the new stuff had kept me fuller than I had been when I'd drunk only a bag of government blood every other day. And the new stripes fading fast was good—but it hadn't healed the earlier stripes. The old burn on my arm still hurt.

Amber gasped sharply. Her son had been a vampire. She had killed him. “Damn,” she said. My mom hadn’t told her about the synth samples sent to our house. “It’s ready?”

“Never thought I’d see the day,” Molly quipped, sipping her wine.

Joey smiled a deep, toothless closed-mouth smile. “Our study on five hundred vampires in the Seattle area—some of them volunteers, some collected by you all, thank you very much—just concluded. Daylight blood’s new formula keeps vampires in stasis in a way comparable to human bagged blood, and calorically and nutritionally is nearly identical. It’s the first synthetic blood to hit the market. It’s a big market. We aren’t approved for medical human markets, which of course would be great in the future—but our primary goal, from the very start of this, wasn’t about that. It’s to meet this pressing need, so that humans can rest easy and vampires can be more human. June, you’ve been instrumental to our project from day one. We’re about to eliminate vampires as we understand them. By giving them something else to eat.”

Miss Marketing Copy.

“Like Twilight and True Blood,” Shelley said, smirking. “How ’bout that. It’s the age of vegetarian vampires.”

We all sat in silence at that, imagining—sarcastically, I could tell, in Shelley’s case—a world where our services weren’t necessary. Where nobody would get turned the way I did. I watched Brid watching Joey.

“They won’t need any blood?” Molly asked.

“If they drink three of our packs a day, they will find themselves nourished far better than if they subsist on the government's blood rations. Our packs are cheap to produce, and in the short term, we can feed every registered vampire in King County and be under our production capacity. With a new factory in Tacoma we're putting together, we can easily meet Seattle's demand, unregistered vampires included. If we begin working with other factories and share our formula with our ingredients suppliers, we could soon extend to the entire West Coast. Some vampires will probably prefer traditional blood for some time, but this will remove the illusion of having no choice. They now have a choice. They can be monsters, or they can be men. Or women. Or they/thems. Citizens," Joey corrected himself, and coughed. "The hardest part of this was actually just the red tape. It took us a little bit to convince the government to allow our imports, given we do some manufacture abroad to avoid US regulations on blood-related products. That was the result of our kerfuffle last year that you all ah, gave us some flack over. But we've gotten it sorted! We're about to partner with the city's vampire department to begin distribution of Daylight blood next week."

"Next week. And you didn't think to tell us," my mom said. She'd been complacent enough until now—there was a wrinkle appearing in her brow.

"We've just been approved to announce it," said Joey tersely.

"What happens if they don't like the fake blood?" Amber asked.

"They're going to do a gradual phase-out of medical human blood, to conserve that supply for where it's most needed, in humans. They'll be able to observe the effects in each population at each distribution center as the switch happens. But the vampires who drink our product won't be desperate or blood-hungry. They'll feel full and satisfied."

Amber raised a hand. Joey inclined a wrist toward her. With his other hand, he passed his pink bag of fake blood to Shelley, who was closest. The blood began to travel in a circle, toward me.

"I think you're misjudging vampires," Amber said. "They're not going to take this and be happy with it. They want real blood. We still need to kill them."

Joey made a pleasant grimace. "We'll see how this goes. We do need you these first few months. We ask you to be strategic, going forward, about who you target. We will need slayers to help contain the populations of vampires who continue to be violent. But vampires do have a real incentive to use Daylight blood. It's in the name. What prevents vampires from working, going to school, getting name changes, getting apartments, the most?"

I looked back at the blood, changing hands, moving slowly around the circle. "Daylight," I said, in a monotone.

Joey beamed at me, and I thought: Is that guy wearing pore concealer? Not that I have anything against gay guys, but had he done his face to give us this sales pitch in a garage full of crossbows?

Flo almost leapt to her feet. "It can let them walk in the day? And not get burned?"

"This seems dangerous," Shelley said. "If they stay bloodthirsty, all we've done is given them an extra set of powers and more food. You got your PR team thinking about responses if they go full I Am Legend?"

I tried to ignore Shelley. She had given me a stuffed tiger when I was six that I'd only just gotten rid of. I didn't want to think about how she thought of me. So I spoke:

"How fast does it work?"

Joey seemed discomfited to address me, though he must have known I was a vampire, that I was one of their trial subjects. My mom had told them. "Our estimate is six weeks for total immunity" he said, not meeting my eyes, looking at my mom. "But the reduction in sunlight fatality in this latest formula is near-immediate and burns decrease in severity with each week of use. If they stop using it, they will gradually become vulnerable to sunlight again." He smoothed down his sweatshirt. I decided I hated the narrow shape of his nose.

"The stuff with gov distribution is better than I was hoping for," Mom said. "If it's true." She looked at the pink pack.

"It's true, Miss Sorkin," Joey said, now showing teeth. "This is the kind of change that I want to be part of, you know?"

We all just looked at him. The slayers know bullshit. This guy probably made 90k a year.

"I'm announcing, effectively, that this whole group probably will see a reduction in demand fairly soon, after this phase-in era is over. We believe that for the majority of vampires, once they see that this works, and that they can integrate into society as a whole again, the problems of crime, and blood sales, and assault, will go away. No more slaying necessary. Maybe it will take a bit, but there will be a day when you girls hit a Friday night and can just—" here Joey shook his head, as if letting his hair down—"Relax! Hahaha!" He glanced around to see if we liked that. We didn't. He adjusted. "But! We do have some strategic actions we want done in these first couple months."

My mom sat up straighter. I wondered if she bought this whole thing, now it was happening. She had always said Daylight products wouldn't ever fix the vamp plague. "What's that?" she asked. I was holding the plastic blood bag now. I looked away from her eyes as they fell on me.

"Well, as I think you're aware, there is a booming parallel market of black-market blood. Expired medical blood, seller blood, and blood smuggled from around the world. To encourage people to make the switch, we're going to have to do more to combat that market, and to curtail the so-called Free Blood movement which advocates reckless fluid-sharing. That is, I think, going to need to be a somewhat rapid push here in Seattle. We don't want there to be an option of using both illegal blood and our product. That would defeat the point!"

Amber was looking excited again; she scratched her chin. "You guys got weapons for us?"

Joey didn't like saying the word weapon. "James in our supply department has authorized a shipment of some of the products you have worked with before. We also want to emphasize, as much as possible, that vampires now, pre-launch, are quite vulnerable to sunlight. So—"

"You want us to drive them into the sun." My mom was smiling. "Would you authorize a couple large strikes on centers of activity?"

"I think that we know that our mayor won't see it as a loss if a few centers of unregulated vampire activity disappear. The police haven't been able to take down the U District cluster. So, yes, June."

But Brid shook her head slowly.

"I'm not sure," Brid said, "that it's a good idea to outright raid this community clinic place." I met her eyes across the room, and she gave me a look full of meaning. I was startled for a second—maybe she intuitively understood something about what I had learned about vampires being kind of complicated, and knew what I was feeling, and after all this time we still had a connection. But then she added, practically, "it's like, you know. It's a huge potential source of information. And if they think it's a safe space, a non-infiltrated space, we can conduct who knows how many raids through it."

Amber frowned; Brid usually doesn't speak up like that. "Stacey almost died trying to waste that wino vamp in the tunnel. We need to strike another big, indiscriminate blow. It's been months. Cain's probably sitting back pleased as punch right now."

My mom raised a hand. "Here's what I think. We know that the clinic has particular hours, regulations, and clientele. And some of the vamps who use it aren't our biggest targets, though of course we wouldn't mind if we scored a few. They're mostly registered vampires who are a little hungry but don't want to hunt. They'll get on the Daylight stuff. What we need is to jump one over. The tunnels, and the shelter. The shelter vamps are who's gonna be attacking college girls. Some of the most violent incidents we're seeing reported are around the college, with new vampires. That girl who got bitten at the frat party, for instance. So, if we can locate the shelters, bars on the Hill, and then from there find a few squats, that's more effective military tactics than just getting the clinic." Her voice lilted up the last few syllables, a hint of the sunny California girl accent she'd carried north with her. Her perkiness is one reason she's remained the leader. An idea she brings to the table has a ring of beachside optimism.

"I agree with June," said Molly, who always agrees with my mom.

"Me too," said Shelley.

Diane scowled.

Amber shook her head. "June, we love you, we know you trust Rachel, but we have enough intel to strike. And for once, we actually have support. We don't need to keep sending a vampire out alone on solo missions. She could run off on us."

"No offense, Rachel," said Brid, rolling her eyes at Amber, which I appreciated.

"No offense, but Rachel is a vampire," Amber said, as if I wasn't there.

And she was right to say it, because as much as part of me had been thinking, I could infiltrate the shelter and report back, another part of me had been thinking, with some excitement, I could just run off. I could be normal, now the Daylight blood was here. I could escape my mom's orbit, drink synth blood, walk in the daytime, and maybe, just once in a while—I could drink someone's blood, like I had with Fawn. Just a little. Just with someone who knew what she was doing.

Amber knew.

"What's the big? She can kill vampires." Another glance at me—and Brid moved her legs, so I could see the edge of her upper thighs under her skirt.

Flo raised her hand. I noticed that as she looked around the room, she studiously avoided meeting my eyes. I had felt her eyes on me before, though, when I was looking down.

Amber inclined her head toward her.

"We could just have the authorities close the clinic once we have intel on the shelters, couldn't we? No need to kill a bunch of non-hunting vamps—just call it in to the cops once we have what we need on the other spots. Then they get legally punished, it's not our business."

Everyone was silent for a second.

"I doubt we'll just call it in, since Amber's strategy is to bomb every spot we surveil," Molly said.

"I do say bomb it," Amber said. "Report it so the hospital blood running leaks to the papers, but burn it down. Send a message we aren't playing around."

"Be strategic," said Molly.

"Regardless of how we get rid of the clinic, I say the old Rachel intelligence plan re: the shelters isn't bad," Shelley said. "One more recon night, she can get the tunnel location or the shelter address. We figured out we could trust her. We've already wasted three or four of those vamps coming out of the clinic, and six more going into that sewer on the hill. Come on, Amber. Let Rachel find the shelter for us, leave the clinic alone till after."

"Just want to reiterate: she's a vampire," Amber said again.

My mom did a quick calculation of who would vote with who. Brid would vote with her mom. Stacey would vote with her mom. "Put it to a vote," she said.

Amber, sensing the wind blowing against her, said, "All in favor of Rachel doing more recon, then a daytime strike with the objective of destroying the shelters and eliminating the clinic."

Vote: yes.

Amber was giving me stink eye. I looked down.

I typed a draft of a text to Erica. *My mom is getting weird. She said all vampires are evil. Can I come live with you lol*

I didn't send it.

They dropped me at the clinic again, to get the address of the shelter. My mom was parked at the grocery store; she would hit the bridges and hill on the other side of the highway, then come back for me. Now I knew the drill, I gave the guy the ten, nodding politely. I felt old hat. I let my ridges morph outward from my brow bone.

There was something happening tonight that hadn't been happening last time. Some kind of show. When I came in, there was a girl onstage, her brow ridges large, slicked with some kind of red gel. The wetness surprised me, unnerved me. She was lipsyncing to The Smiths' "Still Ill," pointing at people, handing around a bucket. Halfway through, she took out a container of red Jell-o and dropped it over her own head, where it jangled down the white collar of her shirt and into her tits. Then she took off her shirt to reveal that she didn't have any tits: they were silicone cups that fell away. She pulled off her wig, and then went to sit down, the green and red lights of the stage slipping off her so she looked—except for her sticky brows—just like any other gay man in too much makeup. She was laughing.

"All proceeds from tonight's open-mic go to the clinic coffers," said Frankie, wiping his protruding forehead as he waddled onto the stage. He looked down at the scattered, sticky gelatin. "We love the avant-garde happening, everyone, but if you can, please minimize mess. Our next number will be on in five. Sherry, get the hell back here with the paper towels."

Laughter. Sherry, who was taking a drink from her bag, gave him the finger, but caught the towels and spray bottle thrown in her direction and knelt down on the low stage to clean the Jell-O.

The girl from my school was there, watching. Whitney.

"Hey, Rachel," she said, waving me over after I accepted a blood bag from sweaty, harried Frankie, who practically tossed the bags at five or six people gathered around the counter. I had been looking forward to this blood all day—all week. The synth blood didn't make me feel the same, even if I wasn't hungry. I looked for Erica, but she wasn't there. I walked over to Whitney. She was with two other people my age.

"This is Angie and Jay," Whitney said. "I met them here a few nights ago. Angie did a poem on stage."

Angie was a fat, big-shouldered girl with a wide face and a pug nose and dyed blue hair; her ridges made me think of an ankylosaur. Jay was a skinny Latino kid, six feet tall but still with baby roundness to him, dark eyes under heavy brows, teeth too big for his mouth. They had already drunk their allotted blood, the bags spread on the seat adjacent to the foosball table they congregated around.

"I'm Rachel," I said.

"Angie's a few months old, Jay's brand new," Whitney said. "They live in this punk house down in Ravenna. I was just saying I still go to school."

"We don't," Angie laughed.

"Cool," I said.

"We just had to move, because of stupid here," Angie said, gesturing to Jay. "An incident."

Jay gave her an angry glance, but then laughed. "I can't deal with that psycho Ned," he said.

"Wait," I said. "I've met Ned here. The older Asian guy. He's psycho?"

"He just," Jay said. He glanced at Angie. "He lets humans help run the shelter. They put a human in with us, a seller. I don't know what he's playing at. You know? I'm not trying to hurt anyone, but it's crazy hard to sleep next to a human like that when you're hungry, and then she's a seller."

"No way," Whitney said. "Ned seemed so chill. I love that bakery, too. He told me if I ever need to stay I could."

"So the shelter is really a business?" I asked, trying to piece together the story, and the implications. "Like, to help sellers?" To get kids hooked on fresh human blood?

"Not really," Angie said, waving her hand like she was swatting a fly. "None of the kids who stay there have money. It was one girl who showed up out of the blue, he just stuck her in with us. It was dumb, though. He could have put her with older vampires and not made so much trouble. How long you been in this?"

"Few months," I said. "It was harder at first, I guess."

"Where are you at?" Angie asked.

"Home," I said. And then I said, "I may need somewhere else to stay soon. I was thinking about the shelter. Even if it's weird."

If I didn't let my mom know about where the shelter was, it would take her a minute to find out. I could leave Seattle.

"You gotta get out of home for sure," Jay said. "The pandemic shortage could happen again. And I read this thing last week about a grandma in Tacoma lit up her grandson the summer after he turned, he was sleeping in the basement and she dragged him out, locked him into the greenhouse, he was messaging people trying to get help and then just stopped messaging back when the sun was up, they called the cops but he was already burned up too bad to make it."

"The cops don't give a shit about vampires," Whitney said, jangling one of the silver chains bobbling over her bound chest. She looked ill at ease. She lived at home too.

"You guys hear about the slayings on the hill?" Jay asked.

"Let's not talk about slayings," Whitney said. "I'm wigged out enough getting home on the bus."

Another act went on. This one was a young-looking woman with long dark hair wearing a sweatshirt with a photorealistic bluejay on it, who took out a drum.

"*Klahowya tillicum.* Don't worry, I don't have any Jello." She laughed. "Hey, so, I'm here for a public service announcement and a song. I grew up around here a long time ago. They didn't get me in 2020 because I never trust the government. I'm Jane, I'm Duwamish. Same way these tech guys are displacing everybody into the camps in the woods now, they did that to my family when I was a kid. My mother said, we aren't going. The Suquamish and Duwamish and Nuu-chah-nulth men were working the mills. Bosses needed them. But they didn't like us being in the city. They knocked down our houses. I ate the men who knocked down my mother's house after she died. And I turned that white vampire who bit me back into a bat. Qəbqəbayus."

A few awkward laughs.

"I'm up here to make a statement. Duwamish culture is all around you, in the ground we dig the tunnels in. Same thing happening to you now happened to us first. You're digging a vamp tunnel, you find a bone or a midden, you gotta stop digging the tunnel, tell Frankie, right, Frankie? Because then the tribe can come get that stuff and the state doesn't take it. Don't mess with bones and stuff. You can make another tunnel. I got people complaining, oh, I can't make another tunnel, too hard. You don't want my people against you. History is long. Remember Fort Lawton. More fights going on now. We will break down the dams. We will never die. And there is a future if we respect the land we're on."

She began to sing in a language that wasn't English, hitting the drum. Three men in blue jeans and beat up sneakers sitting in a corner sang with her, for about five minutes, banging on their table. Frankie, who seemed to know the words too, sang from the back, turning in a small, shimmying circle. She grinned at him. Maybe her speech wasn't as aggro as it sounded. The bucket came back around; I put in a dollar, feeling guilty and also annoyed and also shaken. I hadn't thought about how vampires being old meant that the pioneers were like, yesterday.

When I looked back up after the woman had finished her song, Angie and Jay were at either end of the foosball table, knocking the ball back and forth. I sidled over to them. "Okay," Angie said. "Let's talk about the crazy outfit Amelia wore at the show we went to last night."

"Oh my god," Jay said. He turned to us. "Okay, so, she had on these big foam forms she'd made. It was like, lips, and her legs were the teeth? Like long white stockings, pointy shoes. Her whole body was the mouth and the legs were the teeth. She made it out of foam from that weird foam store down past the Ave near Trader Joes. Amelia's in this band, the Redtones."

"I haven't been to a show in ages," said Whitney. "My dad doesn't know I go out at all. I just sit around and watch X Files and my dad gives me different stuff he thinks will cure me of needing blood. He's like, a thousand percent convinced there's a cure."

"There's the synth blood," I said, but Angie and Jay looked at me with stink-eyes.

"Run away from home," Jay said, clapping his hands on the beat of the words.

"You should come with us next time," Angie said. She smiled at Whitney, and I wondered if the invitation was extended to me. Whitney did look cooler than I did; she had on a black shirt with silver chains over it, and I was wearing a pink Gap sweatshirt. "There's free-blooders who go to some shows, though you got to get to them before they're out for the night and they mostly all have older vamps they want to give blood to. Now, the best place to see a show is Cyland, but that's down in South Seattle. But it's safe as hell. There's still places downtown and Wallingford—I'll text you." She reached out an expectant hand, for Whitney's phone.

"I left my phone at my house," Whitney said apologetically. "My dad has a tracker on it."

"We could maybe fit one more at our house," Angie said, specifically to Whitney now, for sure. I was putting off bad vibes or something.

Whitney turned to me.

"How was the bar you went to with that lady?"

Angie and Jay looked more interested in me. "Uh, she took me to this woman's house, actually," I said. "A—a seller. She thought it was safer."

"Sugar mommy," Angie said. "Lucky."

"I mean," Jay said with a tone of magnaminty, "Sellers aren't really for us. Not like, the broke kids. We die or we go to clinics or we find the people who love us. Sellers don't love anyone they sell to, they just are meeting a viable economic need."

Angie laughed. "Find the people who love us. That really is the scenario. And then you discover that Free Blooders are mostly a bunch of people who all think they're god's gift to vampires."

"Who turned you?" I asked.

Angie and Jay just looked at each other and laughed.

Whitney took out a pack of bubble gum, and I watched

Angie and Jay sort of recoil when she put a piece into her mouth and blew a snap-quick blue bubble. "My dad cut me off from the lady who turned me. Her name was Hoa. I wish I knew if she was okay. She was really old. She got turned in the 1950s by a French guy. She survived the war in Vietnam, got out with some other vampires in a container ship. I met her when I was volunteering at the community center."

"That's not old," Jay said.

"No, but not a lot of the older ones are left now," Whitney said.

"You know, in ancient Egypt they worshiped us as gods," Jay said, batting the foosball into its plastic trap.

"Okay, Anne Rice," Whitney said sharply. "I don't know if early agricultural feudalism is really my deal. Some guy forces some other guy to give me his blood to please the sun god and help the harvest? It sounds lonely."

"Not forces. The guy would be super excited to. It was an honor."

The foosball skittered off the table, up into the air, down between the legs of a woman with gray hair and a batlike nose that reminded me of Cain's, who watched it and then looked at us for a moment before returning to her friend's conversation.

Angie waved her hand as Whitney went after the ball. "This is all bull," she said. "Free blood is about the future, not the past. It's never existed perfect before, sure, but it's a way of solving a lot of problems. It's recycling. We drink, and they heal faster—It's like the fuckin' loaves and fishes. It's like the oil miracle at Hanukkah. It's something from nothing. It's the maximum efficient use of energy. It's ancient magic, new use. That's how climate crisis is gonna be solved, plus ending the meat industry and natural gas, obviously. More people become vampires, the less food has to be grown."

This was the propaganda my mother had told me about.

"Is that really how it works?" Whitney asked. "Don't people have to eat way more when you drink from them? Doesn't that cancel out?"

"I forget the calorie breakdown, but it's real," Jay said. "And our teeth help kill disease."

Feeling attracted to Whitney's critical scrutiny and angry at Jay—though I wasn't exactly sure at what—I got up, and went to the counter. Frankie, fangs glistening under the purple light, turned to me as I approached.

"Hon, sorry, but no doubles tonight, not even if you have cash. We're short stock."

"Actually, I was wondering about the shelter," I said. "Ned's thing. See, my mom—" I stopped. "She wants . . ." I looked to the side and the ceiling. "She's not really chill."

In my head, I was thinking: They will raid eventually, regardless of me. But I can warn them. And I can get out. Fuck Diane. Fuck Amber.

Frankie inclined his head slowly and solemnly, as if this was the ancient chorus. "Okay, honey," he said, holding out a stubby finger. "Ned's not here, but I can get your information down. Is it an emergency? Like, you need a spot before dawn?"

I thought about it. My mom didn't know where the tunnels were or where the shelter was, yet. If I went back to her, I would need to tell her. I didn't know if I could lie to her. "Um, maybe?" I asked.

Frankie wiped at his red, sticky brow, held up a pause finger to his purple-haired associate, and waddled stodgily out from behind the bar. I followed him around the corner into a low-ceilinged office with a glowing colored lamp. "Now," he said, shuffling a business card out of a drawer. "You just go to this address, between nine p.m. and seven a.m. Path through the tunnels on the back. Overland it's a bakery, underland it's a Scorpio symbol on the door. There's no waitlist, but if they're full you might end up in a broom closet. We aren't the Plaza." He chuckled darkly.

I took the card. "Oh," I said.

I thought about how long my mother was likely to take to come back.

"The tunnel's right here," Frankie said, kicking open a grate hidden behind the counter. "It's drizzly out."

"Rachel?" I heard Whitney say behind me; I turned and caught her looking at me like a gay girl.

Someone new was on the stage with a ukulele.

"This one's something my sire taught me," he said. "It was a work song in the camps where the Hoover Dam was built. I've chosen to adapt it to ukulele, as that is the only instrument I know . . ."

"Let me in the tunnel," I said. I saw Whitney's eyes dance to me and then to Frankie. I let the closing door obstruct my vision. Whitney was hesitating, returning toward Angie and Jay.

Water that I hoped was rain dripped from the ceiling of the dim cement tunnel, but it was more a trickle than a downpour. My boots in the dark tunnel splashed. I heard a noise behind me, and I was able to pretend it was just a distant splashing rat, until—

Whitney ran splashy up behind me, and her hand on my shoulder made me jolt. "Rachel," she said. "Wait up."

"Sorry," I said. "I just had—I have to get going."

"You got the card for the shelter. Let's go together. We can't go home again. You heard Angie and Jay. My dad's been making me drink pig blood."

"We—no, I wasn't," I said, idiotically. I felt like trying to stop Whitney from going to the shelter. I didn't want her to follow me in case someone was watching us. I also didn't want her to be there when I said to whoever ran the shelter that I had been a slayer, that everyone needed to leave.

"Yes, you were," Whitney said. "Why are you lying?"

I knotted my hands in my pockets. We were still walking, downhill into a deeper tunnel. I thought I heard more footsteps. Probably another vampire, I thought, there were thousands who must use the clinic through these tunnels—

—A strange noise, a strangled cry in the dark at a distance. Whitney looked up at the noise. I knew what it was.

"What's going on?" she pressed. "You're acting all panicky."

"I'm sorry, you should go back inside," I said. "I'm worried about . . ." I trailed off. I knew my mom or any of the MAVIS members might be around. They were probably watching.

"I was really glad to see you there tonight," Whitney said. "I feel like I have to get closer to people, now I'm a vampire. I gotta find some new friends and stuff. I also . . . you know. I figure, we could hang out. Even if you don't go to the shelter now."

I looked at her, and her red irises gleamed purple-black. She had a sweet face. I was still feeling the buzz of the blood in my body, and I felt myself lean into her when she took both my hands in hers. It stopped me walking. A rat splashed in the dark. I thought about dodging around her and running, but I couldn't bring myself to.

"I think you seem cool too," I said, desperately. "But I have to go."

"We have no idea how long we're here for now. It could be a really long time," she said. "I don't want to have forever without a community. And I have to confess, I think you're really cute."

"You're cute too," I said, feeling a pit of dread well up inside my mouth. By then I saw Brid. She was approaching from behind Whitney, from deeper in the deep circular hole that disappeared around the bend, her wide swagger unmistakable. I didn't do anything. I stood there, frozen, staring through the dark that hid nothing. She made eye contact, winked, raised an arm. I let out a yelp that was more strangled peep, but it was too late. Whitney screamed and became a fanged skull as the stake stuck through her, back to front. My mom makes sure all the stakes are about eighteen inches long enough, big enough to punch through vampire torsos. She orders all the crap we sell on Security Sisters from China, but she makes the stakes herself.

Whitney dissolved into ashes, heart last.

Brid licked the stake, base to tip, blew a kiss at the crumpling form, and the air of her living breath scattered the dust towards me. It stuck to my clothes and hair as it fell to the wet sludge beneath.

"Cheating on me, Rachel?" she grinned.

I felt my mouth open and close, the tears springing to my eyes.

"Brid."

We hadn't been unsupervised in the same space for months. She was here smiling at me. I thought for a second when her hand came up again that she was going to stake me too.

Brid moved forward, taking a big step and turning me, so my back was to the brick wall we had been passing. I squeaked. My hand spasmed into a fist. But her movements were soft, affectionate. She was stroking my shoulders now, stake in hand, pushing her body against me. There was nobody else in the tunnel, but surely—

"Brid, that was so scary."

Her lips brushed mine. "Whatever. I just wanted to get some special time with you in between when you left the clinic and when we were back under Mommy and Mommy Jr's supervision. I can't even fucking send you a text these days, she checks my damn phone all the time. And then I saw you had brought me a present. Or were you trying to get laid with her?"

She stashed the stake in her belt. Brid's hips angled in, brushing my leg, and her hands ran through my hair. I had wanted this for so long, and now it was here, in the tunnel that smelled bad, and there was something in me that didn't let me like it anymore. I had wanted it. Now, I didn't.

She kissed me, and didn't let me respond to her question,

and her hot mouth was so familiar, and I felt angry and hot and cold and scared. I wasn't very hungry, but I would have dug my teeth into her neck if I hadn't frozen and stopped moving in response. I felt my body tremble against hers as I tried to hold myself perfectly still, felt my arms close in a tight, frozen hug around her back. I felt the jangle of pain and desire bounce through me. I didn't know what to do.

"God, your lips are so cold. You taste like iron."

I was kissing her back. I started moving. I felt my body brush against her warm body. I don't know why. How could I know why? I was desperate for something. I clung to her. Whitney had settled into a pile of dust gradually dissipating on the wet tunnel floor. There were tears on my face, and Brid brushed one off my cheek, showing me that it was red. "Sick," she said, and licked it. "You think your tears will turn me too?"

"That was a girl from my school," I said, finally. "She only drank at clinics. She didn't hurt anyone."

I felt the hard push into the curved wall with my eyes closed. Brid's mouth was on my neck. "She would have eventually," she said. "Just like some part of you probably wants to hurt me, right?" Her hand went into my back pocket, and I felt her draw out the card with the map to the shelter. I grabbed at her hand, but she pulled back that arm. She pushed her other hand down the front of my jeans, and her smile, when I opened my eyes, kept me pinned until she let me go a couple minutes later. Brid panted triumph over me.

"I wondered if you'd feel the same," she said. I heard what I wanted to.

"I still feel about you—the way I felt," I stammered. "But I'm scared . . ." I trailed off. I was mostly scared of her. I saw I could not say that to her.

In the long silence, a rat skittered.

"I don't know if I still want what we were doing," Brid said, wiping her fingers on my shirt, pocketing the card. "You are harboring a demon soul, you know? No personal baggage or whatever, just how it is. But I do like what we can do together. We can wrap up this vampire shit once and for all. That stupid twink Joey's right about that. There's going to be a big storm before it all clears and the world is normal. There's a lot of vampires who have to die before it's all over. You gonna help me, Rach?"

I looked past her, up through the grate to the night I wouldn't reach.

12.

FAWN

I didn't know if Richeza's protection was real, or if anyone respected it, but I knew I had to go to the fish-smelling vampire bar under the grocery store, because Silver was probably there. I would be firm that my blood was only for one person. I knew where Damalbi's was because of Google Maps: it was near the water, and I knew the water was downhill from where I was staying. Right now, here, at four in the morning, I was in Ballard. I had gotten eighty dollars from Richeza. I walked eight blocks through streets of small homes and tall metal buildings like Richeza's and took the light rail back to the station nearest my house. A cold, almost blinding wind started up and blasted my face and hands red as I walked the last half-mile past cranes and the park. I fumbled with the copied keys. My coat wasn't enough. When I got back to the apartment, it was cold inside too. Raina wasn't there, but Roxy was. I felt electrically charged and not hungry, but I remembered Raina's talking about iron. I thought I should probably eat something. I was eating one of the packets of mac and cheese from a well-stocked box in the pantry, realizing I was really hungry after all, when Roxy walked in and looked around, putting her hands on her hips.

"Are these your dishes?" she asked, gesturing to the sink.

"No," I said, shaking my hands to warm them. I looked, to make sure: a mug, a half-full bowl of cereal. "No."

"Okay. Just want to make sure you know, this is an empty-sink house," she said. "Raina forgets sometimes, I believe you that it isn't you. We keep tidy."

I felt the sting of an accusation, even though she left after that. I did the dishes in the sink, then returned to the futon to check my email. A message waited—from Flo.

Flo's said:

Fawn, I'm in Seattle. I'm upset with you, but I can also forgive you. I know it had to be scary to face this alone. I've joined an organization that tracks unregistered vampires and kills them. They're working with a company that will cure vampires once and for all, by giving them a blood substitute that lets them go out in the day and act normal. They're highly secretive, but I can get you in. We can do this together. The Silver we knew is dead and has become a monster. Cain hurt both of us, and he's hurting Silver too. You were right, we can't just go on with our lives. We have to fight this. We have to kill the monsters or turn them back. Please talk to me.

I felt a terror creep down my spine: a new urgency. I felt the urge to throw my phone away, but I couldn't do that. I also couldn't ignore it, because that would be like telling her it was okay.

I emailed Flo back: *Flo, what group have you joined? Killing vampires? What a terrifying thing to send me. I don't want to kill Cain. I hope you don't want to kill Silver.*

I threw the phone away from me. I thought about Flo in a black trench coat, a knife or a wooden stake at her belt. It would look good on her: she was slender and carried herself like someone who was already the protagonist of a TV show. The theme song would be so punk.

I covered myself with a blanket and read the rest of the bad vampire novel I had gotten at the thrift store. It was about a vampire who killed himself.

I texted Silver just before falling asleep: *I'm in Seattle. I want to see you. Talk to me. I've been getting my blood drunk. I'm ready for who you are now. For what you are.*

But when I woke up, there were no new messages from Silver. Instead, there was the noise of a shower, and, echoing on the fiberglass through two thin walls, the voice of a woman crying. Sobbing, the keening, guttural noises sloshing under the noise of the water. I couldn't tell if it was Raina or Roxy. It was disturbing. It sounded like a sick creature screaming. I put my head around the door when I heard the water stop and peered into the empty kitchen. I was nervous about eating from the pantry when she might come in and tell me something wasn't allowed, so I ate three packets of instant oatmeal very fast and then waited for her to appear, listening to her sobs grow softer and then silence. The lock of the door clicked, and Raina appeared, freshly dressed in leggings and a long sweater, hair and eyes wet.

"What's wrong?" I asked.

It took her a second to respond. She squinted at me, as though I shouldn't be there.

"Slayers found the clinic on the hill," Raina said, rubbing her puffy, red left eye and walking past me into her room. "And the shelter." Her voice was flat and haggard.

"The shelter where I was?" My heart sped up. I followed her and stood in the door of her room, waiting for more. Raina looked over her shoulder at me, seeming unable to keep her eyes open. She walked into the kitchen and started making coffee.

"Millie's okay, and ten kids got out, but the tunnels got firebombed first thing this morning. Probably some dead. The clinic was set on fire after it closed. There's fifteen or so missing still. The news hasn't covered it yet except as a fire on a residential block. Bet they say it's an accident, don't even mention casualties. Ned's shop is going to get shut down, and he has to figure out what to do. He wasn't there last night, he was out. But fifteen—we don't know where they are. Millie took some kids into the tunnels, they're still hiding out somewhere, she doesn't want to tell me where in case the slayers have the line. They could have anyone's line."

I felt like dropping to the ground, crying, *Silver, Silver!* but that also felt overdramatic. He probably wasn't there. He was with Cain. "Is this—how often do they do this?" I asked. "Slayers attacked the van I was in. On the way to the city."

"They do it as much as they can. I think they have police funding. Police don't raid these places themselves, mostly.

But our side's gotten better, with security." She looked at me with some suspicion. "Or were supposed to. That shelter is supposed to be secret. Not many people are allowed to know about it."

"I haven't told anyone about it," I said, feeling myself assess how far my shoes, the door were.

"I don't—no, why would you." She blew her nose. "Just . . . those poor kids. These slayers are evil, inhuman people. The cops won't find them, won't charge them. I bet a couple are cops."

"What can we do to help?" I asked.

"You can't do shit. You're new. A child," Raina said. "There's going to be a lot of hungry people coming to us, though, probably. I don't know what to do. I can't really cut my rate much. I mean, I guess that's terrible to say, but I can't. I can't feed everyone."

I sat with that. I didn't feel like I couldn't do shit. I had learned so much, so fast.

"I can try to help," I said. "Tell me what I can do."

"Sorry to be curt, but I really need time to myself right now. Can you leave the house for a bit? Leave me alone? I just—for my peace of mind, I need space." She shut her bedroom door, and I was left staring at its grooves. The coffee machine bubbled.

I had lost all track of time, but I thought I should walk down the hill, down Pike, looking for the grocery store and the bar beneath it. Whatever had happened, I could learn more there.

It was warmer than I had expected and sweat built up on my back when I started walking. I turned myself in a new direction—downhill—and set off, passing an old man and a dog sleeping on the doorstep of Raina's house. I didn't feel like I lived there for real enough to tell him to move, and I didn't want to anyway, though I wondered if Raina would be mad at me for not evicting him. The further down I went, the more the hill was covered with large, boxy buildings with fancy apartments that had no window blinds inside, and a few boxy buildings that were SROs, and the kind of businesses that didn't make any sense to me, called things like Ruddr and Knoll and Beanbag. They had white lights inside and strangely shaped geometric furniture, with people sitting around on laptops. They were intermixed with empty storefronts whose naked interiors yawned. A few places were recognizable as coffee shops and restaurants, and then there was an axe-throwing place, and a bar, but when I went into a cafe that was still open, a muffin cost 8 dollars and there wasn't a bathroom, so I left again. Cop cars seemed to be parked somewhere on nearly every block. At the break in the street where it became a bridge over a steep shrub-covered cliff and the highway, I saw a pile of tents, descending down the trash-strewn rocky hill towards the rushing cars, one wasted tree leaning over them like a protective claw. A man shot past me on the sidewalk on an electric scooter. The tallest skyscrapers of the downtown weren't finished yet: yellow and orange cranes sprouted over the shells, touching the sky over their bony outlines. Behind them, the water glimmered in the light of late afternoon.

I looked up Damalbi's on my phone. It closed at ten. The bar probably wouldn't be open until after that.

I went to Gefen's on Cherry, which meant turning around and walking back uphill. It was an old silver-walled diner. The outside of it looked like a quilt, with beaten metal instead of cloth. Inside, the dimming sun hit the faces of a few customers. Almost all were older than me, but human. They looked professional in a work-from-home kind of way. The sun was still up. Inside, there was a long, narrow Formica counter, and a wide workspace behind. A glass case had six kinds of cream cheese and piles of cold fish and deviled eggs and something that looked like cornbread, cut in half with a crumbly white cheese in its middle. I went to the counter and showed my bracelet.

"Richeza gave this to me and told me to come here for a free bagel and coffee," I said as confidently as I could, to the short Latino guy working. He was fat-bellied, middle-aged, with a tattoo of a bird's wing spreading over the back of his neck and heavy wrinkles over his eyes. He was human.

"She acts like Pola's still here running the shop instead of me," he snorted, but he turned to grab a paper cup. "Sugar?"

"No thanks. I appreciate it." There was a social script and I was inside of it. Richeza was real. I hadn't dreamed her.

"How is she," he said. "Still look like an albino bat? So glad she never got registered. She'd be dead."

I no longer knew the script. "Good," I said. "I just met her, really. She's nice. Do you know what she does for work?"

"She has some ancient gold buried somewhere still. Sells a piece of it at a time. She's a weird one, but she's got some old, old friendship with Pola."

"They knew each other in Bukovina," I offered.

"It has to do with helping her buy the building, years back. Think they knew each other in Ukraine, though Richeza's Albanian or something. Pola's given orders we feed anyone who's Richeza's friend. She's not in the shop much anymore. She says the Board of Health would notice she hasn't aged." He set a paper cup of coffee on the counter, face serious but voice gregarious. "What kind of bagel? Some lox?"

"Uh, everything. And everything I can get." I wasn't used to bagels. He turned and took a bagel out of the steel cage that held them.

"Yo, so. You heard about the clinic last night," he said, as he fed the bagel into a conveyer-belt toaster. "There's another, down in South Seattle, but it's going to get crazy now."

"I heard," I said, thinking about Raina crying. "The shelter too."

"Kids dead," he said, in a low voice. "Nothing in the news. You on the Discord server?"

"No," I said.

We both went quiet as another customer came in. They picked up a remote order in a plastic bag from the counter next to me. Other people eating were sitting farther down the counter. Maybe they knew Pola was a vampire too, or maybe they didn't listen.

He pulled the bagel from the conveyor belt, dipped a

knife in white cream cheese, took more pink fish than I had expected and spread it across the surface of the bagel before folding it quickly in tinfoil and sliding it toward me.

"Richeza and Pola both talk shit on the U District kids a lot, but they'll be devastated. It's like a world nobody else knows about, happening right alongside the real world, on fire all the time, people dying. Every time they're both in here, they just list people they know who are dead. I can't get the two realities to gel, ever since working here."

"Yeah," I said. I looked at the counter and took the bagel. I turned to put milk in my coffee, and then chanced a glance back at him. He had been staring at me.

"What's your name?"

"Uh," I said, and hesitated. "Fawn."

"It's interesting. Usually Richeza doesn't go for boys," he said. "Drank from me once, then told me she liked women better so I couldn't have a bracelet." He laughed. "She's broadening her scope."

I felt my tongue knot in my throat. My mouth clenched.

He was making an expression as if he had expected more insight from me, or a joke, a wink-wink. But when I didn't say anything more, he shrugged, turned, and then—while I sat down at the counter, and for the hour after—paid me no more attention than he did anyone else. He cleared trays strewn with trash off nearby tables, and the sun went down.

My phone vibrated.

I had a text from an unknown number. *Hi, this is Rachel who met you at your house. I'm kind of new at this, but are you free tonight? I don't know where to get blood now the clinic and the shelter are gone. Do you know how to get into the Pearl? I'd pay you to be my guide.*

I shouldn't be free tonight, because I'd already had Richeza drink too much blood yesterday and I hadn't eaten much. I should be careful, if what Wanda had told me was true. And I didn't really know how to get to the Pearl. But I felt a buzz in my body, and I wanted more of that buzz. I also was harboring some questions about what Richeza had said—about neck-blood, about wings.

Face pic so I know you aren't cops, I sent.

The picture I received in return surprised me—mouth tight, tiny, pouty. She still looked like a girl who would have bullied me at school.

I can meet after 8, she sent. *Do you know a place?*

According to Richeza, in order to turn, she'd had to want to turn. True? Who knew.

Richeza's power came from her weird intensity, but this girl was so awkward and also had a power over me. I had a different response to her than to Wanda; with both, I buckled under instantly on seeing them, wanted to give them something, wanted their approval. I hadn't felt like that about the girls at my school who looked like Rachel. I'd been too scared of them. But she had looked at me that time as if she wanted me, beyond just needing my blood. Even if she also ran away and didn't text me back.

I replied with a picture of my face and neck, with Richeza's teeth-indents purple in my skin. I looked like I had looked: goth, androgynous, round-faced, with eyebrows too heavy, but I found myself liking my own scowl.

Had a client yesterday, I said, trying to sound mature, busy. *But if you can buy me dinner, I can probably see you too. The Pearl is under a grocery store near Pike Place.*

A couple minutes passed, then:

Meet me at Pike Place Market 8:15?

Sure.

I sent Silver the bite-mark photo too.

Would he be hungry?

Then I left the bar, walked down, down the hill that dropped down to the narrow gray sound, and sat in the cold on the stoop in front of a store that sold umbrellas until they told me to move. Night didn't come fast. I moved down to the tourist farmers' market and wandered there, up and down, and ate cheese samples, as the rest of the crowd dwindled and eight p.m. grew nearer. I was wondering the whole time how many of them had their blood drunk on the regular. More than zero, right? There were many levels to the market, because it sat on what was essentially a hill at a forty-five degree angle, and on a lower floor, an orange-walled food court that was flanked by candle stores and Mexican Folk Art stores and a store selling incense and one selling comics, there was an automated fortune teller in a glass case. You could pay a quarter to get a fortune from it. I had a quarter in the bottom of my backpack. The apricot-colored dummy, which was wearing a wig in a gray perm and a cloak held shut with a brooch, clanked back and forth with one finger over dusty Tarot cards while I looked at my reflection in the glass. There was nobody behind me in the food court except for one shop owner dragging the gate of her store shut.

I felt a hand on my shoulder, even though I didn't see anyone behind me in the reflection on the glass, and at the same moment, the slot at the base of the puppet's torso spat out a piece of paper.

"Don't trust those machines, they steal your money," the voice at my shoulder said.

I turned around and found the pouty, evil-looking, pretty blond girl, shorter than I had remembered from when she came to Roxanne's house. She was wearing a hoodie and jeans, which only managed to accentuate how much she looked like an airbrushed, fourth-gen Disney princess, an Elsa slightly smooshed and plumped to be even more perfect adorning a keychain.

I looked down at the card. I squinted at it—there was far more writing on it than I'd expected. *Beware a beautiful woman, and look forward to meeting an old friend,* it began. *Lucky numbers 80, 34 and 23.*

"Seems applicable to me," I said. "I'm even hoping to see a guy I know in this bar."

She was appraising me with a mix, I thought, of mean-girl scrutiny and that same look of want and nervousness. A part of me worried about what she saw, in my hands and jaw and shoulders.

"You sound Southern, kind of," she said. "Didn't catch it before. You're not from here."

"I'm not," I said.

"I thought I'd take you to the Chinese bakery place upstairs?" Her sentence ended with a question, as if waiting for my approval, but I knew from her voice she was also used to getting what she wanted. The contented certainty.

We walked up two flights of wooden, shellacked stairs, and took tables with wooden booths next to the misty, dirty window in the Chinese bakery. The boat-lights on the water shone. Many of the shops in the indoor part of the market were shut, but the fragrant steam from the pans and hot case still rocketed around in this place.

She said what I had been worried about her saying, but it didn't hurt as bad because she needed something from me. "You're trans, right?"

"Yeah."

"Like, a . . . transfeminine person."

Oh, god.

"A girl." This had been my worst day so far, in terms of how people spoke to me. The counter guy—it ultimately hurt worse, after I realized he was gay. It wasn't better at all. She'd bitten me, her teeth in my arm. A golden-colored girl saying *person* in that voice made me furious enough to throw something, and my shoulders knitted tight. I felt like asking her to go, to leave, but I didn't. How did she think about me?

Rachel nodded and glanced to the side. "Okay. I'm not transphobic, I just wanted to know. I totally support trans rights. So, have you been to uh, the vampire bar before?"

My bluff was called. "No. Just heard about it. I wanted to go tonight anyway, to find out what happened with the clinic. I feel like people will talk about it. My friend might be there."

A series of expressions—panic, maybe, fear, disappointment—crossed her face, so I turned, got up, and ordered two steamed chicken buns and a tea from the woman at the counter before Rachel could leave.

"You were hoping I'd show you the ropes," I laughed, turning back to sit.

"Yeah," she said, tucking a strand of hair behind her ear.

"Are you living with your parents?" I asked. She could be in college, maybe. She could be a very young eighteen. She acted Mormon or something. What was up with her?

"What have you heard about the clinic?" she asked, not answering. "I was there last night—"

"Oh my god," I exclaimed. It hadn't occurred to me that maybe someone had tried to kill her since I'd last seen her.

"—before they got it, and it was normal. I only found out—" she paused. "Sorry, no. I didn't see anything. That's why I'm asking. I found out this afternoon when I woke up."

"Me too. My roommate was really upset. She's a seller, too."

"Roxy, right?"

I nodded—suddenly wondering, with a flash of paranoia, if I should trust this girl. There was something off. But maybe that was just me smelling the definite slight cringe she'd had when I confirmed I was trans. And maybe she was just literally so born yesterday that she'd never thought about it before she saw an actual trans person, and now she'd be so normal.

"I can't figure it out," Rachel said. "Sellers, I mean. What I think about it."

Oh, no. "What?"

"I mean Erica took me to see you, so that's easy, I didn't have to think. I was using the government blood bank, a bag a day. Then they told me the government doesn't give me enough to live, so I went to the clinic. Now the clinic's gone. There's people at the clinic who hate sellers, and then people who think other stuff—that's like, it's bad to drink from people. And now there's synthetic blood, so I don't have to and shouldn't. But when I drank from you, it felt so good. It just felt right. I just *want* it. But it's so dangerous."

"I know some people hate sellers and people who buy, for sure," I said. "Not everyone. I haven't run into trouble yet." *I just want it.* I felt the zap-zap.

"How did you feel? When I drank?" she asked. She leaned forward, voice grave.

"Good," I said. Then I thought I'd be a little bit more candid, because of the way her teeth were elongating over her lips. "I mean, really good. It feels like stars."

"It didn't feel like—degrading?"

Okay, weird. "I liked how it felt."

Another expression of panic from her.

"I realize I'm being weird," Rachel said quickly. "I don't—I'm sorry, I don't think there's anything wrong with you."

"Would hope not. Might commit suicide if you thought I was bad," I said, grinning at the bizarre tension on her face—the fangs and her pursed, scrunched frown—and she looked offended—a deep, incredulous, panicked scowl—until I laughed, and then she laughed too, nervously.

"I also don't think you're bad," I added.

I felt superior again, and also felt a pang of anxiety for her, and for myself—having to look after her. One of Cain's troubled "children," like Richeza said. Young vampires without guidance, like Wanda said. Where'd she come from?

"No," Rachel said slowly. She covered her mouth with her hand. Her brow furrowed and unfurrowed. "Hey, I have something for you to take with us into the place. In addition to uh, the money." She pulled a glittering small electronic device from her pocket. "It's a taser. In case anyone drinks from you who you don't want to."

The side of the taser said *Security Sisters* in looping cursive.

Again, something kind of off but also really earnest in her voice, her face, the way she looked at me. Maybe it was just that she was confused.

"Uh, thanks," I said. I put it in my pocket and ate my bun, looking away from her at the water, feeling like Chihiro in *Spirited Away*. The free food at least was a good gig. "You gotta give the money to me before we go in too."

She nodded solemnly and pulled out an envelope, passed it across the table. I could book it now, if I wanted, I thought. But I felt beholden to this vampire who thought I was going to be able to help her.

I checked my phone to make sure I understood where Damalbi's was, where the bar was, and to see if Silver had texted me or seen my text. He hadn't. I led Rachel after me up the stairs and outside, mostly silent, up a short, steep hill. At the cross section where the grocery store sign flickered, I looked down between my feet at the tiles of thick purple glass in the sidewalk, where electric light glowed, and at the closed metal storefront. Next door was an abandoned theater, its cracked marquis announcing a movie that had premiered in 2015. A car and a delivery cyclist skidded by on the damp street, and I was briefly distracted, watching him vanish up the hill. I could be a delivery cyclist, that would be how I could make money.

Blond, little Rachel hovered uncertainly at my arm. "What now?"

I looked around, trying to project competence. The area was mostly deserted. There wasn't a big line of vampires going to the same place. I didn't know how to get inside. I stretched my neck by turning my head side to side, drew my necklace out and looked around for someone who would notice and let me in on the strength of my bat-heart. Then I jumped.

Across the street, I saw a girl looking at me who looked a lot like Flo. It was dark; I couldn't see her face after a shadow fell across it, and I knew I had to be seeing things, because even given her note, what were the odds? She wore a long coat, which wasn't like Flo, even though it looked good. When I looked again, she was walking away from us down the street. Her walk was Flo's. I felt my heart spike into the back of my tongue. I thought about the threat of slayers. Richeza, talking about the Castle.

"Did you see that girl over there?" My voice was high and tight.

"I think that's the door over there," Rachel said, pointing. I looked, and saw a yellow flash of light in the metal trapdoor in the street, just starting to close. When the long-haired man in front of us saw us coming behind him, he held the door open with his free arm, and flashed red eyes at us as we scrambled after him

"Don't let it stand open too long."

We slid in. He was grey-haired, with a small, focused mouth, holding a big box; he turned to descend a long, spiral staircase in a strange, tiny, arched hallway. The brick walls were plastered over near the door in scuffed white, but then the plaster stopped and they were only caked in glitter, so that every step on the metal sent a little cascade of gold dust down on our heads, its shine illuminated only by a red bulb at the first curve of the stairwell. We followed the long-haired man down, echoing. At the base of the stairs, he turned around, free hand held in a claw, and said, "Boo!"

His nose flared out, batlike.

Rachel jumped, and I didn't. He loomed over us a little, his head almost on the ceiling, his eyes red. No webbing between his fingers; only two fangs were pointed.

"First timers," he said, grinning. "Here because the false safe place is gone. Welcome to the real underworld. Ten bucks."

Rachel looked ready to pass out, so I held her hand, and I felt her grip mine back. I handed over the cash from the envelope. Sixty bucks left.

"I'm Fawn," I said. I took out my necklace and put it over my shirt. "This is my friend, who's going to drink from me tonight."

His expression changed a little.

"Haven't met you before, Fawn. Welcome. You are needed tonight. Here." He handed my ten back. "A lot of folks are very scared right now, and will be hungry soon. Are you ready to help? Had your dinner?"

"Yes," I said.

"This box has some cookies and sandwiches from the Vietnamese place over a few blocks, if you need a pick-me-up later. It's hungry work. They'll be over on that table. I'm Ryan. If anyone drinks from you too long or you need to go home and you need a drive, talk to me or one of the other people with a white armband. Remember, don't give more than three pints tonight or you might have to go to the hospital and then there's a chance we'll all get busted. You can hang out after you're done giving, just move to the fainting couch for a bit." He gestured to his arm: a white handkerchief was tied around the upper part, and then to a series of futons on the other side of the long red room. "And who are you?"

Rachel stammered. "I'm Ray," she said, after a second.

"You look half-starved. Remember, what we are doing here is practicing abundance. Even in emergency. This is where we drink freely, according to our own appetite, instead of what someone tells us to. We have a security system, so don't be scared. This isn't the clinic."

He walked away to put the box on the table.

"What does that mean?" Rachel said. "Abundance? There's only so much blood in your body."

"We'll find out," I said, in a low voice. "I guess it depends how many humans there are."

Purple fairy lights and dim red bulbs glowed in a wide, dirty room with brick walls and old hardwood flooring. Along the walls—my eyes focused and unfocused on them, trying to make sense of it—there was a system of wires, interlocking pulley mechanisms, and piping, all of which looked more or less DIY. The music in here sounded like kickdrums in a distant basement being pounded over and over with electric bubbles on top; the lights were so low that it felt like being in the photography darkroom at school. There was a long bar, and I could see two fridges behind it. A handful of mismatched armchairs stood in corners. The whole space was long and low, the ceiling barely two feet over my head covered in dusty bare boards, and looked as if at least two other rooms had been here; huge wooden beams bisected the wide room. I searched for another clearly marked exit and saw a distant door, unmarked and closed, at the other end of the hall-like room. The air was stale. I did smell, immediately, something metallic. There were only maybe twenty people inside with us, but above us, I heard more feet stomping down on the metal. I pulled Rachel to the back of the room, near the closed doors, and we stood against the wall.

"This is weird," she said, turning to me. The ridges on her forehead were out. "Drinking here. I guess it's cooler than the clinic." She pushed her hair back and giggled again. She was really on edge. "Would it be crazy to drink from you right now?"

"Seems like it's what the space is here for."

"Are you okay if I do? I'm, um. Ready." Garnet eyes. And the feeling again—I am useful, for someone, for something. I'm needed.

"Sure," I said.

She set a six-minute timer on her phone, then awkwardly kneeled and took my hand, as if she was proposing, but bent her face so a few strands of gold hair slipped over her forehead. Her eyes were closed, and her tongue seemed prickly, like a cat's. Her hand reached up to stroke my stomach as her fangs sank into my wrist, which I didn't expect—nobody touched my stomach. I felt her shiver as she prepared to bite. Her touch made me warm, and without thinking, I grabbed the back of her head, to hold her to my wrist while she drank. She growled, and twisted her head in such a way that there was a brief jolt of real, deep pain, but then her lips moved more, and I felt the galactic space overhead open, a dreamy wave that made the lines of my body shiver. It didn't feel like when Richeza had drunk from my neck, and nothing like Wanda. There was a cold xylophone being played on my spine. But I felt the timid want she had, felt the rush of need she was feeling, despite her embarrassment, and I saw, inside her, the place that Richeza's strange electricity came from.

When she looked up, I could see her nose change a little. The edges of her nostrils had begun to flay away from her face, like a Star-nose mole's. As I watched, they receded, and she looked like a young Margot Robbie again.

"*Drink more*," I gasped, as the timer went off. It was a command, though I hadn't meant it to be.

But she pushed me away and leaped up, turning, covering her face again, as scared as she had been at Roxy's. "*Nnnope*, that's enough for me," she said.

Someone heard her and moved toward us. "Too early in the evening to say that," the girl who sidled up to us said. She was a Black butch woman in a maroon tweed suit jacket and black turtleneck and half-heart necklace, holding a juice box. When she smiled with eyebrows raised at Rachel, no fangs showed—she was a human. Maybe a few years older than me. "Take a drink from me too, hon."

Rachel put a hand to her chest. "I'm—I'm new," she said. "I think I need to wait a little. Uh. I don't . . . want to go too hard."

"It can feel overwhelming. But that's why the space is here. This is where you can let loose." The butch, whose cheek held one perfect dimple, held out her hand, where a gold ring sat on her second-to last-finger. "Jess. Haven't seen you before."

I felt unexpectedly moved-in-on. I had wanted to get rid of Rachel a few minutes ago, to look for Silver—now I felt the anxiety of having something this woman wanted. And Rachel, I thought, was her own valuable, nervous kind-of-beautiful woman. Even if she was going through it right now, maybe she would be exactly the right kind of person on the other side of it.

Rachel retracted her hand behind her body, looking down at the ground. Jess tensed. So did I. Rachel's posture was crouched as if Jess was the one who had blood running down her chin.

"I'm sorry," Rachel said to the floor, and I saw she was visibly shaking. "I—have to go." She backed away from Jess toward the stairwell and then, pell-mell, pelted up it heavily and blunderingly, against the tide of bodies coming down, having to elbow and push in order to get through. Jess watched her go with an expression on her face that felt recognizable to me.

"She's scared," I said.

Jess scoffed. "Fuck that noise. Something I come here to avoid is when they're scared."

There were a rush of people who had made it downstairs. Some looked comfortable, and some looked nervous, like Rachel. Maybe from the clinic. Ridged brows, but also smooth ones, different ages and sizes—though you had to be kind of agile to get down those steep steps. The humans were mostly young. They were moving around the space now, around us. Most looked no older than Jess, but some eyes flashed red. There was no scream, no roar—but the music increased in volume, and the lights dimmed. People started dancing around us, and Jess made no move to join, just sulked against a wall, looking across the room, browsing. The growing crowd's taste in clothing leaned toward the glam end of Gothic or toward all-black sweatsuits. I saw more than one shabby black velvet coat, bandeau made out of black tape, more than one sequined shirt, more than one set of fishnet fingerless gloves—though some were in patched black jeans and t-shirts. I was not completely out of place, just too young. I felt eyes on me, on the blood on my wrist. There was an anticipatory buzz in the air. I saw people hauling amps past through the dancers, though it wasn't clear where they were going. I couldn't see Silver anywhere.

"Go eat something," Jess said to me finally. "Your girlfriend might come back."

"She won't, I think," I said, feeling a rush of confusion in my stomach about what I'd wanted Rachel to do. It was stupid to want her to drink more. I wanted to save the rest of my blood tonight for Silver.

Jess looked at me with a smirk—down at the heart necklace, and up at my face, and at my neck. She hadn't looked at me hard before and it made me sweat. I felt my hand go to it reflexively, and she laughed.

"You like when they bite the neck, huh."

"I'm Fawn," I said, and held out my hand, readying myself to talk about the clinic again. But though she shook, I felt her eyes were already flitting around the room. Sure enough, in a second, she'd walked off toward the table of food, where in a second she had found another tall woman to talk to.

The hum of general sociality and music and dancing around me made it seem like it would be easy to talk to people, but I felt as alone as I ever had. It was more crowded. Everyone was in small circles. Some were in circles around two figures, one of them probably drinking.

The man who'd let us in was tinkering with an electrical panel. I watched him, wondering about where I might have seen his face before, when I felt a cold hand on my arm.

"What are you doing here," Silver said.

Silver, alive. White as snow, his two moles high-contrast, his black hair blacker than night, the same length as the day I last saw him.

I turned toward him, expecting him to fade into the air. But he was solid. He wore a leopard-print blazer, a ripped black tee shirt, and baggy black jeans. He was sullen, red-eyed, ridged, fanged, clutching my wrist. He looked—I couldn't tell if he was angry. He always looked angry.

"I came to find you," I said, gasping, suddenly feeling more dizzy than I had a minute ago. I reached out for his other hand, and to my delight, to the endless gratification of the buzzing imperative that had made me chase him, he took it. "I texted you."

His ridged brow furrowed and he dropped my hand. "I didn't ask you to."

"Well, why not," I said, feeling a jolt in my heart. What? "What the fuck. You up and left me. You left Flo. You left everyone."

"I had to go."

He scowled at me in such a familiar, sullen way that my heart did somersaults. It had been so long since I'd seen his scowl. We stared at each other, furious, seething. And I also felt confused.

"Are you—did someone hit you in the head? Look." I grabbed my phone, pulled it out, showed him where I'd sent him the picture of my neck. "See, right here. I say, Silver, I want to see you."

"You want to see me," he said, with the kind of contempt I'd only ever heard him use toward teachers. "But you always looked down on what I wanted. You thought it was a game."

"No. I was in it with you." His face was papery white, his skin more like vellum than it had been, but he was himself. He hadn't been replaced with another person. He seethed at me.

"Whatever," Silver said. "So, what, you're here to give blood now? You love vampires now?"

"Obviously," I said, pointing to my neck. "I came here. I found you. I found others too. Just drink my fucking blood already."

He turned away from me. I leaned forward to grab his arm, pull him in. He turned, flashing his fangs as if to scare me and lunged for my neck. I took a step back to absorb his weight but put up no arms to stop him, and his face collided with my shoulder. My heart was pounding. I put a hand in his hair, thinking about Flo being right outside, about to burst in with a crossbow. If she came in, God damn it, she would see me holding Silver, never letting him go. Even if she shot him.

"Drink," I said. I growled. "You're such a monster, then drink."

He sputtered, looked at me, and bit my neck. My knees weakened. I felt the necklace jangle as he pushed the chain to the side.

He was not as desperate as Rachel, but he was hungry and imprecise like her, scraping and nuzzling my neck with his teeth. He'd bitten my neck with his human teeth before just this way. I felt drunk, letting him pull me down slightly, my spine bent so he could reach. My head was red fog, but the mist was like a sunset on a hot evening, and my legs went soft and rubbery with the full song running through me. Silver, mine.

I heard a whistle from behind us, and Silver did too—he started to pull back, but I clutched at his head. "Get wings," I said. "Drink until you change."

He gurgled, swallowed, sucked to the beat of the double kickdrums coming over the speakers like my heart. Over Silver's shoulder, I saw Jess, and Jess was looking back toward us now. In this room of vampires, there was mostly chatter and rhythmic dancing; our bent forms were the locus of the corner we were in, and I heard fingers snap behind us and more low hoots of encouragement.

He slowed, his tongue moving a little against the bruise he drank from. "I thought you hated me," he whispered.

The confusion of this statement blurred like charcoal as soon as he said it, because he was holding me. "I missed you."

Now he was clutching my shoulders, his nails digging into me, and his tongue seemed to grow proboscically thin, dipping between his teeth into my skin. The moon rose and set in my head. It was a magnified version of the feeling I'd had the first time he'd cut himself and I'd drank: we were impossibly close. I flowed into him, and I felt it as he drifted up off the carpet. His teeth multiplied, became sharper, his mouth wider. As I tangled my fingers in his hair, I felt his ears, long and batlike, stretch and thin, covered by white down. His nose pressed to me, wide, flat, flared and cold.

He pulled back, and his face was a white bat's—furry with a damp phosphorescence, as if he was a fish in the deepest part of the sea.

"I've got to get ready for my show," he said, through a bat mouth that had little sharp teeth around his big fangs. "Tonight's important. We're going to trap the slayers. Find me later."

He licked his bloody lips, coughed, and hailed someone behind me. I turned to look. Cain stood there, white hair towering on his head, a red Elizabethan collar blooming around his throat. If he saw me, he didn't acknowledge it. He grabbed the mic.

13.

RACHEL

I stumbled out into the misty, half-drizzly night, breathing hard, trying to feel the breath so my face didn't look like a monster. I couldn't remember how to hold the breath in my lungs. My face was burning, buzzing. The blood had been the most intense I'd ever had. I felt like I was three glasses of wine deep, but spinny, flaming wine. Or two strawberry Svedka shots, or—I stood in the night, looking out at the lights of big dark transport ships on the bay, catching sight of my mother's silhouette on the roof of a nearby building. I couldn't leave now. She'd see me.

As I stood against the building, panting, my phone buzzed. It was time, and Flo sidled up to me as naturally as she could have. Her dark jacket flared in the wind; under it she had on a black halter top and jeans.

"Sup," she said. "Seems like it's time to party, but you're not in the party."

"I—uh." What to say? I got scared? I tried to flee before this all went to hell? "I wanted to check in," I managed.

"Not running?"

She knew I had been seeing if there was a way to get out. She was going to make me go back in. I said nothing.

"You made contact with Fawn, I saw." Her voice was low. The vocal fry in it crunched like gravel.

"She's in there," I said. "I got her in there. It's my fault she's in there."

Flo studied my face. "We'll rescue her. Not that I'm sure she wants to be rescued. You've got blood on your mouth."

I wiped my mouth. "It's Daylight blood."

"That's not Daylight," she said, the note of disgust in her voice obvious. "That stuff's brighter red. I saw it. You really drank from Fawn. That wasn't the plan. I thought you were able to control yourself."

Up the dark street, there should be two women in alleyways with stakes. There would be Brid. "I had to," I said. "I had to, they were making me." I felt tears jump to my eyes, and I knew they were red, dark.

"Whatever. Get me in there," Flo said.

But when I turned, there was a man on the other side of me. I made eye contact with the rubies on his boots first, flashing in their holsters, studding the interior circle of bright, sharp steel spurs. Up the leather pants, rhinestones gleaming like Liberace, dark velvet red coat flapping, bright red collar like a starched Brillo pad. He had a face that was way younger than the long white hair would have told you. Ridges crowned his eyebrows like the spikes of starfish. He was baby-faced, middle-aged, and ancient all at once.

Cain.

"You baby bats want a smoke?" he asked. He held out a pack of Camels to us. If he recognized me, he gave no sign. "The party's about to get started in there, but I need a moment out in the moonlight before I emcee all night."

Rings on his long fingers flashed. Flo blanched, and I felt like running. I could stab him here and run. It wasn't the plan, but my mother wouldn't hate me for it—she'd understand it was a mistake, a vengeful lapse, and I would be killing her oldest enemy. The problem was that I had no weapon. It would have to be Flo, and then she would get the credit. Could he really not recognize me? I had no stake. I looked to Flo, who regained her composure and took a cigarette. "Thanks," she said. I copied her, feeling the paper stick to my hands in the blue mist. I didn't like the taste of tobacco; I missed weed. My mom had ransacked my room and thrown out everything she'd found, which had been everything, except a half-pack of gummies I couldn't digest. The tobacco tasted like licking a street.

"You young demons been to our sumptuous lair before?" Cain drew in a breath, exhaled it away from my face. "You look familiar, but you also look nervous." His eyes didn't flash meaningfully. He genuinely looked as if he was trying to place me. Could it be that he didn't remember me? This, somehow, spooked me even more. I tried to steady myself.

"It's my first time," I said. "Since the clinic burned down."

"I've never been," Flo said.

"Shhh," Cain said. He put a long, white finger to his lips. "Bad luck to discuss that austere place here. Here you'll get better blood than you ever would at the *clinic*. In an atmosphere of brotherhood, sisterhood. One of beauty and glamor." He leaned in and, without warning, kissed my forehead. We were both cold, but his lips shocked me. He raised a hand and petted my hair. I was too surprised to do anything. "Young, gracious monsters, supping together. An aristocracy of night."

He laughed—it was a high, keening laugh that rolled up the sides of the buildings. It was louder than it had any right to be. He pulled a rose from his lapel and held it out to Flo, who didn't move to take it.

"I *just* realized you're human," he said to her. "Do you know who I am?"

Flo nodded, once, curtly.

"Your face is beautiful. I thought I'd seen you before, but I think it is just that you remind me of a woman I met in Spain in the reign of Louis I. She, like you, had deep, black eyes. Thank you for coming here to share with us. There's going to be some *killer* drag later."

His eyes opened wide, and in their red irises I could almost see the circles spinning. "Exciting," Flo said.

Cain threw his cigarette into the wet gutter, where it was extinguished. "Come in, darlings. The real show is in the theater. We can get you good seats."

I looked over my shoulder at my mom's ledge. I couldn't see her there anymore. If she'd had the chance, she could have taken a shot—but then, the plan to drive the vampires into the sun wouldn't work.

We followed Cain as he clattered down into the reddish darkness. Flo grabbed at my hand, and I held it.

"No," she hissed, and I realized she was trying to manipulate my hand back, to the stake hidden at her belt, in her coat. I allowed her to guide my hand back, and I grasped the blunt end, keeping my fingers away from the point. It was smaller than my mothers' stakes, so it could be hidden. I looked at Cain's white hair piled on his head, bobbing downward in front of us—he shuffled awkwardly, as if his legs were shaped wrong. Maybe I could take him out by breaking his knees. I both wanted and did not want to be here. I wanted to leave, but I also wanted to kill Cain. That was the one thing I still knew my mother was right about. It was nearly six hours before the sun rose. My mother would kill anyone coming out, but we had to transmit to her where the exits were. There were bound to be more than one. I figured I could get out of one I forgot to tell her about, and she would think I was killed in the rush.

I jammed the stake into the pocket of my pants. Just the blunt tip was visible, but not if I pulled my sweatshirt down.

Cain turned back toward us, his sharp teeth gleaming. "It's a special night. Come with me."

He didn't seem to suspect us. As he rounded the bottom of the stair, a tall middle-aged man with horn-rimmed glasses met him, opening the buttons of his shirt, and Cain wrapped his arms around him, lips parting, biting into the tan skin of his neck. Flo tensed behind me. The man hissed in pleasure, his eyes rolling up, and they spun twice fully around as if they were slow-dancing. Cain's forehead sprouted long, spindly whiskers with little lights on the end, his face clouded with dark fur along his temples, sideburns like a nineteenth-century president blurring into animal fur. When he dropped his arms from clutching the man's sides and pulled back, he let out a prom-queen laugh, turning a totally bloody grin towards us.

"Thank you," the man said to Cain. Cain turned back and kissed him on the forehead.

The man offered his bare, bloody neck to me in turn. I held up a hand as if to say no. Cain narrowed his eyes at me.

"Maxwell has plenty to share, my dear. I estimate him to contain two gallons."

"I—I just ate," I said.

"You still look like you're an Edward Gorey dead child, honey. You haven't eaten enough," Cain said delicately. "I *insist,* my dear dead one. If not from him, then from your friend there."

The blood smell—could I drink more? I knew I could. But Flo would think me more of a monster if I did. I could feel her drawing back, away from me.

"I'm—waiting," I said awkwardly.

Cain raised eyebrows, a frighteningly polite toothy grin on his monstrous face, but waved a hand for us to continue on.

"Come on in, then."

A group of other young people followed us in his wake as we crossed the room. One handed him a bag of blood. I began to see how a vampire got to be fat like him. He ripped the plastic with his teeth and drank it down in two long gulps.

"Aurelius isn't here," a girl said to him, taking the empty bag back from his hands and licking the edges. "I'm worried. He's our security."

"He texted me earlier," Cain said. "He'll be here. He's safe."

"Cain, security tonight—there's nobody inside the door," a short mustached boy said. "It seems like we need extra tonight, if anything—there's so many new people—"

Cain turned to look at the boy, and his furred face was now unmistakably lavender, his nose flaring, flat, the nostrils filled with fine hairs. "Shh, my dear," he said, his voice lower now, a garnet drop leaking from his mouth. "It's a night to be welcoming. The austere idiots have lost their way. We welcome them with open arms. Feed them, feed them, and feed them some more. We turn nobody away. And humans—the more of them, the more we all may eat. They can leave if they don't like it."

"Cain, security . . . the slayers—"

"We are prepared for whatever they throw at us. Come, children."

And he looked directly at Flo, and I knew, suddenly, that he knew who we were—or at least, why we were here. She didn't see him, knowing. She was gauging the exits, and the system of wires and pipes on the walls—I saw her note a trap door, a spring-loaded pulley, saw her pull out her phone.

"Flo," I whispered.

She didn't respond. She was texting my mom as we walked.

He was turning away from us, though I had seen that look, and at any time he could lean and whisper to one of the young vampires at his side. I could turn and run, pull her with me, but then they'd all lunge for us. I realized I might not make it out of here alive. My best chance was to leave soon, before MAVIS launched the attack. That would mean abandoning Flo.

I considered it.

Cain didn't stop to drink from anyone else, but led a procession back through the room, to the back doors which had been closed when I'd drunk from Fawn a moment earlier. We walked with him. I was practically at his elbow, between him and the other vampires. He opened them with a silver key from his wide black belt, and they creaked open on a space much larger than I had been imagining.

It was a dimly lit, vast old movie theater, surrounded on all walls with the same network of ropes and pulleys and wires that lined the walls of the other room, with rising rows of worn velvet seats sixteen deep and a graying screen. Peeling paint decorated the Art Deco pillars on the walls. The room smelled of sweat and mold. Three doors on the aisles seemed to indicate exits—I saw Flo counting. I had a mounting feeling of dread. A screen hung from the ceiling over a raised stage of naked wooden beams, with sawdust beneath. The light that was there was purple, from spotlights somewhere hidden in a back room.

"Find your places," he said to the boy who had been worried about security, and the boy and his friends made their way to the front. More people were filtering in behind us, the doors opening signaling that a show was about to start. "And you two," Cain said, turning to me and Flo. "Up here, at the front. I have something to show you."

He beckoned with a long, clawed finger.

Who was I? Was I someone to run? I would stab him in here, then die. I would stab him, then run.

I followed him. Flo did too. She might die if I stabbed him. Well—she said she wanted to fight vampires. I felt a rip that had started somewhere in my heart tearing further. A lot of the vampires in here were normal.

I did have to kill Cain. It was for me, not Mom. Damn the consequences.

Maybe Flo had a flamethrower in her boot.

Cain climbed the steps to the wooden stage. I was at his ruby heels. He turned to face me at the top, and that was when I lunged, grabbing the stake from my pocket. Briefly, I saw him look at me, his red eyes wide. At the same time as I lunged, something wide and leathery hit my face and side. I lost my footing, slipped on the stage, and fell sprawling, flat. I heard Flo scream, and heard the screams of the two vampires sitting in the front seats. I scrambled, hearing my stake clatter down from the stage to the floor, and looked up into the purple spotlight that fell on me. Cain was above me.

He had wide, wide wings.

He was up in the peeling golden rafters, wings beating, holding Flo to his chest. His teeth were sunk in Flo's neck. She was scrambling for her own stake, but her hands were flailing. I wasn't yet to my feet when two of the vampire boys who had been following after Cain were on the stage, pinning my legs and arms. One had tight dark curls and dark skin that seemed purple in the purple lights; one was pale and had too much greasy dark eyeshadow ringing his eyes.

"What are you doing here, Slayer?" the pale boy said, his knee on my neck. I struggled, but both were stronger than me—both foreheads ridged, teeth long, cheeks furry.

"She killed *Sam*," the other boy said. "This is the Sorkin girl. The daughter."

"Ahh," Cain said, with a wet smack above us. A great, leathery flap. His boots touched back down. Flo was limp in his arms. "At last we drop the charade, my dear. Julius, darling, hold her down. I'm going to get the switch over here, and we'll see if this mechanism Aurelius and Idris built does its little job as well as Sam's."

I couldn't see anything. A creak above us, and a metallic jangling, and two thuds on either side of the stage. I was wrestled to my feet. I bit the hand of the boy nearest me, my sharp teeth wedged into his dry, cold flesh, but he held me even tighter. I was pushed headfirst, and landed on cold metal. It stung my skin. I scrambled to my feet—heard the clang of a door.

I found myself inside a cage, staring back at Cain, who was pushing Flo into a similar one on the other side of the stage. The bars were wide enough apart that I could put a hand through, but the door was shut.

"If you'd had a decent dinner, dear, you might have fought better," Cain said, turning to me with a face that seemed genuinely pained with regret. "One pint is not enough." His great wings were folded behind him. He shut the door of Flo's cage, and returned to the side of the stage, where he pulled a lever. I heard a creak, and felt the floor rise beneath me. It was like a cartoon: I was trapped in the iron prison, swinging above the stage. And as I looked around, I realized there was a vast mechanism around me—of chains and pulleys, and above . . . "That's the first lesson my sire taught me. Always eat *well.* I said it to you, when you first drank from me. It pains me how so many today forget due to their shame."

There were, above us, a series of interlocking springs, and above that, a pulley system braced with axes and spears, ready to fall.

"I never wanted to be like you," I screamed. "You hurt people."

He looked up at me. "I suppose you're in your mother's pocket, still. That's why you killed Sam. You do not think we are people, or that your violence is real violence."

"You ruined my life!"

"I made you a new one," he called up, shading his eyes against the lilac spotlights. "Much better than being a child trained to be scared of everything and never do anything but kill. You had so many options, and you stay clinging to that evil ideology. Oh well. Now you are bait in the trap."

He picked something up from the stage. I realized, with a pang, that it was my cell phone. I looked over at Flo. She was looking around her, like me, eyes narrowed. I remember Amber saying she wanted to go into STEM. She was tying up her hair, smoothing bloody tendrils from her neck.

"Dear mummy," Cain said, in a high, singsong voice, tapping at my phone. "I think they're onto us."

He hit send, pocketed the phone, and held out a hand to the boy who had tackled me. The boy gave him a small wooden whistle, which he blew into, hard.

"Show's starting!"

The gray-haired man I had seen when I came in entered the theater area, carrying a big cardboard box on each shoulder.

It was not an immediate flow, but a gradual creep—the people in the other room made their way in, towards the purple seats, and perched on them in different places. There were thirty, forty of them. Not all of the people outside came in. They looked up at us with trepidation mixed with humor. I thought about crying out to them, but if the other vampires had recognized who I was, it might not get me anywhere. Also, my cage was starting to spin slowly, and I couldn't stay oriented.

"Get Silver!" Cain hissed. "Where is that boy?"

A microphone screeched, and I heard the thick noise of a cord being plugged in and unplugged. Below me, Cain spread his wings wide, and began to laugh into the mic, a low rumble that made my hair stand on end but didn't seem to faze any of the vampires. For them, this was normal. The purple lights dimmed, and there was a vague murmur. Other conversation slowed. I was looking the way they were looking. Cain's wings were like a dinosaur exhibit. They stretched past the edges of the stage, toward the wall. This was, it seemed, not ordinary for Cain's routine.

"They're real, darling," he laughed into the mic. "I don't get them out for just anyone, but it seems the ideal time to remind some of you what we can be." He turned, showing the wings from the back, and they swooped a big shadow over the younger vampire boys in the front row. From above I could see each joint was tipped in a claw. "*Ask* me how."

There was a mixed laughter—some loud, some uncomfortable. Cain flapped the wings, and they carried him up, away from his mic stand. He caught the side of my cage, making it tilt, and I did scream, once, even though I was trying to be stoic.

"Ask me how!"

Now there was a gasp as he flew—really flew—up and over the seats, kicking a little ungracefully off the top row, feet fumbling against someone's shoulder, and flapping three more times, back to the stage. A red light came on, the spotlight unfocused, then narrowing in on him. Another mic screech.

"It's about eating *breakfast*!" Cain spread his long fingers out over his stomach. "You, my dears, even if you look well fed, you are starving. Especially you clinic vampires. You've had one, two bags a day for too long. Even two is not enough. Who wants wings?"

Silence, cut with a few giggles. Cain was clearly anticipating a roar—but he'd insulted everyone here who wasn't a Free Blood psycho. The cage spun and faced the wall. I couldn't see who wanted wings. I thought about like, was there any world where I wanted to be what he was?

"Come up to the stage. Come up here. Yes, you."

The crowd that was here didn't totally trust Cain. One younger vampire climbed to the stage—it was Jay, from the clinic.

"Who wants to give Jay wings? Two donors will do it." Cain asked. Hoots and whistles, but scattered—a predominant, uneasy silence.

The Black butch woman Jess I had seen earlier raised a

hand in back—she hadn't found anyone to drink from her yet.

Where was my mom? Had she gotten the text? I looked around, and the logic of the pulley systems seemed just slightly clearer—above each exit, weapons braced. The stage below, I realized, was shaped like a giant mousetrap: a great spring on one end, a great guillotine-like blade elevated, hovering like decoration above the performers but ready to drop, the mechanism for setting it unclear to me. In line with Cain's camp, I guessed. To get my mother, we were the bait. Flo—she seemed to be calculating something, turning, looking up. I saw her take a small screwdriver from her pocket and look at her watch.

"Thank you, Jess, dear. Someone else?"

A man raised his hand. He was taller than Jay by a head. He climbed to the stage too. They weren't setting off the big mousetrap—something else would, something Cain was counting on.

"Are you prepared to be feasted on?"

"I prefer that to nibbled," Jess deadpanned, which got a deep laugh from further into the audience, beyond the front-row seats.

"We have to will Jay to ascend into a truer form. Everyone, stomp your feet, and picture beautiful big wings coming out of this boy's back. Three pints won't give you wings, though it will feed you—but three pints from the neck. That will, if we all believe. Here we go."

Vampire Tinkerbell. Gag.

I closed my eyes tight—"Crimson and Clover" started to play over the speaker system, and then, three excruciating minutes later, the Cramps's "What's Inside A Girl." I didn't really want to look because I knew it would make my salivary glands burn, to see someone drink and drink like that. Jess had come up to me, wanted me to do that. Was this high vampire art? Was this a hazing? I was rotating in horrible circles, seeing Flo's face against the back of my eyelids on blinks and then seeing her for real as she stood in her cage and began to work on something—she had a wrench tied to a piece of string and was swinging it toward one of the wire-and-pulley systems on the nearest wall. I glanced down once—and caught the eye of Jess, looking up at me, standing to one side waiting her turn, head cocked. I could see that I didn't compute for her.

I didn't see Fawn in the crowd.

Jay was holding Jess, his once-beautiful face a Wolfman mask of fur and cranial bones and teeth, his clothes shredding off his shoulder blades to make room for the seriously enormous half-feathered, half-furred wings that were bursting, totally wet, from his back. They were blood-red, vast. He screamed like a football player, raw and harsh. The crowd cheered, more with him than they had been with Cain, though some sounded a little nervous.

I remembered Tammy. Not all vampires were like Cain.

Jay paused, panting. Jess was holding him like all of that had really worked for her.

Cain minced forward, embraced Jay and Jess and planted kisses on Jay's cheeks. Jay's red tears ran down his face on either side. Jess clutched his chest, staggered against him to her feet, and I dug my knuckles into my eyes. I decided not to look down anymore—to turn into a monster, he had to have hurt her—but then I did anyway.

"They tell you never to drink more than one pint at a time, is that right?" Jay yelled. "This is why! This is our true form! This is what we're meant to be *like*!"

He let go of Jess, and she stumbled and fell. He did reach for her in surprise, to his credit.

Was Jess dead?

She got to her feet—and then kept rising.

Jess was floating. She lifted from the stage like a dust mote. Jess was floating up, past him, her eyes starry. Her back was to me. The crowd's hollers silenced into hushed reverie. She had moonbeams in her hands, the way the purple light was hitting her, and she flexed and unflexed her fingers. She was as high as I was, ten feet off the stage. She reached her arms up toward the peeling plaster, laughed, and then, for the length of three breaths, descended again. Jay caught her, helped her down off the stage. She sat down. Someone handed her a Coke.

Applause. Like it was Taylor Swift, the opera, a musical. This was exactly what my mother had warned me about. And yet I was feeling as confused as the crowd—it was a lot of blood, yes, but Jess had liked it—my cage's chain trembled—I found I was clutching the bars, staring at Jess, at her dark face, flushed and happy. She chugged soda, burped. People were staring at me, too.

Was now time to scream?

"We haven't gotten the festivities started yet," Cain shouted into the mic, crackling. "Our dear human friends tonight will give their blood, so take it. Though not any more from Jess, I think. Two pints, and then let them rest and eat. If you're here, whether you are coming for the first time or the hundredth, know that we love you. But vampires, know that what our individual human friends give you isn't all you have. The sky is the limit of what you can drink; we need physical power. Take still more, too. I've got what the clinic hasn't. Not expired. No cover. Let's *get* it. Get strong. And if my son can hurry up sometime in the next century, we can see some drag."

He spoke like someone who knew he had an army behind him, and I did think it didn't look that way from where I was standing. Maybe he had once.

There were more vampires on the stage now—a man in a top hat, a woman in a T-shirt and black leggings—throwing bags of blood into the audience. Clawed hands reached up. More ridges, more furs in different shades were going to appear. I felt my own ridges, not going away. Fawn's blood had only made them bigger.

Now I saw Fawn again.

She was in the back, looking unsteady, holding a Capri Sun and a granola bar. She was squinting uncertainly up in my direction, but I could see she was also staring at Jay. Between her and me, there was a scrambling through violet light for bags of blood. Three new figures took the stage with Cain. When the boxes were empty, Cain kicked them to the side. Bowing, his wings folding in until they were only a lump again under his cloak, he handed the mic to the dark-haired boy next to him. Drag was a strong word for the outfits happening on the stage—more greasepaint and thrift store than anything, with velvet Halloween cloaks and long, spiderweb-patterned dresses and dangling collections of Halloween plastic bones hanging around their necks.

"Hi," the boy said. His voice was high. "Me and Idris and Aurelius have composed a set to Idris's music. We're going to thrash. You should thrash too."

Unbearable noise started booming from every speaker, and some of the more-into-Cain people still lounging leaned forward, over the backs of chairs, moved like a tide of spiders toward the stage. I saw Flo clutch her head as the blast of ragged, thundering sound made the walls tremble. She looked around, taking in the scene, down, at her hands, and over at me. I gestured to her, trying to tell her I no longer had a stake. She shrugged, looking furious. I wondered if she had a plan. She was eight steps ahead of me. She would, I could see from the sharp, calculating glance she shot me, sacrifice me in a minute for her own escape. Below us, Silver and his two friends unfolded their wings.

This was the kind of situation in which my mom had always told me portals to hell could open. Big snakes, fat demons in bathtubs, men with no eyes, and spiders would follow. Dry-mouthed, I watched the vast leathery appendages spring forth from the boy who had spoken and from his two friends. They were dark and had fine, little sharp spines on the tips of their ridges. The flesh that stretched batlike between the finger bones was identical boy to boy—dark, baby-rat fuzzy, translucent. They grappled with each other on the stage to the noise, which sounded like a washing machine falling apart over a high voice singing in another language and a thudding, insistent kick drum. Other vampires rose on the seats to stand and headbang.

After a minute, when no glowing circles on the wall opened, I re-evaluated what was going on. This was just vampires being weird and stupid. The secret to their underworld, to Cain, was that they wanted to drink a lot of blood and *thrash*. Looking down, it was like I'd opened the lid of a trash can and sent rodents scattering. They were like any other dirty punk. No wonder my mom had never unlocked a master plan. Why did she think these people had power?

I stared at Fawn.

She stared at the boys. I saw that she had new, fresh marks on her neck—she was far away, but the bruises were red and clear.

I felt jealous, thinking of her blood on my tongue. Something in the way she was soft and hard at once—the tough front she'd put on over text and her street-smart talk, combined with the way she seemed to melt under my mouth for a second . . . She was so different than me. I wanted to get inside the softness I could feel there, to make it mine, to wrap it around me. I had seen her looking at me with something like sympathy. But that was stupid, because we didn't have a bond. She was in these vampires' corner. I was on the wrong side.

The music disintegrated into a tangled mess of sobs and wrenches clattering down a fire escape, and Silver was sweating blood beneath me, grabbing the mic.

"Don't trust Daylight," he yelled. "The secret is to be a real monster. You have to listen to your elders and the old ways, not trust humans who want us gone. You want to know something?"

He paused, and he seemed to note, at the same moment I did, that he was talking over a party, not speaking to an audience. They hadn't come here for a lecture; they talked to their friends, turned away from Silver. Cain was watching from the edge of the stage, his hands clasped proudly before his chest.

"I went out in the sun today," Silver said. The mic he was wearing shook against his face and spat static.

Every head turned back to him.

"I went out in the sun, because I drank a bunch of blood from the *necks* of Livia and Owen and Maddie and Francisco. When I drank, I grew wings, and they floated with me. Like we're meant to." He flapped his wings for emphasis, bared his fangs. "Everyone who's convinced our liberation is going to come from a bag—it's not. It comes from being bold, and being unafraid to want what you want, to take it from people happy to give it. They exist. I walked down the street today in the sunlight, and no harm came to me."

He turned and gestured to the projector screen behind him, and a shaky video appeared, of Silver, Idris and Aurelius strolling down a street in the U district. Their bloodred eyes were the only clue; they looked like college freshmen. The music had completely died. In the hush, you could hear the humans in the audience breathe.

"The clinic is gone, so what," Silver added, as the point of view of the video changed, and rose, to show the sun above them, shining through a white cloud.

At this, several people stood pointedly and strode angrily out of the theater. I thought, *I hope they're going to the tunnels.* I realized that I thought it. I didn't want any of them to die. I looked to Jay, who was staring up at Silver, rapt.

Cain stepped forward, kissed Silver's cheek, and gestured for Silver to step aside. Briefly, Silver stood there, sweating, not letting Cain take the mic. But he hopped awkwardly down, into the audience. Cain cleared his throat, and his flutelike, campy voice strained the sound system again, twanging upwards.

"The U District clinic's loss is of course tragic. Our foul enemies know no limit to their evil. They've stalked us since the beginning, burning our homes and our shelters, with the help of the cops. They kill us over and over. I helped build those tunnels. I remember what it took. I remember the Castle, La Fang, Crocket. I remember the past days, before yesteryear, when our Parisian catacombs were raided by this devious slayer's noxious predecessors. The friends we have lost will never be forgotten. That loss will be carried with us in our blood until the end of days, because every vampire contains a part of every other. The point is, and what we must live by, is that we cannot be killed if we are *brave.* They will have a hard time beating us when we are not emaciated and frail. Don't limit yourself to a pint a day. Or two. Make more friends. We have a world of friends to make. They want it too, even if they don't *know* it yet," Cain said.

A few cheers—from who? Hard to say.

He looked up to Flo.

"Speaking of slayers. We caught two infiltrators earlier," he added slyly.

"I don't know, Cain," Flo called down, louder than expected, shaking me to my senses. "Who's catching who?"

Cain's brow furrowed slightly as he squinted up into the lights—and at the same time, Flo, who—while everything had been going on below—had been throwing different projectiles at the wall, hooking twine and wire together from her cage in a way that had looked totally aimless everytime I glanced over, pulled.

Her cage door swung open, and she threw, with calculated and astonishing accuracy, a stake down onto one specific point on the stage. There was, somewhere in the darkness, a distinctly metallic twang. Several things happened too fast to precisely follow. Cain, when he heard the *thunk*, leaped, grabbing Silver, pushing him off the stage and onto the floor, rolling under the elevated platform. The other vampires around them scrambled, inadequately—but the stage's mousetrap blade fell, with a dreadful whoosh, down toward the stage. *Thrak!* At the same time, there was a clattering from all around the room, as knives, axes, and various heavy weights thudded and collapsed in cascades over exits and levers and pulleys leaned one way and then another. Most of the weapons fell without hitting anyone, though I saw one weight collide with a vampire's shoulder, and one vampire threw themself out of the way a second too late and had a spear embed itself in their arm. The stage's blade itself nearly fell on Jess. Screams rang out through the audience.

"You call this a security system?" Flo called, over the

commotion. She projected very well, I thought. Almost like Mom. She tossed herself out the side of the cage, somersaulting over herself, ponytail twisting, landing on the disarmed mousetrap blade with two feet. That was also something Mom would do. On landing, she threw a stake into the audience; vampires flung themselves out of the way, towards the doors.

Cain was on the floor. People hopped over him.

"You thought *this* would catch June Sorkin? A couple bobby pins and some Joann's Fabrics. Rube Goldberg ass janky demons. You all run out of money?"

Cain drew himself up off Silver, who was staring open-mouthed at Flo as some vampires in the room fled and some stood, uncertainly fanning wings out and baring teeth, waiting for Cain's signal. I was doing more or less the same thing, inside the open door of my cage.

The long-haired man pushed through the crowd in the doorway. He had a gun; he pointed the gun at Flo.

"Wait!" Silver cried, unexpectedly, flailing his arms. "Don't hurt her!"

He leapt up, pushing Cain off him.

I could only see the top of Flo's head; she sneered, and walked along the top of the great blade to pull at another lever on the side of the stage. With a creak, my cage came crashing down from a great height unceremoniously. The pit in my stomach reached up to the top of my head during the fall, and the bone-rattling crash on the other end of it left me on my side in the cage, the door open. I could feel where my fangs had bit through my lip. I took a second to figure out where my legs had landed. My back hurt.

Silver was back on stage, grabbing at Flo, catching at her sleeves like a child, his bat-face puppylike, his wings bent back in a way that looked painful from his fall.

"Flo, you found me. I never expected to see you again." He turned to Cain's bodyguard. "There has to be a mistake. She can't be with the slayers."

"Oh, I am," Flo said, and wrapped an arm around Silver in a headlock. He didn't expect it—didn't seem to understand it was happening as it happened. She had a stake pressed to his chest. She was grinning. "It seems like vampires are a lot easier to take out than everyone has been telling me."

"Silver, get away from the slayer!" Cain shrieked over his shoulder hurriedly, his white hair streaming in several directions with static electricity. "We can still deal with her." He was scrambling to his bodyguard, through a dwindling, panicked group of undead making for the doors. His bodyguard handed him a sword, and he turned around, disheveled and desperate-looking, toward Silver.

Flo cocked her head. "Silver, I thought you were dead. Now I find out this freak has you in his pedo clutches and you're attacking people to drink their blood."

"I missed you. I missed you, Flo." His voice was choked; he was still on the mic, and his sob reverberated through the sound system. "You don't really want to hurt vampires. I know you don't get it but give it a minute. You can be one of us, now, or you could live with me." His voice got softer.

I saw Fawn in the crowd, trying to fight her way forward through the many vampires currently attempting to exit—some pushing each other into the tunnels, the hundred vampires in the room melting into dozens, the noise of fear and screams.

Cain was not losing a moment for showmanship. He pushed forward with his sword to Silver, and sliced toward Flo's neck on her unprotected side, forcing her to let go of Silver to fight him. She raised her arm and used the stake to block his blade. Silver looked unsure of whether he wanted to be moving away from her, even as he rolled away across the half-destroyed stage toward me. I was trying to figure out how to get out without Flo seeing me. If she was engaged in hand-to-hand combat with Cain, that seemed like a good time. Silver was looking at me, now, as if seeing for the first time I was there, and free, and not doing anything.

Flo knocked her head back into Cain's nose and teeth at the same moment that a loud alarm began to sound and something fell from the ceiling down into the mingled mass of undead in purple chairs. An asbestos tile shattered over the heads of some fleeing vamps in the first row of seats.

My mom came down, ziplining towards me.

14.

FAWN

First, Jay had been on the stage drinking, and that had been bad enough. Now it was Flo, who was dressed like the protagonist in a streetfighter video game, and Silver was tenderly grasping at her hand even as she held a stake to his heart. He had lurched forward and attacked my neck and then dropped me again to go do his show. I'd had a brief moment of triumph, seeing the great wings fold out from his body—this is what he was always meant to be, and I'm here with him—

Flo was a slayer, and yet, if Cain tried to hurt her, Silver would try to stop Cain.

That straightened some things out for me, I guess, though it was the kind of straightening where someone maybe grabs both ends of your spine and yanks it out of your body. Goodbye, visions of a life in a house in New Orleans with kudzu swirling up the windowsill, us sitting on a porch in the moonlight watching lightning bugs over the street, our house full of red velvet and gargoyle garden statues, me bonded to him, his life, his lover. Hello to whatever else you did after your best friend showed you that you didn't actually exist. Life on the margins, chasing people who will drink from you for a second. Unloved.

I saw Rachel, in the cage—and she was with the slayers too, it seemed like. My head was half white noise.

The first huge piece of fiberglass fell next to Flo with a noise like cracking rocks in a quarry, and she jumped back from the shattered fibers of the ceiling tile and lost her footing. The voices around me were becoming confused in the rising din, people turning and moving toward each other, back from each other, toward the doors. Cain was looking up at the hole spreading across the ceiling. I stumbled and fell too when someone elbowed my side. My head was a little light. Between Rachel and Silver and Richeza . . . how many pints was that I was missing? I was maybe being super stupid.

Three women holding on to leather straps slid down a length of wire from the hole in the ceiling, landing on the stage with the poise of skinny panthers. The first one, the blondest, did look a lot like Rachel, but older. She wore black stretch-pleather leggings, a canvas utility belt, and a spandex athleisure black top. She pulled a crossbow from off her back, loaded it with a stake, and pointed it at Cain in a motion that took maybe three seconds. The mic screeched.

"Slayers!" Jay yelled, his wolfish face like a panicked child. There was no game happening here. There was suddenly a bottleneck at the door, the remaining people who had been moving toward the stage now turning to the door en masse, shoving against each other—the gray-haired man who had let us in getting pushed against the lintel, shouldering his way back in, springing forward with his gun. He took one shot, wide, towards June and then got kicked in the head. I saw one girl, young like Jay, vanish in a puff of dust. I followed a line of sight back to the stage, where a darker-haired, solidly built slayer in blue jeans had landed and was reloading an improbable bazooka-like doohickey with another wooden stake. Poof. Another puff of dust.

I flattened myself to the floor.

Silver was still onstage, clutched in Flo's arms.

"Party's over, old man," the woman said onstage.

Cain sneered back, a pile with no composition after he'd fallen on his ass when the slayers landed. He staggered to his feet, between June and Flo. He hissed up at her—he was shorter. I thought that if Silver had wanted to get away, he could have.

"I dare you, June. We've come face to face again and again, and somehow you always have a reason not to stake me. I think you *like me*."

A thwack; a glowing arc of fire extended from the third woman's flamethrower and lit the screen on fire behind him. His smile dropped as he dodged. The twenty or so vampires who had waited to see if Cain had a secret weapon were now cascading past us, fleeing the flames, thundering. Poof: another fluff of ash.

"That's never been true. You know what your problem is, Cain? You've got a major Peter Pan syndrome. Always needing to chase your childhood."

My heart was beating fast—I was bleary.

"Don't monologue at each other, kill some vampires already!" Flo shouted. She kicked out wildly—Cain winced.

A woman next to her had grabbed Silver's friend Idris out of the air as he flew toward her, pinned him, and was holding a stake up as if to stab him. Silver screamed and jumped in their direction. He was well within flame-ing distance, or stake-throwing distance. I didn't want him to die. Even if he sucked, I didn't want to see him gone. That was why I'd come all this way. My heart was small up in my throat.

I moved my legs. A crossbow bolt rocketed through the air where Silver had been a moment before, but it cut through cloth, arced up and stuck in the tiles above us. Suddenly Cain was billowing upward on his great wings, grabbing at the chains that had held the cages, dragging Silver with him, Silver's wings flapping, obscuring Rachel and Flo and the slayers. A middle-aged slayer was pulling at Silver's legs, tugging his hand apart from Cain's. He fell to the ground. Rachel, still in her cage, was gesturing at June, yelling too. Flame followed Cain but only smoked at the end of his cloak, smoldering an Art Deco pillar. His ruby boots flashed. The bat-boy named Aurelius was flapping his wings wildly, leapfrogging off the wall to catch up. Cain and Aurelius scrambled through the frayed gap between the tiles. Silver was on the floor—he reached toward them, trying to stretch his arms out, weighed down. June Sorkin's crossbow tracked Cain's flight but didn't fire. The stake came down into Idris's body, and he was ash and a lingering scream. Silver howled, his wings flapping like a pigeon. Flo was rolling off the stage toward me.

I was almost the only one left in here, everyone else gone toward either the steps to the street or some other tunnel. Flo caught a stake in her right hand as she ran—I didn't see who threw it.

I tripped her, and when she rolled expertly, as if made of well-greased springs instead of horse-girl bone, as if she had come into a set of supernatural powers during the few weeks we'd spent apart, I followed her, jumped on top of her, holding her arms, pinned her to the ground. I remembered Rachel's taser and pulled it out. I was marginally heavier. Flo struggled, elbowing my gut, but I'd been jumped in the boys' bathroom before, and I shifted my weight to slow her and pushed the taser against her skin, turning it on. It buzzed. She started, but it didn't seem to do what tasers were supposed to. Flo jabbed me with the wooden stake enough to make me cry out, then kicked me in the crotch. I dropped the taser, pushed my elbow down on her back, but somehow she got an arm around my arm, and pulled my hand, and then flipped me onto the ground. Her hair was wild. Something in her eyes was bright and ugly.

"You cunt," she hissed. "Did you just try to tase me?"

"Silver still loves you best," I said up into her face. "Don't worry. Even though you can never give him what he needs."

She spit on my face with a vehemence that would have been funny except that she had access to a bunch of weapons. She knew: Silver wanted her more, but I understood him more. That's what she was mad about.

"You're the reason he's like this, that he's a monster."

"Say it like you mean it," I said to her. I kicked her crotch—fair's fair—and we rolled for a full revolution again, hands at each other's arms, necks, fists in each other's pelvises, and my world was sticky carpet and purple light and the face of my former friend, rolling into the edges of the rows of seats and down over the low steps until two manicured hands pulled us apart.

"Flo," June Sorkin said. "She's not a vampire, she's a victim. You don't need to beat the crap out of her. We've set the place on fire, it's time to split. We'll take her too."

I had a black eye. I was someone's victim for sure. Was Silver alive?

Flo turned away with a grunt of frustration. I couldn't see what I'd done to her face, but her nose was bleeding.

"Catch, kid," one of the older slayers called to her. Flo caught the flamethrower and turned to the wall nearest us, which she set on fire.

I lay on the floor looking at the dim ceiling for a second, until June was bending underneath me and lifting me under the arms, hauling me up.

"You're safe," she said to me. "We don't kill humans. You may be majorly brainwashed, but you're not our enemy. We've got to get out of here. Hang on tight, now." I looked around, saw an unconscious winged form—Silver hadn't been ashed.

June began to rise up from the ground on a rope dangling from the ceiling, where they'd come through, where Cain had just escaped into night air. We ascended—and I say "we" because my arms wrapped involuntarily around June as the floor disappeared beneath my feet. Her arm was a vise, as solid as a roller coaster's safety bar.

At the top of the rope, she swung me easily up and through the narrow attic to the roof outside. It sagged in places—this was how they'd busted in, I saw, with a sledgehammer—but was connected to a fire escape, where a silhouette waited and beckoned to June as she emerged.

"The van's down below. It's too bad we didn't get sunrise on our side," the woman said. "Hours still to go before these vamps would toast. Who's this?"

"Victim," June grunted. "Three bite marks in her neck. We got Cain's new boy, too. Hostage."

Under us, smoke was beginning to billow up in earnest through the hole.

"How do you know she hasn't turned?"

"We don't. But we'll know in about five hours. Can bring her to Daylight till then."

The skyline of the trees and harbor and water was still beautiful. You could see it from the roof. There was no evidence a battle had just happened on the empty street outside.

"Well, let's get the poor motherfucker to the van."

I was a sack of meat, pushed between June and this new short-haired, ginger woman, who turned to me curtly as we descended the rickety iron stairwell, put out a hand, and said, "I'm Amber."

"Fawn," I said, and I saw her demeanor completely change when she heard my voice. She made an expression of mild disgust, where before she'd had the grim manner of a battlefield nurse with a patient who might not live.

"How'd they get you, Fawn?" she asked.

"Nobody got me," I said. "I came with Rachel."

We were still descending the stairs. Tung, tung, tung.

"You sell blood."

"I do," I said, and found a grain of deep, angry pride as I said it. "People need blood."

Amber tsk'd at me. "They're rolling in handouts and they want more. These guys in here, they're just greedy. They want everything. They want to drink people dry. You love demons."

"I think we have different opinions about this," I said, and, because I had no choice, started down the ladder to the street, June at my heels, with the crossbow still on her back. When I dropped to the uneven paved ground, I tried to run, but my knees gave out, and Amber caught me by the arm. She was as strong as Flo's mom; maybe she kept horses too. I wondered what Flo's mom was thinking about her daughter's sudden departure. She was probably worried. Flo's mom was nice.

"No you don't," Amber said. "We have to keep an eye to make sure you don't turn bloodsucker too."

"Awesome," I said, and, maybe because I'd run out of things to do, I fainted.

When I came to, I was in the back of a van. Stars were dancing in front of my eyes, but if I focused they disappeared. My hands were zip tied together, though my feet were free. My mouth was dry. Around me, there were four figures who had sacks tied over their heads, moving with various levels of success against the metal handcuffs locking their hands to their feet.

The van jolted through the dark. Through the back window, I saw we were on a highway.

"Hey, is anyone awake?" I said. "Are any of you awake? Silver?"

There was a muffled noise from underneath one hood. I saw his wings had vanished.

"Okay. Good. I'm Fawn, for those who don't know me," I said. "Good news is they haven't staked you guys yet, and they told me they wouldn't kill me. Bad news is I have no idea where they're taking us."

Someone knocked against the back window of the cab, which looked through a grille into the area where we were being jolted around. A girl's face peered through. Not Rachel, not Flo. She had freckles.

"Don't talk to them," she said. "They've gotten in your brain. They'll hypnotize you more."

"They probably can't hypnotize me with a bag on their head," I said. "Who are you?"

"I'm Stacey," she said, and snapped a piece of bubble gum in her mouth. "Don't worry, we've got you tied up but it's just in case you start getting bite-y. June says five hours, but honestly if you're still breathing in three I feel like it's for sure you're not vamped. Rachel got turned and her heart stopped like that, so if your heart's still going, you're fine probably."

"So like, what, in three hours you'll let me go?"

Stacey's face registered uncertainty. "Well, you're a blood seller, so that is illegal, so we have to report you to the cops." She hesitated. "But, like, you're so young. I'm sure the cops will know you're being exploited and you won't get in trouble."

"Oh, I see," I said. I felt like being mean to her. "That's

really nice of the cops. Will I be zip tied until you guys report me, or am I maybe gonna get some of these fancier shackles and a head bag?"

Flo's head appeared next to Stacey. "Don't be a bitch, we saved your life," Flo said. "We could have left you in the burning theater."

"Flo, not to be a bitch, but what the hell is wrong with you?" I asked. "I thought you were going to college and stuff. Silver leaves so you literally become a supervillain? What are you guys doing?"

Stacey looked between me and Flo and snapped her gum again. A sharp gleam jolted in her eye. "Wait, you guys know each other?"

"She fucked my boyfriend," Flo said flatly.

"Or you fucked mine," I said, though at this point, after everything, I could admit he'd never been my boyfriend really. He wasn't even that nice to me. He was just the first person who made me feel a certain way.

"Well, you convinced my boyfriend to become a vampire."

"I didn't convince him, I just knew that's what he did," I said. "You didn't, because you didn't even really like him."

"You both wore that Free Blood necklace. Yeah, I know about that now. It's because you have some kind of sick desire to get your blood drunk. You want to prove you're like, this weak damsel or something," Flo said. "It's honestly so sad."

"Do you guys know each other from like, high school?" Stacey asked. "Who's Silver?"

I wanted Stacey to be up to date. "Silver's Cain's new lackey," I said. "He turned into a vampire just a bit ago. He's tied up back here. We're all from Maryland."

"You made him like this. I told him it was weird that he wanted to drink my blood. You told him it was fine."

"It is fine," I said. "To me."

"Doesn't it hurt?" Stacey asked, wrinkling her nose. "And don't they like, disrespect you?"

"It doesn't make you real, to get your blood drunk," Flo said.

I knew what she meant by that. All through her sympathetic noises in high school, I could feel that somewhere inside her, she thought that. Now she'd found a way to let it out. All I could do was laugh. I felt Richeza's bracelet on my wrist under my zip tie, and it was suddenly a huge comfort to think of her. I was special. She barely met me, and she wanted to give me a free bagel. I was looking around the van at the same time for anything that could cut through the zip ties. We turned off the highway—I could see the lights disappearing behind us. I had established I was a genius under fire in vans. I had to get us out of this. I still felt dizzy.

"When I thought he had died it was fine," Flo said, mostly to Stacey, fake tearing up. Or maybe really crying, I wasn't being generous. "To know he left me to become a monster and drink innocent people's blood . . . probably, like, innocent girls. And to know I'd loved someone like that, I knew I had to kill him."

"Word," Stacey said to her emphatically, empathetically.

"I mean," I said, loudly, feeling with my foot for any loose jingly keys on the ground, having ideas. "Okay. Let's dig into this. Are the victims innocent, or do we have a sick desire to get our blood drunk? You're saying different things here."

"Shut the fuck up, Fawn," Flo said. "There are people besides you in the universe."

"Quiet down back there," Amber's voice sounded from the front of the van. "You're gonna get all those vampires frothing at the mouth the way you all are bellowing."

"I am pretty hungry and weak," I yelled, at a volume I thought Amber might be able to hear. "I think I've had about, I don't know, maybe three pints of blood drunk? Shouldn't you guys take me to a hospital?"

"We'll get you on a drip when we get to Daylight," Amber said in response, which was not really a great sentence.

There were some frantic, muffled sounds from another vampire, cuffed under their hood. My hands were secured, or I could have pulled the bag off. I tried to rub against a sharp uneven screw in the floor, to cut the zip ties, but the van bounced. I was beginning to feel sick.

"Quiet," I said to Silver, when he moaned. I turned around so my back faced the other vampire and used my hands to tug at the bag on their head. It was, I realized, secured with a cord around his neck—*mmph, mpph*—but if I lay with my ass in their face, blocking Stacey's possible view of their head, I could feel around for the edges of the cord, and the knot, and pull. It undid; the bag slid. I felt the vampire's ridged face, the cloth binding something into their mouth, the stifled sigh. I pulled at the cloth in their mouth too, and they spat.

"*Shh.*" I turned painfully over again. Her face was young and pug-nosed and round. Angie from the shelter.

"You're—" she started, in a whisper.

"Yes."

"Fuck," she whispered. Her eyes darted to the other prisoners. "Ned's not here, but I saw they got him. I hope he's in the other van and not—"

"Will you bite my zip ties?" I asked.

She nodded, and I rolled around again to face the grille, felt her chew at the plastic. They broke. I could barely feel my hands but felt at her handcuffs. Locked . . . there was probably a key. They wouldn't put it in here with us if there was—it was probably with Amber. But there was a YouTube video I had watched a long time ago that I was remembering.

Silver was making a frantic gesture toward his shoe, under the hem of his spiderweb gown.

I scooted toward him, trying to make it look like my hands were still tied.

"What are you doing back there?" Flo called, and squinted into the darkness. "Shit, Amber, she's got one of their masks off."

"Don't matter as long as they're still chained," Amber said. "Maybe she wants 'em to drink from her."

"We should stop, they could be up to something."

"We're almost there."

I pushed my fingers into the boot, had to pull it slightly off his foot to feel what he was showing me. A big dagger. Was I willing to hurt someone? Flo? Would he want me to hurt her? I wasn't sure. Once I pulled a weapon, I was pretty sure their weapons would come out too. And I couldn't fight them all alone.

I took it and rolled back to where I had been. Why hadn't they chained me like the vampires? Did they trust me more? Did they just not have enough cuffs? I stuck the blade into the lock for Angie's cuffs and twisted, but the tip of the point was too big to maneuver in the keyhole. Was there anything else I could use? Paperclip. Paperclip. I felt around in the dark as we bumped along. There were pieces of dirt and trash in the back of the van—a granola bar wrapper. A receipt. Then, I found it. In the corner, against gritty dust, I found a hard, thin metal shape. A nail.

We were at a light. Then moving, turning, slowing. I pressed the nail into the keyhole of Angie's cuffs just as we stopped—but it was the right shape to maneuver. I could twist and feel the mechanism. There was a click, and Angie looked at me, moved her arms slightly apart. The cuffs opened. I handed her the dagger—she would need it more than me, and maybe be brave enough to actually use it. I undid the handcuffs of the others, pulled off two more bags, exposing the face of a middle-aged Asian man and a nervous-looking young white woman whose hair was singed half off on one side. I wondered why Stacey wasn't looking back here, and what would happen if she did.

We stopped moving. The front door of the van slammed.

I was moving toward Silver's handcuffs when the back of the van opened.

"Jesus shit a brick," Amber said, as Angie rocketed at her—though it was more of a fast stumble, and as she leapt out onto her it was more of a fall. But she got the blade I'd handed her into Amber's side. Amber screamed and became less intimidating. I tried to pull Silver up, still fumbling—I got his handcuffs off—but something was hurting him, and he was limp and heavy against me. He let out a moan of pain. Shit. Amber was holding her side, clinging to the opening of the van. Angie was sprinting away into the dark. The two other vampires were running after her. Angie tore her windbreaker off, threw it to the ground, unfurled big, leathery wings, and leapt into the air, blocking the moon. The Asian guy leapt into the bushes—he didn't have wings. The other vampire woman collapsed into dust as a stake caught her through the back.

Stacey was pulling Amber away across the parking lot of the brightly lit glass building we were parked in front of. Flo was leveling her crossbow at me and Silver.

"Why didn't you run?" Flo asked me.

"Flo, please," Silver said, looking at her with puppy dog eyes.

"You're asking me why I didn't leave you alone with Silver after you said you'd kill him."

"Stay still, or I will shoot you. I don't care what June or Daylight says."

I stayed still. I could feel Silver next to me shaking. Where had his wings, all that blood-power gone? His fur was still there. I looked down, saw for the first time that one of his legs was a burned mess. He was shivering.

"The synthetic blood company?"

"There's a vampire! Right there," I said. "Quick!"

Flo glanced at Rachel. "You know, Rachel, that's a fair point."

"Don't shoot," June said to Flo, turning back from the Amber crisis. "Your trigger finger's looking a little happy there. We don't kill humans, Flo, even if they're really pissing us off."

"She helped that vampire girl stab Amber," Flo said.

"She thinks she's doing the right thing," June said. "She wants to be a hero. I get it. I really do. Get up. Move." She gestured to me with her hand. "Re-cuff them."

There was a crossbow pointed at me; I raised my hands in surrender and slid toward the end of the open bed as Flo scrambled in to renew Silver's bonds and put his head back into the bag. She hopped in and pushed Silver forward until his legs found the end of the truck bed and slipped down onto the pavement. I got handcuffed by Rachel, who murmured sorry. Silver stood unsteadily.

We shuffled across a wide, empty parking lot, toward the glowing doors of a building with silver struts. Around the edges of the parking lot, there were tall trees; there was a hint of foggy suburban street past the stop sign that marked the exit. Amber was sitting on the curb of the sidewalk close to the yellow light spilling out through the glass, holding her side, blood coming through her fingers. Stacey was tearing apart a t-shirt, handing wads of fabric to her. Another figure in chains sat hooded on her other side.

"We lost three prisoners," Amber said through gritted teeth. "Jonathan and Joey won't be pleased."

"We have Cain's boy," June said, sort of defensively. "It's not really about their test subjects."

"You could have *shot* Cain. You were right there. Flo told me. *I* could have shot Cain, but you told me to stay in the van," Amber griped. "He taunted you and escaped again.

Like he always—*fucking*—does." She wheezed around gritted teeth.

June sneered. "You'll do what I tell you to do," she said. "We didn't get him this time, but we knew there was a chance he'd prioritize his own escape. We killed ten vamps. More with the firebombs in the tunnels by now, probably. And we got the Pearl. It's gone."

Firebombs in the tunnels. If anyone did get down, out—I thought of the full hall. The attitude that had been in there, of like, we are throwing a big party, it's safe here. Had Cain even tried to keep the other vampires safe? He hadn't even saved Silver.

"Ten. There were a hundred in there. If you'd waited for the sun to rise, like your precious, incorruptible *plan*—"

"Rachel and Flo would be *dead*!" June shouted. She turned away from me completely, though I could still feel Flo at my back. June had her hands balled into fists at her sides. "My daughter would be dead, and I would have abandoned Flo to the vampires, and even if we killed all two hundred or whatever with the sunlight, I would have failed. My job is to keep the people I love alive."

"Your daughter is already dead," Amber said. "You failed. Now, is Stacey allowed to take me to a hospital, or is that against the plan too?"

Stacey had been silent, staring steadfastly away from the argument; now she nodded eagerly, reassuringly at Amber. "We're going to a hospital really quick," she said. "Right away. I'm just waiting on my mom for the keys."

June raised a walkie-talkie to her mouth. "Diane, get Amber out of here before I have to slap her."

"June, you're off your rocker. I'm calling a leadership vote next meeting," Amber said, her tone dead.

"You do that," June said icily. She flipped her head back around to me, her vivid gold hair bouncing. "Okay, move it."

Inside the foyer, we moved past a garden of large, spacious fig trees in pots and benches that had backs with LED lights in them. June unlocked a red door, and the corridor was instantly industrial white. I had a bad feeling that I'd just missed my chance to save my own skin. The hallway echoed as June stepped into it like it went on a long way.

We moved down one set of stairs, through another hallway, and abruptly were steered through some doors into a small white room with two chairs bolted to the floor. They were not uncomfortable chairs—kind of a pleathery, dentist's waiting room vibe, only there was nothing on the walls or cabinets, just a ceiling vent and a computer with a dark screen on the wall. I got handcuffed to the chair, June taking a new pair of cuffs so that each arm was anchored to a pleather-topped steel arm. The nail had dropped to the bottom of the car. Silver got clipped to the other chair, bag still on head. June tugged at my cuff, then Silver's, then nodded.

"How about that IV drip you promised?"

Crossbow still pointed at me, she left the room.

I stared at Silver in his bag in white silence, at his burned, raw leg. How many minutes passed?

I could see a camera in the corner of the room. I wondered what was coming next. This was a science-y place. Was it funded by Bezos? By Bill Gates? Peter Thiel? What did they want with Silver?

A guy in scrubs with a tablet and a clipboard came through the door. He blanched when he saw us both anchored to the chairs, and exited, closing the door. After a minute he came back and took the bag off Silver's head and the gag out of his mouth. His shoulders were tense. I felt relieved to see Silver's face: just a few bruises, a lump over his red eye and flared, batlike nose, and one section of fur that had burned away. The same awkward, narrow pale face beneath, tired eyes. He saw me and gave me a brief pained, uncomfortable look before looking at the doctor.

"Apologies for the way you've been conducted here."

"What the hell," Silver spat, his speech slightly slurred around his fangs. "Are you guys going to kill me, or what?"

"No, no, no," the guy said. He hadn't really looked at me at all. He was looking down at Silver like he had never seen a bat nose before. "I'm Doctor Nychall. You've been selected to be part of our study."

"Your study on how to kill vampires?"

"No. On how to provide a better food source. I imagine you're tired of having to drink blood. Daylight is working on an alternative."

"They just killed a guy outside. They killed my friend Idris. You're a sicko creep."

Doctor Nychall went pale and still for a moment. Silver's tired, leaden eyes gleamed with righteous fury. He was never a person to back down in the face of authority, though I wasn't sure if he knew what he was doing.

"You did agree to the study. We have the consent form."

I felt a chill go through my body.

"Get me the fuck out of here!" Silver yelled.

Silver was only looking at the doctor. Was he thinking about me? Was I supposed to be making use of the doctor being distracted?

"Ma'a—si—I'm just going to proceed with the questions before we do any more of this. Did you drink non-synthetic blood from a live human donor in the last two weeks?"

"Hell yeah."

The venom in his voice was real, and I thought about the ancient creatures hiding in wells and stuff. I did love him.

"Last two weeks . . ." There had been a moment of hesitation, and it was gone now. The man in scrubs let his stylus hover over a tablet.

"My most recent meal is here. She's sitting right behind you." Silver looked directly at my eyes for the first time as the doctor turned to stare at me, as if fully assimilating my presence, craning his neck.

"That's me," I said, realizing for the first time how much my split lip and black eye hurt.

"You look rough," Silver added, his scowl becoming a little contrite. "Flo got you. I didn't realize she was . . ."

"A dick. Your leg okay?"

"It's okay. Cain will come for us. I'll get more blood and be fine. You'll be safe too." His voice was tough, certain. I wasn't so sure Cain would be back.

"Excuse me," Doctor Nychall said. He waved a hand in front of Silver's face. "We are as of now going to wean you off of blood and on to Daylight product. We'll need to keep you here for observation and perform some tests."

Silver pursed his lips defiantly. The longer he sat, the more his burned leg looked pink-white rather than charred and his fur faded, his face returning to that of a scrawny eighteen-year-old boy who hadn't gotten on testosterone yet. Just the bat nose stayed.

The doctor took out a vial and drew some of Silver's blood into it. Then he turned to me.

"I'm going to take your blood pressure," he said.

I said nothing and let him wrap the cuff around my arm. He frowned at the number that appeared.

"We should get you on an IV drip. Your blood pressure is very low."

"Oh, that just runs in my family," I said cagily.

The doctor left the room.

We sat in silence for what felt like ten minutes, Silver staring past my head. I had a lot of thoughts.

"Are you and Cain dating?" I asked, finally.

Silver's frown became guarded, like at the theater. "What? No."

"Is it *not dating*, the way you *weren't dating* me?"

He shook his head. "It's much more arcane. Why *didn't* you leave me in the truck? You could have run."

"I didn't want to. I was going to try to get you out."

"After you'd had two pints taken? Humans are so stupid."

I felt warmth glow in my chest. I loved him. I was so glad he was alive. "You love being able to say *humans*, don't you. You've been waiting for it for years. You gonna move into some abandoned Scottish highland ruin next?"

His face scrunched more.

"Silver, you could say thank you to me."

"You didn't do anything."

I was still mad at him, but the anger was like soapsuds

on water, with lots of space in between. "I gave you my blood and I tried to save you from the slayers, you dipshit. I chased you across the country because I love you."

"I didn't ask you to."

He hadn't, but I felt, in my warm love for him, a slight icy thrill. "You sure made out with me a lot. You left the necklace."

"Yeah. I thought . . . I guess I thought *someone* would find it, and like, learn about vampires."

A shiver in my heart, now. "You didn't mean for me to find it?"

"Fawn, you were going to go to Pratt in New York for design. I was leaving. Why would I think you would follow me?"

"My parents couldn't afford Pratt, I told you that. I was going to have to go to state school. But I decided I wasn't doing that either, because my insane best friend faked his own death. Did you think about how you committing suicide would affect me? I'm not Miss Mental Health."

Silver's scrunched brow and pout didn't waver. He either couldn't let me be right or he was having a hard time unscrunching because of the life-or-death situation we were in. I watched his fanged mouth twist.

"I guess I really didn't think you'd do some crazy shit like that," he said finally. "I thought you were going to be the one who went and had a normal life. You were going to get out of Jarlsburg and go on hormones and pass and be like, a graphic designer lady."

"That's so offensive. You thought I was going to live a *normal life*?"

"Yeah, 'cause you're pretty and smart. You *got in* to Pratt."

"You think that does anything for me?"

"I don't know!" He strained against the chair as if through gargantuan effort he could upend it. He thrashed, and it didn't move. "I knew you didn't feel how I felt, didn't wish you were a creature. I knew you got me, sort of, but you didn't want to go where I did—I was lonely. You weren't there."

I loved him, but I was eighty percent angry.

"I *was* fucking *there,* you freak," I snapped.

Click-clack: shoes tapped down the cement corridor outside. The doctor came back with a cart of equipment and a fluid IV. He set up a strange ring-shaped lamp in front of Silver. Silver flinched. It turned on, illuminating him like he was about to start filming a commercial.

The doctor put an IV in my arm and held a juice box in front of my face until I'd drunk the whole thing through a plastic straw.

Then he left again.

"Is that light meant to hypnotize you?" I asked Silver.

"To test my sensitivity to sunlight, probably. It's like, some kind of ultraviolet, I can feel it. Don't worry, I've been drinking a ton of blood. It'll be an hour or two before I get burned."

"If you hadn't been drinking fresh blood at all, you'd get fried?"

"I'd hurt. Only real sun can turn us to ashes."

I didn't feel like watching Silver get gradually more burned. I strained against my cuffs, the way he just had, but then I heard footsteps in the hall again.

Rachel came in. She immediately unplugged the light facing Silver.

"Uh, okay, cool," Silver said.

"She's with the slayers," I told him. "She used me to get in to the Pearl."

"What?"

"I'm trying to help you," Rachel said, and she sounded like a high school mean girl. "Shut up."

"If you're coming to drink more, I'm plumb out," I said to Rachel. "They're preparing my gravestone already."

"A vampire with the slayers?" Silver looked at Rachel. "Are you stupid?"

Rachel blanched, but then seemed to collect herself.

"We don't have much time," Rachel said. "Fawn, I'm so sorry. I didn't mean for you to get caught up in this too. I know it's—" she teared up, her nose crinkling, her hands rising to her face. Her tears were red and got on her wrist. "I tried to get out earlier, and I couldn't. And it just kept cascading and cascading. Cain's evil, but it's . . . There's tons of vampires here that my mom brought them to test on. They've burned some of them. I've seen them. They grabbed Ned who runs the shelter. They're going to give the Daylight blood to everyone, but they're going to have Mom kill anyone who doesn't take it. I can't believe I thought they were good."

"Can happen to the best of us," Silver said. "Just last Tuesday I accidentally joined a hate movement that hates me specifically. D'oh!"

I laughed. "You mean your ex-girlfriend did."

Silver snarled.

"Please. I have the key to the cuffs," Rachel said. She held up a key and went to work on Silver's cuffs. "Fawn, I've been trying to get out. June's my mother. It's hard. I saw—there was this girl from my school that Brid killed, and I realized then. I should have done something then, but I'm doing something now."

"Aw, I hate it when my murder friends murder people," Silver grumbled, but he freed his hands and rubbed them gratefully.

"I'm going to try to get you both out of this. The vent above you leads to these huge air ducts. I know they have to vent the air in here. And I've seen the ducts go through a hallway at the end of the floor, it's a tight squeeze but it's big enough for a person. If it doesn't go directly outside you should be able to get into the staff area four rooms over and leave from there—" she pointed down the direction of the hall, then right. "I think you can get out that way. You could do the door, but Flo's out there."

I tried to imagine scrambling up into the air ducts. Like a '90s movie. Bending, Rachel undid my cuffs, handed me a Phillips head screwdriver. I yanked out my IV and held my finger over it. Rachel saw, turned, rummaged in a drawer for a bandage.

"How do we get in? It's shut," said Silver.

"I'll lift you and you can unscrew it," Rachel said, and hurriedly wrapped her arms around my knees. She was strong, and the ground disappeared from under me. I let out a yelp as I was hoisted toward the ceiling.

I'd put together a bookshelf and a birdhouse. The screw turned. When the grate on the vent came off, I wasn't sure if I'd fit through the hole, but Rachel pushed me up anyway, as if I were as light as a doll. My shoulders got stuck, but the space beyond the opening was big enough, and as I felt Silver push my foot too, I unstuck and slid up. I had just pulled up my boot and was turning around to reach down to Silver when we heard more footsteps, fast. Click-clack.

"Shit," Rachel said, and blocked the door with her body as someone banged against it. "They'll know I did it."

"Come on," I yelled to Silver. I held my arms out to him. He was short, but our hands just met if he stood on the chair. I pulled at him, feeling that I was still dizzy and tired and he was too. He dangled, swung. I slipped forward. Rachel stopped holding the door and gave him a boost with her shoulder as I braced a foot against the hole, and he clambered up, me edging backward to make space inside the dark, dusty air duct—

—but then there was a crash below.

"Brid," Rachel said weakly. I couldn't see who she was speaking to.

"Hiding something, aren't you?"

"Come on," I said to Silver, and started crawling, but he yelped and fell forward onto his hands, clutching at the slick, sharp-edged metal, his fingers sliding backward.

"They got my foot," he said. "One of them. They're gonna kill me—"

I grabbed his arms again, and pulled, but he slid backward, pulling me with him, screaming. Sharp metal cut at my shoulder as I slid against the wall of the duct. I scrambled with my feet for purchase, but was slipping too.

"Fuck, fuck, fuck don't let go," Silver said, and I hated

the desperation in his face, the weakness. I didn't, but his hands were slippery, and I heard the angry growl of another unknown teenager in the room below. He slipped back, falling, and a moment later a crossbow bolt impaled itself in the metal above the duct opening. I scrambled back on my hands and feet like a crab, into the darkness.

"I'm coming for you too, you snowflake motherfucker," the girl who wasn't Rachel yelled up. I was terrified I'd hear her swing up after me, but as I moved forward on all fours, their voices receded.

It was noisy when I moved and there was an immediate feeling like I was breathing in a ton of dust. It wasn't clean like in the movies, and sharp edges rose at the seams of the ductwork when I moved my hands and the metal buckled under me.

I had to get out.

15.

RACHEL

Brid looked at Silver's form, slumped on the ground. He looked way more pathetic than he had in the club, under the fluorescent lights. She'd hit him on the back of the neck with the side of her hand in a precise way that had made him drop, unconscious. She'd always known how to do that better than me.

"So, you were helping this hostage escape, huh."

"Brid," I said, and wondered if I could just run out the door. I closed my eyes so I didn't have to look at her. "I don't think what you're doing is right. And there's no reason to keep Fawn here. She's human."

"When you summoned us to the theater early, I thought it might be a trap, that maybe you were in it with Cain. Flo was texting me some crazy shit." Brid let her hand, with its uniform manicured fingernails, trace up my arm. "But if it was a trap, it didn't go so good for you, did it?"

I made myself open my eyes and look at her. Her hazel eyes, which had once stared down at me in the park, under the leaves, off the trail where nobody could see us. She had a perfect little turned-up nose. Her hair was strawberry blond naturally. Mine was bleached. I hadn't had to touch up the roots in months, since it had stopped growing as fast. Or maybe at all.

"It wasn't a trap. Cain put us in cages. He was going to kill us. He wanted to lure Mom there. But when Mom burst in and you all started just setting people on fire, Cain didn't get hurt. Everyone else did."

"Everyone thinks you're going to go over to their side at some point. All I can say is, now you're rescuing vampires. Feeling conflicted, huh."

Silver groaned, and Brid kicked him hard in the ribs.

"Mom's going to kill me if I stay," I said.

Brid's eyes sparkled. "That's not true, Rachel," she said. She drew close, so I could smell her breath, which smelled kind of like sour milk. I could hear the beat of her heart, feel the brush of her stomach. "I'm going to kill you before she does."

She took my face in her hands and kissed me, gently and deeply. I could feel her tongue tracing over my fangs, exploring my upper and lower canines. I moved against her out of habit, then stopped as the chill hit my bones.

We heard more footsteps in the hall. Clicking closer, then bam, the door again. Brid released me.

"What happened here?" Mom asked. Jonathan the non-twink Daylight representative was at her side, Diane trailing behind them with a bag of stakes—I guess just in case. Mom looked between Fawn's empty chair to the unplugged lamp and Silver on the floor to the open ventilation duct, which had been pretty brutalized in the struggle. Jonathan was in a businesslike grey turtleneck. He had a faint ginger beard—new, since the last time I'd seen him.

Brid stepped between me and my mother. "Rachel came in and found the air duct open. The blood seller trans kid had already climbed out the ceiling. This kid was trying to follow them. Rachel called for help so I came. We pulled her down."

I noticed her pronoun, for Silver.

My mom looked to me.

"She's still probably in the building," I said weakly. I could misdirect them? But Brid knew where Fawn had gone, and who helped her. She was holding it over my head that she knew. When would she let the shoe drop? Maybe at the meeting when Amber called for a leadership vote.

Unexpectedly, my mom waved a hand dismissively. "Human genderfluid kid can get lost, for all I care. They weren't turning. Just dumb."

"What if they go to Cain?" Brid asked. "They're in his whole cadre of human victims."

Mom smirked. "That would be great. We want Cain to come here, after all."

I was pretty sure by now that Fawn didn't really know Cain, or like him. She would be heading—hopefully as fast as possible—in the opposite direction.

Cain would know he wasn't safe anywhere. I didn't know if he cared about anyone, let alone the baby vampire supremacist nerd curled miserably on the floor in the white room, but my mom's guess that he'd try to have a battle to the death with her for the umpteenth time was statistically likely.

Jonathan looked uncomfortably between all of us, clearly realizing there was more happening here than he'd bargained for. "Sorry?" he asked.

"We've got what he wants. Blood, his captured little friend. Perfect time to strike. He doesn't have an organized posse right now, we just routed his friends at the Pearl. He's got all kinds of chances to try to be a hero. We let him in, and then we don't let him out. Once he falls, the Free Blood movement is just a few kids running amok."

Diane looked with discomfort at my mother and at Jonathan—my mom was getting into monologuing mode. This was her weakness. Daylight wasn't supposed to know all this yet.

"I don't know that my supervisors are going to be okay with a confrontation at the lab itself," Jonathan said, as if talking to a child. My mother ignored him.

"Rachel, good job keeping Silver here. We've got to secure him in another room, and then there's plenty of work to go round preparing for the battle."

I saw the way Diane was looking at my mom. She would follow orders, but Amber was effectively sowing doubts. Maybe just the way my mom was was sowing doubts too. I had always thought of her as such a classic leader, before. But she bossed everyone around and let people get hurt.

"Battle?" Jonathan asked. "Miss Sorkin, we really appreciate your operations, but I need you to press pause for a second here."

"The dead don't sleep, Jonny," my mother said. "I don't think you understand the ways of vampires like I do. They're good at hiding and sliming around after we kill a few of them, but we escalated something tonight. Cain's coming here, and we can beat him, but we have to be ready. Let your bosses know and I can fill them in."

She breezed out of the room, leaving Jonathan looking at Silver on the floor.

"Young lady," he said. "Can you stand? We're going to relocate you now to a more secure room."

We marched out with Silver at the front. There were four long hallways in the experiments part of the Daylight building. I'd been here before. Behind each of the doors was a vampire who either thought things were normal and they were here to get their blood tested or a vampire who was getting held against their will. Daylight had some vampires they'd deprived of blood for a while, and not given Daylight packs to yet, and they had some vampires who had been given Daylight packs at longer and longer intervals while the lamps shone on them, to find out how much Daylight fixed you so you could see the sun. We'd brought all of them here.

Silver staggered. We moved him to another white room, deeper into the labyrinth. He was chained again, and a new lamp pointed at his face. I had to think quickly about how I'd stop him from getting hurt. But I didn't know. And Brid was right behind me. When the door shut on Silver he was shooting me a curious glance, and I should have given him a confident one back. But the keys—that was my only brave thing. I couldn't figure out another one so fast.

It was two in the afternoon before the higher-ups could be scheduled to meet with us about the fact that the leader of the vampire underworld might want to break into their building. There was nowhere to shower or change, and we sat in the staff room for hours in front of a tiny TV, my mom talking the whole time and me tuning her out and Brid on patrol with Flo and then coming back to look menacingly at me. I was hoping the whole time that Fawn had gotten out, gotten away. My mom was in business mode. She'd had Stacey buy everyone coffee while coming back from taking Amber to the hospital. Stacey looked terrible. The Starbucks plastic cups wept into the little holster they'd come in. We were talking to the people more important than Jonathan who didn't usually meet with us, and Jonathan still looked nervous, and Brid still hadn't told on me, but was shooting me scary secret smiles every time our eyes met. I tried not to have them meet.

"We need to secure the warehouse areas," Mom said. "If Cain conducts a raid, those are going to be where they hit. Ideally, we want to let Cain into the building but prevent him from accessing product or test subjects."

I desperately wished I could drink coffee or sleep. I watched my mom sip the cold brew. I tried to comfort myself. After all, in a few hours I would probably be dead.

"We can station a few more contract security around," said the man whose name was Brad. "But we're familiar with

Cain. He won't operate during the day. More importantly, maybe we should work on rehousing you and the other MAVIS members temporarily. Your homes could be targets, now that you've taken out two major vampire spaces."

"Which we appreciate," said the man named Arnold. He was in a casual suit that truly rich people wore, and I could tell he had more money.

"Vampires can't access our homes without invitation," Mom said dismissively, waving her hand. "Happy to stay in a hotel, but frankly, it's not going to get that far. This is a tonight or tomorrow thing. This is not a weeks-away situation. This is tight. Think about a movie. We're in the last thirty minutes. They're almost beat, but this guy is always popping back just when you think he'd slink off."

"He has totally been popping back a lot, hasn't he?" Stacey piped up, and my mom looked over at her sharply. She'd been talking to Amber.

Arnold gave Stacey a patronizing look.

"Well," he said, "You girls sure are enterprising. I guess I can have Jonathan give you all a tour of our refrigerated warehouse areas, and you can direct our security team. I'll let you have ten more guards tonight, and we'll see if anything odd happens. We're busy with launch logistics this week, we've got Times interviews, new stuff going on with HBO for a documentary, so we won't be around, but we can hop on a meeting the day after tomorrow."

My mom smiled her cheerleader smile that was more tense these days, like a rictus. "Sure thing," she said. "I think twenty guards would be better. We had one of our crew get stabbed earlier, so we're down one."

Brad looked disturbed. Arnold looked peaceful.

"Ten," Arnold said. "They're not going to be able to get inside."

I knew Mom would make sure that they did, though.

She took me aside in the hallway, after Arnold and Brad walked away, with Brid standing right there, and it would have been the perfect time for Brid to rat me out for helping Fawn, but Brid stood there saying nothing.

"Baby," Mom said. "I want you to know how brave you're being, helping us with this. I just want you to know that we're going to get through it, okay? And when Cain is dead, and Daylight is normal, we can just be a normal family. We don't have to do all this anymore. I'll take you to the movies all the time."

It was like she knew there was something wrong with me, but she was pleading instead of getting angry. She was scared of losing me. She was scared of what I could be if she lost me. She wanted me on her side. I felt sad, suddenly. She would be so sad when I died, whether she killed me or not.

"That's okay," I said. "I mean, it's always been like this."

Brid loomed like a lightning bolt.

"You're so brave," my mom said again, and kissed me on the forehead.

Diane said, "Maybe the girls can do a tour of the storage facilities, to scope it out for security tonight. They'll know better than the contract guys what's going on."

Brid nodded. "So true. I think Rachel and I should tour the freezers. I saw them earlier. I think they're pretty secure, but the loading docks are a point of weakness. Don't you think, Rachel?"

"Yeah." I felt numb.

"Okay, great. You guys get to it," Mom said. Diane handed me some of her big bag of stakes.

"We need an authorization key. Jonathan?"

"He gave me one. This should be the uber-access code for the building. If it doesn't work, page me." The paper was handed to Brid.

All business. It was like a million other moments. I knew that Brid was going to do something when we were alone. But if someone else came along, they might gang up on me.

Down three flights of stairs, entering the access code four times at four increasingly heavy doors, me following Brid, holding the cross-body stake-holder and the stake bazooka. I wondered if she was going to kill me now. She was the most beautiful girl in the world, but it was pretty stupid of me to be in love with her. I noted that there were security cameras all over the place. I didn't know if they'd share the footage with my mom if Brid killed me, but at least someone would see her attacking me unprovoked. That wouldn't get her in trouble, but someone would know, no matter what she told people.

"It's really cold down here," I said. There were echoes of screams coming from somewhere. Tortured, strangled, monstrous. I wondered if Fawn had got out. If that other vamp was burned yet.

Brid opened a door to a heavily sealed room off a white-and-gray cement hallway. It hissed and frost-steam came out. "You won't like it in here, then, Rache," she said.

I followed her in. I don't really know why. I guess I was

just used to following her. And I wanted to know what she wanted to show me. She could have outed me in front of everyone as a double agent and executed me, and instead she had something to say. I wanted to know what.

It was blastingly cold inside the room. Colder than I had thought was necessary. After all, Daylight synth blood was shelf stable for months. Brid began to shiver almost immediately, even with her coat. I could feel my own body slowing down—I was starting at a colder temperature, and I didn't shiver.

"What's in here, anyway?" I asked. "If it's synth blood, it doesn't need this cold."

"I thought the same thing, when I came in here for the first time," Brid said. "I'll help you solve the mystery in a second." She shut the door behind us, but it couldn't latch from the inside. There wasn't a handle. A bare white line of the hallway showed in the crack, leaking cold.

"What are all these boxes?" They had writing on them in a bunch of different languages.

"Okay, Rache," she said. She snapped her fingers in front of my eyes. "Focus. We're getting there."

"Why didn't you tell Mom about what I did?"

Brid sat on a box. "Basically because I don't trust your mom."

"You don't? But she's the leader."

"I'm saying, let's face facts. You're a bloodsucking monster, and you're only going to lose more of your humanity with time. Your mom is totally duped. She thinks you're incapable of harming another soul. Flo told me you drank that trans kid's blood at the club and tried to stop Flo fucking with Cain's Death Machine. You've probably been drinking tons of blood this whole time. You're not the girl I fell in love with, even if you look the same. They've got you. And your mom is letting it rot her brain."

"I don't *want* to suck anyone's blood," I said, though I was lying. I was looking at her neck even as I said it.

"See, you're lying. I know you're lying. I just told you I know you've been drinking blood. You can't stop yourself. You'll never be normal." Brid was tearing up. "I know you want to be, but you aren't. I can't believe you're just gaslighting me, saying you don't drink blood. The Rachel I know *wouldn't lie* to me."

"Brid," I said, desperately, because her hand was on the stake at her belt. "Okay, I admit it. I drank. But you have to understand why I didn't tell. My mom has said all vampires should get staked before. And you know Amber. June's only giving me the benefit of the doubt because I'm her kid. I don't want people to think I'm a monster before I've even gotten a chance to prove myself."

"You've had a chance."

"But now Daylight is gonna come on market!" I watched her long fingers with their purple short acrylics, stroking the stake. "Daylight blood could literally help me be more ordinary than I was before! Once it hits the market, I could just drink it every day, and I wouldn't be hurting anyone. I wouldn't need to pay sellers, I wouldn't need black market blood. Neither would anyone else I think most vampires just want to be *normal*." I knew from her face that she was unmoved—how could I move her? "That's all I ever wanted. I thought that was what you wanted too. I just want to lay in the sun and laugh."

Maybe I was still beautiful. She was looking at me intently.

"I thought you wanted to be a prosecuting attorney," Brid said, scrutinizing my face. "Send vampires to jail via due legal process, so vigilante gangs didn't have to roam the streets."

She moved toward me in the cold, and the steam came from her mouth and also seemed to radiate off her in waves as she grabbed my throat and pinned me against the icy wall. "Is that not who you are anymore?"

"I don't want to be just who my mom was but worse!"

Brid grabbed a handful of my hair, pulled my head forward, and banged my head against the metal wall. Then she let me go, backed up, turned away again. "Your mom fucked up, but it's because this is her life's work and she thought it was about protecting your future. As long as you're here being a vampire, she's going to be confused."

I reeled, the thin fluorescent lights turning into twos and fours. She walked between the cold-storage bags of Daylight blood. She trailed her hand along the tops of the cardboard boxes, her sneakers squeaking on the metal floor. She flipped her ponytail over a shoulder. I could run. At any time, I could run. Where?

"It's a fantasy that Daylight is solving the problem," she said to me. "You asked why they have to keep this in freezer storage? Good question." She lifted a box, held it up to the dim white light, turned it so I could see. There were Hebrew and Arabic letters on the exterior of the cardboard. A series of barcode stickers. "Come close. The English lettering down here."

BIOLOGICAL SUBSTANCE CATEGORY B, the letters said. On another side of the box, it said, EXEMPT HUMAN SPECIMEN.

"The code here," she said, tapping the barcode. "I looked it up. It's plasma. Which, if you open one of these up, it's not red. It's like, yellow. It looks gross."

"Plasma," I said. I thought about the Daylight blood—how it made me feel good, but in a different way. How it had a different flavor, but didn't taste as bad as every other not-blood thing.

"I don't know how it goes in the Daylight stuff. It's altered structurally somehow for storage. I don't know the details. But Daylight can't operate without human victims, same as any other blood supply. I came down here first when I visited Daylight with your mom, back when we were keeping you in the dark. I guess they thought we just wouldn't look at the fucking storage room? Or that we're dumb blondes?"

"How does that make any sense," I said. "Blood from abroad is already on the black market. Why would they use plasma from abroad?"

"Maybe it takes less plasma to make the juice than it takes regular blood. Just a little dot of plasma and dilute. There's other stuff in some of these too, in addition to plasma. I don't know what all the codes are."

I thought about how Cain said that drinking enough blood let you withstand daytime sunlight too. Maybe if Daylight was working the same way, it was just because there was enough concentrated blood-adjacent stuff in their product. From lots of people. It did eerily cohere.

"These boxes are from Israel, from Ecuador, from Indonesia and India and Ghana and Brazil and the Congo. There're different ones at different times. I don't think Daylight is probably too keen on anyone asking questions about their precise procurement process. But they think we're dumb muscle. Jonathan gave June the access codes."

"It's wrong," I said. "You're wrong. All this must be for something else. Their blood doesn't even taste like blood."

"And you would know how blood tastes."

"I got the baggies from the government! Of course I know! But this—this is obviously sketch, but maybe they're using it in the experiments, not the actual product."

"The supply problems they were having," Brid said. "Remember? Why would they have supply problems for their stuff if it was synthetic?"

"Chemical supplies, I guess," I said, though I saw what she saw. "Are you sure these are like, used in making Daylight?"

Brid leaned back comfortably on the boxes. "I'm so sure that I've already leaked a bunch of photos to the press. Times, journal, post, mail, whatever. Local and national. There's so much angst around here about the vampire spike, and the government's turning over the whole supply to this sketch company that's buying war blood or whatever from abroad, just to feed our demon problem. Big story. Unless someone high up kills it, it's going live next week."

"Mom's gonna kill you," I gasped, but as I said it, I realized that Mom was on her way out. She wouldn't be killing anyone soon, especially after this story broke. She'd pushed the alliance with Daylight. Now everyone would turn on her, even Diane. And Brid was careful. She would find a way to not implicate MAVIS in all this. Amber was the one who was after Mom, but she wasn't likable enough. Brid was going to be the new leader.

She was going to fuck Flo, I suddenly realized. Maybe she already had. It would be how she kept Flo in check.

I was struck with how smart she was. How on top of the Nancy Drew mystery of it all. But there was a bigger problem.

"I thought I was going to be okay," I said. My voice sounded small. It cracked. I hadn't realized how much I was actually banking on not needing to find blood from people, quenching the thirst that I knew burned in me, unquenchable. "I thought I wasn't going to need . . ."

Brid's hazel eyes studied me. They were big, luminous eyes. They were meant to stare out from a magazine or a children's biography of the first woman president. They weren't sympathetic, but they were tender. She reached out for me. I let her take my upper arms in her hands. She brought her face close to mine, brushed my mouth with hers.

"Oh, Rachel," she said softly.

Her voice was low. I had often touched the small of her back. I wanted to now. I let my hand creep around, feel her blue veins brimming, feel the gentle bumps of her spine. She was so warm in the dark, even though she was shivering.

"Please don't kill me," I said.

"I showed you this because I wanted to help you understand. I didn't want you to think that I wanted this. But I saw you help that trans freak. I know what you're doing." I was still hanging onto her back, and her hand was bringing the stake up between us, pointed at my heart. "There's no way you can live except by blood. What kills me is you could have just let him kill you. Instead you drank."

"I had to," I said. I was still holding her, letting my hands slip around her hips.

"You know there's only one thing to do."

Brid has a way of always being right. And I knew she was. There was only one thing to do, and I did it.

I had drunk Fawn's blood, and I was stronger than I had been for a while. I grabbed the hand holding her stake and twisted it. For whatever reason she didn't expect it: her grip loosened, the stake fell, and I lashed forward and sank my teeth into her neck. She fought against me, screaming, pulling against my grip, and her blood flowed hot against my mouth, filling me with new strength as I did what I had been thinking about doing every time I saw her since I turned—though it did taste different, feel different, I noticed. It didn't feel as good to get it like this. I couldn't kill her, either. I tossed her backward, skidding across four frozen boxes, toppling the last in the line to the next aisle. Her feet went up, and she made a beautiful grunt. I grabbed a box of plasma and ran for the door.

When I got there, I shut it behind me, wiping my mouth. The handle was only on the outside.

The latch flipped up. I didn't have the access code to get out of the long hallway, so when I hit the EXIT sign door, the alarm sounded. It rang long and loud as I went up and around three flights of stairs. I ran into Diane on my way up, when I was back on the level we'd come in on.

"Where are you going?" she asked.

"I have to take something to Mom," I said, gesturing to the box.

"She's up with the prisoner," Diane said. "Leave it with me."

"Sorry," I said. "She was specific. I gotta go find her."

Diane let me go and turned to her phone. She was texting someone rapidly.

I wasn't sure why I was clutching the box, what I was doing. I had been, for a second, trying to find my mom. Now I wasn't. I ran past two people in scrubs, down the hall, into the sunlit glass lobby. I had been drinking the thing made from plasma from people from around the world, and also my ex-girlfriend's blood, so the sun didn't hurt me when it shone in dazzling sparkles across the mica-studded marble floor. I pushed open the door to the parking lot and went outside.

16.

FAWN

Not all air ducts lead outside. However, after crawling through twenty or thirty feet of buckling duct that crunched and bent as I traveled, I scrambled to the nearest vent, punched through it with a screwdriver, and kicked it until it gave way and I dropped to the floor. Nobody saw me, though I created enough of a racket. I was lucky. I could hear people in a room adjacent to me, yelling. I found myself close to a fire exit that was propped open. I shouldered it and no alarm sounded. A guy in scrubs outside on the gravelly pavement was smoking and looking at his phone, and he didn't look up when I passed. A big truck was parked lower down, near a loading dock, and it was making so much noise, with its backing up and beeping, that nobody looked at me. I didn't want to just walk across the parking lot, so I walked to the edge of the woods where the other vampire had run when it was still dark. It was a scrubby hill; at the bottom it ran into a suburban fence. I climbed it, feeling my arms turning to jelly.

There was a dog barking at me, but it was small, and I got around it and to the street as an old woman peered at me from a window across the street. At the bottom of a cul de sac, there was a bus stop.

I had eighty dollars in my pocket still.

Wait—

No I didn't. They must have taken it back from me when I fainted. Against paying for blood on policy.

I had my phone. It was on 8 percent.

The first thing I did, not because I necessarily thought it would work, but because it seemed like some kind of obligation, was call 911. When they picked up, I said,

"It seems like there's a torture lab in Daylight Inc's headquarters in North Seattle. I just got brought there with my head in a bag and they're like, burning vampires and keeping them locked up there. Just thought you should know."

The operator started to ask a question, but then my phone died.

Richeza was first on the list of ideas I had. I had to get to her house, and from there to Cain. What an exhausting multi-step process. I looked nervously around myself while waiting for the bus. My hair was in knots. My clothes were dirty from the van and the brush. There was one middle-aged woman walking her dog that I had no doubt wanted to kill me, but she didn't. The bus eventually came. I didn't pay the fare, but the bus driver said nothing.

It was an uncommonly sunny day, and the bus ride through the arteries of the highway and back to the hill was sweaty. I was dehydrated. I needed liquids. I probably needed food in general. When I stood from the bus seat, I reeled again, stars swimming. I needed to eat. I remembered the walk to Richeza's. Up the hill, through the park. Near where Roxanne and Raina were hopefully fine. They would probably not enjoy seeing me.

When I got to Richeza's, I could feel the prickle under my armpits and the ache in my head. I galloped up through the ominous carpeted stairwell and then almost collapsed at the top. I was winded, and I did not feel good. I was dizzy and nauseous. My skin was cold. I didn't have enough fluids in me. I retched, then caught myself on the wall. Leaned on it, walking, until I reached her door, and rang.

She opened it, and her ears perked up and she grinned a terrible *Where The Wild Things Are* grin and her eyes flashed—and then her face fell as, I guess, she took in the mess that was me. Behind her, a record player was playing opera music.

"Oh, you are not looking good," she said, pulling back from the door and crossing her arms. "This is why I don't like young people, you're stupid. What happened?"

I held up a hand to say I'd explain when I felt less dizzy, and she glanced down the hallway and pulled me inside, her long twisted fingers holding me up until I sat down on the bed. It felt so good to sit down that I laid down. She went to the sink and got water in a cup, and then dug under her cabinets. She came over with a protein bar and a Gatorade and perched next to me.

"Start with this," she said. "It won't fix you immediately. Ah, I'm going to turn off this music. Forgive my love of opera. My sire, before he passed, was there at its dawn, in the days of Jacopo Peri. So why are you coming to me? You must know you can't give more blood. What are you looking to me for? Are you in trouble? Were you attacked?"

I held up my phone. "My phone's dead. Do you . . . ?"

She went to rummage in a drawer. "I know I have one of this kind of charger. I took it from the library."

The one she drew out of her drawer had a lot of exposed wire showing, like it had been chewed on. But my phone started charging. She went to the mini freezer and brought back an ice pack and gestured to my eye.

Her interest in me seemed at once caring and also had a kind of prurient quality—she leaned in to stare excitedly at my bruise as she brought ice.

I chugged the Gatorade and held up a finger to say wait a second, feeling so grateful for her ancient, stonelike, alien, feline face. It was a relief that she'd let me in. I didn't know what I would have done if she hadn't. She was peering at me from the corner, wrapping herself in an afghan at the same time.

"If it was a vampire that drank too much, I can deal with them," she said seriously, as she waited for me to catch my breath.

"Slayers," I said, finally, having finished the Gatorade. "Raided the Pearl. Last night. A lot of people are dead, I think."

"They hurt you?" Richeza seemed to be calculating whether she could do anything about slayers. I realized I probably looked pretty bad. I could feel my eye swelling.

"Yes. But also I gave too much blood to my friend."

She nodded slowly. "You asked about the bar, and I told you to be careful, that slayers can show up. You remember?"

"I know," I said. "But I was right. My friend was there. He escaped alive when everyone was getting staked. Now I need to find Cain and get him to help me rescue Silver."

Richeza drew her hand back from my knee and waved it furiously in the air. "No, no. I will help you kill the slayers after you recover, as I am sworn to protect any human I signal favor for, and I am true to my word. You hear me?" She waved her fingers in front of my open eye, snapped them. "I am true."

"I hear you," I said. "I don't need you to avenge me."

"No, I will kill whoever hurt you. But I will not talk to that man."

"Okay, okay," I said. "Calm down."

"Don't trust him. He says he was on the House of Lords and holds up this picture that looks like him now, the beard. He says, this picture is from 1872. But he didn't look like that. I know. I met him then. He didn't have a beard until—maybe 1985, because then he got the injections, the testosterone." She pronounced it like macaroni, with some humor. "In the 1970s, he was just turned, just starting to live as a man. He looked like Mercedes de Acosta. He lies like a rug. We all must lie sometimes. But he tries to make a movement and it is all stories."

"Where's his money from, if he's so young?"

"He ran a check fraud scam at one time in the 1980s. He got in on the dot com boom, for one minute in the 1990s. It's mostly gone now. You saw the club."

I started eating the protein bar, processing this information. I wondered why it hadn't come up before, that Cain was trans. This also seemed to imply some things about vampire endocrinology I had been wondering about. "I don't need you to talk to him," I said eventually between bites. "Just tell me where he might be, if you know. Where he might run to after a fight. I'll try to convince him."

"Convince him what?"

"To go rescue my friend. He's at Daylight. And there's other vampires trapped in the Daylight Inc. building. They've been doing experiments on vampires, burning them. I got brought there because they thought I might turn into one of you. I escaped."

Richeza was now looking at me over long fingers folded in a temple. "You were kidnapped by Slayers and lived and got out. To me, that is enough. You need to leave town for a while." I couldn't tell if she registered the Daylight Inc. thing.

"I think the lead slayer's daughter is on our side. We might be able to defeat them if she works with us."

"Don't trust anyone, Fawn," Richeza said.

"I've been trusting people this whole time," I said. "It's how I got here. It's why I'm alive." I saw what Richeza meant, but I meant what I said too. Rachel had seemed confused and flighty, but she wasn't all slayer either. I had felt the need she had, when she drank. A lot of ifs. A lot of bad ideas. But if bad ideas had got me here . . .

"You've been very lucky. But you must leave Seattle. The Sorkin woman's crew is bad news. The clinics and the shelter and now the Pearl. They're declaring war."

"It's the Daylight Pharma thing. The synthetic blood. The city's switching over the supply to this company. Everyone who's getting it from the government has to switch. And they're—Daylight's paying the slayers to destroy vampire spaces where people get anything else, to force everyone to take it." I sounded a little insane, but the day had been insane.

Richeza squinted at me. She reached under her bed, and pulled out a phone. It looked incongruous in her hand. She went to the camera and opened the roll to a screenshot of an email.

"That is very interesting. My friend Sigo got this. He sent it to me. I don't use . . . phone apps. He's registered. It says they're acquiring synthetic blood from a new supplier beginning Friday. This must be the thing what you're saying."

"That's it," I said, glad that she had confirmed that some of what I was saying was true. I laid back on the bed and closed my eye. My head was throbbing. "Can you hand me my phone?"

I logged on to Tumblr.

Cain, I sent. Hope you're alive. I am alive, if you care. You are a cunt, but I need to talk to you. Been to the Daylight headquarters and escaped. They have Silver. He's alive. I can help you break in. We need to destroy the supply so they can't switch vampires over to synth blood. Here's my number.

Richeza looked for something else for me to eat, and found a can of garbanzo beans, a jar of peanut butter, and a packet of ramen. I took the peanut butter and a spoon.

She sat on the floor and drank a pack of blood. I looked around as I ate at what she'd been doing before I came: on the little folding table in the corner, she was cutting apart old National Geographics and arranging a lot of small photographs of coral on a new sheet of paper, in a spiral that spread outward.

"Do you have someone out of town who can come get you?" Richeza asked. She changed the record.

I dug Wanda's card out from my pants. Richeza looked. "Oh, Wanda Olejnik," she said, with some approval. "Strange you know her. She is good. She might be somewhere within a day's drive."

"You know her."

"It is a small enough world for the old." Richeza raised an eyebrow.

Richeza called Wanda.

My phone was buzzing too. An unknown number was calling me.

His voice, over the phone, was staticky, like he was in an area with very little service.

"—Nd the f—"

"Who is this, what?" I strained to hear. There was mainly the noise of distortion.

"Fawn. Fawn, can you hear me?"

He came into focus, and I felt odd relief at hearing that high, villainous voice.

"I can hear you."

"I thought I would die," Cain said, his voice cracking. "He's alive? I have been walking around with a stake pointed at my chest."

“And here I thought you didn’t have a heart,” I snapped. “Look, cut the theater.”

“Fawn, I am so sincerely sorry. I will tell you, last night didn’t go as planned. I meant to trap June in a big mousetrap, but it didn’t work. It was that stupid boy Idris’s fault. The mechanism failed. Since Sam died, I trusted it all to him. Oh, tell me that Silver is safe.” His voice fluttered between hysterics and droll gravity, each sentence lilting up.

“Silver is not safe,” I said. I was annoyed that he had slipped so easily into accusations. “We’ll save him. Tell me where you are. I’ll come to you.”

“Oh, dear girl. Do come to me. We’ll put together a plan. You can feed me . . .”

“Don’t do that,” Richeza snapped, loudly. “Stay here until Wanda can get you.”

“Who’s with you?” Cain said. His voice instantly darkened into suspicion.

“A vampire who hates you,” I said. “I’m not too hot on you myself, but we’ve got to fight the slayers. We have to free the vampires that Daylight has in their building. I think you have the power to do that.”

“If we have allies . . .” Cain said. “Oh, dear, I just got the most splitting headache. I am awash in agony and relief. Agony, my friends are mostly ash or have turned on me. Relief—my Silver is alive and I have you. I worry that I will never see him again. We have not a minute to lose.”

“I’ll try my best, Cain. My friend is telling me to stay put for a second. I’m still recovering from having two pints of my blood drunk yesterday and then having the crap beaten out of me.”

There was a brief muffled silence, where Cain seemed to be formulating an idea.

"Can you go by Home Depot on your way here, for supplies?"

"Where are you?" I pressed.

"We're in the crypts at Cavalry. Me and the young Aurelius. Where are you?"

"I'm at 1005 East Roy," I said. "Near the top of Cap Hill."

"You don't have a car, do you?" Cain asked, as if it was likely.

"Suck a *dick*," I said venomously. "God, you're useless. You don't know a single person who could lend us a car?"

"You may be unaware, dear child, of how hard it is to get a car or driving license when one has been officially dead since 1874."

"I've only been in this scene a few weeks," I said, remembering Richeza saying Cain lied about his age. "There's gotta be someone."

"Alas . . . maybe it is time I simply fell on this stake after all. Oh . . ."

I let out a strangled frustrated moan. This man was worse than useless.

Richeza, who was still waiting on Wanda to pick up, shushed me.

"Cain," I said. "I know you have some kind of complicated psycho-whatever thing going on with my friend. I don't think it's good for you or him, even if it's less creepy than it looks. Even if he makes you feel good about yourself and vice versa. I think you suck. But deeper than that, I believe in a world where you can get what you need, and where I can too. And people who don't believe in that world want to kill us. And I think you might be the only one who can kill June. So I am going to fight with you and whoever else against the slayers, and I will fight till I am dead."

"Forget about it, Fawn. I will just perish, knowing my son will follow me soon to that great Hell in the sky, beyond the moon . . ."

"Shut up. You're both still alive. We have shared material interests in defeating these people, and we have to defeat them before Daylight monopolizes vampire blood supply."

"If we have no car . . ."

"June knows where you are," I said. I didn't know this for sure, but it seemed a good guess. "Get her before she gets you."

It got Cain. He was silent. "Shit."

"I'm going to get to Calvary," I said. "I'll work on the car, you piece of shit. You try too." I hung up.

I turned to Richeza.

"I am going to go fight the slayers," I said. "Question one, do you have a car. Question two, what do I need to know about recovering from losing two pints?"

Richeza was tapping her phone angrily with her thumb. When I spoke, she shook a finger at me with her other hand without looking up. "You should be drinking the fluids, the Gatorade, and resting," she said. "You're being stupid, little one. Look, I can't go with you in the day. I am not drinking enough blood for that kind of energy. Can you wait and rest, and go seek this asshole at night?"

This was a possibility, but I had a feeling Silver wouldn't appreciate it. And if the other slayers figured out Rachel was sort of on the other side now, she wouldn't last long either.

Why did I have to be a hero, instead of just waiting here for Wanda to show up and sweep me into the sunset and a life of certain poverty and crime?

But the slayers would eliminate every vampire in Seattle who didn't obey them if someone didn't stop Daylight and June Sorkin.

"I have to go," I said. "I'm gonna sit here for twenty minutes and eat the rest of the peanut butter, but then I have to go get another bus."

Richeza shook her head, and briefly, her fangs and fur emerged. "No, no, I will have Pola send someone with a car. She has a caretaker, you know. I will ask."

She put a finger in her mouth and held it out to me. "Drink a drop of my blood with the venom in it. No more, or it will overwhelm your immune system and start your transformation. But this will get you through today."

I tasted the black pinprick of blood. I did immediately feel a jolt.

The person who showed up with the car was not the same guy who had misgendered me in Gefen's. It was Millie from the shelter. The windows were blacked out, so I couldn't tell till she rolled one down. She had a brace on her neck. I felt kind of relieved seeing her, since it was confirmation she was alive.

"It's you," she said to me through the window.

"It's me," I said. "You work for Pola too."

"Only so many vampires can pay for work," she said drily.

"Uh, thanks for finding me housing."

"Let me get this straight," she said, when I swung into the car. "I'm taking you to the Calvary cemetery, and then I'm dropping you off at a medical facility because you are fighting slayers? Single-handed?"

I wasn't sure on her thoughts on Cain. "I'm grabbing a couple friends," I said.

"It's a pretty suicidal mission. Enough people have died. I'm surprised Richeza's down for you pulling that shit."

"They don't hurt humans," I said.

"That's not exactly true," Millie said, and gestured to the brace on her neck. "They didn't stop to check whether my heart was beating before pitching me down the stairs. I think they're also not super keen on trans people."

"Right. But they're not supposed to kill us."

"I think this is dumb," Millie said. "With everything happening. I'll drive you to the cemetery, but I am not into this."

"I'm going to try to rescue Ned," I said, since I knew she knew Ned. "I have a girl on the inside."

True? I should probably text Rachel, though that could also blow her cover.

I wasn't sure how much I wanted to involve this random woman in the scheme I had going, or even if I had a scheme sort of adequate to the stakes, so to speak, but I also needed the help.

"They have *Ned*?" Millie asked, turning to me, her tone immediately grave. Her whole demeanor changed. She'd been about to pull out of the parking space. "Is there any chance he's still alive?"

"I think so. They have vampires being held at the Daylight lab as test subjects. They have some of them there willingly for the study, but when they took me there I saw hallways where there were like, people yelling behind doors, super scary."

Millie took out her phone. "Hold on. Before we go on a suicide mission, we need to like, get you saying all this. Before they impale you. I need to let people know what's happening. Where Ned is. There's a listserv, there's a Discord. For human allies and the unregistered vampires who have phones. We can try to see if anyone else wants to help."

This was a more useful suggestion than anything Richeza had said.

She hit record, capturing me probably not looking my best. I didn't want to know how greasy, pale, puffy, beat to hell or unwashed I looked. I stuttered for a second, then tried to summarize, as best as I could, the raid at the Pearl, how the Slayers had infiltrated, then busted in through the roof, how I'd been captured, and what I'd seen at the lab. I left Rachel's name out, but I mentioned that she'd hired me and used me to find the entrance. Millie turned the camera around on herself.

"If anyone is doubting this girl, I can say she's a real seller, I've met her before all this went down. She's got literally no reason to put herself in harm's way over this. I don't advocate for taking actions where you could get hurt, but if you can help her, and can stand the sun, and feel like starting a riot, head to Daylight Inc."

She posted it to a private channel on Discord and then to her Insta story, covering my face with a big emoji.

"Is it safe for Facebook to have that?" I asked. "I feel like they have access to the un-emoji version."

"No," Millie said. "But it won't matter by the time they flag it."

"Thanks for your confidence," I said, feeling my stomach flip.

"I can't fight," Millie said, pulling out of the parking space into traffic. "I am not interested in fighting a bunch of cis women wielding sharp sticks. But I can park outside and drive. If you get out, I can drive you somewhere and drop you off after. If cops show up, I am moving the car, but I'll text you."

Walking between where Richeza lived and Ravenna would have taken me about two hours, assuming I was well enough to walk that long. A bus would have been forty-five minutes. In a car, it took fifteen minutes. We slid onto the highway and off it, and drove past a mall, up the hill to the cemetery. The gates were open; it was a big, dry lawn, interspersed with gravestones. A looping car path tracked in a rough circle, with the rows of graves in between. Millie pulled over under a blooming cherry tree, its pink blossoms scattered on the rough yellow grass. I wondered how, exactly, vampires got past the regular security people. Maybe they had a rent system. I texted Cain.

He called me within seconds. "Head to the big sarcophagus next to the St. James monolith, human girl. We've got a staircase there."

I saluted Millie, who was looking increasingly like she wanted to turn around, and looked around for what he was talking about for about eight minutes. Eventually I found it—a brown marble arch with a little pope guy on it, labeled St. James. I texted, *I'm here.*

A tile, about a foot and a half wide, slid solidly aside behind the marble arch. A hand waved from the dark, square hole—in the weak sunlight, it didn't burn.

If I turned my body diagonally, I could just slide on my ass down the tiny, steep stone steps embedded into the tunnel below the trapdoor opening. I could make out the shadowy figure of Cain in the darkness, stooped under the low tile ceiling. He moved away into the tunnel, beckoning silently for me to follow.

How did Cain get down here? I wondered, looking up at the hole I'd just crawled through.

I walked down the completely black corridor into the subterranean cold. The walls were slightly clammy when I put out a hand to feel for them. At the end of the hall, a green lightbulb shone from beneath a black-shaded lamp, plugged into a generator. I went inside the eerily lit stone room. I peered in. There was a figure that must be Aurelius, Silver's other friend, huddled in a corner, under a quilt, his wings spread over him. A box of blood packs sat in the middle of the room on a low table. Cain sat himself in an antique rocking chair next to a gramophone, holding a pack of blood, which he was rolling up like a tube of toothpaste as he drank from a hole in the top. His face was half-shadow, half-green. His fingers were long and talon-like. His wings must not have been out. They would have hurt on the straight-backed chair.

"Hello, human savior," he rasped. "I hear you have a plan to make all right with the world. I was experiencing, it must be said, a moment of devastation, but I am ready to help you. Tell me about how you will redeem our hordes from irreparable destruction."

"It sort of depends," I said. "How many vampires do you think would still do what you asked them to do?"

Cain's face grotesquely crumpled. He bent his head and began to softly howl.

"Okay," I said, watching the unmoving lump of Aurelius. "Does that mean twelve? Does that mean zero?"

Cain shook his head sharply. "Girl," he said, and then hiccuped. "Once, I could command a legion of thousands from here to Santa Barbara. From here to Monterey. My howls are for those lost in the war against the *wretched* Moms."

"Okay," I said. I leaned in to look him in his face, close. This was the man who people spoke about like he ran things. There had to be power in there. "How many?"

He paused, seeming taken aback, considering. "Many will leave town after last night. I don't blame them. I think we are likely to be able to get about thirty younglings who will be willing to fight MAVIS. Their elders and I have too much dark history."

"Let me register," I said, "that the thing where you don't have anyone your age who likes you indicates something negative. But thirty. That's fine. Thirty is more than the slayers. They've got like, what, ten?"

Cain shook his head. "They have Shelton and Tacoma and Spokane people too, perhaps. They've got at least twenty-five active slayers in the county."

"Thirty versus twenty-five. Not bad."

"They love to indiscriminately kill," Cain said. "We do not. No matter what they say about me, I love blood, not death. We cannot let more die."

"You could have worked harder to stop the slayers last night, or to have better exits for emergencies" I said. "And you could have made it harder to find."

Cain began to howl again like a wounded animal, putting his long hands up into his long hair. I was sick of his shit. I continued.

"We'll try to minimize the casualties. Are you all vulnerable to guns?"

"It's going to hurt. Unless our body is blown apart, it won't kill us," Cain said, snapping out of his howl. "A shotgun would be worse, but I don't believe MAVIS uses those. They're too messy and loud. A machine gun would seriously hurt us."

"So, the biggest problem is stakes and those crossbow things. Has anyone ever tried wearing like, armor against that?"

Cain nodded. He lifted his shirt, showing me that he was wearing a chainmail shirt under his piratelike frock. "Most don't enjoy it because it's so heavy," he said. "And expensive. I had some made years ago. It won't stop a crossbow, but they can't tip or weight them with metal, so it'll often blunt against the armor and won't penetrate my heart. It's more ribs broken."

"There don't happen to be wholesale suppliers of these who could get us thirty in the next couple hours?" I asked.

"Not a chance, dear," Cain said. "It's custom. A bullet-proof vest would be better. But motorcycle jackets work okay for non-projectile stakes. And most of us have some kind of motorcycle jacket." He waved a hand. "I have five chainmail vests," he said dolorously. "We can distribute them."

"Here?"

"Down the hall. And sunscreen."

"Cain," I said. "I am going to go to get that stuff. Can you work on summoning your Lost Boy army or whatever? Can you contact people to come to Daylight and fight?"

He snuffled through his batlike nose. "You are noble, little Dawn," he said.

"It's Fawn," I said. "Get it right or I'm leaving you here to stake yourself." I paused. "Can you make sure Angie is there? Or ask her? I feel like she might be useful."

Millie was waiting against the car when we emerged from the hidden tile again, dragging two duffel bags that barely fit through the hole. Aurelius was still sleeping; it was decided he would stay hidden, with a note next to him to explain where we had gone.

"No way," Millie said, when she saw Cain. He had de-morphed for the purpose of striding across the graveyard, so in his charred velvet vest, long white hair and rectangular sunglasses he looked, if anything, like the author of a steampunk webcomic about to give a talk at a convention, but he still wore a hooded cowl and had long, long fingers. Again, I wondered how the graveyard staff could possibly miss it—unless they were vampires, too. He was carrying a flowered handbag filled with packs of blood and ice packs.

"He can walk in sunlight, Millie, and he's got wings," I said. "If you know anyone else with those qualities, feel free to ask them."

"I'm not the only one who can walk in sunlight," Cain sniffed. "Anyone can, if they feed well enough."

"You're a terrible influence on kids. You make them act in dangerous ways," Millie said to Cain, as he climbed into the back seat, checking the skin on his hands. It was fine.

"My dear," he said. "People have been saying that to me since I was a child myself."

Millie looked at me sternly. "You did *not* mention him."

"I know," I said. "It would have been counterproductive. Are you out? I can drive."

"I'm not handing my car off to *him*," Millie hissed to me in a whisper. "I drive, but I am not guaranteeing I'm waiting around for him if he's the last out. Pola doesn't pay me enough."

Cain heard. He brushed his hair back from his tall white forehead. "My darling," he said, "We will fly, if necessary, on the way back." He sounded a little better than he had before; an antagonistic audience brought something out in him. "I've asked the young ones to join us. Human Free Blood youth and vampires. There is a fair bit of risk, as you have acknowledged, Fawn. Not everyone is interested."

I thought about the mixed crowd at Cain's bar. People had trusted his space; they'd discovered it wasn't safe. They'd seen him flee. Only a specific kind of person would come out of that burning theater with a quest for revenge against MAVIS, rather than Cain.

Millie turned the key in the engine. "Okay, so are we picking anyone up?"

"There are three humans who can take a bus. There are six vampires who have sun immunity and can fly. There are four vampires who need transport," Cain said, counting on his fingers and looking at his phone.

"Flying in daytime?" Millie asked drily, pulling out of the cemetery onto 50th.

"Blood will allow it. We have a couple human donors. We are all interdependent, and the slayers hate our delicate, beautiful, reciprocal network," Cain said, resting his head against the glass of the window and closing his eyes. There was something mildly sardonic in his voice.

"They want me in jail or something," I said. Flo would kill me if she could.

"Humans could also just come out themselves. The goal is to stop the operation of the lab, right?" Millie asked. "Does anyone know how to make like, a low-grade explosive? Or something to contaminate the product? Are we trying to destroy product or steal it?"

"Stealing it would be good," Cain said. "If only we had a truck."

I had an idea about Wanda. I opened my phone to text

Richeza. Then I realized I could just text Wanda—her number on the card was engraved into my memory. I started to type.

"I think a good idea would be to start a fire," Cain said. "As they did to us. Drive them out, rescue our people. Have an attack team, a rescue team. I shall be on both. I will disarm them. Fawn, do you know where in the building Silver is being kept?"

"I think he was probably moved. We'll have to search. Do we need to wait until nightfall?"

Cain shook his head. "My young ones who have confirmed are available now. Here are their addresses."

"But the vampires we're trying to rescue won't be able to safely leave the building when it's light out," Millie said, squinting at the first address and typing it into her phone for navigation with one hand. "They haven't been blood-maxing like you two. And Daylight blood takes a while to give protection."

Cain checked his watch. "The sun will go down in about three hours. But it's also supposed to rain. I see a heavy cloud. We can get there an hour before sunset."

Millie put the clicker on as she prepared to turn. "I think we have time to make a few Molotov cocktails. I'm going to stop for some supplies."

17.

RACHEL

Running down a suburban street while holding a frozen cardboard box of plasma felt too conspicuous. Probably in the next hour, someone was going to notice me and Brid were missing. What could I do?

There had been sunlight pouring down when I left through the doors, nobody turning to stop me.

Now a cloud passed over the sun, and I felt a few drops on my head. It hit me that I was entirely alone in the universe. There was nobody who liked me. There was nothing for me. I was recognizable as the daughter of a woman who had tried to kill vampires, and vampires everywhere would continue to recognize me. Brid knew I was a traitor.

I wanted to live.

It was at that moment a small Subaru with blacked-out windows screeched to a halt on the side of the wide, empty road that led through the neighborhoods to Daylight. A door opened.

"Rachel!"

I turned, holding the box. I saw Fawn's face. I staggered backward. She was in a car, and the car had other people in it too—I saw multiple sets of glowing red eyes in the shadow of the door.

Fawn got out and came toward me. "Rachel, we're going to get Silver out. We're going to free the other vampires. We need you. Are you leaving?"

"I don't know what I'm doing," I said. Without thinking about it, I set the box down and ran forward. I threw my arms around her. "I'm sorry for not saving Silver. I'm sorry."

"This isn't over yet," Fawn said. She didn't hug back. Instead, she pushed me back a little, but gently. It hurt my feelings more than I wanted it to. "We have to dismantle Daylight."

"We have to get *out of here*," I said.

"There's still people inside," she said. The tone in her voice told me she thought I was totally evil and stupid for ignoring that. Maybe I was evil and stupid. Maybe I'd been raised to be evil and stupid and now I was stuck. But what was I supposed to do? There wasn't a big red button that opened all the doors.

"Brid tried to kill me," I said, by way of explanation. "I had to leave."

"Well, you have to go back in," one of the red-eyed, shadowy figures in the backseat of the car rasped. "We've got to get in there."

"Little Sorkin," a familiar voice intoned. I stepped back, a big step. "I am pleased to learn that you are considering assisting your own kind."

I saw the ruby shoes flash in the bottom of the backseat.

"Him?" I asked Fawn. "Him? He's the monster who turned me!"

She glanced into the car. "Cain?"

I turned around, crossing my arms, and walked away a few paces like I was thirteen and throwing a tantrum at the mall. I knew I looked ridiculous; I felt so much shame and anger. I realized that every minute I spent standing here was a minute that my mom was probably putting pieces together. I wished I had wings so I could just take off into the sky too. Maybe they'd already released Brid by now. Maybe they were looking at the security camera footage. "I won't work with him," I said to Fawn. "The slayers are bad, but he's bad too."

"Okay," Fawn said. "Well, it makes sense that you were attacked if you were a slayer. Work with me, though. If you're changing your mind about what side you're on, stick to it. We have to rescue the vampires in there."

Through the air above us, there came the unexpected flapping of enormous, leathery wings. I looked up, rain getting in my eyes, as four figures caught low tree branches in the Douglas Firs that lined the road, bouncing a little before descending with four thuds in the scrub on the side of the street.

"Rachel," Angie said. She was the biggest of the winged teen vampires before me, recognizable even though her nose was flat and her face was hairy and distorted. She had a split lip and a bruise on her forehead. "Surprised to see you here." She glanced at Fawn. "We doing in the slayer vamp first?"

"No," Fawn said. "She's a friend. She's changed sides."

"She killed that girl Whitney, I know it. Didn't you?" Angie stepped around me, got up in my face. I looked back into her thick, round, confident one, sharp-toothed and possibly homicidal.

That was my girlfriend, not me was a weak defense. I hadn't stopped her. Whitney was dead, and I had pretended I was powerless. I could think of hundreds of times where my hand had held the stake, where I'd thought of the person on the other end of the point as an it. The weight of it was like a wave that threatened to sweep me under. Angie's pug nose and beady, intent eyes didn't let me sidestep it, the way I'd been doing for so long. "The slayers do kill people," I stammered. "I killed people. And I hate that. I thought vampires were cursed to be evil, but now I don't. I don't want to be one of the slayers anymore."

"And we're supposed to trust you," Angie said. "That's a stretch."

The three other vampire teens with her weren't people I recognized. I didn't see Jay, and that made me worry, even if Jay had annoyed me. I had seen how vast the fire was.

"Angie," Fawn said. "You can do something totally unrelated to Rachel. You don't have to rely on her."

"So we know she's not communicating with June?"

Fawn looked at me appraisingly. "I do think the best thing for you to do, Rachel, is go back inside like nothing has happened, talk to your mom to distract her, and wait for the signal, and then help us get in the back after we cause a distraction in the front."

I didn't have a chance to say what I thought of that.

There was another flap of wings, and another set of recognizable boots landed in front of me. The tall woman who wore them was wearing sunglasses, a hood, and a KN95 mask and gloves, and held herself like she maybe had a pain in her leg, and she staggered a little on landing. I looked up into her face nervously. Her red eyes were keen and bright behind the sunglasses; when she pulled down her mask for a second to wipe her nose, her fangs showed white against her sienna skin. I felt so guilty I might fall into a hole.

"This is where the party starts, then," Erica said. She squinted at the car. "I read on Discord from Millie about the Pearl, that they had Ned after the raid on the shelter, and that things were going down here. I saw Fawn's video. I wanted to find out exactly what was up. Some ragtag idiots without a clue what they're doing, it looks like. That you in there, Cain? You running this show?"

I didn't want to look at her face. "Erica," I said. *You have wings* was the thought in the front of my mind. She must have drunk more blood than normal to get them—whose? Roxanne's? After that in my head was the image of her bending over Roxanne tenderly, the feeling of wanting the warmth that would include me in its glow.

"Rachel," she said.

"She's a slayer," Angie said. "She's June Sorkin's daughter."

Erica shook her head. "No she's—"

I bit my lip; she saw. Existential terror. Erica's eyes widened. Then she clapped her hands and spun in a circle, came back to looking at all of us.

"Okay. I don't really know what to think, but as long as

we're on the same team, we can sort it out later. Where are we at? What's happening? Is anyone paying attention to a bunch of bat-winged vampires hanging out on the side of the road?"

Millie climbed out of the driver door. "They're going to be in a second," she said. "I'm going to re-park the car." She went around to the back of the trunk and opened it. She handed Fawn an empty glass bottle, and then a rag, and then moved to hand the same items from her bag to the winged vampires. "Gasoline tank's in the back here," she said. "Bic lighter for everyone. Hammer for everyone. Fawn?"

Erica balked at the Molotov supplies. "Millie," she said. "That shit's gonna get you on federal charges."

Millie's face was close and guarded. "Play it safe then," she said. "But they have Ned in there."

Erica took a bottle and a rag, and let Millie fill the bottle with gasoline. She pulled a KN95 mask out of her pocket and handed it to Millie. "At least don't let them see your face."

Fawn stood up a little taller, like she was a general.

"First wave, you go at the front, you smash some glass, you throw the incendiary device, and you bite anyone who comes out to look at you. If you can break into the building that way, do. But the goal is to be a distraction. If you want to set fire to cars in the parking lot, that's probably fine too. Especially one that's a big blue van."

Cain stepped out of the car, drawing his long cape and cowl around himself like a bathrobe, tottering in his heeled shoes. He did not look as dangerous as he had the previous night. He looked queasy.

"Those of us who can fly should land on the roof and make some holes in the glass on the upper stories," he said.

Fawn nodded to me. "Rachel, again. The best thing you can do right now is go inside, find your mom, and distract her for a while as we get started."

I looked at her deep brown eyes, and the purple bruise that made one eyebrow swell and droop down. Her face was elegantly lopsided. She looked like an adorable dog about to win a street fight. I could not stand against her, and I wanted her love.

"Okay," I said. "What's my signal?"

"When you hear someone scream, 'Oh my god, vampires,'" a vampire boy behind Angie said.

"All the way in the back of the building where the loading docks are," Fawn said. "We need you to open an exit door."

I picked up the defrosting box of plasma. I held it against my hip as I walked back up the slight hill toward the Daylight building. I made a few quick decisions.

I texted my mom, *Mom, I've been looking everywhere for you. There's something important I need to tell you.*

There were lots of cars in the parking lot, since it was day. I allowed myself to marvel again at the way my skin wasn't burning. I thought about how many concentrated body part essences were in the stuff I'd been drinking, that let me live that way. Did I deserve sunlight? Did I deserve it if it came via shady war bone marrow or plasma or whatever—or Brid's blood? When I re-entered the building, one of the front desk staff nodded me through the glassy lobby. I wondered if she had seen me run out with the box before.

She did let her gaze linger on it for a minute, but decided it wasn't her business. I walked back through the halls where the screaming and moaning could be just vaguely heard. I had meant to leave forever.

My mom met me by the staff room.

"Brid's not with you?" she asked, anxiously.

"Um," I said, "That's actually what I need to talk to you about. Have you seen this?"

She looked down at the box in my hands. "What's that?"

"It's a box from the storage areas. Look at its label." Part of me wanted to expect the best from her.

My mom studied it. "Human plasma." She looked up and made eye contact with me.

"Mom. Daylight's not synthetic. It's just a composite. They're getting human blood and other stuff delivered from war zones all over the world, and then they're doing something to it that makes it shelf stable and concentrated or diluted or something. It's a scam. There's tons of these boxes down there."

My mom stared at me blankly for a second. "Daylight's our sponsor, Rachel. They're making it possible for us to fight on this scale."

"Yeah, and they're a scam. Mom, I had to tell you. Brid found out about it first. She already leaked the news to the press. She may have talked to Amber too. There's gonna be legal stuff, with how they're marketing it, with distributing it. It'll probably put the rollout on hold. It isn't going to look good for MAVIS to be connected to them."

"Brid is betraying us?" Mom staggered back. "Amber is . . . But she wouldn't. She would have come to me first."

"She just told me," I said. I thought of Brid freezing slowly somewhere downstairs and felt a flash of guilt.

"Where is she now?" My mom looked back and forth down the hall, as if Brid might be there. She looked panicked, like she had in third grade when I told her I had to have a trifold for the next day's science fair.

I felt desperately sorry for her.

"She left," I said. "She showed me this and then said she was out."

"Diane!" my mom called down the hallway. "Diane!"

Diane's head emerged from around a corner, just as an alarm sounded throughout the hallways. Water started pouring from a sprinkler system. A voice over the intercom said, *Fire. Fire. Please evacuate the building.*

My mom was carrying the box now, bending close to confer with Diane, who might be on her side but who might not be. She turned to me. "This doesn't look good. Find Flo and get your weapons from her. She's on the third floor."

"Okay," I said, though of course Flo was the last person I wanted to find. I ran down the hall, turning a corner and racing toward a fire exit, which was already open because people were evacuating from their workplace. Nobody was making any effort to open any of the locked doors where the test subjects were held. There was a crowd growing outside grumbling; a security staff member was standing by the door. I hadn't expected that, and I guessed Fawn hadn't either.

"Head on out, little lady," he said to me. "There's a fire."

When I stood at the door, hesitating, he gestured again for me to come out, clearly confused about why a teenager was in the building.

"Come on. Not safe. There's some kind of commotion at the front of the building."

I saw, in the shrubs and scraggly woods that divided the back parking lot from the neighborhood next door, a few figures hunched, waiting.

I did something I hadn't done since I went to Girl Scout Camp and got to be a junior counselor. I put two fingers in my mouth and whistled, loud.

Then I turned to the security guy and bit his neck.

I crunched through tendon—it wasn't a precise bite, and probably unsafe. But my fangs were sharp and opened a non-arterial vein, and I drank.

He fought against me as I bit, which pulled at my teeth, but it had the desired effect, which was that everyone gathered outside because of the fire alarm began to scream and scatter, creating an adequate pandemonium. Someone ran forward and hit my head with their water bottle, which was metal, and did hurt. I kicked out at them as I drank, swinging the security guy around in the process, and they ran away again. I drank for maybe a minute. It was easier than with Brid.

When I released him, he ran. There was no way I had drunk enough to really hurt him, and that could be a comfort to me. I felt my nose change shape on my face, my ridges come out. The figures in the brush ran toward the door I'd opened. It was Fawn, Cain, two humans, and one younger vampire I didn't know. I wondered what was going on at the front of the building.

"You're in," I said to them. "Most of the staff is already evacuated. Open the doors, get the vampires out. Someone's probably calling the cops."

Cain smiled. "Dear one, will you show me to your mother?"

I didn't like the way he looked at me. Huge creep. Maybe everything we stood for was wrong, but this guy was definitely a huge creep. "She's at the front," I said. "Focus on freeing people, right?"

"Where's Silver?"

I gestured down the two right-angle white hallways lined in doors. "There's the test subjects. Here, see."

I opened a door and immediately regretted it. Inside was a woman vampire with burned, charred skin sitting in a chair like the one Silver had been sitting in. Her face still moved under the burns as she turned toward the sound of my voice. Her fangs were exposed because her lips were retracted. Cain blanched. I did too.

"They need a safe place to go out of the sun," I said. "Since they're not immune. Do you guys have a plan for that?"

"Millie's having some friends with cars drive over," Fawn said, using a nail to pick at the lock of the cuffs the woman was wearing. The woman opened her mouth and made a terrible, rasping noise. "For now, we can cover people in something to get them outside and into the bushes. Even if the cops show up, there's no way they're supposed to be doing this to people. We gotta find covers. Blankets? Sheets?"

Cain opened a blood bag and offered it to the woman, who drank from it ravenously. As she drank, the burns on her face became more scabbed over, the flesh of her face filled out just a little.

I didn't know where blankets or sheets were. But the younger vampire found some in a cabinet. The group of them—of us—traveled down the hallway, opening doors. Most of the vampires weren't in the same state as the woman in the first room, but several of their faces radiated blood hunger. Cain handed them bags of blood, like he was the Candyman.

I heard my mother's voice in the distance. "Rachel!"

"I'm going to go hold her off," I said, wiping my mouth with a sleeve, concentrating on smoothing the ridges and folds of my forehead, and ran down the hall. I turned a corner. My mom had been close to looking around it, seeing her worst enemy smuggling a burned vampire in a bedsheet toward a fire exit. She grasped me to her chest.

"Where are your weapons?" she asked, apparently not registering any blood on my face. "Here, take this." She handed me a long stake, grabbed my hand, and pulled me back toward the front of the building. There weren't any staff in the hallway, just the loud alarm and the intercom voice. When we went through the heavy door into the glass atrium, the acrid smell of smoke hit my nose, and I saw what the other vampires who had come with Fawn had been doing.

Many of the glass walls of the atrium had been shattered with hammers; vampires with big wings fluttered like great moths back and forth along its length, smashing new holes. A Daylight custodian was recording them, holding his phone, a safe distance from the glass, near the back stairwell. Outside, other Daylight employees were running to their cars, peeling out of the parking lot. It would be easy, in the confusion, for new cars to come in without being noticed, and in the background, I saw a figure in a bedsheet being escorted into a sedan. My mother wasn't watching for that.

The first few holes that had been smashed had been entry points for Molotov cocktails, and while the marble floors weren't flammable, the uncomfortable couches were smoking, and the big secretary desk was ablaze.

My mom's walkie sounded with Diane's voice. "Stacey, patrol second floor."

Flo stood in the smoke, pointing her crossbow up at the glass. My mom reached out and gestured for her to put it down.

"You can't hit them through the glass," she said.

"I'll go outside, then," Flo said. She ran toward the doors.

"Wait!"

The instant she opened them, two vampires—one was Erica—dropped onto her from above, kicking the crossbow out of her hands. She spun and kicked out at Erica, hitting her in the solar plexus, and Erica kicked her back, knocking her down. Neither tried to bite her, which I thought would have been smart, but Erica was wearing her mask. They did both start kicking her. My mom ran forward, but by the time she reached Flo, both vampires were back in the air. My mom hurled a stake with a fair amount of accuracy, but without a bow it's hard to hit a moving target, and the stake only glanced off Erica's knee. She scrambled on the ground for the crossbow. I had stood there the whole time frozen. If she'd managed to kill Erica, I would have been standing there frozen.

"I said we needed to have a shotgun," Flo said to my mom. She shot me a look; she would be wondering where Brid was.

"This isn't right," Mom said, holding her. "Vampires don't ever do stuff like this. Daytime raids, pointless vandalism. What's the goal? There's something up here. I don't see Cain."

Behind us, three more security guys jogged up.

"Ms. Sorkin," one said. "There're intruders on the lower levels. We picked them up on the security cameras."

"Two plus two is four," Flo said. "We've been distracted." She turned with her own weapons back into the white hallways.

I hoped Millie was fast with that car. I heard sirens outside.

"Make sure the cops don't come into the lab area here and snoop around," Mom said to the security contractors. "They can help get rid of the vampires, but there's proprietary stuff going on. Our sponsors don't want it leaked. If firefighters get in here, don't let them to the lower levels."

The security guys glanced at each other nervously.

My mom sprinted off again, down the hall, leaving them to stare up at the fluttering vampires with hammers. I knew she knew that Cain was in the building.

I followed her.

By the time we were back in the hallway where the vamp invaders had started off, everyone was gone. Doors were open, prisoners gone too.

"Shit. They've liberated the test subjects," Mom said. "If we had another driver we could block the parking lot entrances, there are only two. The cops could do that." She turned back, as if she was going to go back again and tell the guards her thoughts, but I could tell she also wanted to stalk and kill Cain.

The sprinkler system had stopped, but the floor was wet, and I almost slipped.

"Where's Stacey?" My mom asked into her walkie-talkie. "Where's Diane?"

There was the sound of commotion from a ways down the hall, answering at least one question.

"June!" Stacey yelled over her shoulder, as we approached. "This is totally not fun to do alone!" She was engaged in a battle with a teen vampire—Silver. She landed a kick, but he blocked her stake arm, knocking the stake to the ground. When she scrambled for another from her belt and went at him again, he fell, and the miss was closer.

My mom fumbled with the crossbow. Usually she's really elegant with it, but her nerves were shot.

"We need backup," my mom said into her comms channel. "I expected to have a tight squad and I've got a teen girl battling a loose vampire hostage here alone."

Diane's voice registered. "Brid's missing. Shelley and Molly were patrolling on the third floor. There're intruders."

"Typical," my mom growled. "One girl in all the world . . ."

I stood next to her as she leveled the crossbow at Silver. It was difficult for her to take the shot, because Stacey was right there.

"Stacey, back up," she said.

Stacey staggered back a few steps, giving my mom room to fire. She shouldered the crossbow.

That's when I jumped forward and took the crossbow from her. It went off, embedding itself to the middle of the shaft in the linoleum ceiling. My mom looked at me in confusion, and opened her mouth, probably to ask what I was doing.

"Run!" I yelled to the boy vampire. He ran, slipping on the wet floor, sliding toward the stairs.

"Cain went that way," he shouted to me. "I've got to let him know I'm all right and get him out of here."

That was the turning point, obviously. I ran after him, wondering where the hell he thought he was going running away from an exit. The floor was wet, so I had to step sort of precisely in order not to slip, but I had fresh blood in my veins. I was faster than my mom.

Where I was going was another question. Where were my allies? By which I maybe meant just one human girl who hadn't given up on me yet.

I clattered up the stairs, the alarm that went off when I blasted through the door just another noise to echo through the cement hallways. I heard my mom behind me.

"Rachel! Rachel, why did you do that?"

It was obvious why I'd done it. I emerged into the hallway at the top of the stairs to a more nightmarish image.

This long white hallway ended in some flat, wide windows that faced the parking lot. One window had been broken, and there was evidence of a recent minor fire being put out. Flo and Cain were facing each other in front of a white door, Flo's back against it. Silver was at her feet now, her foot on his head. This kid couldn't catch a break. Cain was in his bestial form, on all fours, his long hair standing up in waves from his head, his wings out though not spread. He looked like a wolf, but an ancient, strange, flared-nosed one. Flo was holding one of the multi-stake launchers that Amber had made, trying to get a level shot at his heart, more difficult because of his pose. I saw Molly at the other end of the corridor, pinned under Fawn.

"Just let me retrieve Silver, little one, and I'll be merciful," Cain said.

Flo saw me and my mom emerging from the stairwell, because by now my mom had caught up with me.

"Rachel! Shoot him!" my mom said to me.

And I could have. Cain wasn't Erica. It would have been satisfying in its way. I still hated him. But even the worst vampire in the world was maybe better than the thing we'd all been doing for so long.

Instead, I ran past him, so that Cain stood between me and my mother. I turned and shouldered my crossbow, pointing it at Flo and then my mom. Flo started sardonically laughing. My mom screamed—in agony, and fury.

"Rachel, that's not useful!" she yelled. "Take the shot at Cain!"

Flo turned her head slightly toward my mom. "She's on the other side, June."

"No, she's not. She's not! Rachel!"

"Get a grip!" Flo said. Flo shot Cain with the stake gun, and the hawthorn stakes shot through his lower abdomen, one after the other, making three ragged holes. I flattened myself to the wall; the stakes clattered to the floor. If they'd hit his heart, he would be dead. Most vampires would still crumble if you hit them with that many projectiles in any case.

Cain didn't collapse into ash, though a few pieces of him flaked away. He started cackling; he beat his wings, and odd cold blew through the hallway. The holes spun with dark energy and began to knit back together. You could still see Flo's face through the holes.

"You never learn, June," he cackled, and then, very unexpectedly, dissolved into a black smoke that dropped to the floor in a smoggy wave and began winding its way along the floor in several directions.

"Cain, help," Silver called desperately. I saw the trust leave his eyes—he didn't know if Cain was still intent on saving him.

I didn't know that was an option. How did you start turning into smoke? It would be good to know right about now.

The sound of a door. Brid appeared with Stacey, emerging from the stairwell. She was holding a sword. Two white women cops accompanied them—I guess the security guards had let them in after all. They had guns drawn. Brid's face was white as a sheet and looked as murderous as the last time I'd seen her. Behind me, I could hear Molly gradually holding her own against Fawn. A glance back showed Fawn's human teeth were embedded in Molly's arm and her feet were kicking wildly, while Molly took haymaker swings at Fawn's face and pelvis. Fawn didn't have slayer strength. I didn't know if anyone else would come to stand between me, my mom, Brid and Flo and the cops. I didn't know where the rest of the vampires were.

"She tried to kill me," Brid said to my mom, pointing at me. "She's a monster. She bit me and locked me in the freezer to die."

My mom looked back and forth from Brid to me. "Who let the cops in here?" she asked. "Officers, you need to stand back."

"She tried to stake me!" I shouted, though at this point who I was arguing with was kind of beside the point.

The cops looked at everything going on and hesitated.

Flo took her next shot at me, but I dodged against the other wall, and the stake intended for my heart instead lodged itself in Molly's calf. Even if you aren't a vampire, that kind of massive splinter hurts. Molly howled. Fawn leapt on her and held her down again.

"She's the enemy," Brid yelled again at my mom. "The one who's been among us all along, who you weren't willing to fight. You coward."

She ran at me, sword leveled with my stomach. It's hard to kick a sword aside when your hands are full of crossbow. I jumped over it, but overshot, colliding with Brid's chest and head. She didn't lose her grip and swung up at me, but the angle was wrong. I spun to the ground, having miraculously avoided setting off the crossbow. On landing, a bolt embedded itself in the ceiling.

"Everyone drop your weapons," the younger cop said. Her gun was pointed at me. Her partner's gun was pointed at Flo. "Everyone here is under arrest."

I looked at Brid, who was slouched on the ground,

breathing heavily, holding her sword. She looked at the cops. We both dropped our weapons. Flo didn't drop her weapon.

My mom took the ID badge from her belt. "Officer, I'm a friend of Officer Barden, and a dedicated supporter of the Seattle Police Foundation. We were hired to protect this building from a gang of vampires run amok."

"Everyone is under arrest," the cop repeated to Flo. "Drop your weapons."

My mom clearly made a snap decision. In two quick blows, she hit both cops on the back of their heads with the blade of her hand. They didn't react fast enough. They dropped to the floor. My mom retrieved their guns, and pointed them both at me. She never feels comfortable without a weapon.

"What the fuck was that for," Brid said, turning from me to look at my mother with unmistakable frustration and hatred. "We work with the cops, June."

"Not right now," we don't," my mom said.

I took the opportunity to leap at Brid and sink my teeth into her neck, pulling her in front of me at the same time so that she'd form a shield. She screamed, long and ragged, clawing back at my face with the hand I couldn't pin. I drank from her, as she struggled against me, the second time I had done the thing I'd been so scared of doing. I had wanted her blood. I wanted to taste how she felt inside, what she had wanted from our days spent in the sun together, what she remembered of playing under the piers. I didn't understand her. Mainly I could taste her fear, her hatred. It wasn't at all like drinking from Fawn. Her adrenaline was somehow palpable. It made my gut twist uneasily; red tears came to my eyes. But the blood that hit my tongue also made me feel powerful. Powerful enough to do what I needed to do.

"Kill Rachel," Flo yelled. "Brid's going to die!"

Stacey, who had clearly been holding it in, screamed. She didn't stop screaming.

"Rachel," Mom shouted. "Are you really working with the vampires?"

I looked up at her, blood soaking my chin. I could feel my nose flaying away from my face, the ridges rising. I felt, for the first time, something change in the blades of my shoulders—an itch, a new ripple in my skin. I felt the wings unfurling. It felt kind of indecent, unguarded, uncontrollable. They spiraled out of me, an extrusion of bone and leather. They cast no shadow on the floor. I began to float.

"Mom, I am a vampire," I said. "Whose side should I be on?"

"Diane, please, the third floor," my mom gasped into her walkie talkie.

The walkie crackled. We all waited. Diane's voice came through.

"June, Brid told me some pretty disturbing information. I can't take orders from you."

My mom was white.

I dropped Brid to the floor. She hadn't lost enough blood to faint, but she had been in an icebox for a while before I drank from her.

Mom, who looked much older than her forty-two years, fired two rounds into my chest and stomach. She could have fired at my head. The bullets went through me. I felt one scrape my heart. They hurt, but I felt, after they'd torn through the flesh, that I wasn't disintegrating. I dropped to all fours, as Cain had, and felt my arms elongate, my fingers spreading long and spindly like spiders. I was quick. I moved toward my mom first, knowing Flo might fire at my back. June seemed disarmed by how quickly I scurried, my leather wings flapping, and her next shot went over my head. I pinned her arms against the wall next to the exit stairwell, my face inches from hers. My long fingers secured her hands. She was taller than me, but I was able to float, my legs parallel with the floor, so I looked down on her.

Flo took her shot. A stake tore through one of my wings, pinning it to the wall above my mom's arms. The pain was neon bright. But I didn't let go. I put my feet on my mom's shoulders and pulled back, tearing the skin of my new appendage, ripping it open, freeing me. Blood sprayed; Stacey and Flo ducked, as if it could burn them. Stacey began moving, head down, toward Brid. Flo ran down the hall to claim Brid's sword.

At that moment, Cain emerged from smoke, consolidating upwards, holding Silver in his arms like King Kong and Fay Wray. Silver was clutching at his chest, his skin pink and peeling. He looked relieved, desperately tired. Cain saw me, my mother, Flo, arched his neck toward Brid.

"Well," Cain said. He smiled, with long, piranha-like teeth—not just the two canines, but all his teeth were sharp. "You seem to have things under control here. I'll be seeing you."

He ran toward the window, where the broken glass

spread out like stars, pushing aside Flo, Stacey, and Brid along the way. In his wake he left a trail of the smoke he had been before. He grew wings as he jumped. His wings beat twice on the exit, black against the dark, rainy sky, and he disappeared up above the roof.

He was an overgrown boy who ran away when things were tough. He probably only really cared about a handful of people. He hadn't minded hurting me, just like I hadn't minded hurting Brid.

"Way to help us out," Fawn called after Cain.

Stacey was pulling the unconscious Brid back toward the stairwell. She shouldered open the door, clearly intending to descend the stairs.

"Hold it," my mom said. "Help me."

Stacey looked at my mom. "June, I'm sorry, but like, this is sort of between you and your daughter."

The door slammed. Now it was just Flo, with a sword. She probably wasn't on my mother's side, but she was very into killing me.

Fawn released Molly, who was now clutching her injury against the wall, and came toward me. Flo glanced in her direction. Fawn was limping a little, and I could see her breathing was heavy. "Rachel," she said. "We can get out through the window, too, if you can carry me."

"Flo," my mom called. "Kill her. Kill her. I realize I was wrong. Help me."

I couldn't figure out a good way to get to the window, since my mom was still holding the guns, even if her hands were pinned. I could try to bite her hands off. I looked around to try to get a bead on Fawn, and saw Flo racing toward me with the sword. If I stopped her, I'd have to let go of my mom.

"Rachel, I know this isn't you," my mom said. Her usual confidence was gone. I could see that she was just a woman. I had never needed to be afraid of her. "You aren't this monster. Please, come back to me."

Flo. The sword.

Fawn's leg stopped her. She tripped her, and Flo fell to the ground.

"Come on!" Fawn called to me.

My hands weren't free. My wing was bleeding. I kicked my mother in the solar plexus and used the moment to grab one gun from her hand and pitch it down the hall away from us, then, as she scrabbled at my neck, I kicked the other one. Clumsily, I trampled Flo, catching a slice of sword in my shoulder but pushing her to the wall. I grabbed Fawn in my arms, and barrelled down the remainder of the hallway toward the window. I felt my toes extending through my shoes as I ran.

My mom has speed and strength unmatched by almost any human. She recovered fast, even if she was alone in the world, abandoned by everyone she had trusted. She grabbed the sword that Flo had dropped and charged after us as we raced toward our freedom.

When we passed through the open pane, a few stray sharp pieces of glass still embedded in the frame cut me on my wingtips and scraped against the taloned toes that had emerged from the front of my Converse.

My mom leapt after us, holding the sword.

I went up.

She went down, and down.

18.

FAWN

Being held in a woman's arms as she leaps from a window with wings powerful enough, despite the laws of physics, to carry both you and her, is heady stuff. If she dropped me, I'd fall to my death. I held on. We rose above the roof of the smoking building, circling the parking lot, the rain coming down in a haze that wet my hair to my forehead. Faint purple and wine-colored light marked that sunset was nearly here.

I had not known if I could trust her, but it had been made clear to me again that it pays sometimes to trust.

The outline of June Sorkin, splayed on the pavement, was clear from where we flew. Cops in the parking lot circled around her form. There were eight police cars down there, and two more blocking the entryway. Rachel wasn't looking down. She pumped her wings harder, and they carried us into the lowest levels of the misty clouds, so that water molecules obscured where we had just been.

Ahead of us in the clouds, there were the shadowy forms

of other winged beings. The red and pink light danced off Rachel's face above me, monstrous and beautiful, her bat nose flared against the wind, her blond hair blown back from her face.

We hadn't managed everything we'd set out to do. There was too much product in the building to destroy, and we didn't have what we needed to steal it. But there was a truck being loaded when we'd begun the raid, and the driver had gotten out to see what was going on, and Millie had gotten in. I didn't know where she'd driven it, but she'd pulled out of the parking lot before the cops had gotten there.

Rachel clearly intuited enough to follow the other vampires, because in the wind my voice got lost against her sternum. They flew over three neighborhood developments, and then over the water, a thin line of bridge below us.

The wet and the cold woke me up; I was still weak and had also just gone up and down stairs a bunch of times and had needed to bite a girl on the arm, which I hadn't needed to do since I was four.

Skimming under the lowest clouds, you could see the Seattle roofs and gray buildings, and the sound, twinkling dark in the coming night, the cold air blowing from it inland.

The other vampires circled down around a narrow road leading to an overgrown cul-de-sac. There was a big freighter truck parked there, next to a Subaru with blacked out windows and a U-Haul van. We followed, banking down, flapping awkwardly after we dropped under the altitude where air currents helped buoy the vampires' wings. I realized one of the vampires ahead of us was Silver.

Rachel clearly didn't know how to land. She beat frantically as we approached a tree, extending a leg to kick off of it, and then spiraled sideways, falling toward the ground, breaking our momentum just enough that we crumpled to the pavement rather than splatted against it.

The hole in Rachel's wing was not bleeding when I looked at it again. It had not knitted closed yet but was pulsing a little. I looked up at her face, and found her eyes, red and huge, looking back at me.

"Did anyone die?" she asked me, after we both scrambled to our feet.

"I'm not sure your mom made it," I said.

"Well, yeah. I mean our team."

"I'm not sure," I said, jarred by how easily, now, she named her new allegiance. Was she mainly motivated by self-preservation, or honor?

"I've never felt more alive," she said to me earnestly, as I began to turn to look at the other figures who had landed in the cul-de-sac.

I knew what she felt, looking at me, and it was really nice, in a way, that she felt it. But she was really complicated, and unpredictable. Only roughly thirty-six hours ago she'd more or less participated in the raid on The Pearl. I squeezed her hand.

"Thanks for getting us out of there," I said earnestly, but when she tried to catch my face in her long fingers, I pulled away.

"Fawn, let me kiss you," Rachel said—voice pleading, insistent.

I'd had too much blood drunk in the last day. I had almost died several times in a row. She'd nearly gotten me killed, sort of saved me, then done both again. I didn't want to ride the high of being her refuge. I would faint. I was dizzy. How could she ask me for that?

"Um, not right now. I'm sorry."

Several kinds of pain wrenched her features around.

"Fair enough." She looked livid and tearful.

I had to turn away and trust that nobody around would let her change sides a second time. I couldn't be safe with her if she was this easy to enrage. I needed a second, didn't feel like giving.

Erica and Ned were checking each other for injuries; when Erica saw Rachel, she moved toward us.

"Rachel," Erica said. "You got out. You fought for us after all. I wasn't sure if you would." She moved forward, then held herself back, looking like she wasn't sure whether to touch Rachel.

Rachel burst into tears and knelt to the ground. It was Ned, not Erica, that moved to put an arm around her shoulder and crouch with her to the asphalt, speaking in a low, level voice. I wanted to move toward her, I felt drawn to her, sorry for her, curious about her, but again—exhaustion in every part of my body. I needed someone to take care of me whose goal wasn't just to escape her mom's cult and get strong off my blood.

Two vampires I didn't know, both burned, sat under bedsheets next to Millie's car. Around us in the dim twilight, a few wingless humanoid figures had been moving, carrying boxes from the Daylight truck to the U-Haul van. One of them was tall, and bulky, and butch, the most beautiful woman I had ever seen.

Cain and Silver were crouched near Millie's car in heated, quiet conversation next to Angie and Jay, who were scrupulously ignoring them, in conversation.

I went over toward Silver. For a second he didn't look up at me.

Jay, who looked exhausted, gave me a small salute. "Hey, human girl," he said. "Sorry for that crazy shit I pulled a while back. Angie told me that you were the one who helped get us all out today."

"Thanks for saying that," I said. The ground threatened to move up toward me. "It's been crazy."

Silver saw me and stood up.

"Silver," Cain said crossly. "I was *talking*."

I looked at Silver. He looked up at me.

"Thanks for saving me, Fawn."

"No problem." I put my hands in my pockets.

"For everything. Now I want you to see this."

He whirled back toward Cain, pointing a finger at him. "According to the ancient law, I charge thee, sire, with *negligence*."

Cain's face wobbled in that strange way it had, between imperious power and bereft structurelessness.

"I saved you, boy, from fates worse than death. I carried you from the building."

Silver's face was not quite monstrous, not batlike, but his eyes flashed and his fangs were over his lips. "You let Idris die. My brother, and your son as much as me. And I know it is not the first time you've let your children die. Not the first time you've decided it was our fault, and not yours. I cannot trust you, sire, with my protection. According to the ancient law—"

Cain became less and less before me. He had been crouched; he leapt to his feet, but it was a limping gait he used as he lurched forward. "Silver, please, don't finish this oath, you don't mean this," he hissed quietly. "Please, I know I messed up."

"—the bones thirty thousand years old and older, back to the dawn of time," Silver said, rising so he was taller than usual. Cain's white hair blowing in the breeze looked, right now, lank. "If a sire produces a new child of darkness and does not care for them, love them, teach them to live on the rich earth in nighttime, the bat-child may take without giving, drinking from the sire's neck, and not let up until the sire is in its smallest form, so that they may know humility and suffer the world as a predator made prey, eating wood-lice and flies. You taught me these words. I believed your vow. Make good your vow to me."

A hush had fallen across the vampires.

Cain whimpered. "I promise, Silver. I promise that if I ever let anyone hurt you again . . ."

"No," Angie called, from where she stood by Jay. "You heard the oath. You heard it as you said it to him, before you turned him. Before you turned me."

Cain stood surrounded by his children.

This was all gibberish to me, but I guessed I had been researching estrogen instead of learning the vampire vows.

Cain looked at Silver a long time and bit his lip. "Please, then. Let nobody say I am not honorable. Do what you must. Only allow me to be with you again, in humility, when it is done. I love you, and I did not try to hurt you."

Silver had a streak of red tear down his face and more

clouding the whites of his eyes. "Cain, you made me. I owe you my life. But you're crazy, and I need a break from you."

He reached forward, grabbed Cain's shoulders. Cain let him sink sharp teeth into his throat.

After the first minute, I tried to turn away, move off. But when I awkwardly averted my gaze, I realized everyone else was standing and watching still, like this was a funeral, or a wedding, and the main event was going on. I didn't want to watch Silver suckle at Cain. I didn't know if there was some kind of wacky reconciliation happening, or what—

Rachel suddenly was next to me. "He's getting smaller," she breathed.

And he was. Cain was no longer the size of a short man. He was a small child—or a very large bat. And then he was a smaller bat, wings flaring wide. Silver, meanwhile, was growing. The monster-form that Cain had claimed was bubbling up from his relatively small body, wings spreading, hands becoming claw, until a big dark winged wolf held a little brown bat in its hand. A wisp of white hair trailed from the bat's head.

Wanda sauntered over. She squinted at the tiny bat. "He had that coming," she said.

Silver had blood ringing his toothy muzzle. "Okay, so, now this is done, I do feel bad," he said, looking down.

"He'll be fine," Wanda said. "I was a bat through most of the 1890s. We can bring him along if you want, but he'll need a box or something."

The bat squeaked.

The great beast gave a flit upwards with its claw, and the bat rose, circling. It peeped again at us—and then took off, faster than I would have expected, in wide frantic circles above us.

The great beast that had all of Cain's power looked at me.

"*I'm* going to lead the vampire revolution that saves the world," it said, in a voice that was still Silver's but lower.

Me and Silver were from the same place; we had found what we needed, together, far away. We were also very different.

I had thought he was cooler than me, but that wasn't even close to true.

"That's pretty funny to think about," I told him.

"You want to start over as friends?" he asked me, long bloody tongue making his voice indistinct.

"I'll think about it," I said. "Are you leaving town?"

"Me and Angie and Jay are, with this woman who came with the smaller truck. We gotta clear out now we've flown around and burned a building."

"Millie," I called. "Did we save everyone?"

"Folks got everyone they could find," Millie said. "We didn't get down in the basement, though, so there may still be people down there. But the cops were going to search the building. If there's vampires there, it'll look bad for Daylight. We're taking most of our injured up to John's in Bothell."

A gull cried.

"Guys," Wanda called. "Let's get it moving, or we won't be out of here before the cops trace the truck."

She registered me now, as she turned from squinting at Cain's bat-form circling. Her eyes brightened.

"Wanda," I said.

"Figure I may as well resell some of this synth stuff down south while I can. Novelty. You probably shouldn't help me load, given all those bite marks in your neck. I told you to be careful," Wanda said.

"I found a lot of trouble," I said, as her arms circled around me in a tight hug.

"Climb in the passenger seat if you want to. Figure you might want to hit the bricks. I'm heading down to California. Taking the teen vamps with me. Seems prudent. Gonna see if they want to try to make it in Santa Carla. We'll switch trucks in Eugene."

Rachel was hesitating, watching us. Wanda gestured to her.

"Vamps ride in back. There's a few big trunks serve as beds."

Rachel looked at me. She was scared.

I climbed into the back, with Rachel, who staggered. We sat next to each other in the back, in the big plastic trunk; there were enough fleece blankets for us each to have one.

The moon was shining through the clouds by the time we hit I-5; the tarp over the back window was pulled aside so its glow spread on our bodies. Silver's beast-form was curled on the floor outside the trunks, huge; Aurelius was in his arms. We were quiet—tired, spent. The open eyes were red in the dark. Rachel bent over, and then she leaned onto my lap. She looked up at me, exhausted. I stroked her arm.

"It's going to be okay. Someday."

Instantly she was asleep.

Her fangs over her bottom lip were beautiful to me, and I thought about her bat-face when she drank from my neck. She had hated it. I wanted her to love it. I wondered if, when we both were less made of electric wire, she would try again.

I wouldn't ask her now.

ACKNOWLEDGMENTS

Thank you to Tal Mancini, Rasheeda Saka, and Ruth Weiner, the team at 7Stories Press who made this work logistically, syntactically, and financially possible. Thanks 7Stories Press for signing onto PACBI. May we someday live in a world that includes a free Palestine. Stop the genocide. If you're not on board with stopping the bombing of schools, universities, and refugee camps, ask yourself why.

This book was mostly written on unceded Munsee Lenape/Canarsie land. It's set in the unceded land of Coast Salish people, particularly the Duwamish, Suquamish, Stillaguamish, and Muckleshoot.

Even more than Anne Rice, I would like to thank Emma Geissler from my 2008 seventh grade class for loaning me Anne Rice's *The Vampire Lestat,* giving me *The Black Parade* burned on a CD, and showing me her sketchbooks full of shadowy-eyed, nude, long-haired bishonen vampire guys who had tails for some reason. It is very rare that anyone is as true to themselves as early and as loudly as she, and while she emanated danger, she held a hypnotic power over me.

Thanks Jolene, owner of world's best laugh, who showed me *Hackers* and *Bram Stoker's Dracula* (1994, the Coppola one). Jolene could save Seattle's vampires through the power of doe-eyed if wary trust and sleepless organizing. But should she have to? And will the vampires be kind to her too?

Thanks Nicholas, my husband, who is a gentle and reassuring presence in my life, and who watched all of Buffy with me in 2022-23. Thank you to Lewis and Chris, and to Nathan, likewise, thanks much for your sincere feedback, conversation and questions. Deep gratitude to Aalon, for showing me *Blade, They Live, From Dusk Till Dawn,* and the Annie Lenox video for "Walking On Broken Glass," all of which were obscurely relevant. Thanks to Mal, beloved friend of 10+ years who offered interesting questions that ended up being the plot sort of. Thanks Josephine Parker, who got me paid during the writing of this book more than I perhaps have ever or will ever be paid again for a speaking engagement, and Spice, for hosting.

Thanks to any teen who has ever read my books. I don't know what this YA stuff is. If it's helping, good, and if it's not, turn me into a small bat.

Cheers to oft-complicated queer forefathers and mothers, including any I have named before, anywhere—Dusty, Luis, Talcott, Sammy, Gil, Aiden. Kate Bornstein, for *101 Alternatives to Suicide.* "Poppy Z Brite," mostly for *Drawing Blood.* Patrick Califia, you made my life/writing possible and I also know a lot of people who you hurt,* though an old friend says you weren't any worse than any other white trans guys in 2005. Leslie Feinberg, thank g-d for *Drag King Dreams,* and other than perhaps denying war crimes in Bosnia because of the subsequent U.S invasion** I

* "Lesbian S/M leads to criminal charges," *Bay Area Reporter,* Volume 12, Number 49, 9 December 1982. https://archive.org/details/BAR_19821209

** Feinberg, Leslie. "Big Lie and the Breakup of Yugoslavia: Lavender and Red, part 114," *Workers World,* November 18, 2007. https://www.workers.org/2007/world/lavender-red-114/

think you're beyond reproach, but you were one humorless sunofagun sometimes. Wish I could have met you.

Thanks to Lee Mandelo and Isaac Fellman for writing trans monsters too. Thanks Rena and Daisy and Glen for bringing back print media. Thanks Dean Spade, for past and future work for all of us, and Jules Gill-Peterson, for theorizing in a materialist way on why so many people are so mean to trans girls.

How do we live and seek liberation, without compromise, without hurting those we are closest to? How do we reconcile gay disorganization with desire for revolution and artistic production? Jeanne might have answers. Thank you to Jeanne for hosting WTF and offering so much space to so many kinds of artists and for the work you've done encouraging me. Cat too.

Thanks very, very much to Kyle Lukoff, whose early notes on the first draft helped me take heart and also revise. Thanks Leo Fox too for reading said early draft, plus Max Zev Reynolds, Aydan, Tom, Sophia Dahlin, and others.

Thank you to the gay woods, where I went after finishing a draft and experienced real if contingent magic.

PHOTO BY NICHOLAS SHANNON

HAL SCHRIEVE is a children's librarian in New York City, where ze facilitates comics and creative writing workshops with young people. Ze is the author of the young adult novels *How to Get Over the End of the World* and *Out of Salem*, which was longlisted for the National Book Award for Young People's Literature. Hal's comics are featured in *We're Still Here*, an all-trans comics anthology, and the zine Very Online. Hir comic *Vivian's Ghost* was on the shortlist for Comics Beat's 2023 Cartoonist Studio Prize Award for Best Webcomic. Originally from Olympia, WA, Hal now lives in New York.